FRANKIE McG straight after leavi out on teenage ma Fleet Street. She fr two children, co newspapers and n *day Times*, *Daily Mail*, *Cosmopolitan* and *Company*. Since then she has worked as an editor, most recently for *Top Santé Health & Beauty*. She has twice been nominated as Editor of the Year. Frankie McGowan lives with her husband and their children in London.

FRANKIE McGOWAN

Ellie

Fontana
An Imprint of HarperCollinsPublishers

Fontana
An Imprint of HarperCollins*Publishers*
77–85 Fulham Palace Road,
Hammersmith, London W6 8JB

A Fontana Original 1993

1 3 5 7 9 8 6 4 2

Copyright © Frankie McGowan 1993

The Author asserts the moral right to be
identified as the author of this work

A catalogue record for this book is
available from the British Library

ISBN 0 00 647312 1

Set in Linotron Sabon

Printed in Great Britain by
HarperCollinsManufacturing Glasgow

FOR ANGELA WITH LOVE
AND FOR JOHN, JOANNA AND LAURA,
WHOM SHE LOVED

Acknowledgements

All books have an input from other people and this is no exception. My grateful thanks therefore to both my friend, journalist Lee Wilson, and John Mullis of Mullis Morgan for their invaluable help while I was writing *Ellie*. I owe a real debt of gratitude to Rosemary Sandberg for acting so swiftly and decisively and to Imogen Taylor and Susan Opie at HarperCollins whose skill, advice and enthusiasm, along with Rosemary's undentable optimism, was frankly inspirational.

In a year in which my whole family had to find extra measures of courage and faith and as always to be there for each other, I was also fortunate to have my children Tom and Amy patiently rooting for me and my husband Peter Glossop, unfailingly encouraging, who had the sense to grit his teeth where I couldn't see him, who wouldn't let me give up and to whom this book is also dedicated.

Chapter One

The office was nearly deserted as Ellie emerged from the lift. Trafalgar Square had been solid with traffic and the journey from Lombard Street to her own office south of Piccadilly had been frustratingly slow.

The taxi driver had kept up an unstoppable condemnation of the life and times of the government of the day. The choice between opening the windows and being choked by the fumes of buses and cars crawling along beside the cab in the late afternoon of London in the grip of a heatwave, or closing the windows and quietly expiring with heat had left Ellie only with a strong desire to strangle anyone who told her how much they envied her busy life.

Only the memory of the private and confidential, handwritten note from Roland Whittington that morning made it all worthwhile.

As she strode briskly to her own tiny domain on the other side of the *Focus* newsroom, she caught her reflection in the glass panelling that housed other specialist writers away from the mainstream of office life, and couldn't decide why the expression gazing back at her was weary and not smug or deliciously excited.

The note had been left on her desk by Roland's private secretary, Dixie, before Ellie had arrived in the office that morning.

At first the sight of the heavy black scrawl had filled her with alarm. But that was not unusual. Her upbringing had conditioned her to believe that all news was bound to be of the worst kind.

Ellie gave a faintly rueful smile recalling the full five minutes she had taken to open the stiff, white envelope. And who could blame her, she silently excused herself. What with all these redundancy rumours, why should she be different?

Shutting the office door, she had instructed Lucy not to put any calls through, and taking a deep breath, had prised open the note.

She would need to be seen unbowed by whatever crushing blow it contained, would need a few minutes to get over the now familiar sickening shaking that had been a constant companion to her since she had first realized when she was only about five or six that life could be a real bitch.

Swiftly she scanned the contents of the envelope and as she did, her hand flew to her mouth and she gasped. She read it again and then clenched her eyes tight, throwing her head back, and punched the air with her fists.

Her own column. At last her very own column. The Eleanor Carter Interview.

And she wasn't to tell anyone until Roland himself made the announcement in a few days' time when he returned from New York.

How cruel, how unfair, how unbelievable. Life was suddenly very wonderful indeed. Of course she told Jed. Trying not to run, Ellie walked rapidly down the corridor, burst into the famous gossip columnist's office, shut the door and handed him the note.

'Wow-ee,' he laughed, grabbing her in a bear hug. 'Celebration tonight, my flower. Champagne on me.'

'Ssh,' she warned. 'Roland will slay me if he thinks I've blabbed. You know how he likes to be king pin.'

Jed dutifully rearranged his features into a frown.

'That better? Good. Wine bar, six o'clock. Well done, flower. But come to think of it, as you're now a star, champagne will be on you.'

Ellie had poked her tongue out at him and departed, wondering how she was going to explain the silly grin on her face for the next three days. But Jed would keep her secret. There was very little she didn't confide in him, except the nightmares of course. Those she shared only with Oliver.

Her brother Oliver understood. Four years older than Ellie, there was a strong bond between them, which even his marriage to Jill could not entirely supersede. Oliver, she knew, confided everything to Jill; but it was Ellie who understood his fears like no-one else could, as he understood hers. Even the distance between rural Dorset, where he now ran a hotel, and London, even the difference in the way they lived their lives, could not shake their closeness.

A stiflingly hot journey across town had taken some of the edge off her deliriously happy day, but these days, her life, hectic though it was, was now the only one she knew, the one she needed.

Nothing, she told herself as she reached her office, could now change that. Of course not. Silly to be so unsure after all these years.

Lucy had gone for the night, leaving Ellie a pile of letters to be signed, a note reminding her of her evening appointments and a message to say that Alistair Bell, the company lawyer, had been trying to reach her all afternoon.

Ellie dumped her bag on her desk and went back to the outer office to see if the percolator was up to a quick hot drink before she tackled the pile of work on her desk. Minutes later she returned gratefully sipping a carton of strong black coffee. Holding the door open with her hip, she hooked her foot around a chair and wedged it in front of it to keep it open.

'Air at last,' she muttered, settling herself behind her desk. Pulling her diary towards her, she slipped her jacket off and checked where she was up to in her busy life. The cluttered pages of her diary proved a number of things to Eleanor Carter. That she led a hectic, full, active existence was indisputable. That her views, her presence, her approval was sought after by so many, unquestionable.

But to the more discerning, the more cynical and the realistic, it revealed, as she herself well knew, only that she was wholly incapable of saying no.

It was a thought Ellie had recently come to find disturbing, not least because approaching her thirtieth birthday she could no longer excuse such wholesale acceptance of invitations as simply youthful enthusiasm for her job.

Interviewing household names from politicians to authors, rich industrialists to City whizz kids, Ellie, while still not ranked alongside the heavyweight political and financial columnists, had nevertheless swiftly secured a valued place in the features team of *Focus*, who were obliged to look out for diary stories and take their turn on the news desk. Ellie didn't mind it, but increasingly she felt frustrated at having to forsake a more rounded, detailed story for brevity and longed only to be able to write more closely analysed profiles.

Ellie preferred people to events.

The features editor preferred Ellie, not just for the quality of her writing, but because she was highly selective about who she suggested for interviews and remained unmoved by pop stars, flashes of fashionable names and those whose only talent lay in getting noticed by the tabloid press.

In recent months, it had not gone unnoticed by either the editor or her immediate boss that if an issue appeared without a profile from her shrewd, analytical pen there would be a sprinkling of letters from readers asking about its absence. When they flagged an interview she had written, sales went fractionally up. In publishing it was enough. Ellie clearly needed pinning down. This morning they had done it.

But for one so discerning about what appeared under her name in the magazine, Ellie was uncomfortably aware that she didn't apply the same discipline to invitations.

Frowning, she flicked through the endless pages of lunches, dinners and committee meetings, some crossed out only to be reinstated at a later date, others firmly lassoed in red biro decreeing their importance; bold, black felt pen underscored those marked 'Must Go' or 'Vital' in an urgent tirade.

Without taking her gaze from the crowded pages, she groped inside her bag until she located a fountain pen. Slowly she unscrewed the top and made some swift adjustments to the pages.

Her frown cleared. That was better. Move Polly to Wednesday, suggest drinks instead of dinner to the new PR at Hogarth and Lejeaune and leave lunch free to fit in a brief look in at Cassandra's book launch. Perfect.

Satisfied with her efforts, she relaxed in her chair and skimmed through the newly constructed week. She could afford to change her mind, shift appointments, alter plans. As long as she didn't cancel completely, Ellie knew she would be accommodated.

Not by Paul, of course – Paul D'Erlanger, travel writer and her colleague at *Focus*. She lifted her head from the page and gazed thoughtfully into the distance. In bed last night Paul had required a great deal of accommodation to compensate for Ellie running late all day, opting out of accompanying him to a first night and not getting back to her flat till past eleven.

The memory was not one she cared to dwell on. Paul's sexual demands and the boundaries of Ellie's commitment to him were on collision course. Angrily she massaged the back of her neck. She wasn't comfortable about last night. She had been tired, not ready for his sulky demands.

Faint protests, an angry exchange and absurd accusations had preceded an act which Ellie hoped she would not be asked, no, would not allow herself to be persuaded into again. What was the matter with her? She was strong, independent. She didn't need that kind of cheap performance. Face it, she sighed, you don't need half of what's going on in your life right now.

'If the rumours are true,' the style editor, Rosie Monteith Gore, had said earlier that afternoon, 'I for one will take the redundo and be off like a shot. What will you do?'

Ellie had shrugged, knowing that Rosie was lying. But better bravado doing the talking than the panic-stricken exchanges taking place in the newsroom. Who would go, who would stay. The mortgage, the alimony and what about, Rosie had wailed, my eyelift?

Roland had more or less assured Ellie that if the worst happened she would be okay, so she tried not to be alarmed. For one thing, there was no slackening of interest in the magazine. Why, there were queues, veritable queues of people wanting to be interviewed. She was unashamedly pursued by those who needed to be profiled by her and she in turn was rarely refused a meeting that she had sought. It was not unusual to find her office, small though it was, awash with flowers, complimentary review copies of the very latest hardback novels, tickets for previews, or samples of perfume. There were some who would have been pulsing with pleasure at being so sought after. Indeed Ellie used to be one of them.

Now she wasn't particularly pleased or otherwise. It had become a fact of her increasingly hectic life that the gravy train would pass through her office several times a week and that she had merely to mention, to comment, to exclaim, to wish out loud to be granted her desire by the bevy of people eager to please her.

But as it was, enjoying the silence that descended at the tail end of such a day, when desk lamps were gradually extinguished, goodnights had been called out, and the cavernous room took on an alien calm, leaving Ellie sitting quietly at her desk, gently easing one expensively elegant shoe off with the toes of the other, she was simply prepared to recognize the rules of the game. And if playing them correctly would keep her from ever again having to endure the struggling years she had experienced on arriving in London a decade ago, she was prepared to play them for all it was worth − and to win. She went where she was asked, said what was expected, was there when required. Her diary was evidence of that.

Some other time, not tonight, I will fix a few days off, she promised herself, swinging long, lithe legs still bronzed and golden from her trip to Antigua earlier that month, on to the chair beside her.

It's so hot in London, that's what's getting me down, not the work. That's what I'll do. Go home to Dorset, see Oliver and Jill and the twins, maybe even drive down to Devon to see Pa and Alison.

She smiled at the thought of her family, admiring their unity, the completeness of their lives, without envying any of it. She had come too far for that. She led another kind of life, now. To be honest, they all did. Such different choices, all wanting different things, and yet still a united family with the kind of closeness that only comes from having stood on the edge of ruin together and stared scandal in the face . . . well, never mind about that.

Perhaps at the end of the week, she would ask Roland for a couple of days' leave. Make a long weekend of it. Get away from Paul, and these ghastly rumours. If she remembered at all that it was only last night and indeed, if she were honest, the night before that as well, that she had embarked on a similar resolution, she seemed not to recall it. Or maybe she preferred not to.

Glancing through the glass partition that separated her own office from the sprawling, shambling chaos of the newsroom, enjoying the gentle reverie at the end of another frenzied but – and she smiled to herself – very important day for her, she checked the time and with a small tsk of annoyance pushed her chair back. Ellie began to scrabble around under her desk to locate her shoes, then shrugged into her beige linen jacket, realizing that, at nearly six thirty, something would have to give.

There was no dispute here. All thought of celebrating with Jed was now abandoned. Anxious only not to be late for her next appointment, she flew around her tiny room, throwing letters into the out tray, giving one last hurried glance around and backing out clutching her bag and briefcase between her knees while she locked the door, before walking briskly down the corridor to tell Jed that he was going to be the latest sacrifice on the altar of her hectic life.

'No-one else but yourself to blame,' Jed Bayley said bluntly, when she told him how much she really didn't want to go, but was now obliged to having said she would, and now it was too late to back off and could they have a drink later perhaps? 'You're always banging on about making contacts. You should be like me. Heartless, ruthless but terribly happy.'

'But you're not,' Ellie protested. Together they left the building that housed Belvedere Publishing PLC and plunged into the sticky heat of a late June evening.

Pushing their way along the crowded pavement they weaved in and out of the rush hour scramble as London's offices and shops disgorged their occupants at the end of the day, and headed for the tube at Green Park.

'I mean, you're not really ruthless,' she argued to his back as he pressed ahead of her. 'You just pretend you are. You know you do. It's just that it's easier for men. Women have to work hard just to be accepted. They . . . *hey*! Where are you going? Honestly, Jed . . . I wouldn't just walk away if you . . .'

'Yes, you would,' Jed called out as he craned his neck for the sight of a cab. 'If I'd said "it's easier for men" as many times as you have, you most certainly would. In fact you wouldn't be as kind as I am. You'd have told me to stop moaning ages ago.'

'*Moaning?*' She was aghast. 'What do you mean, moaning?' Genuinely appalled, she halted abruptly in the middle of the crowded street.

'Really!' hissed an infuriated middle-aged woman, colliding into her.

'Watch what you're doing,' bellowed a man brandishing a bulging briefcase, as Ellie stepped back on him. For a moment she was buffeted between the two.

'How can you say that,' she demanded, outraged, extricating herself from the havoc she was creating at the entrance to the tube. 'No, not you, madam, I'm talking to my friend over there.'

'Easily,' Jed threw back at her without taking his eyes from the more pressing problem of transport. 'Moan, moan, moan. That's all you do these days. In fact I should have mentioned it a long time ago.'

'Oh, should you really?' she shouted furiously, trying to keep him in sight as a swarm of commuters swept between them. 'And why is that?'

'Because that's what friends are for. If you don't enjoy what you're doing, then it's not what you should be doing. Try enjoying yourself – we may not have much longer, the way the rumours are going. And now you've got your own column, think of how many people will be rushing your name on to their list of useful people to be extra nice to. So why not . . . Taxi! . . . Taxi! . . . go for it. Want a lift?'

Ellie shook her head as he reached for the door handle of the black cab that swung alongside him.

'A lift?' she said with heavy sarcasm as Jed dived in and slammed the door. 'What? *Me*? You've got to be kidding. Miss the chance of making a few new contacts on the Piccadilly line? I'd never forgive myself.'

He was laughing as the cab pulled away from the kerb, leaving Ellie frowning after him.

The few curious stares she attracted passed her by. She stood at the top of the steps, a tall, slender young woman, almost beautiful, but not quite. Her serious grey eyes, perhaps too generous mouth and sweep of beige hair secured at the nape of her neck robbed her of classic beauty but Ellie Carter was rarely dismissed as average. The word most people used was 'striking'. But at this moment the expressive features were struck with nothing more edifying than indignation.

Moaning? How dare Jed say that? He was one of her closest friends. Surely he knew her better than that?

'Moaning,' Aunt Belle had said to her many years ago – and Ellie could hear her as plainly as though she were standing next to her – 'will get you nowhere. No-one will help you unless you help yourself.'

Ten-year-old Ellie had listened and believed her. Her life thus far contained nothing that could possibly contradict what her aunt had told her.

Oh to hell with it, she thought, turning abruptly into the station entrance, I *am* enjoying myself. I wouldn't have it any other way. As for the rumours, well, rumours are just rumours. It may never happen. Who cares what Jed thinks? If it gets me what I want, she shrugged, moving towards the news kiosk and picking up an evening paper, I shall moan on regardless.

With which she disappeared down the stairs leading to

the tube that would take her across London to a committee meeting of a group whose declared aim was to persuade women already in powerful positions to help
women who weren't – but would like to be.

But the question taxing Ellie, clinging to the overhead
strap as the tube hurtled through the tunnel, was not
whether the group's intention was worthwhile, but why,
having reached a position of power, Eleanor Carter did
not feel very inspired to help anyone? And yet why should
she? After all, no-one had bothered to help her.

Jed's blunt appraisal of Ellie's attitude to her lot in life
rankled, but in the aftermath of apologies, a hug and a
conciliatory lunch, she was cautiously beginning to
acknowledge that in one respect at least, he had a point.

All comers in Ellie's life got a hearing. Rarely did she
have the heart to turn away anyone wanting to vent their
anger or frustration. She conceded that it was true: she
did things, got involved or just listened, more out of cowardice than compassion.

'We must, simply MUST celebrate,' squealed Polly
down the phone only days later after Ellie had vowed to
Jed that she wouldn't accept any more dinner invitations
unless she truly wanted to be there. But Polly would
instantly see her as a valuable contact and clearly wanted
to move their friendship up a notch, now word had gone
round of Ellie's promotion.

A few days before, Roland had summoned the staff
and, with much champagne flowing, had announced that
he had created a new column – the Eleanor Carter
Interview.

'Well done, ducky,' Jed had smiled, and with a broad
wink had given her a hug.

'T'riff,' beamed Rosie Monteith Gore, the style editor.

'Heav-eee stuff,' grinned Paul.

'My, my,' drawled Judith Craven Smith, Jed's assistant,

settling herself comfortably, and with a familiarity that sent eyebrows soaring, into one of Roland's armchairs and sipping champagne. 'Not just a beautiful face, eh?'

Now Ellie clenched her eyes tight as she held the phone. She had wanted an evening on her own, just to catch up with her own life, but it was always so hard to refuse Polly.

I'll say yes, she told herself. Then I'll find some excuse not to go.

Such deception was normally alien to her. She was surprised to discover that now she felt no guilt, just relief that she was capable of it. Experience had taught her that people like Polly would demolish every excuse if you weren't completely prepared, and she had most certainly caught Ellie in an unguarded moment.

In a day or two Ellie would call her back, sound desolate, shriek with disappointment and promise faithfully that the minute she could draw breath she would, honestly, take Polly up on it. Even though Polly couldn't see her, Ellie blushed at the string of accomplished lies she was rehearsing.

She could hear Jed's advice: if it makes you unhappy, don't do it. It's all right for him, she argued, then realized with an embarrassed start that she had said it again. But Jed didn't understand that if you don't socialize with these people, how can you expect to get on? If you're there for them, they will be there for you. Right?

Sod him, she thought.

Meanwhile Ellie's most pressing concern was to keep Polly from suspecting such a wanton act of cowardice was being perpetrated at the other end of the phone.

'Polly, you are the best of friends, but it really is too generous of you. I've only been given my own column, not the entire magazine...' She signalled to Lucy through the glass window to bring her some tea.

Polly was immovable, just as Ellie knew she would be.

'No, *no*. Don't say another word. It's what you've been working towards and what we've all thought was long overdue. In fact I don't think Roland realizes that if you left *Focus*, he would have a hell of a time replacing you. A little celebration is a must. Just leave everything to me.'

Ellie laughed, trying to make sure she sounded both flattered and touched. As she spoke she scribbled her signature on the last of the letters in front of her and mouthed her thanks to Lucy who had deposited the tea and a fresh batch of proofs on her desk.

'Polly, I can see why you're so good at your job. All right, but don't go mad, will you?' She wrote 'legal' and added two question marks after it on the proof in front of her and waved it above her head to attract Lucy's attention while Polly squealed in delight.

'Go mad? *Moi?* I'll just invite . . . oh, you know, people like us, and we'll have a low-key, fun evening. Now get your diary.'

'Can't Wednesday,' Ellie told Polly, scanning the pages. 'First night of *Strangers*. I suppose I could skip the party afterwards . . .'

Polly interrupted with an envious groan.

'Honestly, Ellie, if you ever decide on another career you should be a critic. There can't be a play in London you haven't seen. *Strangers*, indeed. I can't get tickets until March.'

Friday . . . Friday? No, hopeless. The PR for the newly launched Aristo Airlines was taking a small group of carefully chosen journalists to New York for the weekend and Ellie would not get back until the early hours of Monday morning.

'Polly, it's all looking pretty dire until Tuesday of next week. Provided I can get out of this meeting Roland wants me to go to,' she lied, describing an imaginary conference on Women in Crisis Management. 'Is that any good?'

It was and thus it was all settled.

Outside the tiny office, the familiar hum of activity started to evaporate as the newsroom began to wind down for the day. Through the glass she could see the secretaries switching off terminals for the night, returning from the ladies' where their make-up had been adjusted for the journey home. Small groups of writers began to drift off towards the pub. Lights flicked out, leaving the office suffused with a subdued glow.

There was something wonderfully satisfying watching it all, being part of it, even if the rumours that the company was in trouble were getting stronger. The latest was that Belvedere might amalgamate with Bentley Goodman Publishing.

Maybe it won't happen, Ellie consoled herself as she idly took in Roland Whittington's progress as he strode through the open plan office, through the banks of black ash desks, gleaming white computer terminals and, for reasons no-one was ever able to fathom, since modern technology was designed to eliminate it, bins overflowing with reams of paper and the detritus of office life.

She saw him stop briefly to talk to Judith Craven Smith. Judith threw back her head and laughed loudly and Roland, grinning at their private joke, moved towards the opulence of the quarters that came with his job as editor.

'Can't think what she sees in him,' Lucy sniffed disparagingly as she reappeared to tell Ellie she was off.

Ellie gently ignored the remark.

'Don't forget you've got to be at the preview by eight,' Lucy reminded her.

Ellie smiled.

'I won't. 'Night, Lucy,' and with a great show of settling down to scrutinize the cuttings recording the career pattern of a newly appointed cabinet minister she hoped to interview, Ellie tried to analyse why, of late, her mind seemed to be crowded with ideas for escape when all her life she had longed only to join in?

Putting her elbows on her desk she pushed her knuckles into the side of her head as though the pressure would help clear the confusion . . . no, the conspiracy, that was pushing her further and further down a track not of her making. It wasn't that she felt unhappy. She just felt uncomfortable, restless. It had been like that for too long; not quite knowing what she wanted any more, pushing aside, cancelling and now lying to avoid confronting . . . but confronting what?

That I need to get out of London for a few days, she decided, listlessly pulling a file towards her and gazing uncomprehendingly at Lucy's carefully logged 'Priority' in black marker pen on the outside. It was a word she could so easily apply to herself. She who had spent a lifetime shying away from studying herself too closely, was now being compelled to do exactly that.

There was the Ellie who had been raised on a wing and a prayer by a delightful but impecunious father – an inspired but disorganized artist – and a string of helpful but uncommitted relatives and friends who passed in and out of her life, until at twenty she had left Dorset and arrived in London.

That Ellie had known the horror of having her home removed, knew what it was to feel bewildered and frightened as bailiffs moved in on her father, watching in frustrated anger as he found himself at the centre of a scandal that changed their lives.

Stop it, stop it, she scolded herself. It's over. They can't touch you ever again. Besides you're no longer a child, no-one can try to take you away from anyone or anything you love, ever again.

But of the many uncertainties in her life, it was an unshakeable faith in her father's innocence that had become her one strong security. Oliver's too. They didn't talk about it any more, and the gossip had long since died down. No-one remembered – or, if they did, they never mentioned it.

Then there was the Ellie she had become. Still funny and clever, but sharper, speaking a language that would have been quite alien in the midst of her family. Adopting a stand on issues that were politically correct rather than instinctively embraced. For one so stubborn, so realistic, she had willingly allowed herself to be reinvented.

Ellie was startled out of her thoughts by the phone, which gave a bullying squawk. The interview with the cabinet minister would have to be postponed. Awfully sorry, came a voice that held no sorrow at all. This was something Roland had better know at once.

With a muttered oath, Ellie replaced the phone and stared ruefully at the untouched cuttings in front of her. She shuffled them back into their buff envelope and threw them into her out tray for Lucy to collect in the morning, then thrust her chair back, reached for the trio of gold interlocked bracelets she had slipped off and wriggled them over her wrist.

With the ease of one who has wound down her day in the same way a hundred times before, the light over her desk was extinguished, the top drawer of her desk was locked and the key slipped into the Chanel bag slung carelessly over one shoulder, the Armani jacket plucked from behind her chair was draped around her shoulders and the thick, bulky black leather organizer scooped up as she strolled out of the office locking the door behind her.

As she passed from the newsroom towards the editor's office she glanced briefly in the mirror that lined one wall. Neither pleased or dissatisfied with what she saw, she simply knew that she now looked every inch the Ellie she had become, without a trace of the Ellie she had once been, who was someone she never wanted to meet again.

The newsroom was deserted as she made her way towards Roland's office. No light showed from Dixie's room and Roland's door was shut.

Damn, he must have gone. Ellie looked around for a pad on which to scribble the news that Downing Street had vetoed the interview with the newest member of the government.

Rapidly scrawling the time she had left the message and that she would talk to him next day, she ripped off the top sheet, opened Roland's door and walked in.

Puzzlingly, the room was in darkness, except for a small lamp glowing on the corner of his desk. For some reason, although it was still daylight outside, the blinds were pulled right down. Ellie blinked in the gloom. But in the lozenge of light cast into the room from the outer office, she had no trouble at all in recognizing the large, over-weight figure of her boss.

'Roland, I thought you'd gone, I'm so sorry . . . I had no idea you . . .' She stopped. Why was Roland standing like that, eyes half closed, clutching something to his stomach, moaning softly?

Jesus . . . a heart attack . . . no . . . what? Ellie's eyes travelled swiftly down to the floor where the naked but unmistakable back of Judith Craven Smith was kneeling, hands gripping . . . dear God . . . surely not? . . . her head rammed explicitly against Roland's groin.

The implications of the scene before her took several seconds to hit Ellie. A sharp intake of breath, a gasp that sounded like a scream as she gazed in disbelief at the frantic couple in front of her.

'Oh my God . . .' she muttered, backing out of the door, slamming it shut. For a second, not knowing whether to laugh or feel outraged, she held the door handle as if fearful that the over-excited duo behind it might try to leave.

'After all,' she said to Jed later over a quick drink before the preview, 'what else do you do, coming across your boss with his trousers round his ankles on the point of orgasm?' Ellie took a gulp of vodka and tonic. 'I mean I don't give a toss one way or the other what Judith does, but she can't really fancy him, can she? I mean she doesn't need him to get on. She's so bright. So pretty.'

'And so lazy,' Jed interrupted. 'Judith doesn't see why she shouldn't have it all now. The good life, the restaurants, the discreet weekends in the sun.' He drained his glass and got up. 'Judith just wants to do it the easy way, that's all.'

'*Easy?* You call that easy? It's the hardest route ever invented because it runs out of mileage around the time his wife gets wind of it and then what? It won't get her anywhere.'

'Not necessarily. Judith believes there are two routes to success. Your route, the sisterhood, the networking, eventually, maybe, victory. She isn't prepared to wait that long. Trouble is,' he said, handing Ellie her jacket, 'she just doesn't believe the sisterhood will be there for her when the chips are down.'

Ellie's face made him stop.

'C'mon,' he said hurriedly, 'I'll drop you at the preview, though I don't know why you bother. Debra Carlysle is a lousy actress.'

Ellie regarded him crossly.

'You know I've got to go,' she said. 'I promised I would.'

It was pointless to tell Jed that he didn't understand. Ellie knew the two routes very well indeed. One was Judith's way, relying totally on a leg up for a leg over. The way Ellie had chosen might be longer, but such carefully prepared groundwork was a surer way of staying on top on her own terms.

Control, that's what Jed didn't understand – the need to control what was going on in your own life, being part of the decisions. Not at the mercy of someone's whim in the way that Judith was with Roland and heaven alone knew who else.

Next morning Ellie heard Judith demanding aspirin and black coffee by the bucketful from the exhausted secretary who looked after the editorial writers.

Roland was striding towards them on his way to a meeting and as he drew alongside, Ellie indicated the suffering girl.

'Judith's not at all well,' she told him.

He didn't look much interested, but paused and took in the elegant form of Judith wearing dark glasses and shovelling pills into her mouth.

'What's the matter with her?'

'Poor Judith,' said Ellie, looking with exaggerated concern at her colleague and innocently back at Roland. 'I hear she's got the most dreadful indigestion.'

With which she strolled casually away, leaving Judith glowering at her back and Roland looking thoughtfully after her.

Chapter Two

In the event, as Ellie had half feared she would, Polly pulled the rug from under her and a mere week after she had lied that she wouldn't be able to join her for dinner she found herself making her way to Polly's Camden Town residence.

'Marvellous news,' Polly had giggled gleefully down the phone. 'I ran into Roland and said, you know mock seriously, per-leese don't make Ellie go to that stuffy conference. And do you know what he said?'

Ellie held her breath.

'He said "What conference?"'

Ellie wasn't at all surprised.

'Darling heart, don't you see? He's forgotten! Now you don't have to go and you can come to me. Brill, eh?'

Brill indeed.

Thus it was cursing her cowardice, she punctually presented herself at Polly and Warren Lambton's decoratively correct town house.

Polly didn't care for carpets or antiques. She liked the feeling of being ahead of the game, totally plugged into the look, the feel, the mood of the moment. On the starkly plain white walls, limited editions of David Hockney jostled with a Victor Koulbak, a Lanskoy and some minor Polish artists that Polly liked to think she was 'bringing on'. Banks of lilies, their perfume dizzily overpowering, cascaded from pitch black cast iron pots.

Two long, lean, le Corbusier sofas sat in almost splendid isolation on stripped and waxed beige floorboards. An open, fake log fire was the only concession to warmth in a room that was reeking of chic, throbbing with style but, Ellie thought, too clever by half.

The Lambtons' fourteen-year-old son, Silas, lurched sullenly into the entrance hall as Ellie arrived. Torn, skin-tight black jeans clung to stick-thin limbs. A cotton T-shirt with 'All Fuckin' Mighty' scrawled on it was effectively ripped. His blonde, lank hair touching his bony shoulders concealed his face. He was clutching, as aggressively as such an item would allow, a McDonalds carton full of chips.

'Mum,' he began as he caught sight of his mother bearing down on them. 'Mum . . . ?'

Polly, in a bronze and gold silk jersey dress with bat wing sleeves, her red hair cut in a squared, geometric style that swung crazily around her plump face, rushed forward as Ellie arrived, bestowing hugs and kisses and ordering a great many things to happen at once.

'Warren, look, Ellie's here. Get her a drink. And Paul. Lovely, lovely. What IS it, Silas? Yes, yes, take what you want, but just go,' cried Polly impatiently thrusting her purse at her son with one hand and grabbing Ellie with the other.

'Everyone, she's here,' she called, brandishing Ellie's clasped hand in hers. 'You look so . . . so powerful,' she gurgled. 'That dress is a real Ellie dress. Isn't it, Warren?'

Warren Lambton, who had spent the day desperately rescheduling the loans to keep his import company afloat, agreed Ellie's knee-skimming, midnight blue chiffon strapless shift dress was indeed Ellie.

'Can't be anything else, though, can it?' he said, puzzled. 'I mean it's yours, ain't it?'

Undeterred, Polly swept on. Whoops of delight and little air kisses planted either side of Ellie's cheeks greeted her as the hostess piloted her around the room like a prized investment. Which of course, to Polly, was exactly what she was.

It had been a long time since Ellie had been to a dinner party for pure enjoyment. Somehow during the last two years, her business life had become her social life. But how? When? Could she track the precise day when the two had blurred, merged and become indistinguishable? She could not.

Ellie knew that this evening, like so many other such evenings, would afterwards be recalled, by those present, for the contacts they had made rather than as the day Eleanor Carter had made it. She didn't mind. A year ago she would have done the same. As it was, she was simply reconciled to the fact that their enthusiastic response to her promotion would not occupy their minds for more than a few minutes and long before sitting down to dinner, they would have forgotten it altogether.

Ellie suppressed a yawn, waiting for an opportunity to peek at her watch. If it's after ten forty-five, we can leave. If it's not yet ten thirty we can't, she decided.

At the end of the table Paul was very efficiently charming a formidable city analyst, sitting on his right.

No-one observing the engagingly attractive travel writer as he chatted animatedly with a clearly entranced Beth Wickham, would have guessed he was still sulking having failed, less than three hours before, to interest Ellie in a little pre-dinner sexual activity.

The odd nudge and stifled giggle from the rest of Polly's guests seated around the dining table, on chairs of such a peculiar triangular shape Ellie wondered how anyone with hips larger than thirty-four inches could sit on them, had not been lost on her. For them it was the one bright spot of the evening watching Beth, who had once boasted that she had been a pioneer of separatist feminism, being expertly mentally dismantled by Paul and reassembled as a coquette.

Ellie studied Paul's handsome profile. She must do something about him. But what?

Paul liked women who were ambitious. He liked their independence. He had told Ellie as much when she had finally agreed to have dinner with him after three months of determined wooing.

'Then my charms will soon wear thin,' she had said lightly. 'I'm not remotely ambitious,' and he had laughed, pulling her against him, not believing a word of it.

'You? Not ambitious? It's written all over you. You're destined for the top. I've never seen anyone so determined to get there. And I want to be there when you do.'

Ellie sighed. Paul's punishment for her refusal to succumb to his charms was as obvious as he was. He glanced up feeling Ellie's eyes on him and mouthed her a silent kiss.

She hoped the tax lawyer on her right had noticed. It might deter him, as her frozen look had not, from pressing his thigh against hers, while pretending preoccupation with Liz Smedley, a moving force in the world of TV documentary, seated on his other side.

Liz's preoccupation was how many times she could get to the bathroom without attracting undue attention and, Ellie noted, returning each time marginally more hyped up than when she had departed. And sniffing.

Ellie wondered how she could afford it.

Peter Carmichael, sitting on her left, touched her elbow. She shook her head with a smile at the proffered mints and swiftly stole a glance at his watch, just visible under his white shirt cuff.

Twenty past ten.

Oh Christ. Ellie longed to close her eyes. She could hear Polly claiming a number of things about her relationship with other professional women. Ellie listened politely.

'As we,' Polly smiled pointedly at Ellie, 'have supported Ellie, with wonderful results.'

Across the table Anne Carmichael, who never forgot she was a barrister, nodded soberly even though she wasn't.

That, Ellie told herself, settled it. Ten forty-five and we're going.

Supported her? When? How? Bloody Polly storing up quite fraudulent credit, her clients at Prestige Public Relations now assured of a major profile in an influential news magazine because – Ellie could hear Polly already – Ellie Carter is a good friend of mine. Why, only last week she was over for dinner.

'Women are much, much more loyal to each other,' Polly was saying. 'We relate to each other as real people, not just job titles. Not like men . . .'

'Bilge,' objected her husband bluntly, while unsteadily splashing wine into his own and his immediate neighbours' glasses. 'You're just the same as men. None of you would know each other if it wasn't for your jobs. Course you wouldn't. Load of feminist claptrap.'

Ellie felt a faint sense of shock as Warren, not yet forty, carrying too much weight and the financial burden of his wife's interminable entertaining, drained his glass and set it down with a snap.

'Now who needs topping up?'

A trill of laughter as artificial as her nails erupted from Polly at her husband's blunt dismissal of her flawed argument. She turned smoothly to Ellie with a conspiratorial smile but not before Ellie had caught the flash of pure rage that had preceded it.

'Appalling, isn't he? Go on Ellie, put him in his place,' she coaxed. 'Tell him what we talk about when we go to lunch. It's never business, is it?'

Ellie looked down into the black liquid in the cobalt blue coffee cup in front of her. The rest of the company, gleefully sensing a spot of marital discord, were watching. Even authoritative hairstyles, influential clothes and intimidating job titles were not unaware of the kudos of being in at the birth of a divorce.

Ellie, who had lunched with Polly no more than twice in the past twelve months, knew her duty.

'I wouldn't dream of revealing what we gossip about,' Ellie laughed, turning to the unrepentant Warren. 'You'd be sho . . .' She stopped, transfixed at the sight of her host.

Emitting a gentle grunt, his head slowly rocking back and forth until it finally came to rest on the back of his chair, it was clear that Warren's interest in the evening was finally over.

Polly's face wore a look of pure loathing as she took in her life's partner, his mouth sagging open, his swollen stomach the only obstacle preventing him from completely disappearing under her minimalist table.

The rest of the party were all laughing at some comment about domestic bliss. Ellie looked at Warren, his business problems featuring daily in the business pages of the broadsheets. These tipsy, tired, driven people were her friends. But what did she know about them? Hardly anything. But then, what did they know about her?

'I somehow don't think your mind is on this,' said Paul much later, rolling off her and collapsing back on to his side of Ellie's bed.

'On what?' she asked, folding her arms behind her head.

'Oh, thanks a lot,' he said sarcastically, punching his pillow into a more comfortable shape.

'Oh, don't start, Paul. I was just thinking about Warren.'

'*Warren?* Christ, you're kidding. *War-ren!*'

Ellie shielded her eyes as Paul lurched up in the bed, snapped on the bedside light, hauled himself on to one elbow and gazed incredulously down at her.

'You know something, Ellie. You're not real. You think I'm some kind of machine, that can be turned on and off . . .'

Paul in a temper had all the charm of an overtired two-year-old and about as much originality.

Ellie was relieved that after Polly's chaotic dinner party Paul had recovered some of his good humour. But it had been short lived. Tired, apprehensive, irritated with his behaviour with Beth, she had felt no urge to respond to him, but wanting to avoid a quarrel she had simply allowed him to make love to her.

Paul gazed at her in silence as she lay with long blonde hair in a tousled tangle, her eyes closed. Unmoved by his anger, untouched by his frustration. It was her very indifference to him that aroused him, these days as much by anger as passion.

Suddenly a slow smile spread across his face.

'I know what this is about,' he whispered, experimentally sliding his hand between her thighs. 'It's because of Beth Wickham, isn't it?'

Ellie opened her eyes and removed his hand.

'Per-leese, spare me. Hardly a conquest. Everyone knows she walks around with a For Rent sign round her neck.'

The covers were angrily thrust back. Ellie watched impassively as Paul struggled into his trousers, pulled on his shirt. Once she would have been frightened, would have cajoled him into staying and after a sulky silence, he would eventually have allowed himself to be persuaded.

He was waiting for that now. He glanced at her lying with one arm thrown across her eyes. What was the matter with her? Where had she gone to? He tried another tack.

'I have no idea why I am here,' he said through clenched teeth. 'Tell me . . . why . . . I . . . am . . . here? Just *tell* me.'

'You are here, Paul, because you want to be. If you don't – and in your present mood I wish you would – just go.'

She heard the door slam and seconds later the faint sound of his car starting up and hurtling away into the distance as he drove furiously back to his own flat.

Ellie lay for a long while after he had gone just gazing at the ceiling. She felt scared, relieved, brave, panicky. Paul measured the strength of their relationship by the amount – not, Ellie thought wryly, the quality – of sex they had. In either case neither could be said to have reached Olympian heights lately.

Ellie's sexual experience had begun with a hasty, inexpert encounter when she was working on the local paper before she came to London. At eighteen she was driven by curiosity, and because she thought virginity was overrated. Not surprisingly for a while afterwards she thought sex was too.

Two relationships followed shortly after she arrived in London when she was just twenty – neither of long duration – that at best could be described as physically useful, but left Ellie curiously detached from any mental involvement.

Until Paul came along. Charming, sexy, intense, they had embarked on a relationship that was initially so sexually frantic she tried not to care that his lovemaking often had about as much finesse as a hungry Rottweiler.

Flattered by his unrelenting siege on her defences, lonely – yes, she had to admit, emotionally lonely, fearing to be left – she fancied herself in love with him. In the same way that she had wanted to experience sex, she had wanted to experience love.

What a mistake, she whispered into the dark. What a mess.

Chapter Three

Ellie slammed the door to her garden flat in a quiet side street in Fulham behind her. Carelessly stuffing the letters she had scooped from the mat into the pocket of her white raincoat she took the basement steps two at a time, silently cursing the rain, a mild hangover and the news that had made her late.

Clanging the gate behind her, she almost collided with the young couple who lived in the ground floor flat above her. Bill Burroughs was carefully helping his pregnant wife Gemma into their car.

'So sorry,' Ellie hastily apologized. 'Late for a meeting,' and with a wave she half ran, half walked towards the main road, impatiently knotting the belt of her cotton mac as she went, a bulky leather bag slung carelessly over her shoulder.

Skirting parked cars lining both sides of the narrow street, she crossed through the nearest gap, pulling the collar of her raincoat up around her neck in an attempt to shield herself from the worst excesses of the rain, now a steady downpour driven by a brisk wind which was whipping the soft fall of beige hair against her face. Overnight the weather had changed. A storm in the early hours had still not cleared bringing with it unseasonal grey skies and the first hint of cooler days.

She didn't want to be late; no-one did just now. This meeting was no surprise. The rumours were, as rumours always are, high on content and low on facts. Someone had to say something, and Roland had chosen nine o'clock to say whatever had to be said to his uneasy staff.

Oliver's phone call, from Delcourt, his Dorset hotel, as Ellie threw herself together after a restless night, had been both inconvenient and eventually unwelcome, much as she loved her brother.

'Oliver, how nice,' she said, automatically reaching out to silence Nicholas Witchell reading the news headlines.

Tucking the phone comfortably under her chin, she continued to swig down a repulsive concoction of raw egg, lemon juice and carbonated water, which her ex-flatmate Amanda had once assured her was brilliant for a hangover.

'I'm fine,' she said into the phone. She glanced at the clock. Seven forty-five, still time to slap on some make-up and get to the office before nine. 'You're early. What's up?'

'I know it's early but I did try to get you last night, but you were out and I'd rather tell you myself what's happened.'

Ellie felt a small stab of fright. 'Happened? What do you mean, "happened"? What's happened? Jill? The twins? Oh my God, not Pa?'

'Don't panic, don't panic. We're all fine. It's just that I think I've lost out on Linton's Field, and I wanted you to know.'

'You're kidding?' Relief fighting with dismay that while no-one dear to her was actually at that moment being stretchered into the nearest casualty unit, Ellie knew the impact that losing Linton's Field would have on her brother. It was vital for the success of the hotel for the land running along one of its boundaries, known as Linton's Field, to remain as it was: an unspoilt stretch of open land beyond the lake, a haven for wildlife, much loved by Delcourt's increasing number of visitors. 'But why? I thought you could raise the money.'

'So did I. Just. The bid against me from Oldburns was stiff, but I could just about match it if they stuck at their price. But then last night, I found out that a new bid had come in – and frankly I'll never meet it.'

'But who's it from?'

There was just the briefest of pauses before her brother said simply: 'Theo Stirling.'

Ellie clutched her half empty glass and sat down heavily on the nearest chair.

Her brother heard the sharp intake of breath.

'Are you sure?' Ellie asked in a strangely calm voice.

'Of course I'm sure. I saw the letter on the agent's desk. I nearly fainted. No, no, he's got no idea that I know. It's meant to be confidential. It's just pure chance I found out it was him.

'The agent said Conrad Linton has delayed the sale until he gets planning permission to redevelop the field. He didn't bother when it was just me interested, but then Oldburns started to get keen, forced the price up and Linton can make a killing if he sells it with planning permission. Now this. Stirling's offer is way above mine or Oldburns'. Either way Linton would be a fool not to accept it.'

Nicholas Witchell was now silently mouthing his way through the details of an ethnic riot in one of the grimmer inner cities. Ellie fixed her gaze on him. Inner city riots were normal. The news was normal. Theo Stirling wasn't part of a normal day. She didn't want him to be part of any day. She never thought he would be, ever again.

Oliver's country house hotel in the Dorset countryside had survived the Gulf War, a nervous bank manager and seemed to be making it through the recession. But the danger of a field which ran across its boundary being redeveloped would clearly have a more devastating effect on its future than the unrealistic ambitions of a lousy chancellor or a deranged Arab leader ever could.

However, it wasn't any of those things that were now flashing through Ellie's mind. Just the memory of herself as a schoolgirl faced with a daily choice between lunch or a three mile walk home and Oliver putting a protective arm around her as they listened out of sight at the top of the stairs while their father shouted angrily at Theo Stirling. And then Aunt Belle had come up looking grim and ordered them both back to their rooms.

'Are you still there, El?'

'Yes, yes, of course. I just don't understand what he wants it for? Why now? Of all the lousy . . . Oh my God, have you told Pa?'

'No. And I'm not going to until I have to. You know how he clams up over all that business and besides what can he do? What can any of us do? History repeating itself, El,' her brother said and Ellie could hear the bitterness in his voice. 'The law doesn't protect anyone from a view being spoilt. I should never have believed Linton claiming he wanted to keep the land just as it was.'

'Oh, rubbish,' she said. 'Ever since I can remember Linton has complained about the countryside being gobbled up. I suppose like everyone else, he can't afford to uphold principles like that any more.'

The contents of the glass in front of her had congealed into a disturbing shade of grey. Ellie studied the mixture with disgust. Amanda must be mad.

'I can't believe this is happening,' she said, pouring the remains of her breakfast straight down the sink. 'Look, Oliver, I'll talk to you later . . . and I'll be there at the weekend. We've all got to see Roland at nine. Oh, nothing much. I'll tell you at the weekend . . . all that stuff about closures.'

She looked frantically at the clock. She didn't want to abandon him, but he did have Jill to talk to.

Oliver sighed. 'I understand, El, it's not your problem.'

Instantly, Ellie felt stricken with guilt. Here she was secure in London with only herself to think of while her brother, with a wife and five-year-old twins to support, was facing ruin. For almost her entire life they had faced every crisis together. She knew she couldn't let him down now, but her job was too pressurized just to down tools and rush back to Delcourt.

'Of course it's my problem. I'll think of something. I promise. We'll talk about it properly at the weekend. We can't just watch Stirling walk all over us again.'

'I know. But money talks, El, and Stirling Industries makes the Bank of England look like they're rattling loose change, you know they do.'

He was wildly exaggerating but compared to the resources Oliver could marshall to compete with a powerful property developer like Stirling, it hardly mattered.

They spoke for a few more minutes, Ellie falling into her usual role of stout optimism, Oliver refusing to be comforted.

She felt faintly irritated. There was a touch of the Pa's about Oliver. Not just in looks; like Ellie he was lean and blond, with the same grey eyes and at thirty-four he possessed a maturity and a stability that came from fighting for every chance in life he had ever encountered. But Ellie recognized now what he was doing. She did it herself. If you accepted that the very worst would happen, pitched yourself to the bottom of the cliff, then anything after that could only be a bonus.

A shriek from his sister had ended the conversation abruptly as she saw the television newsclock move inexorably to eight fifteen.

As she careered around the corner with Brompton Road, the sight of the congested traffic pushing its way slowly along the rain-soaked streets gave her thoughts a more urgent direction. She glanced anxiously at her watch and then at the long straggling queue of people packed under the inadequate shelter at the bus stop with the overspill packed into nearby shop doorways. A bus was now out of the question. Squaring her shoulders, she prepared to outwit anyone for the first sign of a vacant taxi.

Suddenly a cab, which had seconds before cruised slowly past with its light out, pulled into the kerb about twenty yards further up the road.

Expecting someone to alight, she started to sprint towards it when the passenger window was pushed down. A blond head ducked out, yelling her name and waving to her.

'Ellie, Ellie. Buck up. Get in.'

'Jed!' she exclaimed delightedly as the door swung open. Scrambling in, she flopped down on to the leather seat beside the lean-faced young man whose considerable physical charms were only marginally more impressive than his choice of tailor.

'Honestly, Carter,' he grumbled indignantly, swiftly pulling an expensive-looking navy cotton raincoat away from Ellie's drenched figure. 'If I had known you were going to shake water all over me, ruining my clothes, I would most certainly have had second thoughts about rescuing you.'

Ellie just grinned and ruffled his hair.

'I was getting a bit desperate out there. Not that it's anything to do with me,' she said, raising an eyebrow at him as he helped her to slip off her wet raincoat, 'but do you ever go on public transport any more?'

'Unlike you,' he said loftily, 'I do not subject my clothes to unnecessary stress like the rush hour, unless forced. Anyway, why are you late? Lambtons' revels went on a bit, did they?'

Ellie counted on her fingers. 'Let's see now. Warren dozed off in the middle of Polly's set piece, Anne Carmichael was drunk, Liz Smedley was high as a kite, I had my thigh squeezed by a slimeball and Beth Wickham behaved like a – no, correction, is – a bimbo.'

'So you had a good time then?'

Ellie laughed. Jed was good for her.

'Absolutely, I took your advice about enjoying myself and went home. Which reminds me, what on earth are you doing at this end of town at this time of the morning?'

'Ah, the most irresistible piece of gossip,' said Jed with a contented sigh slicking back the long lock of hair that had fallen over his dark tortoise-shell glasses. 'Only the knowledge that my lead piece in the next issue is going to be unrivalled would have lured me from Hampstead overnight.'

'Good heavens, Jed,' said Ellie, her eyes alight with amusement. 'Am I going to be let in on it, or have I got to buy a copy of my own magazine to find out?'

Jed gave her a withering look, at the same time leaning forward to slide shut the window separating the driver from his passengers.

'Oh, very witty,' he said sarcastically. 'Seriously though, I was going to buttonhole you this morning, because you may be able to help. Are you still going to stay with Oliver this weekend?'

Ellie looked startled. 'Oliver? Well, I was but I may take a couple of days and go down next week instead. But as a matter of fact,' she continued carefully, 'I'm not sure he needs visitors, right now, not even me.'

For the first time Jed looked properly at the face of the girl beside him. It was hard to tell with Ellie. Friendship with her, as someone once said, was like climbing a ladder. You took one step and then waited to see if you were invited to climb another.

He had known her for five years since they had arrived at virtually the same time to work for *Focus*, when they had forged an instant bond, albeit more out of the rest of the staff's hostility towards them than instant attraction. Fearful of any newcomers, alarmed by an influx of young, bright writers, the staff would have resented anyone.

Ellie, because she had an overpowering sense of justice, refused to be parted from a job that had been hard won and eventually they got bored with trying to dislodge her. Jed took a little longer since the mileage to be got from baiting him about his sexual preference was not to be easily surrendered.

Eventually, others became a target. Jed's private life remained a source of speculation; Ellie was marked down as ruthlessly ambitious.

There was, however, something about Ellie that Jed could never quite reconcile with the outwardly cool elegance, and the undeniable sense of humour that rarely deserted her. A kind of integrity? Not quite. Loyalty? Yes, but she was that sort. It was something else. A fierceness, an anger.

More than once Jed thought he had detected a hint of confusion in the signals she gave about herself and he had yet to have his curiosity satisfied by knowing how, after a childhood being raised in what seemed to be genteel poverty by a charming but hopelessly irresponsible widowed father, she had acquired such a very stubborn streak.

Now, as he looked at her, he realized that someone who knew her less well might be deceived into believing that she simply had a dreadful headache. But not Jed.

'Hey, what is this?' he said, gently patting her hand. 'What's wrong, my flower? Paul playing up again?'

Ellie shrugged.

'No more than usual.' She hesitated. 'Oh well, it's just that Oliver phoned to say that strip of land he wanted next to the hotel might be sold off and redeveloped. Lousy for business. Bit worrying, that's all.'

It wasn't all but a London taxi, bowling precariously along in the morning rush hour, was hardly the appropriate venue to unload her problems. Even if she could.

'Well, who's the bidder?' asked the ever-practical Jed, who was deeply fond of Ellie's family and a frequent visitor to the hotel. 'Let's find out what they're offering and counter bid.'

Immediately Ellie regretted even that harmless admission. Too close to home. Too close. She turned instead to face him, giving him a reassuring smile.

'Don't worry, I'll call Oliver after this conference. He's very resourceful, and I can't see him or Jill taking this lying down. Anyway, tell me this marvellous piece of gossip and what you will deign to let me do for you.'

Jed plucked an imaginary piece of fluff from his immaculate sleeve and tried to look haughty.

'All my gossip is marvellous. This is particularly sensational.'

Ellie just grinned, relieved that she had steered the conversation off dangerous ground and began gently to push Jed back to the safer waters of his favourite subject which naturally, for a gossip columnist, was the indiscreet behaviour of the Good and the Great.

'It concerns,' said Jed, dropping his voice to a theatrically staged whisper, 'Theo Stirling.'

The taxi driver was hurtling through a maze of back streets avoiding the main routes. Ellie felt sick.

Twice in the space of an hour she had heard a name she had learned, since she was fifteen years old, to put to the back of her mind. It had stayed there, not forgotten but undisturbed, waiting for something like this to bring back the pain and bewilderment of a period in her life that had left her forever connecting Theo Stirling's name with hushed whispers, curious stares, bleak, oh God such bleak days, and an uncertain future.

She gazed blankly back at Jed. He was an intelligent man but not immune to vanity, and mistook her shocked look for astonishment.

'What about him?' Ellie asked, her eyes staring fixedly out of the window. The rain was sliding in misty rivulets down the pane but even if visibility had been possible, Ellie would have seen nothing.

In her head she saw only cold blue eyes, a hard, uncompromising mouth, the undisguised irritation of a man who had curtly ordered a fearful fifteen-year-old Ellie Carter off his land.

His land? Land where she had been born, grown up, run wild with her brother and knew for certain would be there, at the end of every school term? The familiar rambling old house, the cracked, overgrown tennis court where she was champion of the world, and the apple orchard stretching down to the stream that held a thousand and one childhood memories that could never be taken away?

At least Theo Stirling with all his money and power couldn't wipe out memories. Good memories. Important ones.

'Er, are you still with me?' Jed's voice brought her back to the present.

'Yes, of course. I was just wondering what on earth you could have found out about Mr Mega Bucks,' lied Ellie, knowing that to Jed, the name of Theo Stirling was simply cannon fodder for the masses.

'Well, he's back in England,' said Jed as the taxi halted at a red light. Ellie stayed silent. 'I found out quite by chance last night when I went to Meg and Gavin's bash – did you know Gavin's looking after Debra Carlysle?'

Ellie didn't, but she wasn't surprised. The actress, who was currently so hot it was said her fee just to leave her house in the morning made nonsense of the Peruvian national debt, only ever had the best. And Gavin Bellingham, overpaid personal publicist, was certainly that.

Jed's column, a mischievous concoction of real news and the spoils from his daily raids into the lives of high-profile media names, derived a certain dignity purely from being found in the pages of *Focus*. Ellie waited patiently. Jed was, she knew by now, incapable of recounting anything without a dramatic build up.

'This is really exclusive stuff, Ellie,' he said gleefully. 'Carlysle claims she's going to marry Stirling. She's besotted.'

'What's that got to do with me?' asked Ellie, who privately hoped that the stunningly beautiful but dreadfully spoilt film star would break Theo Stirling's cold heart and, with luck, his bank balance.

Jed peered through the misted-up windows as the cab began to slow, reaching into his pocket for his wallet.

'Ah well, that's simple. Stirling's going to be based in Dorset and Carlysle is trying to wriggle out of her next film so she can stay with him.'

Ellie stopped herself from wincing. God, Theo Stirling back in Dorset.

'Which brings me to you,' Jed said, extracting some money as Ellie began to pull her mac back on.

'I just thought if you were bored . . . while you were lazing around at Oliver's, you could use some of your local knowledge to find out what he's up to more easily than I could. I reckon I've got about two weeks before Carlysle starts blabbing about the marriage, but it would be better for us if we can find out why Stirling has suddenly cropped up in England.'

Ellie busied herself rearranging the contents of her bag which were already in perfect order because it gave her time to think.

She could have given Jed the best story he'd had in weeks without leaving the office, come to that without leaving the taxi. She could have told him exactly what Theo Stirling was up to. She could have made Jed's day.

'But if you've got family plans,' Jed said hesitantly,

perplexed by her silence, 'I'll wander down there myself and have a dig around.'

Oh, God, thought Ellie. That's even worse than refusing to help him. Mentally she rapidly reviewed, and as swiftly discarded, a string of excuses that might sound plausible enough to dissuade Jed from taking off for Dorset. There was every chance that someone, somewhere in that small and closely knit community of Willetts Green might accidentally drag up the past.

She tried urging herself to stay calm. But all she kept thinking as she sat in the back of the taxi with an unsuspecting Jed was that the last time Theo Stirling visited Dorset her father, Oliver and herself had fallen victim to his selfish ambitions. This time there was every danger it was going to be her brother.

It was the nightmare again. The one where she was running distractedly from one empty room to another pulling open doors only to find each one led to a sheer drop over the cliffs.

She turned and smiled at Jed. 'Let's talk about it after Roland's meeting. You know I'll help if I can. This announcement he's going to make, sounds ominous doesn't it?'

The cab stopped outside the office. Jed was opening the door, handing the fare to the driver.

Ellie, head down against the still driving rain, walked quickly past him and ran lightly up the wide steps which ran the length of the building and led to the white marble reception hall.

The *Focus* offices were on the fifth floor and the lift was packed. Ellie and Jed squeezed in as the doors began to close and conversation was suspended until they reached their level.

It was just as well. On that rainy autumn morning, Ellie Carter, as familiar a name to *Focus* readers as the people she profiled each week, needed all the time she could get to figure out just how she was going to keep her family's name and a very old scandal out of her own magazine's gossip column.

———

Chapter Four

'Mr Stirling never gives interviews,' said the courteous but firm voice of Roger Nelson, Theo Stirling's personal assistant. 'I'm very sorry not to be able to help you.'

'Would you at least ask?' said Ellie. 'It's *Focus* magazine and most of the international names we feature feel very comfortable with the way we handle interviews.'

'I'm sure they do,' came the unflinchingly polite voice. 'However, Mr Stirling prefers not to give interviews. He is, apart from anything else, an extremely busy man.'

'I am aware of that,' said Ellie, rivalling his calm tone. Her mouth was dry. She battled to keep her voice steady. 'But,' she went on, 'even the busiest of men must eat. I would be happy to meet him for breakfast, lunch or dinner . . . or even a sandwich running alongside him,' she concluded, hoping humour might move the mountain that was on the other end of the phone.

Even as she spoke she realized it was pointless. Although Roger Nelson finally agreed to put the request to the chief executive of Stirling Properties and get back to her, she knew it was simply a ploy to get rid of a persistent journalist.

She groaned softly to herself as she replaced the receiver, half relieved, half irritated that she had got nowhere.

Impatiently pushing her chair back, she stood up and walked over to the window. Wrapping her arms around herself, she leaned against the edge of the frame and gazed out over the grey and black skyline, the sharp sunlight of a cool June afternoon reflecting brilliantly on the wet rooftops glistening from the earlier rain.

Now what?

Her brother had brought the past whistling back, one of her closest friends was unwittingly in danger of revealing family secrets she didn't want revealed and, as though in some master plan of collusion to thoroughly disorientate her well-ordered life, her boss was insisting that she interviewed the man she most had reason to fear – the one she had long ago decided she never wanted to meet again.

'Or else I'll interview him,' Jed had said, thinking he was being helpful at the private meeting held in Roland's office earlier in the day. 'But I do think Ellie has a better chance of getting to him.'

Ellie thought she had no chance at all, but after Roland's blunt announcement to the staff that morning that changes were possible, this was not the moment to appear unhelpful.

About the only thing Roland had said that wasn't news to them was that Belvedere was in trouble. Cost cutting, economies and the very real danger that the company would have to regretfully let some people go were cold, unpalatable facts of publishing life. Although they hated uncertainty and had pushed to be told the truth, most of the staff gathered in Roland's carpeted office – if asked to choose – would have happily decided to go back to living with rumours.

Ellie had felt shocked and more frightened than she would care to admit, even to herself. Her security was bound up in Belvedere, the mortgage, her lifestyle.

'At least *you're* safe,' Rosie Monteith Gore had said as they filed out after hearing Roland's unhappy assessment of their future. 'You're too valuable to them to let you go.'

Ellie hoped, and after a bit decided, that Rosie was probably right. It was just that Oliver's phone call had had an unsettling effect on her. There were still some things, some names that could do that, and Theo Stirling was one. She could feel change happening all around her. Not pleasant change. Ellie wanted to go forward, so why did everything seem to be pushing her back?

Roland was not to be blamed for thinking Theo Stirling would be an absolute coup. Just a hint that Stirling was on an extended visit to England would alert the City, the story would be up for grabs and here they were – in on the ground floor.

Distressing though it was, it was an inescapable fact that it would be safer if she handled the interview and just prayed that a way of avoiding dragging up old scandals might present itself. With a bit of luck, she told herself with more hope than conviction, he won't remember me. After all I was still at school. He was, what? Twenty-three, twenty-four?

Now, with Roger Nelson's discouraging tone still fresh in her ears, she wondered if she had promised much more than she could deliver. Turning away from the window she wandered back to her desk, grateful that she had an office on her own. It was a luxury not many people on the staff had, and one that Ellie treasured.

It wasn't deliberately anti-social, but simply conditioning. Brought up in the uncertain hinterland of cultural clout but floundering financially, the Carter children had carved a life for themselves that did not depend on anyone. Instinctively they had grown to realize that the less the world knew about their private thoughts, hopes and wishes, the less chance there was of anyone destroying them. Ellie and her brother had always assumed only their own efforts would ever lift them above the bare necessities of life that their vague and – it couldn't be denied – often thoughtless parent provided for them.

But not so thoughtless that he deserved to have lost the little he had.

It seemed to Ellie that having lost their home, pushed to the edge, her father had settled for a life that was at variance with his flamboyant, dramatic gestures, his need for gossip and wit and to be surrounded by clever people. The cottage and the art gallery in Devon had all been Alison's idea, to get him away, to make a fresh start. At the time Ellie and Oliver had been relieved that out of the mire of debt and near hopelessness, Alison had quietly taken over, gathered together a broken little family and become, for a time, the central force in their lives.

These days if she thought about it at all, she fleetingly wondered how her father had come to marry Alison Goodmayes. Ellie didn't dislike her stepmother; she simply wasn't at ease with her. In the beginning when she used to appear at their home, Ellie had thought she was a local friend of Aunt Belle's, to be treated with friendly disinterest by her brother and herself.

And why not? At twelve and sixteen, they were well used to a string of strangers in their house. They had assumed Aunt Belle was a party to the more permanent sea of faces that proceeded to take over the place.

The old library with its exquisite wood panelling had been crudely divided with plaster board into four bedsits. Aunt Belle had tried for some time to refer to them as flatlets but the impecunious nature of their inhabitants didn't support this description in any way.

The drawing room, music room and the other rooms in the main part of the house which had been closed to save on heating bills had been reopened and rented out to students at the local art college. Only a small suite of rooms near the stone-flagged kitchen had been left for the Carters. The rest of the once rambling, beautiful house was now a lodging house with perhaps the most elegant but unappreciated gravel drive in the county, filled with cars that had seen better days.

All Alison's idea. All piloted through despite Aunt Belle's cries of horror. Ellie remembered the row, the one when she realized that Aunt Belle's reserve had been a thin front for her contempt for a woman who, as she put it, thought you could mend a broken leg with a band aid.

'Someone's got to stop the rot. What else would you suggest?' Ellie had heard Alison demand as the two women confronted each other across Aunt Belle's packed suitcases the day Aunt Belle had discovered that, for a little extra rent from them, she was expected to supply breakfast to one or two of the students.

'I suggest,' Aunt Belle had said calmly, 'that you lie on the bed you've just made – not the one you've just come from – and prepare for a future making breakfast for everyone.'

That Alison was sleeping with her father had never occurred to Ellie, or that Aunt Belle might disappear from their lives. At that young age, all Ellie cared about was that her father no longer feared every knock on the door. At least for a while he hadn't.

Ellie had gone to the end of the garden, climbed over the wall, slithered down the bank until she could dangle her feet in the water of the stream gushing gently along, and waited until the storm had passed. She hated change. Hated it.

Swivelling around in her chair, Ellie dismissed her father's second wife from her mind. In retrospect, all that mattered was that at a time when they didn't know which way to turn, Alison had quietly stepped in and taken her father in hand. Which, my girl, she told herself sternly, dragging her thoughts back to the present, is something you must do for yourself, otherwise it won't just be an interview you'll be losing, but your job.

She pulled her notepad towards her and took stock of

what she had to go on. Trying to get an interview with Theo Stirling through conventional channels was just not going to work. She frowned down at the list of names and numbers, and knew that she was going to have to try another route. Glancing at the clock, she saw it was almost two thirty. Maybe Oliver might inspire a thought or two. She needed to talk to him anyway. Reaching for the receiver she had barely punched in his number when the internal phone on her desk buzzed.

'Ellie? Roland's office, pronto.'

'Okay, Dixie, consider me there,' she said, already on her feet.

She made her way across the spacious open plan editorial office, which in spite of modern technology still managed to retain the air of chaos that the staff found strangely comforting and completely conducive to producing what was required of them. Jed had once joked that *Focus* must be the only office in London where the cleaners were employed to make a mess.

Ellie paused briefly at the door of the fashion room, where the frantic and faintly eccentric style editor, Rosie Monteith Gore, was waist high in a mountain of glittering, glitzy evening wear that had been arriving in her office all day.

'Hey, I've got to see Roland,' called Ellie, putting her face round the door. 'So don't send that Donna Karan back until I've tried it on. I need something for the dinner at Grosvenor House on Friday.'

'My dear,' sighed Rosie, rising from the colourful mountain, her arms festooned with necklaces, bracelets and scarves like a trader in a Tunisian souk. 'If you could find a way of making that overpaid nitwit hired to model this lot understand that cutting her hair the day before the shoot, when she was booked for her flowing tresses, was an act to justify her murder, then I won't send it back. Ever.'

46

'Oh, what a dumbhead,' exclaimed Ellie, sympathetically ducking out. 'Tell me all later.'

Rosie waved a languid hand in her direction as Ellie moved on to Roland's office. It was located at the far end of the corridor and separated from the main editorial activity by two outer offices.

The reception area, with comfortable chairs grouped around low coffee tables strewn with magazines and newspapers, contained a mini gallery of framed covers of *Focus* and photographs of Roland meeting the rich and famous, or picking up yet another award for his magazine.

The other housed his indefatigable secretary Mary Dixon, Dixie to everyone, who gave a dramatic shudder as Ellie arrived.

'Go on in,' she said, as Ellie raised her eyebrows in alarm seeing Dixie's expression. 'I've had strict instructions from Thelma to lock the drinks cupboard and hide the key to make sure that he'll get home in time for her dinner party. I've had to bribe security to say they can't find another key until tomorrow. So we're all suffering.'

Ellie laughed, knowing that Dixie, briskly efficient and with a grown-up family, remained unfazed by her talented but mercurial boss who drank champagne as though he were personally responsible for keeping the vineyards of France in business.

As the door closed behind Ellie, Dixie gave a silent cheer. Now she would have half an hour to herself. Half hours she didn't mind. It was the locked door and hour-long meetings with Judith Craven Smith that she struggled hard not to explode about. There wasn't much anyone could tell Dixie about the comings and goings of the staff of *Focus*.

The ones who thought their every written word was deathless prose and the ones who needed their egos massaged five times a day; others who regularly regaled the office with every detail of their personal life; and the ones like Ellie. Dixie knew Roland would go to any lengths to keep her on the staff, and that he had counteracted at least one attempt to lure her away. She didn't blame him.

Ellie could get the most difficult and evasive of public figures to bare their souls in print. Sometimes seeing their fears and insecurities splashed across the centre spread of the magazine, they would run howling for their lawyers. But few ever tried to take it further. Ellie scrupulously never misquoted and frequently exercised a wiser judgement than her interviewee by carefully refraining from including their more indiscreet revelations.

'I think your client should be aware that Miss Carter applied great restraint describing their meeting,' Alistair Bell, *Focus*'s tough young lawyer, would calmly point out. 'We would be happy to have the case tested in court.'

Then, torn between fury and immense gratitude that Ellie had merely made them look human instead of stupid, nearly all would accept her invitation to lunch to heal the rift and emerge to tell their friends she was one of the few journalists that they could trust.

Meanwhile Ellie, in her editor's cool, carpeted office, was discussing one writ that wouldn't go away.

Roland was frowning over an internal memo.

'It's not libel,' he said as Ellie waited patiently for him to finish reading what the company lawyers had to say, having now taken advice from Quentin Brough, a leading QC. 'We all know it isn't. I think she just wants her day in court and as much publicity as possible to prop up a sagging bank balance.'

Ellie was surprised the case was still being pursued. Kathryn Renshaw, famous for being the former wife of John Carpenter Renshaw, the ambassador to France, was suing over what she claimed was an attempt, in a profile Ellie had written on her ex-husband, to damage her reputation and to brand her an opportunist.

'Ridiculous,' Ellie told Roland calmly. 'He said it, not me. I simply commented quite legitimately that her social life had certainly blossomed after her marriage and that she did, in the end, benefit enormously from the divorce. The thing is, she knows that she stands no chance of getting him into court, but she can go for us.'

Roland nodded and tossed the letter aside.

'Well, let's wait and see. You might be right. She wasn't remotely interested in having space in *Focus* to put her side of things and she's rejected the ten grand we've paid into court. Frankly, if proof were needed that he was right, this is it. She obviously did marry him for a bit of status and she's got quite a good screw out of him in maintenance. I wonder what all this is about?'

Ellie gestured impatiently.

'Revenge and a shrewd notion that if you shout loud enough, protest too long, judges and juries who tend to loathe the press will be on her side, whether she's right or wrong. I think we'd better be prepared for her day in court and just hope that the members of the jury aren't idiots and keep the damages down.'

Roland nodded and turned to light a cigar.

'Is that what you wanted me for?' Ellie asked, rising to leave.

Roland shook his head vigorously, exhaling a blue cloud of smoke.

'No, no. Just happened to arrive as you came in. What's happening about Stirling?'

Ellie tried to sound businesslike as she explained that for the moment it was impossible to get past Theo Stirling's aides.

'Nonsense. Course he'll see you. Ring him back,' said Roland, smiling confidently from behind his vast black-topped desk, his favourite Davidoff cigar clamped between immaculately manicured fingers.

He was a dramatic-looking man of fifty-ish, with a

shock of steel grey hair, an ostentatious dresser with a penchant for strongly striped shirts, red braces and of the firm belief that it was only miracles that took a little longer to achieve. Ellie didn't trust him an inch. But she knew the rules. She smiled at him.

'What exactly makes you so sure he'll eventually see me, when he's turned down all interviews, except for the business sections of the nationals? After all,' she went on, trying to sound reasonable, 'there isn't one direct quote from him in all of these.' She indicated the pile of cuttings lying on the desk between them. 'All speculation, all repeating the same facts. Theo Stirling, thirty-nine, property tycoon, intensely private, divorced, another deal, another takeover . . . another beautiful woman. I mean,' she argued, 'the man is just not interested in talking about himself.'

She didn't add that she could have recounted all those facts without once looking at the cuttings. There was very little about Theo Stirling she didn't know, right from the beginning, when he took over the US office of Stirling Properties Inc.

Straight out of Harvard, he was young, ambitious and keen to prove himself in the family business. While his father consolidated the English side of things, Theo had bought for a song a couple of dilapidated mansions on a central site in Miami Beach.

Once fashionable, the area had become run-down and isolated from the bustling centre of the city. Theo anticipated a revival, but not the one that actually happened. He thought the area would be razed and rebuilt with smart condos and hotels. In fact he miscalculated, but not to his disadvantage. Miami Beach was suddenly touched by fashion. First, artists moved in, drawn by the romantic art deco architecture to say nothing of the cheap rents. They were followed by their patrons, hooked by the raffish atmosphere. Soon Miami Beach was as fashionable as New York's SoHo, with the advantage of all year suntans.

Theo now owned two of the best looking buildings on the whole Beach. And he waited as rents hiccuped, then lurched, then soared. He waited while boutiques blossomed into designer stores bearing the names of some of Europe's finest labels, and cafés and bars transformed themselves into high class restaurants and fashionable clubs. He waited until his secretary had to organize a queuing system to cope with builders, real estate speculators, architects and money-men who besieged his office, begging him to wait no longer.

Within two years he had moved the office to New York and then events in Willetts Green had claimed his attention.

When he arrived in Heathrow at the end of the seventies, he was rich, tanned and more than satisfied with himself. Although the American property market was on the slide, and the north of England heading for recession too, London and the rich south was still booming. He wondered if there wasn't a profit to be made in out-of-town shopping malls, like those he was used to in America.

Ellie didn't want to dwell on the rest of the story, it was too close to home. She gave herself a mental shake and tapping the pile of cuttings with the back of her fingers said, without thinking, 'And they even get wrong what little they have got on him. He's a very unpleasant man.'

'How do you know?' Roland looked at her sharply.

Oh grief, careful, careful, she admonished herself.

'Well, they all say he's well liked,' she said a bit too quickly. 'How do they know if they've never met him? And anyway, few men who get to the top are very likeable.'

'Oh, there is that,' agreed Roland easily. 'But you could get to him another way.'

He smiled mischievously as Ellie looked puzzled.

'Debra Carlysle.'

Ellie looked blank.

'Carlysle? She's even less likely to talk. If Jed's information is right, and she really is going to marry Theo Stirling, he'll take a dim view of it.'

'You know, Ellie,' said Roland mildly, but watching her carefully through a cloud of blue smoke, 'between this morning and now you must have studied this man very closely. You can't know she won't talk unless you ask her.'

Ellie could have kicked herself. Keeping quiet about the past wasn't going to be as easy as she thought.

'Okay, so I get to Carlysle. Then what?'

'Easy,' beamed Roland, taking a puff of his cigar. 'You simply say you've heard she's linked with him which, of course, must be nonsense because you've just been told he's linked to someone else and you thought she would like to put it on the record.'

'You know that's not my style,' Ellie said, gazing impassively back at him.

Roland switched tactics. He knew that look. After five years of moulding her career, he knew she was prepared to lie by omission, but not tell blatant untruths. With any other writer, Roland by now would simply have ordered them to get on with it and produce the necessary two thousand or so words for the relevant issue.

But Eleanor Carter wasn't any other writer. He had never had a moment's doubt about her – and he didn't have one now. He just sensed something was wrong.

He looked thoughtfully at her as she bent over the cuttings, frowning, her fair hair framing an arrestingly serious face. Her clear grey eyes held a hint of laughter and belied the calm composure that rarely seemed to desert her.

She always dressed with a simplicity that was all the

more effective because of its understatement. Simple shift dresses, well-cut classic jackets or, like today, a dark brown silk, knee-skimming coat dress that made her bare, tanned legs seem even longer in her flat brown and white two tone pumps.

All of which merely served to emphasize the tall, slight figure, the gentle curves of her breasts and the fact that Roland was quite frightened of her. Judith Craven Smith had the education, the pedigree, the style. Ellie had the class but she was no fun. Well, not the sort Roland liked twice a day.

He knew that. They both knew it. He needed Ellie but he resented her. He resented the exquisitely polite manner, the studied indifference to him as a man. He thought she was a cold bitch. He wished he could ask her more about herself, but she always politely deflected such curiosity. It annoyed him to think she could give him the brush off and he had no desire to risk it now.

More profitable for him, he decided, to concentrate on pushing Ellie into this interview, than probing her private life. Jed's suggestion that they try for Theo Stirling for the Eleanor Carter Interview was inspired. If they could get him, they would leave their rivals standing and it wouldn't do Roland any harm personally with the Chairman of Belvedere to see that he could still cut the mustard.

At his age, highly paid, the editor was as vulnerable as anyone else. His immediate future was not of the highly secure variety but he hadn't thought it necessary to include himself in the warning he'd issued that morning. Not necessary at all.

'Look, sweetheart,' he said abruptly, seeing the continuing doubt in her serious grey eyes. 'This one is such a coup for us. Just go for it, will you? Trust me. I know you'll get it in the end. You're the best, Ellie, you really are.'

Ellie didn't bother to disclaim such a lavish compliment. If Roland knew her, she was certainly familiar with the unscrupulous tactics he employed to get his writers and photographers to go the full mile, and then bursting with pleasure at his flattery go on to give him half a mile more.

She shuffled the sheaf of black and white prints spread across Roland's desk. They all showed a man who didn't court publicity, but nevertheless managed to attract his unfair share of it. None had him in a co-operative mood.

There were some on the slopes above Gstaad, throwing back his head and laughing, but not for the cameraman hidden a discreet distance away with a zoom lens, more for the benefit of his glamorous companion, a European countess, hotly tipped at that time to be the one who would end Theo Stirling's divorced status.

There was a grim-faced Theo striding through Heathrow, Kennedy, Charles de Gaulle politely declining to be questioned about the end of his two-year relationship with Lady Caroline Montgomery, who had moved out of his New York apartment amid rumours that Theo had refused to marry her.

There he was seated at the wheel of a white Ferrari, driving a ravishing blonde through the flashing bulbs of the Italian paparazzi blocking his way, intent only on weaving a path through the throng. And no doubt clearly wishing he could mow a few of them down, thought Ellie, gazing at the oddly handsome but stern features.

Of course there wasn't a substantial interview with him anywhere to be found. If there was, surely some of the glamour, the mystique that surrounded him would be tarnished?

What would you think, she wondered, looking at her boss, if I told you that Theo had ruined my father's reputation? That Theo's father, Robert Stirling, aided and abetted by his son, had so unjustly accused John Carter of sabotaging Stirling Industries by committing a despicable crime?

A gentle, loving man like John Carter. Anyone who truly knew him would have believed him when he protested his innocence.

But as Oliver said, money talks. The Stirlings hadn't suffered as the Carters had when the dust had settled, but had gone from strength to strength. So much for saying Pa had ruined them. He had done nothing of the sort.

Theo Stirling had taken their house, their roots. But his own life went on. With the Carters out of the way, he had turned his attention to buying up half the empty sites in the county to build his next get-rich-quick project. Ensconced in Dorset to try and arrest the damage the Stirlings claimed had been inflicted on them by John Carter, Theo had moved swiftly in – and on.

Ellie had read the account on the City pages of the more upmarket journals but the background to the piece was flawed, with no mention of the dirty tricks that had operated on an innocent man and his family. Goodness no. What a shocking thing for the Stirlings if that ever came to light.

How much more distressing for the Carters.

Driving to the West Country, having seen the Carters safely out of the county to Devon and his own father en route to New York, Theo had spotted his chance: a large sign by the edge of the motorway offering ten acres of commercial industrial land for sale.

He took the next exit off and found his way back down country lanes to the site. Within twenty-four hours he had taken an option on it. Within a week he had met the local planners, talked to seven banks and had architects draw up preliminary plans.

Theo's success in England had begun. He studied the market. His next business park was bigger and more lavish, bringing in big-name tenants relocating out of London.

He always chose his sites close to motorways and airports and spent a long time matching up requirements of potential clients. If he got the equation right, he could get a quick return of more than three times his investment. The trick was to build and sell, he told himself. Let someone else have the milk. Just be content to skim off the cream. Build and sell. That way you didn't get caught. By the time the recession hit England with a vengeance and the property market in particular, he owned nothing but the millions in his various bank accounts.

Build and sell, Ellie remembered. That way you don't get caught. Unless you were called Carter. Her father's home – her home – had been taken away by the Stirlings. Was it now going to be Oliver's turn?

She knew she couldn't let that happen.

'Get near to someone he cares for,' Roland was saying. 'That way he'll feel obliged either to stamp on it, or talk about it. Either way you have a story.'

'Okay, Roland,' she interrupted. 'I'll try again. I don't know how I'll do it, but this one, believe me, I'm going to get.'

Roland looked up, startled, but instinct told him not to probe the reason for such a sudden change of heart.

'Great, great.' he said warmly. 'I know you'll get it. Take your time. But I want it soon. Now, I need a fortifying drink after that.'

'But I thought the key to the drinks cupboard was missing?' said Ellie innocently, rising to leave.

'Oh it is, it is.' He winked at her, draping an arm around her shoulders and walking her to the door. 'But I have to keep Thelma and Dixie happy. Mustn't let them think I've outwitted them, otherwise my life would be a misery.'

Ellie saw his hand slide casually along the frame above

the door and a small gold key fall into his palm.

Judith was flicking through the *Standard* as Ellie came out. Dropping the paper on to the seat beside her, she sauntered into Roland's office. Ellie noticed that she didn't knock. She just shrugged. Dixie, furiously typing, scowled up at her as they both heard the lock click on Roland's door.

The phone was ringing before Ellie reached the door of her office. She ran to pick it up and was still out of breath as she heard the message.

'Call from someone at Stirling Industries,' said the receptionist. 'Will you take it, Ellie?'

'Put it through, Tess,' Ellie said, preparing herself for the regretful voice of Roger Nelson.

There was a whirr, then a brief silence before she heard the receiver being picked up at the other end and a man's voice asked for her.

'Well, now what message have you got for me from the Almighty?' she said teasingly into the phone, visualizing the harassed face of the unknown Roger Nelson charged with ridding his boss from the clutches of another intrusive journalist.

'I admire your ambition,' came an amused voice. 'But this time I fear you're aiming a little too high. This is Theo Stirling.'

'Oh my God,' whispered Ellie.

'Dear me,' came his lazy drawl. 'You do seem to be obsessed with Him. I thought they said you were from *Focus,* not the *Church Chronicle.*'

'I'm not, I mean, I am. No, what I mean is that I thought you were someone else,' Ellie stammered. Jed, passing her door at that moment, wondered why she was doubled up over her desk with the phone clenched in her hand. Odd girl, he thought and meandered away.

'Obviously I'm a major disappointment to you, which is understandable as you were expecting a more – er, elevated name,' continued Theo Stirling. 'However, my information from Roger Nelson is that you requested an interview with me.'

'Yes. Yes, I did,' said Ellie, desperately trying to recover. 'I was just surprised that you chose to ring me yourself. Do I take it the answer is yes?'

'I'm afraid I must disappoint you again.'

Ellie was puzzled.

'Then why not get Mr Nelson to say so?'

'Because occasionally, just very occasionally,' came the calm voice, 'I think it's worthwhile to reinforce the point that I never give interviews. This is such an occasion.'

There was a pause and then he added softly, 'I think you won't need to be reminded of that in future, will you, Miss Carter?'

'In future?' she repeated.

'In case you think I might not mean what I say. I always do, you know.'

Ellie listened to the measured voice and knew instinctively that his voice held a warning. Rarely was she roused to fury, but she could feel the anger stealing up from her chest, her eyes flashed, and her usually low-pitched, pleasant voice took on a steely edge.

'And there was I thinking you were a gentleman,' she said lightly. 'Silly me. Now let me enlighten you, Mr Stirling. I don't need reminding about anything in the future, or indeed,' she paused and it was out before she could stop herself, 'the past.'

'Exactly,' Theo Stirling replied smoothly. 'We understand each other perfectly. I suggest we pretend this phone call never took place because a meeting between us would be of no benefit to – well, anyone, would it, Eleanor?'

He knew. He remembered her. She felt dizzy with shock. Panic gripped her and panic sent her into an unwise retort.

'Benefit? What the hell do you know about benefiting

anyone, except yourself? Believe me, Mr Stirling, we are playing a very different tune now. No-one, *no-one*, do you understand, tells me what I can and can't do. If I want to meet you, I will. If I want to write about you, I will. I don't, thank God, need your permission for either.'

'There you go again,' he sighed. 'Dragging God into it. It is, of course, entirely up to you what you do. It's no concern of mine.'

'Oh, it will be,' she said bitterly. 'As Go . . . as Heaven is my witness,' she corrected herself as she heard an unmistakable crack of laughter at the end of the phone, 'I will make sure it's your concern.'

There was complete silence. For a moment Ellie thought he had hung up.

'Have I made myself clear?' she said in a calmer voice.

'Perfectly,' he said abruptly, and there was no mistaking the cold impatience in his voice. 'Have I?'

'Oh yes,' she said coolly. 'Just watch this space, that's how clear you have made yourself, Mr Stirling.'

And with that she slammed the phone back on to its cradle and, speechless with rage, hurled his file of photographs to the floor.

Home had never been more inviting. Ellie leaned against the closed door, briefly shut her eyes, and let out a deep sigh.

Sliding her shoes off, she padded into the kitchen, dumped her bag and an armful of magazines on to the nearest work-surface and draped her raincoat across one of the cane chairs tucked around a scrubbed and varnished oak table.

What a day, she muttered, opening the fridge and pulling out a bottle of ice-cold Chablis. Cost cutting, maybe redundancies, a libel that won't go away and after Theo bloody Stirling, I deserve this, she told herself, shutting the fridge door with unnecessary vigour.

As she took a glass from the cupboard and began searching the drawer for a corkscrew, she paused to flick the playback button on her answer machine.

'Ellie, it's Oliver. I'm out all evening, so I'll call tomorrow. Jill gave me your message about Stirling. I can't believe it! Speak soon.'

The machine clicked and a buzz signalled the next message.

'It's me, El. Six p.m. All set for Thursday night? David's invited the most divine man. You'll love him. No, correction. He's going to love you. Call when you can.'

Ellie smiled at the machine, recognizing Amanda's bubbly voice. Amanda had been special in Ellie's life since they had arrived in London together, groaned and giggled through a series of shared dreary bedsits, even worse dates, and finally a flat before Amanda had met David and married him. This was a move that had suited Ellie, because while she knew she would truly miss Amanda's sunny daily presence, she had felt for some time that she needed a place to call her own.

Ellie had never regretted defying her teachers by leaving school at eighteen to start work, first as a junior reporter on the local paper back in her old home of Willetts Green, and then two years later to try her luck in London.

It had been sheer chance in the first place, after the Carters had been forced to move, that there had been enough money left over to at least keep her at school to do A levels and allow Oliver to get his degree at university.

'Give me the money to keep me in London,' Ellie had cajoled her father. 'That's every bit as good an education as university and I can be getting on with my life.'

The weekend that Amanda left for her honeymoon, Ellie, having seen her friend off in a shower of confetti, spent in her newly acquired, uncarpeted, curtainless flat, and it would be hard to say who was the most ecstatic of the two.

The machine buzzed and the next message was from Paul.

'This is silly, you know it is. I promise to behave. Me, wine and roses. How can you refuse? And why were you so long with Roland, the old letch? I'll call for you at eight. Love you.'

Paul. Sooner or later, she was going to have to talk seriously to him. Her relationship with him was far from easy. At thirty-two, Paul was good-looking, eligible and had a stylish charm which few women found they could resist and indeed he found it hard to resist most of them. Ellie knew this, and it rankled. It hurt. But she would not have admitted it for the world, certainly not to Paul.

Sometimes she thought it was because Paul had been the much-indulged only son of a wealthy City stockbroker that he didn't know how to begin putting someone else's feelings before his own. Like so much of her rationalizing of Paul's uncertain moods, she persuaded herself that his parents' lack of interest in his emotional welfare was at its root.

Jed told her it was codswallop.

'Selfish sod, simple as that,' he said dismissively. 'Too much going for him. Looks, style, loot. He knows it too. And no, ducky, he isn't my style at all.'

He wasn't Amanda's either. Ellie grimaced. Never before had she been so at odds with the two people she counted as her best friends.

Paul really didn't need to work, but the life of a travel editor appealed to him, and so too did the perks that went with representing *Focus*. Exotic free trips were all part of his job – and he had no difficulty at all in persuading any number of attractive, usually nubile and always willing companions to go along for the ride.

Thus far Ellie had not been one of them. Oh, of course she had been tempted, who wouldn't be? But something held her back. She wasn't immune to men and certainly not to Paul. But at this moment in her life with her career beginning to take off, she didn't want a permanent relationship either. Not that Paul, when she thought about it, was offering one. But he didn't represent a future of any sort.

It was important to Ellie that she was viewed as a woman in her own right, not as an appendage to a professional charmer like Paul. So then why did she always feel a pang of fright every time he strayed?

Walking slowly into the small, but attractively elegant, sitting room, which led off from the kitchen, Ellie sank down into a small Prussian blue sofa that faced its perfect match across a glass-topped, lime-washed coffee table. Putting her glass down she stretched out her arm and switched on one of a pair of Tiffany lamps perched on a small side table that instantly cast a warm glow over the room.

She liked living on her own. She liked being here. She liked the tiny whitewashed walled patio that just fitted a table and four chairs. The blue and lemon sitting room was filled with her favourite books, bowls of flowers, silver-framed pictures of her family, pretty ceramic-framed ones of friends and paintings by her father which included a watercolour of a country garden that Ellie knew by heart. In the winter the gas fire nestling invitingly in the pine fireplace provided a comfortable homely glow from the flames licking companionably into the chimney.

Her flat was warm, inviting and looked expensive, but Ellie knew it had been put together on a shoestring. After weekends of trawling through secondhand junk shops and antique fairs looking for bargains, she had turned her tiny flat into a stylish home.

To Ellie it spelt freedom. No more nasty shocks, no more fearing that some unknown force might take everything away again. Financial independence and of late — she realized with a start because of the drain Paul was putting on her – emotional independence had become very necessary to her.

Picking up her glass, she got up and pushed open the narrow double doors that led on to her tiny patio. The sun had gone from the whitewashed retreat but it was still warm and the scent from the clematis and jasmine that Ellie had trained to climb the walls was hard to resist.

Pulling out one of the white wrought-iron chairs and swinging her bare legs on to the next one, she closed her eyes to let the trauma of the day fade and to calmly assess her relationship with Paul.

Twice she had insisted it was over. Twice she had relented.

'What else do you expect?' he'd said, a mixture of hurt feelings and indignation when she'd pointed out that she knew he was seeing other women. 'I don't even rate third on your list of priorities. You cancel dates at the last minute and whole weekends and you've even left half way through dinner . . .'

'Only if I have to finish a story or if an interview comes up,' she'd protested.

'Oh, very flattering,' he'd snapped. 'Then you expect me to spend the weekend alone living like a monk? I spend enough of that with you . . .'

Recognizing a familiar complaint and one that she didn't particularly wish to pursue, she'd abandoned trying to make him see that she didn't mind if he wanted to date other women, just that if he did, she would prefer it if he stopped regarding her as his exclusive property. She wasn't entirely certain she meant it anyway.

Somewhere in the back of her mind, Ellie knew it was more than just an unsatisfactory relationship that was causing this restlessness. It was the thought of changes that she couldn't quite cope with. For all Ellie's assertion to family and friends that the charm of her life was the unexpected, in truth the charm of her life was knowing exactly what to expect.

Five years of building a career had absorbed her day and night. Five years of careful planning, cultivating and being cultivated by the right people.

Really she had no right to feel so dissatisfied. Maybe she was becoming spoilt, maybe she was taking all she had for granted and maybe she had become all the things she was so quick to accuse Paul of being. Why else would she have handled Theo Stirling so badly? She hadn't been prepared for such an outright rejection. And it rankled. Especially from someone like him.

Blast Theo Stirling. Oh why, she asked herself furiously, couldn't she have had more control over her emotions? What on earth made her go to pieces and explode like that? It was so unlike her and . . . she suddenly stopped, remembering something that in her anger she hadn't quite taken in.

For some reason Theo Stirling was just as anxious as she was to pretend they were strangers. What was it he'd said? 'Let's pretend this phone call never took place.'

How curious. Ellie could understand that she had a lot to lose, but what was he trying to hide . . . or save? That's more like it, she thought. His reputation, of course. Nothing must dent that. But just who did he think he was, threatening her in that appalling way?

She took a sip from her glass, drumming her fingers angrily on the table. I'll find a way of getting even, she told herself. But how to do it without involving her father and risking Oliver losing his livelihood?

I'll think about it later, she promised. Glancing at her watch, she put her half-finished wine on the table in front of her, stretched lazily and then hauled herself to her feet. Meanwhile . . . Paul.

*

64

Three hours later, and for the second time that evening, she let herself into her flat. Paul had refused to take her seriously when she gently told him she no longer wanted such an exclusive relationship.

It was, she reflected, almost becoming routine now, that after another soul searching discussion, the evening would end with Paul driving furiously away to spend the night in his own flat only to phone Ellie in the small hours to talk it over and sometimes to drive at an absurd speed all the way back again to complete the reconciliation.

Which, as she slipped out of her black satin trousers and carefully hung the white crepe shirt she had worn to dinner back into her wardrobe, she had to admit was perhaps half the problem. She was tired and needed a break from everything.

Sliding between the cool cotton sheets of her bed, she snuggled down to try and sleep and put out of her head a recurring image that was preventing her from doing precisely that. The dark, stern features of Theo Stirling danced before her eyes, invaded her thoughts. Damn the man. Why wouldn't he go away? All day she had been occupied with him.

During most of the meal with Paul her mind had been drifting back to that awful phone call.

Having tossed and turned and for the tenth time punched her pillow into a no more comfortable state than it was in when she had first laid her head on it, she was actually pleased when just after midnight the phone suddenly shattered the silence. She didn't want another lengthy discussion. She would just tell Paul it was all her fault without encouraging him to come over.

'Honeybunch. We're on,' came Jed's voice, momentarily disorientating her. Ellie could not think what he meant.

'Me, you and Theo Stirling,' he said gleefully. 'Roland told me you weren't getting anywhere with the great man, so I made a few discreet enquiries . . . now stop shouting, Ellie, I know I promised I wouldn't interfere, but it was too good an opportunity to miss.'

Ellie, sitting bolt upright in bed, stopped yelling at him and just prayed he hadn't done anything that couldn't be undone.

'Well, I was having a drink with Gavin and he said he was escorting Carlysle to a very private drinks party tomorrow given by old Lady Montrose. You know the one, seriously wealthy, always on about rainforests and saving the planet?'

'I know exactly who you mean and personally I rather like the sound of her,' she snapped frostily, objecting to Jed's dismissal of a very hardworking, if eccentric, aristocrat.

'Oh, she's a lovely old duck and at this moment she couldn't be lovelier because Carlysle is one of the celebs she's rounding up to add kudos to her latest environmental campaign. And Gavin thought it would be a good idea for Carlysle's image if I mentioned she was one of its strongest supporters.'

'Oh, Carlysle's going to love that,' said Ellie drily. 'I can see it now. "Debra Carlysle branching out in new direction . . ."'

'Ell-ie,' said Jed ominously. 'Pay attention. You've got to come with me because the real coup is that Theo Stirling has agreed to be there.'

She barely heard the rest of Jed's message. Tomorrow? That soon . . . ? I can't face him. Amanda's . . . I'll cancel . . . I'll hit him . . . no I won't, I'll be really cool.

'Oh, well,' said Jed sarcastically into the silence. 'For a moment there I thought you were in danger of sounding pleased, even grateful . . .'

Ellie tried to concentrate on what Jed was saying. 'Jed, you are a brilliant, wonderful person. I am so grateful. And if I were to say you are better than a sleeping pill, you will never know how much of a compliment that is.'

'Doesn't sound much like one to me,' sniffed Jed. 'But I assume from that that you and I will present ourselves at Lady M's at six thirty p.m. sharp. Right? Now get some sleep. 'Night, Ellie.'

Ellie replaced the receiver and sliding down in her bed, her face wreathed in smiles, she silently gloated at the discomfort she had in store for Theo Stirling. At least now I'll get some sleep, she said contentedly and as the dawn broke five hours later, she wondered wearily why sleep had still managed to evade her and Theo Stirling was still crowding out all other thoughts.

Chapter Five

'Jed, he isn't going to come,' Ellie whispered urgently in his ear.

Together they scanned the crowded drawing room of Lady Sarah Montrose's exotically furnished town house and reluctantly had to admit that at almost eight o'clock it wasn't looking promising.

Jed, ever professional, had made a mental note for his column that, among others, two cabinet ministers known to have opposing views on everything were locked in conversation in an alcove, an Oscar-winning American actress was flirting gently with a distinguished retired judge and a bestselling author of steamy sex novels was being sternly lectured by a leading feminist politician.

Ellie simply felt sick with disappointment. The elation that had propelled her through the day vanished, and the good-humoured banter as she'd hijacked Rosie's fashion room to get ready, leaving Rosie remarking that anyone would think she was on a date rather than an interview, seemed light years away.

'Rosie,' she had said, solemnly pulling a short red crepe skirt up over legs clad in sheer black tights and black suede high heels, 'You know my work is my only love.'

'Well, I'd say you're besotted,' sniffed Rosie, having spent an exhausting afternoon demolishing the confidence of the model's agent, who had allowed the beautiful but brainless girl to cut her hair, thus practically ruining Rosie's fashion shots. Watching the slim figure of Ellie pulling on a matching fitted jacket with a deep vee, so beautifully cut it needed nothing under it, she sighed and mournfully asked her friend if she ever ate anything more than a lettuce leaf.

Ellie had laughed, saying never, provided it was stuffed with black forest gateau, and had departed with Jed in high spirits.

Now it looked as though she had fallen at the first fence.

To interested observers, and her entrance at Lady Montrose's nearly two hours before had not gone unnoticed, she looked a picture of cool, calm elegance, with her blonde hair swept up into a casually loose chignon, the stray curls around her ears lightly brushing delicate, gold hoop ear-rings. Those plus a slender gold chain around her neck were her only accessories. Almost immediately she had been swooped on by Brook Wetherby, anchorman of the most prestigious talk show on TV, who claimed it was high on his list of ambitions to be interviewed by her, a claim he expounded at some length and with increasing intimacy until finally Ellie agreed to have dinner with him to discuss it. This at least secured her release from the corner he had backed her into and she managed to avoid him for the rest of the evening.

Only one pair of eyes regarded her with hostility. Debra Carlysle, holding court in the centre of the room, had not been persuaded to attend this soiree only to find, however briefly, that she wasn't the main attraction.

'Damn Gavin,' muttered Jed. 'He swore they were both going to be here. And Carlysle has bored the socks off me. Come on, let's get out of here. Oh hell, look out, here comes Lady M.'

'My dears,' said the small birdlike figure of Lady Montrose, descending on them while trying without much success to pull an Indian-inspired fringed shawl round her frail shoulders. 'Have you got to go? I've had no time to talk to you and I'm such a fan of your column, Mr Bayley.

Dreadful rubbish but completely compulsive.'

In spite of her dismay at the absence of Theo, Ellie nearly burst out laughing at the expression on Jed's face. For once he was speechless.

Giving him time to recover from such a confused compliment, Ellie's naturally courteous manner overcame her own disappointment and she smilingly held out her hand to Lady Montrose, saying, 'We must think about leaving. Thank you so much for a wonderful evening – this really is a superb idea of yours.'

Lady Montrose was no proof against such genuine admiration and smiled warmly back. 'I'm so glad you think so. One always gets in such a muddle with these people,' she continued, waving her arm vaguely in the direction of the collection of household names behind her. 'One doesn't always know if they will gel, or even worse, like those two,' she nodded at the warring author and feminist, 'just be furious with each other. I suppose I should intervene . . .'

'Oh, why bother,' grinned Ellie. 'Just think how much more useful they'll be trying to outdo each other supporting your campaign.'

Lady Montrose laughed delightedly and patted Ellie's hand.

'Oh my dear, you're so right. Frightful, aren't they? I can't say I blame Theo for avoiding these occasions, but he hasn't failed me yet. Always arrives for a few minutes before the end.'

Ellie stiffened. 'Theo?' she repeated.

'Yes, my godson. Oh, do come and meet him. There he is.'

Ellie wheeled round and found herself gazing at the tall, lean frame of the man she had last seen when she was fifteen years old. Her fingers tightened around her glass, and she looked swiftly round for Jed. Her mouth felt dry, the room suddenly seemed stifling.

Theo Stirling's arrival was being greeted with shrieks of delight from the Oscar-winning actress who kissed him on both cheeks, a warmly clasped hand from one of the cabinet ministers, a proprietorial one held imperiously out by Debra Carlysle and with obvious affection from Lady Montrose, which was clearly reciprocated judging by the bearlike hug he bestowed on his godmother.

Thank heavens they hadn't given up and left five minutes earlier, thought Ellie, rapidly beginning to recover her composure and noting cynically that several other guests had delayed their departure seeing Theo walk in.

He was talking now to the judge and beginning to move through the room, greeting acquaintances, laughing over his shoulder at something the novelist said as he passed. From her stance by the window, Ellie had time to assess how the years had dealt with Theo Stirling. As she took in the clearly exclusively tailored cashmere jacket, the thick black hair that was perhaps a couple of inches longer than it should be, the even white teeth, the features perhaps more harsh than handsome, Ellie knew, to her annoyance, that he looked good.

But it was witnessing the carelessly bestowed, and in her estimation almost arrogant smile, that Ellie grudgingly had to admit that if looks alone judged a man, time had accused Theo Stirling of nothing more damaging than looking powerful where once he had merely looked authoritative.

She wished Jed was nearer to give her support, yet instantly was glad he had been cornered by Brook Wetherby, who was trying to jockey Jed into a mention in his column. God, he was vain.

She didn't want any slip-ups when Lady Montrose announced to Theo she was there. That particular shock might put this arrogant man in his place, but could be tricky if Theo blurted something out that betrayed they had met before. Drawing near, Lady Montrose smiled at Ellie and then beckoned to Theo to bend down so that she could whisper to him.

Ellie watched as with his hands lightly resting on her shoulders, Theo listened to his godmother and then slowly looked up and stared straight at her.

Their eyes met. Ellie found her legs were not quite steady, her hands were shaking and something close to fear began to fill her mouth as she saw the smile dying on his face.

'And this is someone you must meet, Theo,' Lady Montrose was saying, drawing him inexorably forward. 'Eleanor is definitely one of us,' she told him conspiratorially.

The next few seconds passed in a blur. Ellie felt rather than saw Theo's hand take hers, a brief, cool clasp. A formal acknowledgement of the introduction and then Lady Montrose's attention was claimed by the feminist MP, desperate to steal a march on the novelist by offering to do something first for Lady Montrose's vote-catching campaign. With a broad wink at Ellie, Lady Montrose went off to secure the support of at least one branch of the Labour party.

Left alone, Theo made no attempt to speak to Ellie, but simply glanced idly around the room, leaning casually against the wall, one hand thrust into his trouser pocket, the other clasping a drink.

Ellie stole a look at him, completely unnerved at his silence and lack of reaction to her presence.

'Aren't you going to say "round one to you"?' she asked lightly, unable to bear the tension a moment longer.

'Why? Are you anticipating more rounds?' he asked coldly, simultaneously smiling and raising a hand in acknowledgement to Brook Wetherby.

'Certainly, unless you give me the interview I want,' replied Ellie crisply, but smiling brightly at the judge who had been trying to catch her eye all evening and couldn't believe his luck.

'You know I won't do that. But for someone who looks,' he paused and ran his eyes over her with an insolence that made her itch to slap him, 'as though she would be more at home shopping than sparring with someone who is out of her league, I might be prepared to discuss why I won't.'

If ever I get the opportunity to bring him down to size, I will, Ellie decided. Jed, Oliver and her father could all have told Theo Stirling what that expression in Ellie's eyes meant but, indifferent to it, he continued to let his bored gaze travel around the room.

'Now, you're beginning to talk sense,' she said, adopting a reasonable tone, trying to goad him into a reaction. 'Name the time and the venue. I expect you've realized that I always get my man.'

She felt rather than saw him move. She found her glass being removed, a firm grip under her elbow and she was being propelled through the crowded drawing room towards the door.

'What are you doing?' Ellie hissed in fright.

'Taking you somewhere to discuss why I won't be interviewed,' Theo Stirling said.

Jed was standing in the doorway talking to Gavin Bellingham as Ellie, her smile frozen, approached with Theo clamped to her side. Theo paused and murmured something to Gavin, who looked doubtful, but shrugged while Ellie seized the chance to grab Jed with her free hand.

'I think he's gone mad,' she whispered urgently through clenched teeth. 'Get Gavin to call him off.'

To her dismay Jed simply smiled innocently back and began to move away. 'Gavin? I see no Gavin. Don't be stupid, Ellie. Be nice to him. Let me know tomorrow how you did it.' And with the last chance of rescue gone, Ellie found herself out on the streets of Mayfair, being pulled unceremoniously along by a man who looked for all the world as though he had murder and not conversation in mind.

Theo's hand remained clamped to hers as they headed down South Audley Street. I know now why people don't protest when they get abducted, Ellie thought. It's so embarrassing.

'You might like to know,' she said furiously as he yanked her round corners into Park Lane, paying no attention to curious stares from passers-by, 'I have left my wrap at Lady Montrose's, I am feeling quite chilly and I have no intention of going a step further with you.'

Theo's answer was to ignore her and to march her into the foyer of what appeared to be a private house.

'You have no right to drag me off into the night like this,' she protested as he inserted a key into a lock on the elevator and, still retaining a vice-like grip on her, pulled her after him as the door slid noiselessly open.

'Do you always do this much talking?' he enquired mildly as she finally wrenched her hand free.

'I am now ordering you to let me out of this lift,' she seethed, massaging her hand back to life.

'Certainly,' he said calmly as the lift silently halted. 'After you.'

'Thank you,' she snapped. Straightening her jacket, she stepped out ahead of him into what appeared to be a wide, thickly carpeted corridor, immediately in front of which was the entrance to someone's drawing room.

The vast room with two sets of glass double doors leading on to a wide terrace was in stark contrast to the one they had just left. Where Lady Montrose favoured a strong sense of the ornate, mostly inspired by the decorative style of the belle époque, the owner of this apartment had clearly allowed an innate sense of style and colour to emerge in the timeless and classic beauty of the eighteenth century.

Ellie was utterly bewildered.

'Where are we?' she demanded swiftly as she heard a door sliding softly shut behind her. Double panelled doors now disguised the entrance to the lift.

Without speaking, Theo walked into the drawing room and pressed a button next to a closed door on the far wall before turning his attention to a tray of drinks.

'My apartment, of course,' he said, raising an eyebrow as he lifted the stopper from a decanter and splashed whisky into a glass. 'Unless you prefer to discuss this situation in a crowded restaurant. Or would the street have suited you? May I offer you a drink?'

A series of images flashed uncomfortably through Ellie's mind: Theo with the Countess, the ravishing Italian film star, the heartbroken Caroline. She could feel the panic and just prayed it didn't show. A man like Theo Stirling was not used to being rejected.

'Ah, Joseph,' said Theo as a white-coated manservant softly entered the room. 'My plans have been changed. Would you arrange for Miss Carter's wrap to be collected from Lady Montrose's and make sure I am not disturbed until I say so.'

With a small bow and an impassive but significant glance at Ellie, Joseph withdrew.

'Come over here,' said Theo, holding out a glass of chilled white wine to a now silent Ellie who was frantically devising a way of removing herself from this outrageous predicament.

But why get out of it?

She took a quick glance around. After all, that Joseph person wasn't far away, so she wasn't absolutely alone with Theo and provided she kept her head, what could he do? Swiftly she revised her strategy.

'Thank you,' she said, moving forward and taking the

glass from him, feeling for some unfathomable reason suddenly out of her depth. What was it he had said? 'Not in your league.'

Well, let's see about that, she thought. Instinct warned her that it would be a mistake to let him see she felt nervous. Casting wildly round for something to say, her eyes lighted on the terrace and beyond it a magical kaleidoscope of colours of London after dark.

'What a . . . what a marvellous view,' was all she managed before disaster overtook her.

Turning to smile in what she hoped was a relaxed and friendly manner, she was unnerved to find Theo closer than she thought and instinctively took a step back.

She felt the sharp edge of a carved wooden plinth displaying a complex arrangement of white camellias press into her back, which promptly rocked unsteadily as she collided with it and, to her horror, toppled over sending a cascade of icy cold water down her back.

As the shock of water hit her, Ellie just closed her eyes and reasoned that if the good Lord decided to take her there and then, she would not protest. Without even looking she could feel that the impact had sent the contents of her glass flying and not only was her back sopping wet, but the front of her red crepe suit was now drenched in a perfectly chilled and very chilly white Sancerre.

'Dear me,' Theo said, clearly barely able to suppress his laughter as she stood silently dripping water on to his carpet, not even attempting an apology, waiting for his outrage to hit her. 'And there was I wondering how to cool you down. I think you had better get out of those wet things, don't you?'

As he spoke he led her through into a softly carpeted, white marbled hallway.

'Look, I'm so terribly sorry,' said Ellie, scarlet with embarrassment. 'I'll replace the vase and . . .'

'Forget it,' Theo smiled. 'I'm glad you're not hurt. Stupid place to put flowers anyway, they were bound to get knocked over.'

Relieved at his generous reaction but somehow not surprised, Ellie smiled gratefully at his back and followed him to the end of the hall, where he threw open a door and stood aside for her to go in.

'The bathroom is through there.' He indicated the other side of the bedroom. 'You'll find a robe on the back of the door. Don't worry, I'll have you driven home.' With that he closed the door and left her.

Ellie looked around. Despite heavily swagged dark blue silk curtains and a pale grey carpet, the room had a decidedly masculine air. A Georgian mahogany dressing table, a writing desk, several silver framed photographs and two deep armchairs flanked a king size double bed above which hung a set of equestrian engravings.

She wondered if Carlysle was sleeping here these days? Or did he go to her place? Jed said they weren't actually living together. She was too damp and uncomfortable to care particularly.

The door to the bathroom opened at her touch. She ran her hand down the wall until she located the light switch, revealing dark blue tiles and pale grey fittings, efficient, luxurious but again uncompromisingly masculine. No feminine hand could be felt anywhere in this apartment.

Slipping out of her shoes, Ellie stripped off the sopping wet suit and tights, folded them into some sort of order and looked around for something in which to wrap them. The promised bathrobe and some fluffy, dark blue towels were not really suitable so she padded barefoot back into the bedroom, hugging the robe around her as she went. Good manners prevented her from searching too intimately for something to pack her belongings into but she felt it wouldn't harm if she borrowed a shirt to wear. A towelling robe was simply not adequate in a strange man's apartment.

The closet door swung open to reveal a row of at least two dozen freshly laundered shirts. She ran her hand rapidly along the rail searching for something casual and lighted on a blue denim one, which seemed harmless enough. Hastily she slipped the shirt on and shrugged into the towelling robe once more. Then she looked at herself in the mirror.

'You're going to wake up in a minute,' she said to her reflection. 'You are just in a nightmare. All this is a bad dream.'

'I know you're a fast worker, but I take it you are still alone in there,' came Theo Stirling's voice.

Blushing furiously, Ellie swung the door open to find her host leaning lazily against the far wall, arms folded across his chest. He had removed his tie and Ellie, against her better judgement, found herself smiling. Debra Carlysle wasn't daft, she decided.

'Mmm. That's so much better than the fierce scowl . . . but I had no idea you felt so cold – a shirt *and* a robe . . .' He laughed at her stricken look as her hand flew to the shirt. 'I'm just teasing. I'm delighted my wardrobe was of some use to you.

'Come and finish your drink,' he went on. 'And we still have to talk.'

It was as though a light switch had been pulled, plunging them back to reality. Ellie visibly stiffened and her smile faded. Have you gone mad, Carter? Are you crazy? This is the man who wrecked your father, could wreck your brother. And you're falling for the oldest trick in the book. He's being charming. He wants to manipulate you, like he does with everyone else.

Just be pleasant, she calmed herself. Just long enough to get out of here without causing any further scandal. Let him think you've fallen for it.

Doubts on a fairly impressive scale had of course assailed her. Who would sympathize if she found herself being attacked? Who would believe her? She felt very vulnerable and suddenly very stupid.

Meekly she followed him back to the drawing room where in her absence he had poured her a fresh drink and the discreet Joseph had removed all traces of the now demolished flowers.

As Theo handed her the glass, he took in her dishevelled figure.

'I suppose a brandy might be better for you? To get over the shock?'

'Ugh.' Ellie wrinkled her nose. 'I can't stand the stuff. Tastes just like cough mixture to me. Not that I think that's what yours would taste like,' she amended hastily.

Theo just laughed and gave her the drink he was holding.

'So,' she said, perching herself on the edge of a pale cream silk sofa, crossing her bare legs and smiling up at him from under her eyelashes in what she hoped would pass for confidence. 'As you say, let's talk.'

For a moment she could have sworn there was a flicker of surprise in Theo's eyes, but as he settled himself on the same sofa, one arm lazily resting along the back behind Ellie, and stretched his long legs out in front of him, his expression was once again inscrutable.

'Why do you want this interview so desperately?' he asked abruptly. 'You must know it isn't at all wise in the circumstances.'

Remembering that she was now playing his game, Ellie smiled archly at him.

'I don't agree,' she said pleasantly. Giving Theo the full benefit of her most engaging smile she moved back to a more comfortable position so that she was half reclining on the mountain of cushions behind her. 'I keep my personal and professional life quite separate. No-one has interviewed you. I want to know what makes you so ambitious, so successful. Why are you one of life's winners?'

He looked at her, his eyes narrowing. 'You've certainly changed,' he said. 'At fifteen you wouldn't have known how to manipulate a man, but now . . . you've certainly learned how to use what you've got. Tell me Eleanor, what is it you really want?' he asked softly and she felt his hand move against her cheek in a caress so slow, so sensuous that she had to use all her willpower not to flinch.

She turned and gazed at him from under her lowered lashes.

'I've told you, an interview that will reveal the way you tick. The way you . . . er . . . persuade people to further your aims.'

'And you don't?'

Ellie swallowed hard. 'Not in the way people like you do.'

Casually he leaned across her and put his glass on the table beside her.

'What are you doing?' she asked, betraying the first signs of nerves as he removed her glass and placed it beside his.

'Doing, Eleanor?' he mocked. 'Why, I'm trying to be what you have already decided I am,' and before she could protest, he pushed her back on to the cushions, holding her flailing wrists, and brought his mouth down on hers as well as most of his body.

In the deepest recesses of her mind Ellie knew she could have stopped him, knew she should, but she didn't. It seemed such a childish thing to do, was how she explained it to herself later. But of course she knew it wasn't true.

She felt his hand moving under her robe, caressing her stomach, moving upwards to cup her breast in his hand, his mouth sliding down her throat. The room began to swim, she felt the weight of his body on hers and her legs beginning to part under him and she gasped softly on the edge of a moment that was sending her spinning, whirling down into a well that was engulfing her and then . . . then she was struggling against him, pushing him away shivering with loathing and rage.

'Get away from me,' she choked. 'You arrogant, conceited . . .'

Abruptly he moved away, and she heard him laugh, reach for his drink and recognized the sharp clink as he refilled his glass.

'Thought so,' she heard him say and felt him sit down beside her as she opened her eyes. 'Not your league at all.'

She was silent and he tried again, openly amused.

'Is the scenario going the way you planned, Eleanor? Is this the moment when I'm supposed to say, "You win"?'

Inside the fury that Ellie had tried to control snapped and, pushing away from him, she struggled to her feet and treated him to the full venom of her feelings.

'How dare you,' she breathed, crossing her arms in front of her body as though to protect herself from further harm. 'How *dare* you force yourself on me?'

'Force myself on you?' he hit back. 'That's rich, coming from you. Isn't that what you came for?'

Ellie gripped the back of a chair, leaning slowly forward, her face betraying the incredulity she felt. Her voice came in a whisper.

'Came for? *Came* for? Are you so rich, so spoilt, so disgustingly sure of yourself, that you can't see when you might actually be offensive?'

Theo shrugged – a bored, indifferent gesture that made his words almost superfluous.

'You always get your man, you said. I see now what you mean. Your success in life doesn't surprise me at all.'

'And yours,' she said, almost spitting out the words, 'fills me with contempt. The only reason anyone would want to interview you is to expose you for your ruthlessness, your selfishness and your blind ambition.'

He whistled softly, swirling the liquid in his glass. 'All of that? Is that what you think? Ruthless, selfish, ambitious? Is that how you see me? Why?'

'Why?' she shot back. 'You know bloody well why. There is not a scrap of evidence to show you are anything else.'

'I could easily say there is none to prove it either,' Theo said evenly and Ellie noticed that he never took his eyes from her.

Too far down the path of venting her rage, she ploughed recklessly on with a speech that even as she uttered it she knew she would regret.

'Okay, I'll provide all the proof you or anyone else would need. You nearly ruined my father. You took away my home. Now you're going to do the same to Oliver. Why do you want that land? Oh yes,' she said bitterly, the flicker of surprise on his face not lost on her. 'I know you're the bidder. Why don't you let Oliver buy it instead of building some God knows what on it and ruining his business?

'I didn't want to interview you at all. I can't imagine anything less pleasant. But if I hadn't, Jed Bayley would have. He found out about you going back to Willetts Green. The great Theo Stirling going back to his roots.'

'Is that who told you about my interest in Linton's land?' Theo asked sharply.

'No. He hasn't a clue. If Jed had got involved then all that stuff about my father might have come out. He's suffered enough because of you. At least this way, saying I would do the interview, I had a chance of protecting everybody.'

Theo hadn't moved. He sat watching her, his eyes narrowed.

'You call this protecting them?' He didn't even attempt to disguise the incredulous note in his voice. 'I don't know why I thought you would be different . . .' His voice sounded regretful.

'Different?' echoed Ellie, momentarily diverted.

'No matter,' he said, refilling his glass. 'Now let me tell you a couple of things. I will buy whatever land I want, when I want. You would be well advised not to repeat to anyone what you know. I'm not even going to ask how you know, I'm simply going to advise you once more: stay out of this or you'll end up getting hurt and so will a lot of other people.'

'Oh, I've no doubt in your hands, we all will,' said Ellie. 'Except of course for you. You don't know what it is to be hurt and you're too loaded ever to be in danger of finding out.'

He shook his head impatiently. 'Christ, you're a typical journalist. Typical career woman, too, using charm to get what you want and then screaming foul when your victim oversteps the mark. Clichés and assumptions . . .'

'*Assumptions?*' Ellie interrupted furiously. 'I *never* assume anything. But I tell you this. If you go ahead and your plans ruin Oliver, then there is no reason for me to remain quiet. I'm going to write a profile on you that will expose you for the heartless man you are. And, my God, no-one will be left to assume anything.'

'Now you can see why I never allow myself to be interviewed,' Theo said as she stopped, trying to recover her breath. 'I expect it will be a highly selective account. Just like those of most of your colleagues. Perhaps you should take lessons in accuracy,' he drawled, slowly rising to his feet and walking towards her, 'instead of relying on your other charms to get what you want.'

Bereft of anything else that could have conveyed the

83

rage she felt at such a studied insult, Ellie lifted her hand and aimed a stinging slap at his face, which by now matched hers in cold fury.

'Don't touch me,' she breathed.

His face bore the red marks of her hand, but he didn't so much as try to massage away the angry evidence of her rage.

'Touch you, Eleanor?' he said quietly. 'I wouldn't dream of it. I was merely going to say, write what you like, it won't affect my plans. And then I was simply going to open the door to bid you goodbye.'

Tears stung her eyes. Grabbing her handbag, she turned and ran from the room. Wrenching open the door to the elevator, she blindly collided with a very angry-looking Debra Carlysle, who was about to step out.

Turning, Ellie flung one final contemptuous look at Theo, standing silently where she had left him.

'More in your league, I think,' she said acidly and was gone before he could reply.

It was only when she reached the corner of Park Lane that she realized why she was attracting so many odd looks.

Tossing her head defiantly, Ellie drew herself up to her full height, and proceeded to extract what little dignity she could from finding herself alone, shoeless on a chilly June night, trying to flag down a taxi in Park Lane, clutching an evening bag and wearing someone else's towelling dressing gown.

Chapter Six

Jed slumped back in his chair, wishing that Ellie would sit down or even just *calm* down.

'No good,' he said, referring to the phone call he had just finished. 'Says Stirling was tough but professional. Has nothing but praise for him. Likes the man personally too.'

Ellie acknowledged Jed's remark with a brief nod, still listening to Judith's very county accent trying to prise a comment out of the beautiful young Austrian Baroness, Gisella Hohlen-Spier, who had once been significant in Theo Stirling's life.

'Oh c'mon, Sella,' she was saying into the phone. 'Of course I won't quote you, but you were linked with the guy for nearly a year, you must be able to say *something* about him. It's just for background. Okay, I understand. No, honestly, I won't even say you picked up the phone. But Sella, darling . . .' Judith paused and, staring innocently at the ceiling, purred: 'I ought to perhaps warn you that Jed might not now have the space to mention your charity ball, but I'm sure you understand. Byeee.

'Stupid cow,' she said, sticking her tongue out at the mouthpiece as she slammed the phone down. 'She was ghastly at school as well. Sorry, Ellie,' she went on, seeing the frustration on Ellie's normally sanguine face. 'I've tried everyone I can think of. Gisella was a last resort and she doesn't want to say a dickie bird about him.'

'This is really hopeless,' muttered Jed. 'They either think he's terrific . . .'

'Poppycock,' snapped Ellie.

'. . . or they don't want to say anything at all,' said Jed wearily.

'Paid off,' Ellie said curtly.

Jed and Judith exchanged a swift glance. What had got into Ellie?

'Ellie,' said Jed, carefully rubbing his eyes, 'we have been through every name in the book for the last two days and we are getting nowhere. Why don't we just take a break and then this evening I'll buy you dinner and we'll come back to it with less dog-eared brains.'

Ellie looked at them gazing hopefully back at her and was instantly contrite.

'Oh, I am sorry,' she said ruefully. 'You've been wonderful. I couldn't have covered so many contacts without you. Tonight, however, I am having dinner with the great Brook Wetherby. And you needn't look so relieved,' she laughed at Jed.

'Well, I am,' he said frankly. 'Supper with you in this mood isn't my idea of relaxing. Mind you, Brook moved fast, didn't he? You only met him last week at Sarah Montrose's.'

'I know, but he rang the next morning and said he was prepared to be interviewed but it would have to be over dinner. *Prepared*. I could only get away from him after guaranteeing to do it.'

'Watch him,' warned Judith. 'He has absolutely no views on anything but when it comes to roving arms, he makes an octopus look under-endowed.'

'Well, he can't do much in a restaurant, can he?' said Ellie practically. 'Okay, okay, I'm going,' she protested, as Jed began to push her from her perch on his desk.

'Sorry, but Roland's waiting for my copy,' he said, glancing at the clock. 'And if I'm to keep Sarah Montrose happy, I really must write some more compulsive rubbish.'

Ellie blew him a kiss, waved an airy hand at Judith

who was back on the phone asking a famous countess if there was any truth in the rumour that her eighteen-year-old daughter had moved in with the drummer in a rock group, and walked slowly back to her own office, hands dug deep into the pockets of her skirt.

Lucy followed her in and, as Ellie seated herself behind her paper-strewn desk, she deposited a steaming mug of coffee in front of her boss before reeling off a list of messages that had arrived.

Mostly they were routine: PRs confirming interviews that Ellie had requested, lunch dates from theatrical agents bent on getting prestigious coverage for celebrated actors, Polly offering her an exclusive under the old pals act, a couple of invitations needing urgent replies and a request to help judge a young writers' competition.

'. . . And Paul says can you let him know what time you'll be back this evening. Think that's all,' finished Lucy, frowning at the list.

'Can you ring him, Lucy, and say probably around ten thirty, I can't imagine I'll be any later. Er . . . anyone from Stirling Industries?' Ellie asked casually as she signed the last of the letters typed that morning.

'No. 'Fraid not,' said Lucy, consulting the list again. 'Although a woman rang. Husky-sounding voice, but wouldn't leave a name. Said she would ring back.'

'How odd. Anything else?'

'No, but I can't see you getting away for a break with this workload,' said Lucy.

Ellie gave her a tired smile. She liked Lucy, who was enthusiastic, gossipy and, at nineteen, mature enough to handle three quite different bosses. Ellie's instinct that she was impressively well organized had not been wrong either.

'But she looks so odd,' Paul had complained when he'd heard that Ellie was pushing for Lucy to be joint secretary to her, Paul and Jed. 'I mean what is it going to look like with my contacts? They expect me to be organized, she doesn't look it.'

In a rare moment of agreement Jed had sided with him.

'To be honest, Ellie, she looks like a direct hit on an Oxfam shop,' he said bluntly. 'I don't mind that but what if her brain matches?'

Ellie sat back and gave them both a confident smile.

'Tsk, tsk,' she said. 'Fancy you both being scared of bleached white hair . . .'

And thus it was settled.

Above all, Lucy was fiercely loyal to Ellie, who was very well aware that her relationship with Paul had remained discreet, thanks in large measure to Lucy who refused to discuss her bosses' love lives with the other secretaries, saying it was unethical.

Privately it was because Lucy, who in spite of her frivolous appearance was an ardent feminist, disliked womanizers like Paul and saw no reason to add to his reputation by linking him so strongly with an obvious catch like Ellie.

'I'm going to Oliver's this weekend, Lucy, so that will be a break,' said Ellie, handing her the pile of signed letters. 'Don't worry about train reservations – I'm going to drive down.'

'Well, I'll shoo you out of the office dead on five, then,' said Lucy, making a note and disappearing to her desk in the main office just outside Ellie's door.

When she had gone, Ellie sat gazing out of the window with a frown. Her fury with Theo Stirling had long since been overtaken by anger with herself for letting the situation get so out of control. The morning after her disastrous evening at his apartment, she had given Jed a carefully edited account of what had taken place after her hasty exit from Lady Montrose's, in what appeared to be a very intimate manner with the most eligible man, not only in the room, but in town.

'I can't tell you how stupid I felt, standing outside Grosvenor House trying to flag down a taxi . . . and shoeless,' she told him. 'Honestly, Jed, there really isn't any need to make such a noise . . . *Jed*! Really, stop it. It wasn't funny.'

For a second Ellie gazed at the convulsed figure in annoyance but the sight of Jed's shoulders shaking made her mouth start to twitch, her natural sense of humour overcame her and she began to rock with laughter.

In the outer office bemused colleagues attracted by the shrieks of mirth – an unusual sound these days in their rumour-stricken world – gazed through the glass window of Jed's office and brought Roland in to share the joke.

'It was Debra Carlysle's face, when she saw her lover disappearing out of the door with a mere journalist,' Jed explained quickly, knowing there were certain things one told the editor and others, including describing his star writer fleeing a property tycoon's apartment clad in not much other than a towelling robe, which you didn't trouble him with.

Jed swiftly provided a very truthful but tactful account of the glamorous, flame-haired prima donna's behaviour after Ellie had left the party with the man generally accepted to be the one Debra was linked with.

'Gavin tried to explain that Ellie simply wanted a quote about some property deal Stirling's involved in, but she clearly didn't believe a word of it and demanded that they leave the party immediately. At that point dear old Lady M tottered over to talk about her campaign and what Debra could most usefully do. All of which delayed their departure for such a long time, that finally Debra just shrieked, "I don't care if the entire bloody rainforest falls down, just let me out of here," and rushed out pushing an appalled Lady M flat against a rare jardinière – which fortunately I managed to save from crashing to the floor.'

'And did you get your interview?' asked a smiling Roland, whose mind never strayed far from the object of the exercise.

'Not exactly,' said Ellie carefully. 'But believe me I will. I'm working on a different kind of profile and I believe once it is compiled, he won't have any option but to make enough comments to complete the picture.'

Roland looked reassured. 'Knew you wouldn't let a little thing like a refusal get in your way,' he said, and exited without another word to the chairman's office for a private meeting.

Ellie and Jed exchanged glances. Roland was spending an awful lot of time with the chairman.

Ellie gave a wry smile and got up to go.

'Dodgy, eh? I wonder when we'll know. Anyway, I've entertained you enough for one day.'

What she hadn't told Jed was that the memory of Theo Stirling's mouth on hers, the strength of his body, was impossible to blot out, that it had kept her awake that night and more than once since then had made her question why it wasn't anger but shock that she felt when she recalled the ease with which she almost gave herself up to him.

And you had only met him an hour before, she chided herself. Even trying to console herself that his behaviour had been outrageous and insulting — treating her like some cheap little journalist on the make — could not eradicate the chastening fact that she had contributed substantially to the whole episode.

Torn between a desire to see him again to prove to herself that it was nothing more than simply a momentary physical reaction to an accomplished seducer of women, and a greater need to get herself back on an equal footing, Ellie had decided as dawn broke the morning after she had been forced to wander shoeless down Park Lane that with or without Theo Stirling's help she would get a potentially ruinous profile together.

She knew even then that it would be her waking thought every morning until she achieved her ambition.

As Ellie gazed at herself in the mirror hastily applying her make-up, she slowly lowered the mascara wand and knew she was deceiving herself. Sod equal footing, she finally acknowledged. It was time she faced the truth. She didn't want to get on an equal footing with Theo Stirling, she wanted to get the better of him.

If he can hold a weapon over Oliver's head, so can I, she told herself, vigorously brushing her hair. He of all people is going to learn that not everyone dances to his tune, she decided as she zipped herself into a beige linen shift dress.

It didn't occur to her just then, but for the first time in her life, anger had replaced fear at the thought of his name.

Tugging her jacket into place, she sped into the kitchen to try to get her muzzy brain working again on several cups of black coffee before leaving for the office.

What she hadn't bargained for was the deafening silence from the people who knew Theo Stirling. For some curious reason he aroused a sense of extraordinary loyalty in those around him.

Or fear, thought Ellie cynically. After all, hadn't she kept silent for so long, never acknowledging for a second that their paths had crossed all those years before? And not just her, but Oliver too. Apart from with his wife, Jill, he had become accustomed to looking blank if the name Stirling had ever been mentioned in his company.

How many others had been forced into silence?

She had decided on the kind of profile she would write in the belief that if she talked to anyone who had ever worked with him, dated him or even slept with him, a picture of the man would emerge with enough critical comment to sting him into an interview and, better still, a deal. A very straightforward one: back off from buying what she now regarded as Oliver's rightful land and she would kill the profile.

Ellie was also perfectly certain that she would not have the nerve or the stomach to print such a damaging profile, but Theo Stirling wasn't to know that. He had written her off as nothing short of a manipulative little tart and if that's what he thought, she might find it useful to let him go on believing it until it suited her to let him see that, unlike him, she was not unprincipled, she had moral scruples and most of all she didn't give a jot what he thought of her.

Which in itself was odd, because if she didn't care what he thought of her, why did it bother her so much that she wanted him to know he was so wrong about her? Even more puzzling, why did it hurt her that he was?

Deciding that the obvious answer was utterly ridiculous, she had tried to concentrate on the task in hand. After a day making fruitless calls to names that Theo Stirling had been linked with either professionally or personally, she had realized that she was too tired to address the problem sensibly. When Oliver phoned to say an old schoolfriend of Jill's had unexpectedly descended on them, Ellie had to admit she was relieved that her visit would have to be postponed, and instead took off for a weekend in Wiltshire where Amanda now lived in rural tranquillity with her husband, dogs and horses.

Once there she had driven Amanda to distraction by doing exactly what she said she wouldn't do: thinking about getting even with Theo Stirling.

By the time she reached the office on Monday morning, and had drawn blanks on four phone calls, she had enlisted the help of Jed, who together with Judith had embarked on attempting to unearth a few choice comments about the mysterious Mr Stirling.

Judith, with her trademark Hermès scarf, Gucci loafers and a list of friends drawn straight from Debrett's, had from the outset declared they were on a fool's errand. With a sinking heart Ellie had begun to believe her.

She remembered Jed saying when he'd hired Judith with no journalistic experience whatsoever, that he didn't give a monkey's about that.

'For a society columnist she has impeccable qualifications – the private numbers of anyone who is anyone are packed into her address book, a mischievous nature, she went to Chartbury and every one of the girls in her year are gossip column names.'

Leaning back in his chair, he'd swung his legs on the desk, and smirked.

'I therefore rest my case. However,' he added, being incurably honest, 'according to her father – you know he's a retired Army General? – it was simply fortuitous that the headmistress's request to remove his daughter from the school coincided with the whole family moving to Washington for a year and the only reason she can truthfully claim that she hadn't been expelled.'

Judith had been a great believer in short cuts even then and, as Jed had so rightly pointed out, she still pursued that policy to get her what she wanted.

Not for the first time Ellie wondered why a girl with a brain, good looks and social connections to die for, should find it necessary to swap sex for a smooth path to the top.

'Honest, Ellie old thing, love to help and all that,' she had drawled. 'But Stirling's frightfully first league and there is this sort of irritating code that if you speak, you're out.'

Codes, Ellie now told herself five unproductive days later, beginning to collect her coat and bag, were not sacrosanct, simply there to be cracked by the enemy.

And in Theo Stirling's life she was most decidedly the

enemy, the trouble being that she had to find someone else who saw themselves in the same role. As she made her way to Roland's office, she reflected that she had to find a gap in Stirling's defence somewhere.

Later that evening over dinner, Roland told his wife that Eleanor Carter sometimes treated him with less than the rightful amount of awe that was his due.

'Nonsense, darling,' said Thelma, who suspected that Eleanor Carter held no-one in awe, especially her husband.

At first she had been wary of Eleanor Carter. With such a striking face and that size ten body, she had fully expected her husband to fall in love with her, which would not have been unusual. But he was given no encouragement to do so by Ellie, who considered him old enough to be her father.

In the end Roland's fragile ego had been restored by a series of excellent profiles which did as much for his reputation as for Ellie's. Thelma had let out her breath and became quite fond of her husband's star reporter. Now she knew he must be exaggerating because Ellie rarely rowed with anyone and was unfailingly courteous.

'Ellie thinks you're a bottomless well of talent, and you know it,' she said passing him the vegetables.

'Well, how do you explain what she did tonight?' he demanded, spooning a generous second helping on to his plate. 'We were having a quick drink before she left the office, telling me about the Theo Stirling interview . . .'

'Ooh, has she got it?' Thelma broke in excitedly.

'No, but she will. Anyway,' he continued. 'She was reeling off a list of people who won't talk about him when Dixie came through and said there was an urgent call for Ellie. So she picked up the phone and just kept saying "Yes" or "I see" and honestly when she put the phone down she looked as though she'd seen a ghost.

'She just gazed at the ceiling with clenched fists and I swear she said "Thank you God", totally ignored all my requests to know what was going on and fled out of the door, leaving me with an opened bottle of champagne to drink.'

'Which of course you didn't,' said Thelma coolly.

'Er . . . which of course I didn't,' he agreed hastily.

Thelma smothered a laugh.

'So what was the matter with Ellie?'

'How do I know,' he said peevishly. 'Why ask me? I'm just the bloody editor. No-one tells me anything. But I'll tell you this, Thelma,' he declared, pushing his plate away and refilling his glass. 'There's something not right about her and Stirling. I have a feeling she knows more about him than she's letting on.'

'How fascinating,' said Thelma, pausing as she started to clear the plates. 'What makes you think that?'

'Something the chairman said when I mentioned it at this morning's meeting. Said he knew Robert Stirling, Theo's father. They were at school together and that he had often spent weekends with them at Willetts Green. I'm sure that's where Ellie was brought up. I'll check it out.'

At the mention of Marcus Margolis, the chairman of Belvedere, Thelma looked up quickly.

'And on that front . . . ?'

'Doesn't look good,' Roland sighed. 'Can't see any other way really. Neither can Marcus. It's got to happen soon. The company is bleeding to death.'

Across town, hastily scrambling out of her work clothes to be ready in time to meet Brook, Ellie was still recovering from the shock of the phone call. She had to admit that much as she disliked anonymous callers, it was a breakthrough.

The husky tones of a woman had said without preamble:

95

'I'm not going to tell you my name. Please don't ask. And don't mention this call to anyone. I know you are trying to gather information about Theo Stirling.

'I believe I have the facts you want. But be careful. He uses women, charms them into submission and then spits them out. Believe me, I know. I will call you another time. Goodbye.'

Ellie had replaced the receiver, her face ashen. It had to be ... it couldn't be anyone else. Only one woman Ellie knew for sure would have a reason to want revenge on Theo Stirling: the woman who had shared his life for two years, the woman he had refused to marry. The gap in Theo Stirling's defence had been breached. Lady Caroline Montgomery was going to talk.

Chapter Seven

Ellie followed the maitre d' to the table where Brook Wetherby was waiting. She had dressed carefully, bearing in mind Judith's warnings about his inability to concentrate on his food, regarding an attractive companion as preferable to a dessert.

However, the discreet and exclusive surroundings of the members-only Belmain Club tucked away behind Grosvenor Square, where Brook had suggested they meet, called for something that looked like real effort. Thanks to Rosie, one of Ellie's favourite designers had agreed to a considerable discount on his evening wear, and she had managed to acquire two or three outfits that might otherwise have never found space in her wardrobe. The strapless midnight blue silk shift dress with a wide black bandeau top that she'd selected this evening was one of them. Casting around for something that would complement the simplicity of the dress while not revealing too much cleavage to the lustful Brook, she had found a black chiffon bat-wing jacket, borrowed from Jill last time she was down at Delcourt.

Seeing the gleam in her interviewee's eye as he gallantly kissed her hand in greeting made her fleetingly regret not wearing chain mail with a key. Clearly Brook Wetherby was not a man easily daunted.

'My dear,' he said. 'We will not even think about work until we have had a glass or several of champagne.'

After which I doubt he'll be capable of thinking, let alone working, thought Ellie.

The next hour turned into a contest between Brook,

determined to keep the conversation at a dangerously intimate level, and Ellie's equal determination to keep his hand off her thigh. By the time they reached the coffee stage, Ellie had all but abandoned any hope of getting more than four sensible quotes from this over-amorous household name and was more concerned with removing his hand from hers without offending him.

'Brook,' she said smilingly. 'Tell me how I'm supposed to pour you more coffee and take notes if I only have one hand free?'

As he leaned forward suggestively she felt someone looking at her and, glancing over Brook's shoulder, found herself staring straight at Theo Stirling who had quite clearly witnessed the whole scene.

Shock kept her features immobile but panic sent waves of chaos through her head. How long had he been there? What the hell was he doing here?

To add to her panic, Brook, wondering what had claimed her attention, turned and spotted him at the same time, delightedly greeted him and urged him to join them for a drink.

Surely Theo would refuse, she thought wildly, but to her horror he said lazily, 'Why not,' and rose from his seat to let his companion go first. It was only then that Ellie recognized the blazing burnished locks of Debra Carlysle who, if anything, looked even less pleased than Ellie at being interrupted and, excusing herself to make a phone call saying she would join them in a moment, disappeared towards the lobby.

At this point Ellie decided that Theo Stirling was obviously mentally disturbed. Reaching their table, he shook Brook's hand and then leaned over to kiss Ellie on the mouth.

'Hello, darling,' he said and as though brushing her ear with his lips whispered, 'You won't even have to try with this one, he's a pushover.'

Incapable of speech, Ellie could only smile icily back at him while he quite blatantly lied to Brook about their relationship.

'Of course I know Eleanor,' he said smoothly, reaching out and squeezing her hand. 'We are very good friends, as I'm sure you are about to become.' With which he gave Brook a very broad wink.

Ellie had never felt so cheap. She marvelled that she found a voice at all.

'Indeed we are,' she said, smiling brightly. 'Sooner than you think, because we were just planning to finish this er . . . interview over a nightcap at my flat . . . is that not so, Brook?'

If it crossed Brook's mind that she had suddenly switched from being puritanical to the point of boredom to making it clear she would not find a proposition unwelcome, he didn't let it trouble him.

'Absolutely,' he said enthusiastically. 'I'll just phone for my driver to pick us up now. Excuse me, Theo. Won't keep you long.' He leered suggestively at Ellie and rushed eagerly into the foyer.

Left alone, Ellie gazed silently at Theo.

'That was a cheap and unnecessary crack,' she said finally in a shaky voice, but delivered with such dignity that she at least had the satisfaction of seeing he looked startled. 'You don't know me at all. Someone like your friend Miss Carlysle might find such a remark amusing, even flattering. But I don't. I find it indefensible.'

Gathering her bag and notebook together, she rose to leave as Brook, pausing only to exchange a few words with an acquaintance, reappeared to collect her. Theo watched her carefully.

'You must have seen he's only got one thought in his head,' he said mildly, politely rising with her. 'You were hardly discouraging him.'

Ellie looked at him impatiently. 'Of course not. I'm not

sixteen. I'm interviewing him. Much easier to be pleasant. He could hardly pounce on me in such a public place. However, until your ill-mannered intervention, I would have managed to deflect him quite easily.'

'So why did you invite him back to your flat?' Theo asked bluntly.

'Oh, that's easy,' she said, not even attempting to disguise the contempt in her eyes as she gazed steadily into his. 'I am just trying to be what you have already decided I am. Goodnight,' she said pleasantly.

'Goodnight, Miss Carlysle,' she added, as Debra arrived back at their table. The overdone lipstick and the cloud of perfume that trailed in her wake bore all the signs of a woman who had decided she was going to have her work cut out to keep attention focused on herself and had used her time in the ladies' to blazing effect.

Knowing that she was being watched by Theo, Ellie smiled encouragingly at Brook, linked her arm in his and swept out of Belmain's hurt to her soul and planning the most excruciating headache in history before Brook could even set foot across her threshold.

Debra Carlysle watched Theo watching Ellie exit from Belmain's with a mixture of irritation and uncertainty.

There was nothing new in that. Most of the time with Theo she never felt anything else. In the powder room she had gazed back at those perfect features, the faintest pout of the lips as she surveyed her handiwork. Reaching into her Chanel handbag she withdrew a small flacon of Jean Patou's 1000. Without removing her gaze from the mirror, she took off the cap and sprayed the perfume slightly to her left. Then she walked through the gently descending exquisite and exclusively fragrant cloud, snapping the flacon shut, knowing that she would now leave an indelible trace of her very expensive presence as she threaded her way back to the table.

Thank God, that ghastly little queen of a gossip columnist hadn't divulged to the world that Theo had left her high and dry at that screamingly boring party when he'd disappeared with a journalist.

Theo's acceptance to join Brook and Eleanor Carter was as surprising as it was alarming. If anything bore all the hallmarks of a repeat performance this was it; and while she had no intention of handing Theo over on a plate to a common little journalist, the greater need just then was not to appear to be unable to prevent another fiasco.

What irked Debra more than anything was that she knew Eleanor Carter wasn't common.

The powder room and a discreet phone call to Gavin to stand by in case she needed rescuing restored much of her command of the situation. Theo was quite another matter. At first she had seen in him exactly what she had confidently believed he saw in her: sexually alluring, untroubled by financial restraints, fiercely ambitious and therefore not dependent on anyone to live life to the full but, most attractive of all, available.

Well, he was now that Serena Castleton had been consigned to the past. Theo had never discussed with Debra his brief, disastrous marriage to the East Coast socialite who was now remarried to a Kentucky horse breeder, but it was obvious to Debra that the beautiful but clinging Serena had made a number of fatal mistakes bringing their brief union to such a messy end. So too had Caro Montgomery. None of which she was going to make.

The fan magazines and the gossip columns therefore found themselves the unwitting messengers of how Debra wanted Theo to view her. 'I need a man in my life, not in my house,' or 'I need a man who does not feel threatened by my success,' became a familiar refrain in all her interviews. They also repeated the one fact that Debra carefully never refuted but knew was a lie.

'I have so many areas left to explore. I haven't tackled Rosalind or Desdemona,' she would confide (carefully omitting Juliet, knowing she had missed the boat on that one) to each show biz journalist allotted their fifteen minutes on the occasions when Debra was required to promote another film.

In truth Debra could not have given a sod about the Bard. What Debra wanted was out. But out with some expensive conditions. A discreet visit to a plastic surgeon had dealt with the first signs of sag under the eyes, and her even more discreet visits to a doctor on Park Avenue back home in New York dealt with details like extinguishing her appetite for days on end when costume fittings loomed.

Debra wanted out all right but out with the protection of a man with all the big Cs: Clout, Charisma and Cash. No-one, absolutely no-one, actively involved in the film industry had any real money. She knew that, she had looked. At least not the kind that Theo Stirling had.

Unfortunately Debra for once in her life had made an error. Two marriages, which had propelled her career upwards but were discarded when their usefulness had expired, had left her with an interesting set of press cuttings but a totally untouched heart.

Theo Stirling, on the other hand, had unfortunately become an obsession. As she approached the table every inch the actress, a smile hovering on her lips, not for the first time did she regret having agreed with him that theirs was a relationship founded on fun, and uncluttered by plans for the future.

Persuading Brook that she had an unaccountably dreadful headache proved more difficult than Ellie had imagined. Unable to prevent him seeing her to the door, she had no option if a very unpleasant scene was to be avoided but to invite him in, but not before a brilliant plan had occurred to her.

'Er, would you excuse me for a moment,' she said. 'I'll just find some aspirin,' with which she fled into her bedroom, frantically dialled Paul's number and got his answer machine.

Keeping her voice as low as she could, she whispered an urgent message.

'Paul, it's ten thirty. If you want to save me from Brook Wetherby's clutches, grab a cab and come over soonest.'

Confident that he couldn't be too far away because Lucy had told him she would be home around this time, Ellie returned to the sitting room, where Brook was beginning to make himself at home.

Nearly an hour later, having exhausted every avenue of escape, she was faced with Brook, the worse now for a couple of whiskies on top of the champagne he had drunk all evening, looking for results. If she had been a more exploitative journalist, Ellie could have made her fortune out of his indiscreet revelations about his private life.

His first wife had divorced him over the woman who became the second Mrs Wetherby and she in turn had been supplanted by the current but estranged Mrs Wetherby who, he confided to Ellie, was nothing but a money-mad airhead who had sold the most intimate details of their relationship to that foul rag, the *Clarion*, in an act of unparalleled spite for a five figure sum.

Ellie doubted the price but had no trouble in believing the motive. Kiss and tell was commonplace and not restricted to page three girls on the make. The more upmarket victims simply wrapped the whole nasty, vengeful business in a more acceptable phrase. Putting the record straight was the usual one. Kathryn Renshaw was no better. However, now was not the time to tell Brook he was in good company, not when she was desperately trying to rid herself of his.

The rest of the whisky was demolished and Brook embarked afresh on his ambition to get Ellie's dress off and much more besides. Come on, Paul, where are you, she thought desperately as she laughingly told Brook she would be happy to drive him home.

'Home, my sweet,' he said, sliding an arm around her bare shoulders while the other imprisoned her waist, 'is where the heart is. And my heart is with you.'

And to think he was paid an annual six figure sum to come out with such crap. Ellie grimly determined to mention something of the sort when she finally described their encounter in *Focus*.

'Brook, you are impossible,' she laughed unconvincingly. 'You know you are out of my league. I'm just a simple, old-fashioned girl . . .'

The door bell pealing brought an oath from Brook and a gasp of relief from Ellie.

It was a very dishevelled Ellie who raced to the door.

'Paul,' she said, thankfully swinging the door open and stopped abruptly, her mouth open. Theo Stirling, lounging against the door frame and holding a long oblong box, looked suspiciously as though he was trying not to laugh.

'Personal delivery,' he smiled, strolling in just like a frequent visitor. 'Hello, Brook, I didn't realize you would still be here.'

The flustered and furious anchorman scrambled as best he could to his feet, hastily adjusting his waistband. Theo appeared not to notice, handing the box he was carrying to Ellie, who still hadn't managed to collect her wits, let alone find anything sensible to say.

'I was just acting as a messenger for Eleanor,' he smiled. 'But I would be delighted to offer you a lift home. I didn't see your driver anywhere in the street.'

Under any other circumstances Ellie would have felt compassion for the embarrassed anchorman, trying to recapture some of his famed charm, having been caught with a girl young enough to be his daughter by one of the City's most respected names, desperately trying to adjust his trousers and not entirely sober.

'No, no,' he blustered. 'I dismissed him. I mean I thought Eleanor and I might be longer than . . . well, it seemed wiser. She has the most dreadful headache, you know. Anyway, I'll call a cab.'

'That won't be necessary,' said Theo, standing aside as Brook recovered his coat. 'My driver will take you wherever you need to go and return for me.'

Ellie felt as though she were passing through a nightmare. How did Theo know where she lived? What was he doing here? And come to that, where was Debra Carlysle?

Too exhausted to care, she allowed Theo to usher an abashed but unprotesting Brook out. The anchorman wasn't too drunk to recall that as to date Theo had resisted all his invitations to appear on his show – 'Insiders' – for an interview, and the possibility would be completely wiped out if he told him exactly what he thought of him ruining his chances with Ellie.

When Theo returned, Ellie was sitting with her head in her lap, her arms wrapped around her knees.

'Aren't you going to open the box?' he asked lightly, but she detected a cautious note in his voice.

She looked up, gazing at him through a tumbled mass of hair. Silently she brushed it out of her eyes and pulled the string off the box. Inside, in layers of delicate white tissue paper, was a replica of the suit she had worn, and ruined, at Theo's flat.

'But why . . . how?' she demanded, looking in bewilderment from Theo to the contents of the box.

'Well, my secretary organized it. I'm afraid my talents

don't stretch that far,' he said apologetically. 'I gave her the size and the designer and she did the rest.'

'I'm impressed,' Ellie said drily. 'It was very thoughtful of you and I appreciate that you have been more than considerate . . .'

Theo groaned.

'Oh my God,' he protested, amused. 'I think I prefer it when you're not being grateful. Yes, I will sit down, and yes please, I'd love some coffee.'

Since Ellie had not offered him a seat or coffee and since it seemed unnecessary since he was now sprawled on the opposite sofa, she just glared at him.

'How dare you do this to me? You got me into that mess . . .'

'And I got you out of it,' he interrupted.

Ellie gave him a resentful look.

'Is that why you came?'

'No, I came to collect my belongings,' he said, laughing at her bemused face. 'I believe you borrowed an outfit to go home in.'

Ellie blushed crimson. 'Look, I am very sorry I slapped you, but you asked for it. And I don't believe for a moment you came to get your things back.'

'Well, now you mention it, perhaps I didn't,' he admitted and smiled with such genuine warmth in his face that Ellie couldn't help laughing back.

'And where are my shoes?'

'Ah well, I thought I would give you everything in stages. Who knows, I may need another excuse to visit you. I always keep something in reserve.'

Ellie regarded him with disbelief. He grinned.

'Oh well, it was worth a try. Actually I'd forgotten all about them. They must be somewhere, I'll get them back to you.'

She rose from her chair, taking the box and the new red suit with her.

'And I'll get your things . . . and some aspirin. I really do have a dreadful headache after all that.'

Relieved that she had washed and ironed his robe and shirt, Ellie disappeared to her bedroom to collect them and some aspirin from the bathroom cabinet on the way.

When she re-entered the living room, Theo was no longer there.

'I'm in here,' he called from the kitchen and as she walked through he was putting two steaming mugs of coffee on the table.

'You are looking a bit done in,' he said sympathetically. 'Tell me how you managed to stave him off for an hour?'

'Tell me how you knew where to find me,' she countered, very aware that physically Theo had the power to attract her and therefore this time on her guard.

'Not hard,' he smiled. 'Brook Wetherby uses a car company and the doorman just checked the address he was taken to. Do you like living alone?' He switched subjects, loosening his tie and lounging back in the chair.

He was, she discovered, easy to talk to. Wary at first, she told him about Amanda and how she preferred being on her own. He asked about her job. She asked him if he liked New York. He said for the energy but not the food. She laughed and they talked about favourite restaurants, plays, books.

An hour passed and not once did it occur to her that this man was an enemy. She kicked off her shoes and rested her feet on the rungs of the next chair. He made some more coffee. She liked seeing him in her kitchen. He teased her about the note on her fridge door, 'I can do without the necessities of life, but I can't live without the luxuries.'

She was laughing at something he had said, when Theo suddenly leaned across the table and took her chin in his hand.

Ellie caught her breath. Her serious grey eyes never wavered from his.

'You know, Eleanor,' he said, tracing the line of her chin; she noticed he never called her Ellie. 'If you stopped fighting me, you could win so much more.'

She stiffened and slowly removed his hand from her face. The husky voice on the phone came back. 'He uses women. He charms them into submission.' Please don't let him mean what I think he means, she said to herself.

'You mean if I drop the fight, you would be, um, how shall we say it? Generous?' she asked lightly, warily, testing him.

She saw a hard blank look replace the softer expression on his face that she was beginning to get used to.

'I wouldn't have put it quite like that. But if that's what you want, why, yes.'

Ellie thought she would never get to her feet. Sickening disappointment swept over her. 'I think you had better go now,' she said, choking back a mixture of rage and despair.

She walked ahead of him out of the kitchen.

'Eleanor, listen to me,' Theo said, swinging her round. 'What . . .'

The sound of the door buzzer broke in and Eleanor swung away from him to open the door. Paul D'Erlanger wasted no time.

Catching Ellie to him he kissed her and said, 'I've just got your message to come over. Sorry,' he said, realizing they weren't alone. 'Who is this?'

Ellie could not bring herself to look at Theo; she felt rather than saw the look of disdain on his face. She heard him move past her, saying softly as he did so for her ears alone, 'That was quite a performance. Congratulations, I almost believed you. Another friend of Eleanor's,' he said, ignoring her ashen face and shaking the younger man's hand.

'Fine, but I'd still quite like to know what you're doing here at one in the morning,' said Paul frostily, looking from Theo to Ellie who appeared to have been turned to stone.

'Oh, that's easy,' said Theo casually, 'I just came to collect these.'

And swooping up his shirt and robe from right under Paul's disbelieving gaze he disappeared into the night.

Chapter Eight

The call had come the morning after a very difficult scene with Paul, who had been furious to find Ellie alone with Theo in her flat in the early hours of the morning. She of all people acting out a scene like something from a Whitehall farce.

In her more honest moments, she could see that from Theo's point of view, who knew little of her lifestyle, instead of it being an extraordinary evening, men coming in and out of her flat like yo-yos at all hours could be par for the course. Tired and angry with the way in which Theo had brought such disorder into her life, Ellie was in no mood to entertain Paul's obvious suspicion that she had slept with him and had stubbornly refused to discuss his presence in her flat.

'He at least rescued me from Brook,' she said heatedly, stung by Paul's visible disbelief that she hardly knew Theo Stirling. 'And if we are going to discuss each other's every move, perhaps we should start by asking where you have been until one in the morning.'

It was a question Paul was clearly uncomfortable with and somewhere in the recess of her weary mind, Ellie realized that she was utterly indifferent to the answer. And so they parted each feeling let down by the other.

The telephone call came as she was trying to decide whether to apologize to Paul for being so ratty or piece together the interview with Brook Wetherby, who had had the wit to send Ellie some roses in case she had taken a dim view of his clumsy behaviour and allowed it to colour her view of him in the profile.

Lucy intercepted the call and reported that the caller insisted Ellie was waiting for her to ring but wouldn't give her name. Ellie sat bolt upright, all thoughts of Brook Wetherby and Paul forgotten.

'Won't you tell me your name?' she asked quietly as the husky tones greeted her.

'No, that's the deal. I have my own reasons for remaining anonymous. You've probably found most people do where Theo is concerned.'

'Are you expecting payment for your information?' Ellie asked, familiar with such requests and knowing Roland's view of these things, ready to inform the caller that pieces of silver were not on tap at the offices of *Focus*.

The woman gave a low, mocking laugh. 'That's all journalists ever think about,' she said. 'No, seeing the truth about him printed would be payment enough.'

Ellie listened, just interjecting the occasional question, experiencing a very odd sensation that while this version of Theo Stirling made sense it curiously didn't ring true with the man she was getting to know.

'How did he hurt you?' she asked gently.

'He used me. I fell in love with him. I needed help and he promised to help me. When I wasn't able to come up to scratch . . .'

'Do you mean in business?' interrupted Ellie, who thought discussing a private relationship with a stranger a very odd way to treat someone you claimed you had once loved.

'I mean in a personal arrangement we had – the details aren't necessary – he abandoned me. Left me in debt. I had to sell everything to survive.'

Ellie felt cold. Except for the names, the story sounded familiar.

'How can I use this information?' she said carefully. 'I have no way of backing the story up.'

'You will,' said the woman. 'I'm going to give you other

names of women he's cheated on, men who would like to see him get what he deserves.'

Ellie needed more. Pushing the woman for information, she grew impatient at the vagueness of her claims and, holding her breath, took a risk.

'C'mon, name names,' she said brusquely, her whole tone altering. 'Who are you talking about? If I don't have that, I'm not interested and we can end the conversation right here.'

There was a brief pause and Ellie thought the woman had hung up.

'Are you prepared to do that?' she repeated.

Finally the woman answered her.

'Okay. Why not? You'll find out anyway. To start with ask him why he threw these men out of Stirling Industries,' and she listed the names of five men Ellie recognized from the press cuttings who had made up the board of the company based in New York that Theo ran personally. 'Their homes, cars, lifestyle vanished. In two cases so did their wives. They know if they talk Theo has the power to damage them.'

Ellie could believe that, but she found the woman's next claim more difficult.

'I think he felt threatened by them. He accused them of cheating the company. The only thing they had left, and to avoid a scandal, was to agree to say they had resigned.'

'And did they cheat on him?' Ellie asked.

'I knew them all,' said the voice that Ellie was irrationally coming to dislike. 'I think you'll find it was Stirling's cheap way of getting rid of people who were no longer useful to him.'

'Like you?' Ellie said pointedly.

'Just like me,' the woman agreed pleasantly. 'I'm going to ask you to take a call from a friend of mine, Jessica. She worked for a mutual friend of ours who was involved with Theo for a long time – Caroline Montgomery.'

'But,' gasped Ellie and stopped herself from saying, but I thought you were Caroline, and changed it to something more innocuous. 'I thought she was out of his life?'

'Oh, emotionally speaking, yes. But Jessica knows what he did to her. So . . . speak soon, okay?'

And the line went dead.

Ellie's brain was working fast. If it wasn't Caroline Montgomery, who the hell was it? She replaced the receiver and buzzed urgently for Lucy.

'Get Scott to fetch these cuttings from the library,' she ordered, jotting down the names of the five men. Ellie looked at the clock; it was eleven a.m. in London, at least another two to three hours before any of the people the mysterious caller mentioned would be stirring in New York or Washington. 'And if someone called Jessica calls – no, I don't have a surname – put her straight through.'

By six o'clock she had heard back from two of the five men on her list. Cautious, unhelpful but clearly bitter about Theo, the first hung up when Ellie said she was a journalist.

The other bluntly announced he wasn't in any position to talk and he would just deny the conversation ever took place. But talk he did.

'It was a long time ago, honey,' drawled Matt G. Harksey, formerly finance director of Stirling Industries NY Inc. 'We took the rap for the incompetent Mr Stirling.'

'In what way was Theo incompetent?' asked Ellie, swiftly taking notes and wondering why she was feeling nauseated by all of this.

'Not Theo, sweetheart, Robert. His father. Anything went wrong, Robert blamed the nearest person. In my case, me. Theo wouldn't hear a word against his father . . . but he also knew if I was out so was Glenn Shuler, his father's deputy, and the plum job in the ole family firm would be his.

'No way was that conniving sonofabitch gonna let that slip through his Ivy League fingers. He called in some private detectives and between them pulled a convincing case against me and Glenn. Next thing you know, Theo is installed aged thirty-one as president of the company. Big deal. Big man. Big shit.'

'Were you compensated?'

'That's a nice word for silence money,' said the drawling voice. 'Sure I was compensated, but I had to say I had resigned. I didn't have the influence or the dough to compete with Stirling when he got going. I had no option. A man of forty-five isn't going to find it easy to get a job if his former employers say he had his fingers in the till.'

Ellie wound up the conversation. She had heard enough. She just wished she hadn't even heard that much. The rest of the evening passed in a blur. A fashionable young artist, having drawn the cream of London society to the opening of his latest exhibition at a gallery in Cork Street, became so unnerved by Ellie's lack of response to his genius that he finally found solace in several glasses of champagne and was heard weeping to the gallery owner, who had invested a considerable sum in his talent, that he knew, just knew, he was a complete failure.

At six thirty the following morning, Ellie pulled on a track suit and, throwing a swimsuit and towel into a bag, let herself quietly out of her flat. She flung the bag into the back of her car and, pausing only to smile good morning to Bill Burroughs who was leaving for work at the same time, drove through virtually empty streets to Covent Garden and the exclusive environs of Blundells health club.

The changing rooms were empty as Ellie quickly wriggled into a black one-piece bathing suit and pulled her hair into a pony tail. Within minutes she was poised on the edge of the pool.

Drawing a deep breath, she dived cleanly through the still surface of the water, plunging down, down into the refreshingly cool depths of the pool, sending waves in four directions. Her blonde hair flattened, eyes shut, gasping for breath, she surfaced with a swoosh. For a few seconds she trod water, vaguely taking in the only two other people in the water with her, religiously clocking up lengths before the clock beat them to the beginning of their day.

It had been weeks since Ellie had found time to go to Blundells, having enrolled in a burst of good intentions at the beginning of the summer with little regard for how many times she would use their facilities to justify the horrendous membership fee. But this morning, striking out in a rapid crawl, her brown arms cutting through the water, her legs kicking out strongly behind, Ellie would have paid twice as much for the relief that the physical exertion gave to compensate for the chaos that was enveloping her mentally. After four lengths of the pool, panting but invigorated, she rolled over and floated on her back, now able to reflect with greater calm and sense on the last twenty-four hours. Indeed, the last week or so. Was that all it was since the phone call from Oliver? Only a matter of days since Theo Stirling had erupted into her life.

As she closed her eyes and drifted silently down the pool, the grubbiness of yesterday's events became easier to handle, the sleepless night a receding memory.

Stupid woman, she chided herself as she gently kicked against the water, allowing the weightlessness of her body to flow at will, it's just a lot of pressure building up. Taken one at a time, each problem was containable. Why, anyone would feel exhausted trying to cope with the uncertain future they all faced, let alone Oliver's problems, or indeed Paul. Turning her body in the water, she swam leisurely to the side. Grasping the rail of the short ladder, she swiftly pulled herself from the water and, squeezing her hair dry, she could already feel her confidence returning, a sense of optimism that if she didn't allow charm and good looks to confuse her, all would be well.

Of that she was certain. She even allowed herself a small smile as she caught sight of her serious face in the mirror as she towel-dried her hair.

Showered, refreshed and restored to something approximating her usual positive self, Ellie drove home, poured a glass of juice, downed some coffee, changed and slapped on some blusher, and was out of the flat, albeit with still damp hair, twenty-five minutes later and heading for the office.

I should do that more often, she reflected as she walked briskly from Green Park tube to the office. The best of all possible ways to start the day.

She was still feeling the benefit of her early morning swim when at five o'clock the call from Jessica came through just as Ellie had abandoned any hope – or fear – that it would.

Jessica was nervous, inarticulate with a peculiar accent which could have been American, cockney or even Irish. She wanted, she said, to see justice done. It occurred to Ellie as she automatically began taking notes that Jessica sounded as though she was reading from a script.

'In what way?' asked Ellie politely, signalling through her window to Jed that he should go on without her to the launch party of a new perfume.

Jed pushed open the door, scribbled on a message pad the name of a bar where he would be later for a drink and left Ellie to her phone call.

'Well, Lady Caroline was good to me,' said the faceless Jessica. 'I think she was treated badly. When she was forced out of the apartment in New York, so was I. I was her maid, you see.'

It crossed Ellie's mind that she didn't sound like a maid who would be given a job in Theo Stirling's household, but then she was learning a lot about Mr Stirling and not one tiny bit of it did she like. Yet she had imagined she would enjoy hearing his reputation being ruined, but she didn't. She would have hated to analyse why.

Jessica's voice whined on. 'She did everything for him. Everything. Entertained all those people, none of them her friends. Pulled in all kinds of people for business for him. And then just one evening she had a few friends of her own in, invited me along as well. Caroline was one of the kindest people I ever met.

'Anyway, we were all sitting around having a few drinks and enjoying ourselves when he came in and threw them all out and Caroline along with them.'

Ellie was frankly sceptical and said so. 'Why should he do that? It doesn't sound very reasonable or rational, and I wouldn't have said he was anything but reasonable and rational.'

The voice didn't even pause.

'Well, he had his reasons all right. It all came out a few days later when he took up with that Austrian woman, Gisella, and now I hear he's with Debra Carlysle.

'Honestly, some women never learn. But Caroline did. None of her family wanted her to live with Theo, she was even cut off without a penny because she did. As a matter of fact, Caroline told me her father loathed Theo. And she was up against Ria, of course.'

'Ria Stirling, you mean?' asked Ellie.

'Yes, that's right, Theo's mother. She was dead jealous of Caroline. Never came to the apartment the whole time Caroline lived there unless it was to report back to Theo what she was doing. So Caroline, who had given everything up for him, found herself out on the street. Well, we came back to England and Caroline went over to stay with some friends in Ireland. We stay in touch. But my livelihood was ruined as well by that stuck-up snob, Stirling.'

Ellie thought the woman was quite vile and refrained from saying if she had been Theo she would have chucked her out as well. Instead she tried asking about the identity of the mysterious caller who had put Jessica in touch with her.

'Well,' said Jessica, a crafty note creeping into her voice as well as a snigger, 'let's just say she is a good friend who wants to see justice done.'

After Jessica had rung off, Ellie sat for a long time staring out of the window. Suddenly she felt out of her depth, delving into a kind of journalism that at best was muck raking and at worst, unjustified.

No. It *was* justified. Oliver, herself, her father, had a right to protect themselves. But not this way.

The argument raged back and forth in her head. Unable to reach a decision, she walked into Roland's office at six, to ask for the next day off. Seeing her white, drawn face, the editor suggested she took a week.

Ellie shook her head. 'No, I just need a long weekend with Oliver. I'll be fine.'

There were times, she told herself as she let herself into her flat, when she hated her job and hated people who were prepared to take part in such a demolition job on a man's character.

But most of all, she thought miserably as she poured a glass of wine, she hated herself and for caring so much that she was going to be the instrument to bring Theo Stirling to his knees.

Chapter Nine

Ellie first heard the news as she arrived at her desk straight from a breakfast interview with a bestselling author who had successfully resisted the government's attempt to have his book banned on the grounds of national security.

She felt elated. Every newspaper in Fleet Street had been trying to get Clive O'Connell Moore. So too had the heavyweight television programmes. But she had beaten all of them. Okay, so she had to make concessions to get it, giving him copy approval of all his direct quotes and agreeing not to enquire too closely into his private life, but nevertheless that was better than no interview at all.

But the compensation was enormous since he had, on what appeared to be a whim as they were parting after a congenial meal together, revealed exclusively to her that the leader of the opposition was telling friends that he was quitting after the next general election.

Roland would be thrilled. Just the sort of exclusive he wanted in these trying times. And just the sort of quotes he wanted to take his mind off the fact that she was nowhere near ready to let him see so much as a line on Theo Stirling.

She had to admit, she was glad of the excuse too.

A weekend with Oliver and Jill, two days of family life, taking her small twin nephew and niece for walks on the beach, playing chase and catching up with their news — anxious though it was — had restored her spirits to their customary positive level. More important, Ellie realized that a weekend away from all the pressures of London had strengthened her resolve not to forget that even the most charming of men could be ruthless in the quest to achieve their goals. Driving back along the motorway the night before, she had congratulated herself that she finally had Theo Stirling in perspective and it would serve no useful purpose to run any kind of feature on him just yet.

The wrangling for Linton's Field had taken on a new dimension and she'd listened intently as Oliver filled in the details over a quiet dinner she'd shared with him and Jill in the pretty hotel dining room.

'Conrad Linton wants to sell, but he's waiting to finalize other deals he's got going before he decides on the price and that will be influenced by whether planning permission is granted and, of course, inflation. It won't make any difference to me. Stirling's bid is still there and so is Oldburns'. But because Linton can't get back here until the spring, planning permission to redevelop the area is dragging its feet.'

Ellie wasn't sure what difference that would make. With two property developers slugging it out, the outcome seemed to her a foregone conclusion. Oliver was just delaying the awful moment. Beating Theo Stirling with his own weapons seemed to her an eminently more effective way to get the result they wanted, and she said so.

But for the first time since they sat down Oliver looked triumphant.

'Well, maybe. But don't you see? It will give me a chance to whip up local sympathy to keep the land as it is. It also means that the chances of all that stuff about Dad coming to light again will be kept at bay. The only danger is that Stirling might win on the popularity vote.'

Ellie almost screamed.

'*Popularity?* What popularity? He – the whole family – just ride roughshod over anyone and anything that gets in their way. Who on earth would find that appealing?'

Really, she fumed, Oliver and Jill had been living in the sticks for far too long. Didn't they understand about ruthless people?

Jill shot her husband a warning look and squeezed his hand, deftly averting a squabble that might have made Miles and Chloe sound reasonable. Honestly, she quietly seethed. Ellie might stop to think that Oliver could be right for once. Instead she explained.

'Jobs, Ellie. Maybe low-level starter homes. That's what he can offer and at times like this, it's potent stuff. Frankly even I would hesitate if I thought some of the people in the town might get a chance to pull through this recession if Stirling Industries decided that developing the land was viable. And don't look like that, Oliver, because you know you would too. It's an awful dilemma because it's our livelihood that would be sacrificed.'

Still feeling wrung out after two dreadful weeks, Ellie was not willing to leave anything to chance.

'Well, let's be prepared. A plan for survival is what you need. And honestly I'll help. Look . . .'

She paused and took in their anxious faces. 'Oh, all right, sorry, I shouldn't have shouted. I just get so mad when I know what some people are capable of. Look, it might not come to anything, but let me tell you what I've found out.'

They'd talked long into the night and finally, walking slowly back to the house where Oliver and Jill lived away from the bustle of the hotel, all three felt that if they eventually went down, at least they were going to go down fighting.

When Jill had gone to check on the twins, Oliver looked thoughtfully at his sister. She had told them about the problems at work, but she hadn't dwelt on them.

Ellie had changed. Oliver knew it and Jill did too. Sometimes he saw flashes of the old Ellie and knew under that cynical, tougher exterior that she presented to the world these days, the same vulnerable, passionate girl still existed.

Pouring her a nightcap he walked over to where she was sitting, lost in thought, gazing into an empty fireplace and handed her a drink.

'El, I know we've got problems, but if push comes to shove and these redundancies affect you, you've always got a home here – you know that, don't you?'

Ellie was startled. She hadn't thought her feelings were so obvious, but then Oliver always could read her like a book.

'You're a pal, kid,' she said, playfully punching his arm. 'But I don't think it will affect me like that. It's just not knowing how extensive the changes are going to be that's causing the headaches.'

What she didn't tell him was that the idea of going back to her roots filled her with dismay. Her whole life, the way she thought and lived was now light years away from Willetts Green and certainly far removed from the few years she had spent in Devon with Pa and Alison. Most certain of all was that the domesticity Oliver and Jill obviously adored held no real excitement for her.

It was still home, but it was no longer where she belonged.

This is where I belong, she thought, as she arrived the following morning at Belvedere Publishing. Independent, but part of a team, belonging somewhere where I mean something.

Bubbling with excitement about her breakfast interview, she halted as she emerged from the lift at the fifth floor and instead of turning left towards her own office she made for the opposite direction, intending to put her head round Roland's door to give him the good news.

The sight of Marcus Margolis emerging from the private lift on the other side of the lobby and heading towards Roland's office changed her mind. What appeared to be his usual posse of acolytes came bustling after him. Shrugging, she turned back and bumped into Angus, the chief sub, striding away from the art department piled high with layouts and proofs, and walked with him the short distance to his office. She nodded over her shoulder to the group disappearing into Roland's office.

'Wonder what brings him down at this hour?'

Angus looked thoughtful. He had been at *Focus* almost as long as Roland. A dour Scotsman, he generally gave little away and now was no exception.

'In the fullness of time, lassie,' he sighed. 'In the fullness of time,' and disappeared in the direction of the production room.

Ellie smiled after him but immediately forgot the activity of the powers that be as she saw the flash of scarlet through her office window.

The bouquet of red roses was visible even before she had opened her door. Already arranged in matching tubular glass vases, the tightly furled velvet buds splayed out in a vivid splash of colour in her tiny office. A grinning Lucy was gathering up the cellophane and ribbon in which they had arrived. Paul would be dropping by later to talk to Roland and would Ellie have lunch?

'Are the roses from him as well?' Ellie asked, moving one of the vases from her desk to the window sill. She knew full well that Lucy would not have been able to resist peeking at the card that accompanied them.

'Um . . . oh well, yes they are,' said an unrepentant Lucy. 'But I didn't read the message, honest.'

Ellie took a swift look at the card. Innocuous enough. Quite loving. Nothing that Lucy could interpret as anything other than a gift from a devoted man.

It occurred to Lucy that Ellie wasn't exactly in transports of delight at such an extravagant gesture, and she was right. The elation Ellie had felt at securing a meeting with Clive O'Connell Moore began to evaporate.

There had been a time when she had been intoxicated with the power of being so enveloped in passion. A time when the making up with Paul was more intense, more agonizing in its depth than the rows that had precipitated it. It had taken her a long time, and a great deal of soul searching, to confront what she had always suspected but feared to test: that Paul was masochistic and at times sadistic.

Other women – and there were at least two she knew about – were explained away in a pleading voice, which claimed Ellie had been uncaring, and he had thought she was trying to end the relationship. Bewildered, Ellie would spend an hour protesting vehemently against the idea, coaxing him back to her side, angry with herself for having so unwittingly hurt him.

Recently she had begun to have the strangest feeling that he hadn't misunderstood at all. It occurred to her that he had wanted to hurt her. He liked hurting her. Once, feeling wretched after a wearying exchange of doubts and suspicions, she had looked up to find him watching her carefully, with a passiveness that belied his claims to be in the depths of misery. It was gone in a flash, but the doubt in her mind took root.

It had been such a long time since she had been able to apply words like tender, sensitive, fun and the sheer joy of being in love, to her relationship with Paul. Sometimes, sitting on the tube, crossing town in a taxi, jogging across the common on Sunday morning, alone late at night, she wondered if those words had ever applied or whether, by just wanting something so much, she had made it seem as though that was what she and Paul shared.

Theo Stirling hadn't been like that. There had been a genuine warmth, a caring directness about him that Ellie's mind wandered back to more than she knew was good for her.

It wasn't sensible to examine her feelings too closely.

Even she couldn't account for the searing wave of disappointment that had swept over her when he had agreed he would be . . . what was it? Oh yes. Generous, if she could bring herself to stop fighting him.

Bad enough having a resentful, accusing Paul on her hands. She hadn't heard from him for five days. Five days of punishing her, and now this. Today, she said to herself, you don't need this. And not for the world would she have admitted that for a brief moment she had hoped the roses had been from someone else.

But then *he* would not have sent anything so obvious as roses and red ones at that.

'Ellie, Roland's office pronto,' came Lucy's urgent voice through the door.

Ellie looked round sharply and saw a buzz of movement in the outer office. Everyone in sight was rising and moving towards Roland's office.

'What is it?' she asked, hastily swinging away from the window. 'What's happened?'

'Not a clue,' answered Lucy, automatically picking up a notebook and pencil and waiting for Ellie to precede her.

Ellie joined the throng making their way down the wide, carpeted corridor to the editor's suite.

'No idea, ducky,' yawned Jed as she caught up with him. 'Dixie just told us all to assemble.'

Ellie looked quickly at his profile. Suddenly she felt panicky and she tugged urgently at his sleeve.

'Jed, you don't think . . . ? I mean is this . . . ?'

He squeezed her hand. 'Probably, ducky. It couldn't go on. Chin up. Don't panic about something that hasn't happened – not yet anyway.'

There wasn't time for any more. Roland's office was packed. The sales staff had come down from the next floor, the circulation manager was there with his staff and so too were the promotion manager and his bright, energetic young team who had done so much to make sure that *Focus* had the highest profile in town.

A soft babble of voices filled the air. Across the room Ellie caught Rosie's eye and lifted her eyebrows and shrugged. Pushing her way through the crowd, she edged towards the window embrasure and squeezed in beside her friend. Judith sat on the arm of a crowded sofa, long legs crossed, looking bored, examining her nails. Jed remained lounging against the door frame.

'Hear the old man's been closeted with Roland since dawn,' whispered Rosie as Ellie sat down. 'Must be heavy duty stuff.'

Ellie nodded. She recalled seeing the lawyer, Alistair Bell, emerging from the lift with Marcus and a man whose face looked familiar but which she couldn't quite place.

There was a rustle and Ellie saw Roland making his way through the crowd, Alistair with him. He didn't waste any time.

'I wanted you to hear it from me, before any announcements are made,' he told them, standing behind his desk, his back to the panorama of London.

Roland spoke evenly, quietly. The room had never been more silent.

'Belvedere Publishing has been sold . . .'

His voice was drowned in a gasp from the entire room. Sold.

Roland waited for silence once more before he continued.

'This morning the proprietor signed contracts with the new owners, Goodman Coopers, and the effect is from now.'

Bentley Goodman. That was the man she had seen with Marcus. It all fell into place.

Roland had half raised a hand to halt the questions already flying at him.

When? How? Who?

'Please let me finish and then I will answer as best I can any queries. You all know we have been struggling; indeed, everyone has. *Focus* is only one magazine in the group, but it is, and I believe this, the best of them all. However, we cannot survive in a recession on reputation alone. While the good news is that Bentley Goodman, the new chairman, has guaranteed to keep the integrity and the title intact, the bad news is that it is going to mean changes.

'The first change is that a new editor, Jerome Strachan, who many of you will know is currently associate editor of *Profile*, is with the new chairman signing a contract to take my place.'

He shrugged wryly, taking in their shocked faces.

'My own position is still a subject under discussion.'

Rosie leaned sideways and whispered out of the corner of her mouth to Ellie:

'Discussing how much the pay off will be, he means. Poor Roland.'

Ellie nodded briefly as Roland went on.

'The sad news is that there will be redundancies. Naturally we are anxious that as far as possible these will be voluntary and all contracts will be honoured.

'I've never lied to you, and I won't start now. We will, of course, have to make our own decisions about terminating some jobs if we don't get sufficient numbers to make not just *Focus* but the entire group more efficient and cost effective.'

The shocked faces of his staff gazed back at him. They had expected some cost cutting, some merging of resources. There had been no inkling that the changes would be on such a scale.

Jerome Strachan. Ellie could hardly believe her ears. At thirty-three, he was generally regarded as a temperamental whizz kid but the stories from *Profile* of his peremptory manner, his arrogance and his blatant self-promotion were legion.

Ellie stole a swift glance at Judith. She was staring ahead, utterly still. Poor Judith. He hadn't even warned her. It was written all over her. What a bastard.

Jerome Strachan arrived the very next day and wasted no time in making changes. Tall, thin, with a shock of blonde hair, Jerome had overdosed on image. His suits came from Italian couture, his flat was a docklands penthouse, his friends were loud and just about famous, his language explicit.

It was difficult to find anything good to say about him, but even his most fervent detractors had to admit he was talented. There was an edge to his ideas Ellie thought truly exciting, but she missed the measured confidence of Roland's ability to exploit them. Where Roland had commanded grudging respect, it took only a matter of days for Jerome to alienate everyone with whom he came into contact.

Within a week he had secured four voluntary redundancies and named the rest. Dixie had been asked, and had agreed, to stay on for the moment with this new young editor, out of a professional instinct that one didn't just jump ship but equally because such high-powered secretarial jobs did not grow on trees. She had moved with Roland as he moved up the ladder. His success was hers and his slide from glory – the unthinkable – caught her in its wake. It wasn't just Ellie who noticed that the good-hearted, motherly Dixie had taken to casting murderous glances at her new young boss which was nothing to what was said about him in hushed whispers throughout the building.

The second casualty of his regime, however, was Judith.

She emerged from her meeting with Jerome the day after his arrival and headed straight for the ladies'. It was there that Rosie found her throwing up, her mascara running in black streaks down her normally immaculately made-up face.

'Honestly, El, I know she's an opportunist, but I wouldn't wish that on anyone,' Rosie confided to Ellie much later, having ushered Judith quietly into her own office, shutting the door firmly until the other girl had stopped shaking. 'I'll give her her due, El, she refused to cry. She's angry – well, murderous is a better description. I think she was planning a march on Bentley Goodman's office when I left her. She said Jerome took just thirty seconds to tell her to clear her desk.'

After Judith, whole departments were ripped apart. Loyal, hardworking employees were summarily dismissed and strangely, for a company looking for reduction in manpower, some new faces appeared. A condition of Jerome's contract was the right to have some loyal lieutenants around him. He had managed to negotiate contracts for two of them who arrived within days and were brash, aggressive and openly derisory about the existing staff.

Outrage at their appointments was not confined to muttered exchanges in the corridors and within an hour of the announcement, a deputation led by Brian Compton, the news editor, and Denton Browne, the talented young photographer headhunted only months before from *Metro*, converged on Jerome's office.

'These are not replacements,' the new editor told them in a coldly furious voice when they asked him to justify his actions. 'Those other jobs no longer exist. These are people with special skills to do a special job.'

Anyone who knew Jerome could also have told them that his fury masked an innate terror of being challenged. Faced with these hotly indignant people he lashed back with the most wounding and undermining reasons that came to hand.

'It's obvious to me,' he raged, 'that if you had all been doing your jobs properly, I would not have had to appoint people from outside to pull this mess together.'

Before the week was out, Ellie's world changed out of all recognition.

Her own interview with Jerome had been an uneasy duel, Ellie trying to get his measure, Jerome telling her what he expected of her. It didn't sound any different to what she had been doing, but Jerome, with a thrusting and belligerent stance, simply relayed his instructions as though he were re-inventing her column.

Ellie watched him as he circled her chair, pulling deeply on a cigarette, pushing his fingers through his hair, taking calls, snapping instructions. He seemed unable to leave the subject of Theo Stirling alone. In a list of forthcoming interviews of some of the best of the Good and the Great, only the possibility of getting Theo into the pages of *Focus* interested him.

Ellie was shrewd enough to see through the hype and the bluster. Jerome Strachan needed that interview to blind everyone to the fact that *Focus* had acquired a new editor because of the new management's desire for their own man to be in place, a grateful man at that, rather than the necessity to improve the tone of the magazine. For *Focus* remained the undisputed market leader. Those who worked for it, read it and invested in it hoped that Jerome Strachan wouldn't ruin it.

A major interview published soon after the departure of his rival – no matter that his predecessor had instigated it – was the clout he needed to silence the gossips who openly queried his abilities.

'I'm not interested in deals with Roland,' he snapped. 'I'm interested in copy, good copy. Do a background piece, anything, but get him.'

Ellie knew he was going down a disastrous path, but she was heading for one herself if she didn't lead the way.

Tomorrow I'll call. Some pretence, anything.

By the time she reached home, she was ready only to take the phone off the hook, sink into a bath, to thank God she hadn't been one of the casualties of the new regime and to think seriously about moving on if it all got too bad. But even as she wallowed, eyes closed, in the soft, foamy, scented water she was uneasily aware that the options for such a choice were slim.

Paul's arrival half way through the evening was not entirely unexpected. After a week away in Europe, there had been no phone call; confident that she would be there, he turned up just as Ellie, wrapped in her housecoat, her hair wound up in a white towelling turban, had just finished talking to her father.

That weekend at Oliver's had put her in a family mood and she missed her father's company, which regular phone calls couldn't replace. It was true he rarely asked about her problems, but they would go for long walks across the hills when she descended on him every few months, and he would be content to listen, enveloping her in an affectionate hug, dragging her off to a marvellous little pub he had discovered or amusing her with perfectly drawn descriptions of life in the Devonshire village that he and Alison had made their home.

Visits by John Carter to his son's home were rare; even rarer were the trips to London to see his daughter. But the trips he did make were memorable, childlike and, just as when they were children, bad moods were forbidden. Trips to the zoo, a boat down the river, the Tower, followed by dinner at the Connaught, a lavish present left behind for her to open, and then he was gone in a whirl of kisses, extravagant promises to come more often; a vague, loving, amusing man, and Ellie suddenly longed for his company.

Her father greeted her call with rapture.

'Darling child, we want you here, don't we, Allie?' he

called and in the background Ellie could hear her step-mother's delighted agreement.

'Okay,' laughed Ellie. 'You win. Tell me when.'

'Ah, when. Yes, well, what about when we get back from Spain? Yes, after Spain. Give me a week or two to put everything in place and then come down.'

Ellie tried not to be disappointed. It was too childish. Her father's trip to Spain was not for another four weeks; two more after that would almost be September. The chances of her getting away would be reduced with the schedule she had lined up.

'Lovely, Pa. Look forward to that. Lots of love to Alison, love you.'

She had barely replaced the receiver when Paul arrived.

Bruised from the unwanted imposition of Jerome Strachan, missing the comfortable familiarity of a life she had grown to love, and disappointed by her father's reaction, Ellie did not resist when Paul took her in his arms, pressing kisses into her neck, trailing his mouth across her shoulders.

There was a desperation, a fierceness, to their love-making that had its roots in their separate needs: Ellie's to blot out the hideousness of her days and Paul's to reawaken in her a need for him which he knew was beginning to recede.

'You know I'm sorry, sweetheart, you know I need you.' His voice was hoarse, as his hands moved to pull the cord from around her wrap, then slid inside, stroking inside her thighs, his mouth moving down to her breasts.

Ellie clung to him, her fingers digging into his back, her eyes closed, waiting, waiting for the familiar stirring of desire to take over, take her away.

Paul was pushing her to the ground, no longer pleading, but demanding, loosening his belt.

'Please, sweetheart. Do this for me. It's just fun. Ellie, please.'

The belt was in his hand. Memories of another such night came rushing back. Then she hadn't been prepared, but now she was. Paul was forcing her around so that her back was to him, her arms pinned behind her. Ellie was no longer moving with him, she was pushing against him. Pushing him away. Fighting him. She didn't like this, she wasn't part of it.

'Hey, tiger,' she gasped. 'Take it easy. Paul . . .'

He ignored her. Ellie struggled. He swore at her. She tried to pull away, as he pushed her face downwards into the carpet, struggling to get control of her arms, pinning her to the floor. He was breathing fast, excited, she could feel the warmth of the belt sliding around her wrists and Paul's knees pinned against her side.

Ellie felt sick.

'Paul, no, not like this. Paul, stop.'

She tried to draw her knees up, struggling to sit up, yelling at him.

'Stop what?' he breathed. 'Stop like you didn't tell Stirling to stop?'

The words acted like a whiplash on her. Fury replaced fear. Outrage supplanted reason. Ellie just caught a brief glimpse of his face as she twisted her head and sunk her teeth deeply and painfully into his arm.

Shock more than pain halted him. It was a split second but all Ellie needed to roll clear of him and sling the belt to the ground. Furious and strangely not at all afraid, watching him as he rolled to the floor clutching his arm, she struggled to her feet and looked down at him. Reaching behind her she recovered the discarded robe, refusing to be panicked into moving at any more than a leisurely pace.

Calmly she spoke to him as he pressed the spot where she had bitten him against his mouth, to soothe the hurt.

'When I say stop, Paul, I mean stop. I'm not even going to dignify your other crude accusations by commenting.

But if you ever, *ever* raise your hand to me once more you will never see me again. Is that clear? Is it, Paul?'

She waited for him to answer, as she slowly shrugged into her robe, and leaned against the fireplace.

Paul sat up and hugged his knees to his chest, beating his head gently against them.

'You don't know what you do to me,' he whispered. 'I can't bear the thought of losing you. You don't know what it did to me, finding you here with him.'

He looked up at her, trying to smile, reaching up to take her hand, his voice contrite, his smile pleading with her.

Ellie's eyes told him everything. He dropped his gaze and mumbled sulkily into his clenched fists.

'Don't look at me like that, Ellie. Haven't you ever known what it's like to be jealous?'

Ellie gazed wearily at him. She had wanted comfort and found pain. Looking for love, she had simply glimpsed violence.

'I'll get us a drink.' She turned and walked into her kitchen. Paul followed her and as she pulled open the fridge door to extract a bottle of wine, she felt his arms slide around her waist, his forehead resting on the back of her head.

'Stupid of me, so stupid,' he whispered into her hair. 'It's just that everything is spinning out of control. It all used to be so good. Don't make me go. Please.'

Sighing, Ellie leaned back against him. She doubted they were talking about the same thing, but she had known him for too long and too intimately to throw him out of her flat and her life. That night, for better or worse, they needed each other.

Later, much later, they lay in bed together. This time he had made love gently, carefully and silently. Their mutual needs remained unspoken. And in any event, their needs had little to do with the intimate act they had just shared.

Finally when Paul fell asleep, his face buried in Ellie's hair, his arm lying across her stomach, she turned her face and looked at the sleeping man beside her.

In that moment she knew her future was not with Paul. But equally — and how she longed for it to be otherwise — she had no idea what lay ahead of her.

Years later she was heard to say that on reflection it was just as well she didn't know.

Chapter Ten

All thoughts of getting even with Theo Stirling were abandoned as Ellie tried and failed to comprehend the enormity of what had happened to them all at work. Who else would suffer?

Judith gone. Roland on leave pending a decision about his future. The entire office felt like a small country, harming no-one and suddenly invaded by these alien forces.

Paul wasn't on the list of those the editor wanted out because he was on a contract and useful because Jerome appeared to like travelling. But Brian Compton, the news editor, was, plus two of the subs, as well as Denton Browne, the brilliant young photographer who had been lured from *Metro* to *Focus* simply because he wanted to work with Roland.

The names were not that surprising. Jerome was settling a few scores and ridding himself of people he had neither the experience nor the willingness to handle.

'My sell-by date must have been stamped, confronting him like that,' said a shaken Brian Compton, as they all grouped in a pub opposite the office when it was learned he was out.

Poor Denton, thought Ellie. He had a mortgage staring him in the face, which he would never be able to manage now that his girlfriend was about to have a baby and had to give up work. It had been obvious he and Jerome were not going to hit it off.

Denton's work had drawn awards and admiration in equal measures, and his own exhibition of photographs had filled the Hamilton Gallery for the three days it was on display. Jerome had told him he wanted something with appeal, and to illustrate this, the new editor had sent a dozen tear sheets from previous issues of *Profile* so that Denton could get the general drift.

Denton's general drift had led to a confrontation that could be heard on the other side of the closed door and beyond, and he'd emerged from his first and last ferocious exchange of views with his new boss with no job, and the threat that his attitude amounted to dismissal.

'He said he would be generous, and count my resignation as redundancy,' Denton told an appalled Ellie and Jed. 'But it's got nothing to do with any of it. He just wants yes men around him. He's frightened of talent, frightened of people he can't control, whom he thinks know more than he does. Pathetic.'

They listened sympathetically and while usually they would have teased him about his arrogant view of his own talent, this time they knew it was what was going to help Denton survive and get back to work again.

He left later that day.

Briefly Ellie thought of Judith, the antithesis of everything she herself stood for, and felt a stab of pity for the girl who had gambled on career sex protecting her from the very situation she was now in. Jerome Strachan wanted nothing of the old regime to obstruct his way. Judith, so intimately acquainted with Roland, was a high risk but easy to dispose of.

Ellie had been more of a problem. She knew that. She knew that Jerome knew that. Her interviews were the best in town, the competition to attract her attention was fierce. Jerome found her difficult to manipulate. Unlike Rosie, who shrugged sheepishly when she found Jerome's current girlfriend, Sonya Harvey-Lloyd, foisted on to her as a 'consultant'.

'She makes Edna Everage look like a class act,' exploded Rosie, slinging her shoes off as Ellie poured them both a drink in her kitchen at the end of the first trying fortnight of Jerome's tenure. 'I can't get any decent girls to model the clothes and the photographers are leaving in droves. No-one wants to know about the rubbish she's dragging in.'

She took a gulp of the wine Ellie offered her and rubbed a hand wearily across her eyes. Ellie stayed silent; she knew the conflict that Rosie was facing. Her son Tom came first. The chances of prising his school fees out of the feckless Rory Monteith Gore were marginally more hopeless than Ellie ridding her mind of Theo Stirling.

Now that Rosie was divorced, sending her son to a weekly boarding school was her lifeline. No erratic help to worry about, just jealously guarded precious weekends that long working hours during the week meant she could keep totally free for her nine-year-old son.

Looking up, Rosie caught Ellie's eye. For a moment she gazed steadily back at her and then with a defeated sigh, closed her eyes and rested her cheek on her folded arms across the kitchen table.

Ellie reached out and squeezed her hand. 'Everyone knows it isn't you, Rosie,' she said.

Rosie lifted her head, a wry smile on her elfin face.

'I haven't any real option, Ellie. There just aren't any jobs, everyone's panicking because of the recession. I know it isn't Sonya's fault, Jerome has just told her she's God's gift – unfortunately I'm the recipient. I've just got to keep my head down and hope Jerome gets hit by a bus.'

Ellie laughed. 'It would have to be a triple decker, he's got all the sensitivity of a navvy's armpit. C'mon,' she said, draining her glass and throwing Rosie's jacket to her. 'Let's go berserk and have one course each at the Ivy.'

Twenty minutes later, a cab dropped them at the fashionable restaurant where Jed had said he would meet them. Of all of them, he seemed to be faring better than most. Jerome's love of gossip and the buzz he got from being at the centre of things made Jed invaluable to him. Moreover, Jed's contact book was the best in London. Jerome hadn't been in the editor's chair long before it dawned on him that society hostesses liked nothing better than to boast Jed Bayley's presence at one of their parties.

'How can you bear it?' Rosie asked him when he joined them at their table. 'That creep and his ghastly girl-friends.'

The waiter hovered behind him. 'Champagne and . . .' Jed rapidly scanned the menu. 'Just scrambled eggs and smoked salmon.'

He handed the menu back to the waiter and smiled straight into Rosie's concerned face, gently pinching her chin.

'How do I bear it, Rosie dear? I don't, but every time he behaves like the social incompetent that he is, I increase my expenses by ten per cent. You know me,' he said airily, as the waiter poured icy cold Dom Pérignon into his glass. 'Art for art's sake and money for chrissake.'

Ellie silently watched Jed as the waiter filled Rosie's glass. As he leaned forward to fill hers, she caught and held Jed's gaze.

Ellie knew the truth of it. So did Jed. No-one was safe.

She was also nowhere near as certain as Rosie that she was indispensable; nor could she believe in Roland's earlier assurance. She calculated that she had a value that on balance was more useful to Jerome than not. But she was wary. Twice in the space of a week she had clashed with him about who should be interviewed for her column.

A newly promoted pop star with a brain the size of a grape had been his first choice. Ellie had gazed impassively back at him.

Nor was Jerome's enthusiasm for the wives of his friends any easier to deal with. Women who seemed to have little to occupy themselves except to be seen lunching regularly with each other in full view of the better-known gossip columnists, were in his view prime candidates for exposure – flattering exposure – in *Focus*.

'I wouldn't mind if they were actually raising money for something, doing something useful with their position, like Lady Montrose and her environment campaigns, but just lunching and shopping. Oh God, spare me.'

Ellie's temper rarely erupted so forcibly, but over dinner with two of her best friends she could not resist the relief of venting her anger at Jerome's blatant hijacking of their columns for his own ends.

The following morning Ellie was treated to another example of how the very little ground they had in common was shrinking fast.

'Perhaps we could think that through a little,' she had deflected him. 'Nigel Barrington is a terribly well known industrialist but I think we need a little more substance for a profile than how Marianne Barrington fits her life around his. It would be difficult to get politicians, ambassadors, financiers to be interviewed if they thought the magazine was losing its prestige.'

Jerome eyed her with ill-disguised fury. Ellie stared coolly back.

'I think circulation is more important than prestige in these trying times,' he said, slamming his pen hard on the desk. 'Putting a household name in your column will do more for it than any number of grey-suited City men.'

Ellie had lost track of his reasoning. At best it was erratic, at worst he seemed to have a plan of his own which no-one else was privy to. Marianne Barrington might be a household name to Jerome in whose house she often dined, but to the readers of *Focus* she was not only unheard of, but of no interest.

Genuinely puzzled, Ellie tried again.

'If the magazine is to change direction, become more mass market, then I absolutely agree with you. Circulation would certainly shoot up. Is that what you intend?'

'Change direction?' he raged. 'Are you crazy? Is that what you think is going on? Why do you think I've been brought in? Just to listen to a lot of crappy ideas rooted in the good old days when advertising was up for grabs? It's because it was drifting from its target audience that I've been brought in, not to drag it away from its unique ground.'

Ellie listened to him in silence. No-one on the staff of *Focus* believed for a second the line that Jerome had fed them since he arrived: that he was saving them.

'And where's that profile on Stirling? That's the kind of stuff we need, juicy gossip, inside track. Sex, scandal, really punching it out.'

If there had been some way to tell Jerome then what she longed to hurl into his arrogant, self-satisfied face, she would have hesitated only long enough to discover which way would hurt him the most. Is that what he thought that profile was about, a scandal-sheet piece of smoking newsprint?

Much as she wanted to prove to Theo Stirling that she had weapons every bit as lethal as his power and money, at that moment she would have willingly consigned Oliver's livelihood to the dustheap rather than give Jerome Strachan so much as a line on the man she had threatened to ruin. Instead she took a deep breath and in a carefully controlled voice explained the special circumstances surrounding the interview with Theo.

Jerome lit his second cigarette and listened intently.

'He won't be interviewed by anyone. I explained all this to Roland. The only way to do it is to get other people talking about him. Maybe he'll relent. But I think it's unlikely. Not just yet.

'Roland trusts – I mean, trusted my judgement,' she amended hastily as Jerome's eyes flew to meet hers. Ellie knew she had accidentally hit a raw nerve. Roland's charismatic presence was a hard act to follow. 'He left it to me to make that decision.'

Jerome ground his cigarette into the ashtray, leaving a spiral of smoke wafting into Ellie's face.

'Let's get one thing quite straight, shall we? You make requests, I make the decisions. Is that clear? I don't know what . . .' he paused and let his eyes flick insolently over her before continuing, '. . . arrangement you had with Roland, but I've always been told the editor's decision is final.'

Ellie couldn't even feel anger. Just irritation. If only he would back off, stop being so prickly. No-one expected him to know everything, or to win their confidence overnight. Talent he might have, but maturity, Ellie realized with exasperation, was still a long way off. What was Bentley Goodman thinking of?

She tried another tack.

'You know, Jerome, I think we may just be misunderstanding each other. I'm more than happy to accommodate what you want. After all,' she paused and smiled at him in what she hoped was a friendly fashion, 'you are the editor and what you want is obviously priority.'

'I want Stirling,' he cut across her. 'I said it yesterday, I don't want to have to say it again.'

Ellie hesitated, torn between loathing and a real fear that he might do her some real harm. Fear won.

'Okay, I'll call his office, see if I can get a colour piece going but then, why don't I round up some other ideas and show them to you . . . I mean I'll get Dixie to fit me into your schedule and maybe we could go through them to see what you want.'

Ellie was beginning to realize how much importance Jerome attached to being held in awe. Where Roland would have dropped by her office, Jerome saw such a gesture as eroding his position.

To her surprise, he suddenly smiled. 'Sure,' he said, reaching out and buzzing for his secretary. 'Dixie, Ellie is just leaving, see if you can fit her in for an appointment before the end of the day.'

Ellie thought he was pathetic. Releasing the speak button, he drew a set of proofs towards him and began running his pen down the first column.

Ellie sat waiting for him to speak.

As though remembering her presence, he suddenly looked up.

'I'm sorry, was there anything else? Dixie will see you on the way out.' The insultingly dismissive gesture was not lost on her. He knew he had scored a point.

Ellie's kept her anger under control and, with what dignity she could, gathered up the files she had brought with her and walked as slowly as the situation would allow from the room, shutting the door carefully and courteously behind her.

'I've got a new way to spell his name,' she whispered into Dixie's ear as she passed her desk. 'It's P.R.A.T.' Dixie rolled her eyes heavenwards in sympathy.

'I'll ring you about seeing him. It's likely to be after five thirty – he's got more audiences than the Palladium lined up.'

Back in her office Ellie picked up her messages from Lucy. Polly, Anne Carmichael, two PRs and Jill wanting to know if she would be down at the weekend.

It sounded like heaven, but she wasn't at all sure she could afford the luxury of a long weekend in the country right now. Reaching across her desk, she flipped open her diary. Friday afternoon didn't look too bad, but at seven o'clock she had marked 'WIN, Soho Square'.

Those meetings of Women Into Networking usually went on a bit, being at the end of the week, with the weekend stretching ahead, no-one in a particular rush. Maybe she could skip it for once. She decided to call Anne Carmichael, who was this year's joint chair with Ellie, and make her excuses. Anne would understand.

That would leave her free to leave the office maybe an hour early to beat the traffic and get down to Dorset. A thought struck her. Why not take Paul? It was ages since he had been down and he loved the atmosphere at Delcourt. Who didn't? she thought ruefully.

Maybe away from London, away from the file on Theo Stirling dominating her thoughts, they could really talk, really relax.

Ellie began to feel better. Just planning a small escape revived her spirits. She was even able to grin at the cheap shots Jerome had fired at that early morning meeting.

She put a call through to Anne Carmichael, who came instantly on to the line.

'Ellie, you work harder than anyone for WIN. Sure, I can manage one meeting. Have a good time.'

Good. That was the first hurdle out of the way. Ellie buzzed for Lucy.

'See if Daniel can fit me in at around one. I badly need to get my ends trimmed and call me there if Dixie rings. I've got to see Jerome at the end of the day. Oh and Lucy, call Paul. Tell him I've been trying to reach him and I'll call before I leave the office.'

Flicking the switch back, she scanned the list of messages again. Nothing from Theo Stirling, but then, why would he ring? Jed had already broken the news in his column that Debra Carlysle and the property developer were an item around town and two or three of the tabloid papers had photographed them at exclusive receptions, looking every inch the sophisticated and international couple they were.

Each time Ellie picked up a paper she held her breath in case news of Theo's interest in Willetts Green had leaked out. Each time she breathed a sigh of relief. His visit was being described as private and on family matters as well as to be with Carlysle, who was filming on location in London.

Ellie gritted her teeth and told herself Debra Carlysle was welcome to him. As nasty as each other. Curiously enough the husky-voiced woman had made no further attempt to contact her.

Frowning, she took from her top drawer a buff folder in which the notes of all the information she had been given on and off the record about Theo were beginning to pile up. She started to flip through it and as she did so she reached for the phone and punched in the number for Stirling Industries. The switchboard put her through to Roger Nelson's secretary. She in turn asked Ellie to hold while she consulted with her boss. Seconds later Roger Nelson took the call, hesitating when she asked him to convey her request to Theo.

'No, don't call back, if you wouldn't mind just holding on. I'm not sure . . . I mean it's difficult . . . look, just don't go away.'

Ellie waited and while she did Lucy buzzed through to say Daniel had said okay, but she might have to wait a few minutes.

'No matter, I can get Jerome's meeting sorted out while I'm waiting. Say I'll be there in twenty minutes.'

Roger Nelson came back on the line. 'Would six o'clock be convenient? Unfortunately, Mr Stirling already has a dinner engagement . . .'

Ellie shuddered. Dinner! The thought made her choke. 'I'm sorry, you've obviously misunderstood, I wasn't suggesting dinner,' she cut across Roger Nelson. 'Six o'clock will be fine.'

Done it now, my girl, she groaned as she replaced the receiver.

Arming herself with a large pad and that day's papers,

she headed for the hairdresser, who fitted her into his busy schedule as much because she was a personal favourite as the fact that he liked to tell other clients that Eleanor Carter had been a client for the last three years.

By the time she got back via Bond Street, having bought a black satin jacket that she had been coveting for some time from one of its more exclusive boutiques, and her hair a shining silky mane just touching her shoulders, Lucy had rearranged her appointments for Friday and informed her that Jerome would see her at five.

'Hope that hairstyle isn't to impress him,' she grinned. 'What a waste.'

'Not on your life, but I hope this does,' said Ellie, brandishing a notepad with a schedule for her column that would satisfy every taste and every voice. 'By the way, can you order a car for me at five thirty? I've got a brief meeting with Theo Stirling.'

She tried to keep a casual note in her voice, riffling through papers on her desk as she spoke. Lucy whistled softly, hastily amending it to a cough when she saw Ellie look up with a frown, and ducked hastily out of the room.

Ellie was still sliding out of her jacket when she noticed the proof of the interview she had done with Brook Wetherby lying on her desk. Something about it made her pause. There was a large picture of Brook's ex-wife on the page. Puzzled, Ellie turned the proof round to study it, sliding slowly into her chair, shrugging her jacket off so that it fell in a heap behind her. She hadn't even mentioned his ex-wife beyond recording that they had once been married, so why dominate the page with this picture?

She soon found out. Half way down the page for no apparent reason there were now four paragraphs that had not originated with Ellie. They read like an embittered attack on Brook's estranged wife, his belief that she had married him only for his money and position and that she was no better than a muckraking bimbo.

Ellie felt as cold as ice. Horrified, she read and reread the paragraphs and as she did so she frantically buzzed the chief sub.

'Angus, what in God's name is going on with this feature? Who put that paragraph in about his wife? It's got to come out. My God, she'll ruin us. Has everyone gone mad?'

'I'm coming round, Ellie,' he said and minutes later while Ellie, ashen-faced, was still clutching the proof, he appeared and closed the door behind him.

'Jerome checked the proof himself while you were in York interviewing Max Culver,' he said. Angus looked crushed with embarrassment. 'He said he would tell you what he was going to do. That you had discussed it with him.'

Ellie was speechless. 'Yes, he did,' she said at last. 'And it's what I told him, but not like this, not with this detail. I simply recorded Brook's belief that his second marriage had nearly wrecked him, that in his view his wife had been more interested in her career than his. Not this. I've never even spoken to her.

'Angus, this is awful, it's so tacky. It won't do us any good and I can't have my name on it. I've already got Kathryn Renshaw baying for my blood, I don't want this as well. I must see him.'

The older man looked alarmed. He was fond of Ellie, but he knew what a delicate line they all walked. 'Calm down before you see him, lassie. No-one wins battles without a strategy.'

His calm good sense stopped her. She was seeing Jerome at five – better to discuss it then.

But her plans came unstuck. Just before five Dixie called through to say that Jerome had cancelled the meeting and had left the office, but would see Ellie at ten thirty next morning. Alarmed and frightened by the way things were beginning to turn out, Ellie ran down the corridor to Angus's office.

'But it's true, isn't it?' Angus asked urgently, glancing swiftly at the clock, aware that a motorbike messenger was waiting to dash the disk to the colour house.

'Yes, but not like this. Angus, please, I've got to take them out. I don't care what you do, make the picture bigger, anything you like, but these words are coming out.'

Even as she spoke Ellie had called the original copy on to his screen and was rewriting the offending paragraphs. Angus sighed and put a call through to the colour repro house, saying the pages were going to be a few minutes behind schedule.

Finally, satisfied that the offending words were removed and a swift, harmless paragraph inserted, Ellie stood aside to let him read it. Angus rapidly ran an experienced eye over the new words, pronounced it 'much better' and the danger passed.

Theo Stirling's suite of offices were on the tenth floor of the Stirling Building, five minutes' walk from St Paul's. The girl on reception, manicured down to the nth degree from her power suit to her black unnervingly high-heeled shoes, directed Ellie to a lift which would take her to the correct floor where she would be met by Roger Nelson's secretary.

The lift glided silently, smoothly upwards, totally at variance with Ellie's frame of mind. Shaken by Jerome's deviousness, apprehensive about the forthcoming meeting, her only consolation as she looked at her reflection in the mirrored wall of the lift was that at least she didn't look dishevelled. Fortunately, she told herself wryly, no-one could see the state of her brain.

The lift doors slid back to reveal a clone of the receptionist who introduced herself as Mr Nelson's PA.

They went down a carpeted corridor, ending with double wooden doors through which she was led into a spacious room, which had a breathtaking vista of the City and the Thames glinting in the late-evening sunlight. The room was occupied by a bank of technology that could easily have rivalled the stock exchange. Far from being intimidated, Ellie was rapidly becoming irritated. She had asked to see Theo Stirling, not the Prime Minister, and with her nerves raw from a trying day at the office, she said so as Roger Nelson came to greet her.

Instantly she was apologetic. He was, she guessed, in his early thirties. Rimless glasses framed a pleasant face that was clearly sympathetic.

'I think the Prime Minister would be easier,' he grinned. 'C'mon, I'll take you down to his office. He's expecting you.'

Ellie deliberately slowed her pace so that the ultra-efficient Roger Nelson would be obliged to appear less so to keep in step. She even stopped to consider a visual display in a glass case of a hotel development Stirling Industries had masterminded in LA and enquired chattily if he worked long hours.

'Not as many as Mr Stirling,' he answered politely. 'But then I am based here in the UK. He divides his time between here and New York . . . ah, here's Ann . . . Ann Winterman, Mr Stirling's personal assistant.'

Ellie, surprised, took in the tall, middle-aged, carefully groomed woman approaching them. Surprised because she had assumed she would be younger, not this mature, elegant figure who was smiling a greeting.

'Ann, this is Miss Carter. Does Theo want us to be present?'

Shaking hands with Ellie, Ann Winterman shook her head.

'Just briefly. He won't keep you a moment, Miss Carter, a rather urgent phone call came in.'

Ann excused herself, needing to attend to some urgent paperwork.

'Why don't you get Linda to do it?' Roger asked her. 'You'll only just get to the theatre on time as it is.'

'Don't worry,' smiled Ann. 'You know how he hates switching over. Besides, I'll grab a cab and get there before curtain up.'

'Mind if I share the ride? I'm meeting my brother and his wife for dinner in Covent Garden.'

'No problem,' smiled Ann.

As she spoke the intercom flashed.

'In we go,' she said, rising and leading the way.

Ellie took a deep breath and let it out again. If she had expected Theo to come forward to meet her, she was disappointed. In fact she might as well have been invisible for the first few minutes.

He was leaning lazily against the edge of a dark oak semicircular desk that filled one corner of a room; an imposing room, not an office, the quiet elegance of the pale grey sofas flanking an ample coffee table, the petrol blue smooth-as-velvet carpet, preventing such an impression.

He was flicking through a file. In shirtsleeves, his tie loosened, he straightened up as they came in.

'Roger . . . good. The meeting with Stockard Billings is to be held for an hour. Tell them I'll get there as soon as I can, but get it under way for me. Ann, I would like the figures for the Blenton contract tonight and when the confirmation comes over from the States, check the figures and then bring them to me at the restaurant and tell them I'm going to be later than planned.'

Ann Winterman's and Roger Nelson's features were inscrutable. Ann scribbled instructions, Roger glanced briefly through a file Theo handed to him.

'Would you like me to let Miss Carlysle know of the delay?' asked Ann.

'Let Max Culver know. My apologies, I'll see them both at the restaurant. I won't make the concert. Roger, take Linda and David with you, in case you need back-up.'

His eyes slid past Roger to where Ellie was standing.

She looked steadily back at him.

'Hi,' he said carefully.

Pull yourself together, Carter, she inwardly lectured herself. There was a silence, brief but significant enough for Roger Nelson to clear his throat and Ann Winterman to shuffle, quite unnecessarily, some papers into order.

Theo glanced at them. 'I thought we might get those instructions carried out tonight,' he said curtly. 'Not tomorrow. Drink, Eleanor?'

'What? Oh, no . . . I mean yes, thank you.'

Roger and Ann had hastily left the room. Neither had protested at the sudden extension to their day, their spoilt plans for the evening. Not by even a flicker had they made it known to Theo that they might like to have been asked.

Ellie, however, couldn't resist it.

'Your . . . secretary had theatre tickets this evening,' she said to his back as he poured her a glass of wine.

'Really?' he replied, walking towards her proffering the drink.

'Yes, really,' said Ellie. 'Terribly hard to get. Roger was dining with his family. He doesn't see them often.'

Theo regarded her with a perplexed look.

'Sorry, am I missing something here?'

'Not a lot. I simply wondered if it ever occurred to you that they might like to have been asked if they would work overtime?'

He eyed her narrowly.

'Their personal lives are their own affair, I don't want to know and if they don't like it they can leave. They are paid extremely well.'

Ellie opened her mouth to argue the moral high ground

she found herself on every time she was in his presence. It annoyed her, but for some reason she couldn't stop herself sounding naive. But before she could speak he was pushing ruthlessly on, driving his argument home. 'Ann has been with this company for nearly twenty years, as my father's secretary before she became mine. Roger has been here for nearly seven — and that as far as I am concerned is all I need to know about them. Now how can I help you?'

Her view so summarily dismissed, she took refuge in taking a gulp of the ice-cold wine in her glass, gazing as coolly as her fury would allow over the rim of her glass.

'Frankly,' she said coldly, 'I'm no longer sure that you can.' The futility of the situation she was in suddenly hit her. She found his attitude to his staff shocking, but her own position even more so. She had thought he was charming. He wasn't. It hit her with inescapable common sense that men like Theo Stirling do not run multinational companies on charm.

She wasn't even sure she had understood why women fell for him. This wasn't the same man who had made coffee in her kitchen, this was a stranger. She was here, she knew, to try and satisfy the whim of a petulant, arrogant young man. She was compromising her family. She was, much more humiliating than the rest, looking every inch the opportunistic journalist Theo believed her to be.

Suddenly she didn't care any more. Life on someone else's terms was too much. She desperately wanted it to be on her own. He was still staring at her, puzzled, impatient. Slowly she rose to her feet.

'I apologise for wasting your time,' she said with a slight smile, replacing her barely touched glass on the table. 'Forgive me. I must go. Enjoy your evening.'

He was between her and the door, staring intently at her.

'What *is* this? Eleanor, what did you want to ask me? Tell me. You must have had a reason for coming. What was it, why isn't it important any more?'

'It just isn't,' she said calmly.

For just a few seconds they gazed at each other, and then he shrugged, stepped aside and opened the door for her.

'Ann? Miss Carter is leaving, please show her out.'

Ellie walked past him, to her horror perilously close to tears. Ann Winterman was on her feet, puzzled but unquestioning.

'Of course,' she said politely, allowing Ellie to walk before her along the carpeted corridor, passing a surprised Roger Nelson on the way. She didn't look back; she knew Theo had simply returned to his office.

Returned to a life that she didn't understand, a man she had quite mistaken.

It could not be said that Ellie slept well that night. Her judgement, the much prized sense of intuition, had utterly failed her.

Not just because she had sought out Theo Stirling – that was an issue she would have to come to terms with much more slowly – but because she had allowed herself to drift so far away from her principles that she had allowed Jerome Strachan to manoeuvre her into making such a fool of herself. Turning up in Theo's office without a reason, hoping one would present itself. Dear God.

Tossing restlessly, she forced herself to address the immediate problem ahead of her: her interview with Jerome. Now only – what time was it? – four o'clock – now only six hours away. Think woman, think, she ordered herself. Strategy, that's what Angus said. Have a strategy ready.

Much as she loathed Brook Wetherby, she loathed even more the fact that Jerome had done something Roland would never have considered doing – would not have needed to do – without telling her first.

As she drifted in and out of sleep, she knew there was no way Jerome would even meet her half way once he knew she had altered the text back to a more reasonable stance.

As dawn broke, she fell into an exhausted sleep, waking with a start to see the hands on the clock approaching nine. Groaning, she scrambled out of bed. A shower and some hot coffee brought her disordered mind into more reasonable shape and by the time she arrived at *Focus* she was ready to fight her quarter with Jerome. She had telephoned Lucy to say she would be there by ten.

Lucy had sounded quiet, but then it was early and no-one was brimming with enthusiasm at ten past nine in the morning, especially these days.

It occurred to Ellie as she walked swiftly to her office that everyone seemed to be subdued. Her cheerful greetings had been returned in a half-hearted way. Too wrapped up with her own problems, she let it slide over her and addressed herself to the meeting ahead with Jerome. She planned to be reasonable, to point out quietly the problems attached to such a sudden switch in style.

She mentally rehearsed how she would dismantle his arguments while at the same time letting him see how she was prepared to listen to his point of view.

The phone squawked on her desk. It was Dixie.

'Ellie? Jerome will see you now.'

Chapter Eleven

Ellie gazed out unseeingly at the profusion of flowers punctuating the ordered existence of Green Park, oblivious to the whispering rustle of the trees swaying in a mild summer breeze. In the distance she could hear the drone of the traffic skirting Piccadilly, an unrelenting passage of purposeful noises of destinations to reach, journeys to complete.

At mid-morning, the park was only just beginning to fill up with tourists, seeking momentary relief from the hot, crowded pavements, nannies pushing their charges in buggies, a handful of students strolling lazily back to their studies. A couple of joggers, sweat bands covering their ears, panted leisurely past. An elderly woman shuffled to a halt in front of her, eyeing Ellie with open interest.

Tattered plastic carrier bags enveloped her. Her feet were shovelled into zipless battered ankle boots, her body encased in layers of torn, filthy coats, a split plastic raincoat ineffectually wrapped around her ageing body and tied with a length of rope.

Finally, having carefully deposited her luggage around her feet, she spoke.

'The Kaiser's got my string,' she announced accusingly.

Ellie dragged her eyes away from the middle distance and looked uncomprehendingly at the dishevelled woman.

'I'm sorry?' she said in a blank voice.

'It was mine.' Finding an audience, the raddled features of the old woman took on a hopeful look. A mind long since separated from the mainstream of life needed no encouragement to pour its many grievances into Ellie's ears. 'It was always mine. Put it away, I did. Nothing to worry about, I said. Nothing. I've got the string to keep it all together. 'Ave you got any string?'

She was coming nearer, hauling her cherished bags with her. Her ambition was quite clearly a closer acquaintance with this white-faced young woman, sitting huddled in the corner of the seat, hands thrust into her pockets, shivering on a day when temperatures were soaring, who thus far had done nothing to discourage her advances.

'That's right,' the woman cackled, as Ellie involuntarily shrank further into the corner. 'Room for all.'

Torn between fear and compassion and jolted abruptly back to reality, Ellie gently eased herself from the seat.

'I'm sorry,' she repeated, taking a slow step back from the bench. 'I have to go.'

The bag lady seemed unmoved. 'Somewhere nice? I used to have nice places to go to. But they weren't really. This is nice. Very nice indeed. Yes.'

She nodded her head vigorously, brooking no argument. Ellie hadn't planned on disagreeing.

Retreating cautiously to the path, Ellie watched as the woman fussily arranged her belongings around her, moving the bags into meaningless piles, rearranging them with a concentration that drove from her mind any further need of Ellie.

Ellie had the oddest sensation that she had seen that same pointless activity somewhere else recently. But where?

She turned and slowly began to retrace her steps. An hour sitting alone and still on a park bench had left her feeling stiff and sore. I ought to run, she told herself as she walked unhurriedly towards the entrance that would bring her back on to Piccadilly. But her legs like her brain felt dead, incapable of responding to anything but a desire to reach home and not have to think ever again.

Somewhere nice? If only. But where was she to go? If only she could think straight.

It was two hours now since Jerome Strachan, not able to meet her eye, had told her that *Focus* was letting her go.

Ellie had felt as though a gun had gone off behind her head. The room was no longer steady. Her mind had gone blank. Letting her go? Go? But where? Jesus. He means . . . he can't. Christ, he does.

Her voice was a croak.

'Why? Because I won't deliver Theo Stirling on a plate just like that or because I object to having my copy tampered with? I've already got Kathryn Renshaw claiming libel and I haven't even libelled her. What you wrote really was libellous. What was I supposed to do?'

Jerome looked surly and tight-lipped.

'Don't be absurd. It has nothing to do with your copy. It's . . .'

Ellie's eyes were riveted to him. 'It's what?' she demanded. 'What is it, if it's not that?' She knew her voice was unsteady.

'It's very sad for us,' he said lamely, fiddling uneasily with his pen, pulling the cap on and off.

'You must have known about this yesterday,' she said slowly. 'While I was discussing the column. You let me go ahead and do all of this . . .' She indicated the schedule she had prepared with a helpless, bewildered gesture. 'Why didn't you just tell me then? So much easier. Why?'

Jerome, confronted with such a reasonable question, took refuge in anger.

'You're being foolish. You know how much you mean to us, it's just another inescapable effect of this damn recession. It's got nothing to do with you personally, you do know that, don't you?'

Ellie struggled to keep her voice under control. Tears

weren't far away. She was horrified at her weakness, but anger sustained her.

Her voice was icy. Jerome blinked rapidly and began to move files aimlessly around his desk, stacking them in brisk, pointless movements as Ellie spoke.

'I can't think who else it has to do with, so, no, I don't know that at all. And no, I don't understand why you have to do it, but yes, I do know how much I mean to you.'

For a moment Jerome's expression brightened, but instantly he regretted it. Ellie's face was wreathed in contempt.

'Yes, I know exactly how much I mean to you. Nothing at all. Now,' she began to rise to her feet, 'if you'll excuse me, I have to clear my desk. I assume that's what you want?'

'Of course it's not what I want. I've told you, I have no option. Cuts are needed,' he said, staring fixedly at the sheet of paper in front of him.

'Well, it's what I want,' she said quietly. 'In fact I've never wanted anything so much in my life.'

She left the room without a backward glance. She heard Dixie calling after her, but she walked on, staring straight ahead. Tears were crowding dangerously close to the surface. If she could just get to her office, grab her jacket, get out of here. She didn't want to meet anyone. She brushed passed Rosie, ignoring her outstretched hand, and glimpsed Lucy rising from her seat.

Oh God, they all knew, guessed. Keep going, keep going, she told herself. The door of her office was open, her jacket and bag were within reach, the phone was going. Lucy was beside her, tears pouring down her face, trying to put her arm around her.

Ellie swung round and grabbed the sobbing girl by the shoulders.

'Stop it, do you hear me?' she commanded. 'Stop it.

Just cancel my lunch date. I'll be back. I've got something important to do.'

Lucy gulped and shook her head. 'Yes, Ellie. What else can I do?'

With the last remnants of self control perilously close to breaking point, Ellie forced herself to try to sound positive.

'You can stop behaving as though it's the end of the world.'

'I don't care,' Lucy muttered furiously. 'They're just sods, the lot of them. Bloody Jerome, he just can't bear to have anyone around him who knows more than he does. Denton was right. That's what all this is about.'

Even through the paralysing grip of shock, Ellie knew that Lucy was right. Jerome found her threatening. He needed women around him – men too – who thought he was God. She put her arm around the distressed Lucy.

'Hey, c'mon, that's enough,' she said gently. 'Have a cup of tea ready for me when I get back, okay?'

Swiftly she hugged the younger girl and, fearful that she might run into Jed, she took the back stairs, ignoring the lift and left the building by the goods entrance.

At last she reached the sanctuary of the street. A few more minutes and she was in the haven of the park. Another second and, safe from prying eyes, tears began to course down her cheeks.

Sinking down on to a deserted bench, she gave full reign to the torrent of emotions that had threatened to overcome her in the middle of the office. Anger and humiliation took it in turns to envelop her. Very little ground was left uncovered, as only those who have lived through the dreadful moments of knowing their carefully constructed life is being slowly torn apart could possibly comprehend.

Unanswered questions, bitter accusations, suspended belief.

Five years of long hours, personal sacrifices, building up to her own column from nothing. *Nothing*. And now this. Out. Not because she wasn't any good, not because she couldn't do her job, not because she had fiddled her expenses, but simply because . . . because what?

She needed to blame someone. Management, the recession, Jerome's obvious dislike of her. Anything would do because she knew for certain that it wouldn't be long before she began to blame herself. It was like waiting for an injection to wear off and the real pain to begin. Anger was sustaining her beyond a point she knew to be reasonable, but just then no-one could have reasoned with her.

She sat until her limbs ached for movement, but she didn't notice. She remained motionless, her face frozen into immobility and she didn't care.

The bag lady had probably saved her from delaying the awful moment any longer, she thought wryly as she headed down Piccadilly and made her way through the maze of back streets to the office. Well, I'm not about to lie down and die. That poor scrap of humanity arranging and patting her parcels . . . She stopped. *That's* who it was. Ellie almost laughed. It had reminded her of Jerome aimlessly pushing files together, not knowing what else to do.

Opposite ends of the human scale, but with so much in common. Both losers.

She stopped in front of the white building and found it hard to believe it was the last time she would be going in as an employee. Redundant. That's what you are, she told herself. Out on your neck. But if it killed her she vowed no-one would know how badly hurt she was.

Today I'll take it as it comes. Tomorrow I'll start again. In a week or two when I'm working somewhere else, this will all seem like the best thing that ever happened to me.

What was it Jerome had said? We will honour your

contract, of course. She almost laughed; honour was the last word she could apply to what had just happened. Three months' money. If he had only been straight with her yesterday she wouldn't have blown a fortune on a new jacket. Ellie knew she should be thinking of practical details like the mortgage and how she was going to survive, but she wouldn't allow herself to consider it, not yet. And anyway, she consoled herself, it probably won't even be necessary to worry.

First thing in the morning I will call Polly and Liz and, good grief, by the time those two had finished it would be a mere matter of hours before the phone started ringing with offers.

Comforted by the knowledge that she had friends to rely on, Ellie began to mount the wide marble steps. Office workers spilled past her en route to lunch, dashing to the shops, the wine bar. A little stab of fear went through her. I'm not one of them now, she told herself. Not ever again.

Oh God, what will I do, what will I do?

''Lo, Ellie,' said one of the advertising reps, rushing past her. 'Got another scoop?'

He didn't wait for an answer, just grinned. He hadn't heard, but he soon would. Ellie forced a smile at his retreating back.

'Not today,' she called. 'Maybe tomorrow.'

C'mon, c'mon. Pull yourself together, the stern lecture reasserted itself inside her head.

I'm not going to be beaten by this, not now, not ever. It was good to know the fighting spirit was still there. No-one could wipe out ten years of hard grind, five of those producing the kind of work she had done. She wouldn't go under, not when she had come so far. She simply wouldn't.

At the top of the steps the black reflecting doors allowed her to watch her progress as she swung jauntily towards them. She saw a woman of thirty, confident, businesslike. And that's how you're going to stay, she whispered to herself as she smiled a greeting to the doorman and walked briskly into the lift.

Squaring her shoulders, she took a deep breath and waited for the doors of the lift to open.

The corridor was deserted, but as she reached the open plan newsroom the shelter provided by the corridor walls fell away. A gentle hush descended as she skirted the desks and computers and headed for her own office at the far side.

'Ellie . . . I'm so sorry.' It was Barney, the art director, matching his step with hers, flinging an arm around her shoulders. 'Rotten, Ellie,' came the voice of the production manager, as he took her arm.

'Hands off, you guys, me and this lady have some celebrating to do.' Ellie looked up. There were Jed and Rosie and Lucy and Dixie, and then she was in the middle of them, caught up in a babble of voices, willing herself to smile, a stern look from Jed warning her not to cry.

'Oh, you lovely, lovely lot,' she whispered in a broken voice. 'No, no, I'm okay, I'm not going to cry. Promise. Truly. I've already arranged to see so many people, you wouldn't believe.'

She was lying as much for herself as them. Jed was moving her ahead of the crowd, urging anyone who encountered them to join them for champagne at the wine bar next door.

'Does that include me?' came Roland's voice.

'Roland!' Ellie exclaimed. 'What are you doing here?'

'Things to be settled,' he said with a shrug. 'So am I included?'

'Of course.' She smiled at the man who had disliked her and made life difficult for her, but had never tried to destroy her. 'As long as it's my company you want, not just the champagne.'

Deftly he moved Barney away and tucked his arm into Ellie's.

'Honestly, Miss Carter, don't you ever give up?'

They were all crowding into the lift; those who couldn't get in took the stairs. Somewhere in the recesses of her confused mind, swept along on an emotional tide of good will, loyalty and anger, Ellie knew this mood was dangerous, misleading. Not for the first time in her life, she felt on the edge of the crowd. She shivered and now it wasn't from sitting on a hot park bench watching the witless wanderings of one of society's forgotten women.

She had never been so afraid in her life.

Chapter Twelve

'Ask her to call Ellie, will you,' Ellie said into the phone. 'That's right, Ellie Carter, I'm at my home number. Yes, she has it. Great, thanks, bye.'

Replacing the receiver, she frowned down at the list in front of her. Okay, that was Polly. Liz and Anne, both calling back. Thus far she had restricted the list to people she knew, who liked her work. Friends really.

She dialled Tony Travers at Metropole Publishing. He had always been wonderful when they met. This time he was truly shocked.

'They must be mad,' he told her. 'You'll be snapped up and then where will that leave them?'

Ellie waited for him to suggest meeting, but whether because he hadn't thought of it, or because he had been unprepared for her call, he didn't. Ellie chatted on for a while and finally, taking a deep breath, said as lightly as she could:

'So there we are. I'm on the loose. An unrepeatable bargain.'

Tony's laugh sounded just a tiny bit strained.

'Ellie, this time next week I'll be reading your by-line in *Profile* or the *Guardian*. Thanks for letting me know. Let's lunch some time.'

Ellie's spirits lifted. She had known Tony for years, and there hadn't been a lunch, a chance encounter when he hadn't expressed his admiration for her work and to let him know any time she wanted to jump ship. She was being oversensitive, that was all. Not surprising really, but old friends like Tony would stand by her. Of that she was sure.

She reached for her diary. 'Great, Tony, I'm free on, let's see ... Tuesday and Thursday next week. How about you?'

There was just the briefest of pauses before an unmistakeably embarrassed voice said it wasn't possible.

'Just so much on, Ellie. I'd love to see you, so why don't we take a rain check just for now and when you're settled, give me a call and we'll celebrate.'

Ellie screwed up her eyes and rocked her body to and fro, trying to maintain a cheerful voice.

'Of course, great idea. Watch this space. Sure, great. Bye, Tony.'

How she regretted making that call. Bad enough to have to say she was out of work, but the humiliation of having to railroad someone like Tony Travers into asking her – or rather not asking her – to lunch. *Jesus.*

Stop it, she told herself. He was just busy. Her own diary wouldn't have allowed anyone to secure her for lunch for at least a month before all this happened. You've just got to be sensible.

But she couldn't, didn't want to, be sensible. She wanted to scream and howl and wreak revenge on Jerome Strachan. Overnight her feeling of shock had been replaced with fear and anger, and now it was resentment.

Lucy had agreed to cancel all the arranged interviews and to call up the lunch dates she had fixed. Ellie was a bit surprised that so many had said to rearrange a date when she was settled, but she shrugged, refusing to give in to an irrational feeling of hurt.

She had cleared her desk and the contents, from five years of working, living, breathing, walking, talking *Focus,* were now contained in two large packing cases sitting in the corner of her tiny spare room. All morning she had passed the door to and from the kitchen making endless cups of coffee, but she couldn't bring herself to unpack. Somewhere there were her cuttings books, the carefully recorded interviews she had done for *Focus*. Under all the books, dictionaries, and the bundle of pictures Lucy had removed from the pin board, there were the personal letters and files she had brought away with her.

The legacy or the debris – depending on how you regarded it – of a career that had taken over her life, and without it . . . Don't be silly, you idiot. It's not over. Just a chapter come to a close.

And somewhere in that pile there was the file on Theo Stirling, which suddenly didn't seem that important. Not now. Not for today.

Everyone had been so optimistic last night at her farewell drink, hurriedly convened when she had agreed to leave there and then. No-one stated the obvious: there was a recession on. When you are out, it's hard to get back. Jed had said, 'Don't hang around, first thing tomorrow get going. Be positive, El. Don't think you can't make it. I'm there for you and so are a great many other people.'

But he wasn't here now. No-one was. The independence, the space that had once seemed so precious to her, was suddenly very lonely. And she didn't know where to begin. Lucy would have known, capable, dependable Lucy. Disconsolately, Ellie wandered into the kitchen and poured some more coffee, taking it back into the sunny living room to drink.

Now come on, she said sternly, think. Be positive. List what you've got.

Okay, so she had three months' money, all her expenses up to date and . . . her coffee had gone cold and for some reason the flat felt very stuffy. She reached out and felt one of the radiators; it was stone cold. For a moment she was puzzled and then realized. Of course, the windows and the door to the patio were shut on a hot summer's day. Usually she was at work and of course they would be closed.

Work. Mustn't think about them any more, she told herself, unlocking the narrow double doors to her tiny walled patio.

Lucy bringing in tea, her messages, organizing her life. Jed putting a head round the door with a delicious piece of gossip. Rosie sitting on the edge of her desk solemnly chewing her latest diet-aid tablet and the phone an unceasing conveyor belt of invitations, requests, information.

Eleven forty-five. Friday morning. The day she had meant to go down to Oliver's with Paul for the weekend. The day ... the familiar feeling of panic that she was beginning to dread rose into her mouth. Stop it, this is just a temporary hiccough. In a minute someone will ring, God knows she had left enough messages. Surely not everyone was in meetings, out, not available?

Almost on cue the phone shrilled out into the silent room. Wait, wait, don't grab it. Take it easy. As it rang for the third time she picked it up.

'Hi, fancy lunch?'

'Jed!' Ellie sank down by the phone, delighted to hear from him, disappointed that it wasn't ... well, anyone really. Any one of the dozen people that she had phoned.

'No, I won't have lunch, but I'd welcome a drink later.'

Ellie resisted the temptation to ask him what was happening and Jed didn't volunteer any information. Of all the people she had spoken to, he was the only one she could be honest with and yet somehow it was too soon for that, even with him. Putting a brave face on it was already becoming second nature.

They talked for a while longer, arranged to meet for a drink at seven and then he rang off, leaving Ellie in her silent room.

Leggings and a baggy T-shirt after eleven o'clock on a weekday. No make-up and her hair scraped into a pony tail. She grimaced at herself in the mirror. The road outside seemed strangely silent and even when a circular was pushed through the letter box, Ellie went to the front door to see what it was.

By midday she had made another three phone calls, drunk five cups of coffee and still hadn't had the courage to ring Oliver to tell him. She feared her own reaction more than his. But she badly wanted to talk to someone. Paul. She stabbed out the number and got his answer machine.

Polly. Why hadn't she phoned back? Maybe she had and couldn't get through. Ellie rang her again to discover after a brief pause that she was still locked in meetings.

'Did you tell her I called earlier?' she asked Polly's secretary.

'I did, Miss Carter, and she will get back to you. She's just very tied up.'

'I see,' said Ellie. But she didn't. It took all her willpower to ring Liz Smedley at Movietone TV. Ellie and Anne Carmichael had taken over the WIN chair from Liz and Polly in the summer, and Ellie was sure that once word got around, she would have some offers pretty soon. Almost to her amazement, so used was she becoming to finding no-one available, Liz came on the line.

'My God, Ellie, I've heard. My darling girl. Lunch. That's what you need. Now get your diary.'

For the first time, Ellie almost cried with relief. Liz was running through her diary. 'Now, what about next Friday . . . no, make that Monday. How about Monday?'

Ellie scribbled it in her diary. 'Liz, you're a pal. Just what I need right now. Actually,' she said with a bravado she was far from feeling, but boosted by Liz's support, 'I needed a break so maybe this is a good time, you know, go at my own pace, look around a little.'

'That's *exactly* what you must do,' came Liz's voice. 'Look, I must dash but see you Monday – one-ish. I'll book. Take care, enjoy the next few days, you're going to be *so* busy after that, you won't know what's hit you.'

Ellie replaced the receiver, feeling her spirits soar. Liz was right. It was early days – well, hours actually. Just give everyone time.

Chapter Thirteen

And then it hit her. Cold grey light seeped through the shutters into Ellie's bedroom, with no sound from the street outside to disturb the silence, no voices to intrude into her thoughts. Shivering, she pulled the quilt up to her chin, hugging her knees, and waited for the familiar noises of the quiet side street starting to come to life to drift into her basement flat.

It was nearly six thirty. Five hours' sleep. That was better than last night. A great deal better than last week, when she'd felt adrift, unmoored from a daily structured life, when nights seemed to go on for ever and days seemed unending.

The sound of a milkfloat making its way down the street drew her eyes to the window. There it was. The comforting clash of bottles as the milkman swung open the basement gate, his feet clattering on the stone steps. The familiar clink as the milk was deposited on the doorstep and then the sound of his feet, retreating up the stone steps, the gate clanging behind him.

The start of another day.

A car revved up, purred into life and moved down the street. Ellie sat quite still, just listening. Soon she would have to move, get up. The flat was cold. Coffee needed to be made, the first of the endless cups that she would drink. The flat needed cleaning.

Her eyes wandered around the room. She could make a start in here. Yes, that's what she should do. Really give it a good clean, turn out her wardrobe. Oxfam would take most of it. Perhaps ... perhaps Nearly New, the secondhand clothes shop, would be interested in the designer jackets she had bought last year. Hardly worn, they would be more useful turned back into cash.

I'll think about it later, she decided. No point in getting too depressed. No point at all. Her gaze travelled back to the shutters; she closed her eyes and let her head rest on the wall behind her bed. Tears began to prick the backs of her eyelids, then the well of misery that she didn't even bother to fight any more took over. Silent tears rolled down her face, salty tears that ran into her mouth, sliding damply on to her neck.

Turning, she pressed her face into the pillow and gave way to the hurt that a month of empty days had produced. Days of phone calls that went unreturned. Letters unanswered. Meetings that proved fruitless, some born out of curiosity from hearing that, of all people, Eleanor Carter was job hunting, some because people were genuinely investing for the future when the economy improved and some because they wanted her to get her come uppance.

Oliver and Jill had been furious on Ellie's behalf and urged her to come home at once. Oliver even wanted to drive up to collect her. She had refused, assuring him that she wouldn't hesitate to turn up, the minute it all got too unbearable.

Half-heartedly, she asked him about Linton's Field and, with a cheerfulness that did not deceive her but she was too dulled by shock to challenge, Oliver told her that no decision was going to be made for some months. She could tell by his tone that while he tried to make light of it for her sake, the worry of it was getting him down.

Amanda rang from her home in Wiltshire, also urging Ellie to come down and stay. Although she kept insisting with little hope or conviction that things would get better, even she ended by saying hopelessly:

'Oh, for God's sake, El, come and starve in the country,

at least it would be better for you than London. Anyway the men are better looking down here. All those green wellies and Barbours. I keep telling David he should be grateful he met me in London, the competition for my hand wasn't nearly so severe.'

Ellie was sorely tempted. Amanda, with her prosperous husband, wanting nothing more than to raise children, ride horses and flirt with the best looking men in the county, made it sound like bliss. But that would be running away. And Ellie had vowed never to run away from anything again in her life. Ever.

At the end of the first week, however, she didn't know which she found more difficult to cope with: the unremitting, if strained, cheerfulness of those who believed optimism in the face of harsh reality was priority, or those who avoided her altogether.

Jed was a constant visitor and a consistent source of new ideas, names to ring, suggestions to make. Rosie, she knew, was always on the other end of a phone.

'Honestly, El,' she groaned. 'If you were in fashion I'd snap you up. But to be honest, it's just as bad in my neck of the woods.'

The promised lunch with Liz had never materialized. She had cancelled at the last minute, leaving a message to say she would resurrect the date soon. She still hadn't phoned.

But it was Polly's defection which had hurt the most. An uneasy lunchtime meeting which Polly had 'squeezed into' her hectic schedule a week after Ellie had left *Focus* had been brief and left Ellie feeling a wave of anger and stupidity that she had allowed herself to be so mistaken in this silly, artificial woman. A woman so keen on feminine solidarity, so insistent on calling a Ellie a friend.

'Throw me out at two, won't you?' was how she greeted Ellie shortly after one o'clock on the appointed day, along with a quick kiss and a hug. She flopped into the seat opposite at the stylish Italian trattoria she had chosen round the corner from her office. 'Client meeting at two fifteen. Ghastly little jerk he is, but the account is a good one. Really, if he gets more of a pain than he is, I might have to let him go.'

Polly gasped, her hand flying to her mouth.

'Oh, Ellie,' she said, squeezing her companion's arm. 'You know I didn't mean that. Oh Lord, what a clumsy thing to say.'

Ellie sipped the glass of champagne Polly had ordered for her and shrugged.

'Why? It's what's happened. Could happen to anyone.'

Polly looked relieved and picked up the menu. 'Now, my treat, of course, so have something delicious. I think I'll just have a salad, anything heavier slows me down and I shall need my wits about me this afternoon.'

Faced with Polly's evident haste, and in truth feeling no appetite at all, Ellie ordered the same.

'Now, tell me all,' said Polly, her eyes flicking around the restaurant to see who she could see. 'Right from the beginning.'

So Ellie told her. Not all, not even right from the beginning. But she did tell her that she was job hunting, that while it wasn't desperate to work this week, she would start to get twitchy if things went on like this.

'Hasn't anyone offered you anything?' Polly sounded incredulous. 'Well, you have shocked me. I thought you would be snapped up. Have you tried Tony Travers? Yes? Well, what about Roland – can't he do anything?'

Ellie didn't miss the quick flash Polly gave to her watch and wondered if it was worth explaining anything more to her. She tried.

'It isn't that there aren't any jobs at all to be had, it's just that there aren't any on my level . . .'

Polly cut across her with an admonishing tone that left Ellie itching to smack her.

'Well, you know, Ellie, in those straitened times you can't afford to be proud. Surely anything just to keep you in the swim of things . . .'

As insensitive remarks went, it was only marginally more offensive than betraying how little she knew about Ellie's character.

As though Polly hadn't interrupted, Ellie continued carefully.

'. . . and no-one wants to recruit someone like me for those jobs because they can get someone with less experience for less money. Pride doesn't come into it. Economics does.'

Polly, whose grasp on economics was marginally weaker than her acquaintance with integrity, looked blank and swivelled away to greet a silver-haired man making his way to a corner table.

'Ian!' she exclaimed, her arm shooting out to grab him as he passed. 'How marvellous to see you.'

Halted by her grip on his pocket, Ian paused and greeted Polly, his eyes sliding towards Ellie.

'You know Ellie, don't you? No? Goodness. I thought everyone did. Eleanor Carter, Ian Willoughby, editor of *Profile*,' beamed Polly, clasping Ian's hand with both of hers.

Ellie smiled politely.

'I didn't say I had never heard of Miss Carter, just that I hadn't met her,' he corrected Polly and leaned over to shake Ellie's hand. 'I heard about your leaving *Focus*,' he said pleasantly. 'Tough times. Don't give up, it could happen to any of us.'

Ellie nodded, thankful that at least he had been honest, not even attempting to say the correct thing and inviting her to make a pointless phone call to his office.

Undeterred, Polly simply looked pleased.

'I thought you must have heard of each other. However, Ian, I would just love to show you our client list. It is so you, you must let me know when you're free.'

Ian Willoughby smiled courteously and promised to phone Polly soon. The opportunity for Polly was too enticing to miss. Get your man in your sights and don't let him go till you've hooked him, is how she once described her working methods to Ellie.

'Look, I'll be back in the office around two fifteen and I've got a free hour, why don't you call then?'

Ellie felt a jolt of humiliation. There had been no client meeting to rush back for. No urgency at all. Just a desperate need not to get trapped by someone who could do Polly no real good for the moment.

Silently she sat until Polly's gushing exchanges had been made and Ian Willoughby had moved away to join his own lunch date.

Polly leaned over the table with a flushed face.

'That really was such a stroke of luck. Now what were we saying, Ellie?'

Ellie hoped that Ian Willoughby never phoned Polly Lambton and if he did it was to say he hated all her clients. Instead, she spoke steadily in a chatty tone:

'I was saying it isn't a question of pride, not taking a job a rung or two down the ladder. It's economics. It's the same as if you were suddenly made redundant, Polly – and as you said it could happen to anyone – you would find in your business that the higher up the ladder you are, the more your prospects shrink. It wouldn't bother me, going down a notch. But it would bother the company. So stalemate.'

Polly agreed it was all very difficult and of course if there was anything she could do.

'Well, yes, there is,' Ellie said calmly, Polly's sudden look of distress not lost on her. 'You could mention my predicament at the next meeting of WIN, just in case I can't get there. Put the word around. Who knows, you might even find a publicist or two who wants a decent copy writer. Now there's something I could do.'

A flash of alarm showed on Polly's face and she shook her head vigorously.

'Oh no, no, no. That would be impossible. I mean . . . well, you know how it is in the business at the moment, everyone cutting back and frankly, Ellie, with your talent you should be in a *big* job, you would frighten the life out of anyone you worked for. Such a threat to their own job having you around.'

Ellie smiled sweetly at her.

'Don't worry, Polly, I was only joking. My goodness, is that the time? I really must fly. Got to see someone at two. Sorry, didn't I mention it?'

She swooped over Polly and kissed her cheek, almost choking with laughter at Polly's startled face.

'Lovely to see you, super lunch. Stay in touch, won't you.'

She swung her jacket around her shoulders, grabbed her bag, blew a kiss and a cheery wave at a PR she recognized on the other side of the restaurant and whirled out on to the street, where she strode briskly away and around the corner.

Out of sight, her shoulders sagged, relief flooded over her. She couldn't help smiling and as she glanced at her watch she saw it was still only ten to two. Bloody Polly. What was it she had said that night? 'Women are friends, not just job titles.' And what was it poor, benighted, sloshed Warren had said? 'Bilge.'

Bilge to you, Polly, Ellie said, and ran to swing on the platform of a number eleven bus that was just pulling away.

Chapter Fourteen

It was the middle of September. Ellie had delayed her visit to Delcourt since that day in July when she faced an uncertain future, but it was time to visit her brother. It wasn't a visit she particularly looked forward to, but it was either that or Oliver turning up in London.

Yearning only for normality, her brother coming hot foot to town to take her away from it all would have been an admission of defeat, proof that the world had won, and Ellie just another loser in the big city. Of course it was an absurd image, but a month into a crash course of being pushed to the edge of everyone's lives had left her convinced she should never have left home.

In her more positive moments, and there were still some, she knew it was absurd. A small, well, smallish, oh all right, bugger it, a major reversal in an otherwise untroubled career, was no reason to regret the entire venture. The problem was, she knew, as she sat alone late at night, just staring into space, drinking just a little too much, eating just a fraction too little and ignoring the phone too often, that she was getting it all out of perspective.

This was a job loss for Christ's sake, not a terminal disease. But the day she knew that no-one was going to ring with the perfect job to put it right, was the day when common sense deserted her and a haunted paranoia set in.

The flat no longer felt like home. It had become a restraining centre to stop Ellie spending money. To keep the world out. Bowls that once played host to armfuls of flowers remained empty. Magazines that had once been stacked carelessly on the coffee table were notable only because they were two or three months old.

Three designer jackets that had cost her almost a month's salary each found their way to a thrift shop, for fifty per cent of the original cost, twenty per cent of that to the shop and the right to return them within three months if they weren't sold.

Ellie had dived out of the shop like one who'd just pawned the family silver. Grief. Three months. All that time before she got anything for them, and meanwhile she had seriously depleted a wardrobe that was unlikely to be replenished for some time. Talk about being a novice at this game. It was so absurd, it even raised a ghost of a smile.

The fridge, however, which once could be relied on to house a bottle or two of chilled Sancerre, underwent a change only in as much as the respectable and drinkable brands disappeared, and quantity replaced quality.

'This is ridiculous,' she exploded one afternoon to a silent flat. 'I am behaving as though there is no-one in the world who will employ me ever again. That I am bound to starve, sink or surrender to social services if I so much as buy a cheap bottle of wine.'

All of which she knew was nonsense but, without any sign of a permanent job being offered to her, she had to tread warily. How much freelance would she continue to get? If any? Everywhere she turned people were retrenching; work that once was farmed out was being dealt with in house.

Late one night at the end of her first month out of work, she sat at her kitchen table, wrestling with a set of figures and a bank statement that had frightened the life out of her. The salary on *Focus* had never been its most attractive quality. With a sinking heart, Ellie began to face just how much she had come to rely on the perks of her job to finance a lifestyle that on her freelance earnings could not be sustained.

After a while, she threw down the pen, pushed back her chair, screwed the paper into a ball and hurled it into the sink. Roughly three months left before the mortgage would become a problem.

Long ago at her interview, Roland had told her that she had a choice about which she ought to be very clear. Magazines like *Focus*, prestigious though they were, would earn her a respectable salary, not a fortune.

'Make your mind up now, because writers tend to get locked into the world in which they start. Nothing wrong with that, but it happens. Not everyone was fortunate enough, as I was, to switch from tabloid journalism to this. But then I wasn't far enough up the ladder for it to matter. I passed through Fleet Street without trace.'

Ellie had found that difficult to believe, but she knew he was making her question herself too. At twenty-five, with a mortgage and no visible means of support except her salary, she could so easily have found herself forced back to the features desk of a middle-market newspaper. The job on *Focus* meant a salary cut, but she reckoned that with a little moonlighting until she got it all together, she could manage.

If Roland ever suspected that his newest recruit was working into the small hours banging out show biz stories and nightclub gossip for the tabloid market using another name, he'd said nothing.

Eventually, as Ellie's career took off, most of her social life was being paid for by the magazine. The people who invited her to first nights, show biz parties, exhibitions and the occasional freebie in some exotic hot spot they were eager to promote, became her friends. The goodies they showered on her removed the need to finance a social life. Expenses were modest but it all helped.

First of all she was brave enough to buy a small car, a

Mini, and as she grew more successful and her bank account showed she was more often in credit than out, she switched to a Golf GTi. It wasn't new, but she loved it, convertible, black leather seats, black leather steering wheel. She hadn't even bothered to take it back to the flat, but had driven straight down to Wiltshire, dragging a startled Amanda out of her cottage. Shrieking with laughter, they had taken off into the countryside.

Parked outside a country inn with wistaria climbing the walls and only the sound of birds overhead to break the silence, they sat on a wooden bench, soaking up the hot June sunshine and just gazed at Ellie's pride and joy.

Amanda sighed wistfully and said how different their lives would have been if they had only had the car when they lived together.

'Just think how many of those creeps would have got the elbow, if we hadn't needed them for a ride back to town.'

Ellie gave a satisfied sigh.

'Just think how more discerning I can be now. Fancy free and on the up.'

'Ahh.' Amanda rose with a superior smile. 'But then I have found a chauffeur for life.'

Ellie tossed the keys to her new car in the air, catching them with a snap and sauntered away, saying: 'But I at least can drive myself home. You will have to ask for a lift. Amanda, stop it . . . no . . . seriously . . . I'll murder you if you throw that drink at me . . .'

The memory of that brilliant, carefree summer came back to her as she replaced the phone a few days later after a sympathetic but realistic assessment of her finances from the bank manager. She hardly knew him, but it didn't take him long to get a very vivid picture of her circumstances. If push came to shove a small, temporary loan? Of course. What, however, were her employment prospects?

'Oh, not so bad,' lied Ellie. 'I would like to freelance for a bit, you know, not be tied down. Getting commissions isn't a problem, I have a lot of contacts. I just thought I ought to let you know, in case some of them take a little time to pay. They often do. Hazard of the business.'

She knew she was sounding positive, matter of fact. The bank manager was prepared to believe her, and said if she ran into difficulties to let him know.

The car was insured and taxed for a year, so there wasn't any point in rushing to sell it. Ellie hadn't slipped so far down the path of pessimism that she had not seen how much she was going to need the car in the next few months.

Twice she had supper with Rosie and left feeling cheered beyond measure.

Once she spotted Polly leaving a restaurant with Anne Carmichael and Beth Wickham and although they all exchanged delighted greetings, Ellie stepped swiftly back so that their proffered cheeks were hastily turned into handshakes.

'Couldn't be better,' she beamed, as they enquired awkwardly and a shade too loudly after her. 'Must dash, so much to do. Leaving for Paris on Friday night.'

So what, she muttered, hailing a taxi she could ill afford and leaping in. Thank God, she had worn her Armani jacket to have the promised drink with Denton Browne, when he rang for the third time, on hearing that she had lost her job as well.

She didn't care to dwell too much on how expensive a chance encounter with Liz Smedley turned out to be. Bored, gloomy and feeling more than a little out of touch, she took off for Harvey Nichols. A stroll around a beautiful upmarket store might well give her spirits a lift, since sitting gazing at the wall of her patio garden or the local supermarket were not having a good effect.

The store was nicely crowded mid afternoon, as Ellie, in a cream linen shift, her hair loosely tied back with a silk scarf, wandered through the store enjoying herself. And then there was Liz Smedley fussily pushing her way through the crowd. Ellie looked wildly around for escape and swiftly turned to examine a beautifully presented bottle of a new French perfume, praying that Liz would sweep past and not notice her.

'Why, Ellie,' crooned Liz's voice. Ellie's heart sank, but as she turned her face was wreathed in a surprised smile.

'Liz . . .' She stepped back to avoid a friendlier greeting.

'Oh, Ellie, poor you. Still nothing? Look, let me buy you lunch sometime . . .'

Ellie resisted a strong desire to tell Liz to fuck off; instead she frowned and looked apologetic.

'How nice of you, but honestly, Liz, right now I just don't have time. As a matter of fact,' she confided with a guilty smile, 'I shouldn't be here, but I just had to try this perfume. Really is superb, isn't it?'

With which she picked up the nearest flacon of perfume, tried not to scream aloud at the price and handed her credit card to a smiling assistant.

Liz eyed her carefully, noting the linen shift that had to be a Calvin Klein and the perfume that would leave little change out of fifty pounds, and began to feel irrationally annoyed. She had expected a small show of gratitude. A scenario of her confiding very discreetly to one or two chums how she had come across Ellie down and out had flashed into her head when she first spied Ellie through the crowd.

Her natural instinct had been to avoid her, but curiosity and the buzz that she would get from imparting some gossip had won. And here was her friendly gesture being treated with a casualness it simply didn't deserve.

While the assistant carefully wrapped Ellie's purchase, they talked of mutual friends, the one eager to get away and the other wondering if her bank manager had a merciful nature. Finally, outside the store they parted company, Liz to soothe her injured feelings by phoning as many of the WIN group she could for the rest of the afternoon, Ellie to face the prospect of eating cornflakes for a week.

It was Jed who insisted she went with him to *Swan Lake* at Covent Garden. And that she couldn't resist. It made her feel better just to get dressed, as she slipped into a black crepe trouser suit with its gilt-buttoned double-breasted jacket. Six journalists had been invited to a special performance of the much loved ballet and to attend a reception afterwards. Ellie couldn't recall exactly what Jed had said the reception was for, but it would certainly make a change from watching TV or totting up how much money she didn't have left.

'This is just brill, Jed,' she told him as they strolled into the reception at the Opera Terrace high above the Piazza, and Ellie, relaxed by the beautiful production she had just witnessed, was pleased that she had made the effort to go with him.

The room was packed. Ellie, content to let Jed work the room, sat observing new arrivals, idly watching the live theatre being performed far below in the square.

It was difficult afterwards to recall exactly who saw whom first, but Jed, returning with drinks for them both, felt Ellie stiffen as she caught sight of the familiar back of Theo Stirling with Debra Carlysle clinging to his arm and his birdlike godmother Lady Montrose greeting everyone at the door.

'Er . . . Jed,' she said casually. 'This reception is for what?'

'Oh, usual stuff, rainforests, I did tell you.' His gaze followed hers and he groaned.

'Oh, hell. Sorry, Ellie, it hadn't occurred to me that he would be here. Do you want to leave?'

'Leave?' she said briskly. 'Certainly not. Anyway, it's too late, they've seen us.'

A few more seconds and the handsome couple had reached them. If it killed her, Ellie was not going to be thrown off balance. She hadn't seen Theo since the evening she had walked out of his office. Hadn't wanted to. Nor did she want to now.

Debra also had Gavin Bellingham in tow and before she had even reached Jed, she was exclaiming.

'Oh, you wicked man, isn't he, darling? Darling, don't you agree, all those indiscreet stories he keeps running.'

It occurred to Ellie that the recipient of her endearments was not overimpressed with her description. He seemed to be focused on Ellie herself, who returned his gaze as calmly as a dry mouth and a calculated expression of indifference would allow.

'How are you?' Theo asked, ignoring Debra's insistent questions. 'What are you up to these days?'

'Oh well, enough to keep me out of mischief,' she replied, but her brain was racing. Did he know she was out of a job? He couldn't know and the longer he didn't the better. How he would relish finding she had been rendered powerless to hurt him? But even as she thought it, she had the strangest feeling that it would not have pleased him at all.

Jed was exchanging pleasantries with Gavin. Debra, her arm still firmly entwined in Theo's, was giving a very unsubtle performance of joining in their conversation while tracking every word that was exchanged between Theo and Ellie.

'I haven't heard your name recently,' he was saying pleasantly. 'I suppose you must have been away.'

Tread carefully, Ellie warned herself. You might just pull this off.

'Mmm, nothing I like more than a break in the country after a hectic summer. And you?'

'New York. It got a bit hectic over there. Some business I thought had been tied up long ago suddenly reared up again. I was just a bit surprised and thought I should deal with it personally.'

Ellie swallowed hard. God Almighty, did he know about the phone call to Matt Harksey? Caroline?

'And you have? I mean, dealt with it?' she said evenly.

'I always do,' he said, turning to include his godmother in the group. 'I thought you knew that. Sally, you remember Eleanor, don't you?'

Lady Montrose did. Ellie was hugged, some general conversation took place in which Ellie played no part and for some reason neither did Theo. They stood silently side by side, not speaking, until the group broke up, Jed and Ellie to a quiet supper at Luigi's and Theo and Debra to . . . well, who cares, she shrugged.

As they turned away, Theo stopped her by lightly catching her arm. 'If you need to talk to me, about . . . well, anything. Just call, won't you?' and he was gone.

'Hi, Jerry, it's Ellie. Yes, Ellie Carter. How are you? Oh fine, just fine. Listen, Jerry, I'm freelancing . . . oh, you heard? Yes, tough, but it could be tougher.'

Holding the phone in one hand, Ellie paced up and down in her sitting room, the handset dangling in the other.

This was the call she had put off making for nearly three months. But it was now September. She hated it, but she hated the idea of no money to eat decently or for the mortgage even more.

A sheaf of bills lay within her line of vision, including the one from the building society. That hadn't been pleasant. She kept them there in case her resolve perished and she told Jerry Mulvaney that the very idea of going back to where she started, well, at least the *Daily News*, made her want to weep but what else could she do?

'Jerry, that would be great. Who did you say?' Ellie reached for a pad and began scribbling. 'Mickey Kerrigan. Right. Remind me, Jerry, who does he play for? Oh, of course, sorry, I was thinking of the footballer. He's in the soap "Beulah Hill". Of course he is.'

It was a start and Jerry said easily: 'Sure, Ellie, I understand. Call yourself anything you want . . . or I'll think of a byline for you. Whatever.'

So she interviewed Mickey Kerrigan, the rising young soap star, and turned in the required piece two days later. The money was a relief.

In its way, going home to Oliver and Jill was a relief too. She had asked Paul to go with her, but he had a deadline to meet and elected to stay in London for the weekend.

Shrugging, Ellie saw him out of the flat. Unusually he had said he needed an early start and he would only disturb her leaving before dawn, so he would spend the night at his own flat.

'Fine, no problem,' she said, reaching up to kiss him. 'Let's have dinner before I go. Is that okay?'

Apparently not. Ellie did not even try to disguise her temper and within minutes they were locked in a fierce row, on her doorstep.

'I can't help it if I'm busy,' he said defensively. 'You're a fine one to talk. Just because you're out of a job, you expect everyone to come running. Well, I won't.'

'Won't what, Paul?' she said angrily. 'Won't or don't want to?'

He threw his head back in exasperation.

'Won't what? I haven't a clue what you mean.'

'I think you do,' she said, backing away from him and leaning against the opposite side of the door, her arms wrapped around her waist. 'Where were you, Paul, the night I was fired? Out. Where were you when I called at midnight, because I felt overwhelmed by it all? Too tired to come over. Why didn't you show up, just to comfort me, put your arm around me, tell me it would be all right? Where were you Paul? Where have you been in the weeks since when I've needed you?'

Her voice was dangerously quiet and he shifted uneasily.

'This is rubbish,' he protested. 'I care very much that you've been sacked . . .'

'Made redundant,' she corrected coldly.

'Okay, redundant, sacked, out of a job, what difference does it make? I just thought you would prefer not to talk about it, I thought you would rather be on your own to sort things out. You've always been such a strong person, always known what to do, how could I possibly help you?'

Ellie felt sorry for him. Poor Paul, so terrified he might be asked to cope with failure. Had she really been so strong, so in control? How little he really knew her. But that wasn't fair. She had let him believe it, because she had believed it too.

Wearily she closed her eyes. 'Sorry, sorry, sorry,' she whispered. 'It's just something I have to cope with. I'll see you on Monday. I'll call you over the weekend.'

She saw the relief on his face that the scene was over and he gave her a quick hug. 'That's my girl,' he whispered.

'Mmm.' She wrinkled her nose. 'New aftershave? Haven't smelt that one before.'

He laughed. 'You haven't been paying attention. I wear it a lot.'

Willetts Green was in darkness when she arrived the following evening. As she drove through the silent village and out along the country roads, she felt a sense of peace and was glad that Oliver had been firm about making her come for the weekend.

Jill was staunchly supportive and within minutes had pushed her into an armchair in front of a welcoming fire that was taking the edge off the first chilly autumn evenings, brought strong coffee and plonked herself down, saying she was all Ellie's.

'We're here for you, you know that? It's just such a bloody rat race, out there.'

Ellie closed her eyes, enjoying the warmth of the fire on her feet stretched out in front of her.

'You're wrong, Jill,' she smiled. 'The rat race is over. Didn't anyone tell you? The rats won.'

Friday night was a particularly busy night at the hotel. Weekend guests arriving, local people having a leisurely, luxurious dinner, winding down after a working week, visitors en route to a more distant destination converged in greater numbers.

Not knowing whether Ellie would finally be persuaded to come down to Delcourt, Oliver and Jill had already invited their own guests for dinner. Ellie had declined the invitation to join them, saying with a straight face that much as she would love to give Jed an exclusive on the historian who was bringing his fourth, incredibly young wife along, she could do without the MP she had profiled the year before and who was still smarting from her unerringly accurate assessment of exactly what he hadn't done for the area.

'Join us for coffee, then,' urged Oliver, knowing she was teasing about repeating details of his guests to Jed. 'He'll have exhausted all of us by then and your arrival might make him go.'

She threw a cushion at her brother and he departed, leaving her to phone Paul. For a moment she thought she had misdialled when a woman's voice answered.

'Is Paul there?' Ellie asked carefully, not wanting to jump to conclusions.

'He's busy right now, can I give him a message?'

Ellie froze. She could hear a hasty hand being put over the receiver, an urgently whispered exchange.

Slowly she sat down on the edge of the armchair, her voice not quite steady. Was she imagining things? Had all the miseries of the last months made her paranoid?

She licked her lips and started again.

'Can you tell him it's Ellie?'

'Actually,' said the woman in a quite different voice, which Ellie knew she was deliberately trying to disguise, 'I've just looked into the drawing room and I think he must have popped out. I'm helping him with his research. Can I get him to call you?'

Ellie knew that voice. It was Beth Wickham. Beth bloody Wickham. It hadn't been aftershave but Beth's overpowering perfume that she had detected on Paul that night. She could feel her face burning with anger, but it was contempt that Beth Wickham heard.

'No, don't bother. Just give him a message. Say Ellie rang to say goodbye,' and she quietly replaced the phone and returned to the warmth of the kitchen.

A mixture of deep hurt and relief fought with each other as Ellie tried to digest the fact that she was now free of Paul. The last link with the life that was fast fading had been severed.

But Beth Wickham, she thought disgustedly as she poured herself a glass of wine and flopped in front of the fire. Couldn't he have done any better than that?

The road from the hotel to Willetts Green village, a mile away, was a favourite walk of Ellie's. The first leaves of autumn were beginning to carpet the hedgerows, the tourists were thinning out, the countryside was being reclaimed by its inhabitants and Ellie absently picked an armful of wild flowers as she went.

It was a habit she had acquired as a child, sent down to the village school, and she remembered Aunt Belle asking her exasperatedly where exactly was she going to put them all, when the same flowers were growing wild in her own back garden?

Now, with the late September sun warm on her back, she pulled off her jersey and wrapped it around her waist, rolling back the short sleeves of her T-shirt.

There was a gap in Ellie's life that had not been created solely by losing her job. It was a gap that required the comfort of someone who would just let her be a child again. Just for a while. Just to soothe her and pet her and tell her it would be all right. But then that gap had been there all her life.

Paul's betrayal, his lies, his weakness, had disgusted more than hurt her. No better than Polly, no better than Liz or Tony Travers. Just there when she had something he wanted. The buzz of being with a strong woman, who would take responsibility for everything and let him stay a child forever emotionally. Well, he had Beth Wickham now, but who did Ellie have?

Well, for sure no-one immediately came to mind. Being a child was a luxury she had never been granted, and really what was the point now?

Jerry Mulvaney had left a message on her machine which she picked up when she returned. Would she do a quick interview with the girl tipped to win the Miss England contest?

Grimacing, she rang to say sure, fine, brilliant, Jerry but she couldn't believe her eyes when the next day the piece on the soap star Mickey Kerrigan finally appeared in the *News*, the most downmarket tabloid imaginable, and it had been completely rewritten.

That was it, that was finally it. Ellie sat down and rocked with laughter, helpless mirth engulfed her, a sound her flat had not heard in weeks. Out of work, scrabbling around for commissions and then she, Eleanor Carter of the Eleanor Carter Interview, had had her copy rewritten by a tabloid newspaper. Tears streamed down her face, her sides ached and she buried her face in the cushion and in the end she didn't know whether she was laughing or crying, and she didn't care much either.

Chapter Fifteen

What frightened Ellie was the way her days were slipping into a new pattern, taking on a permanence that she found alarming. She had managed to sell two interviews to the *Sunday Courier* that she had on file and which Jerome had not wanted for *Focus*, but it wasn't enough to stop the slow, insidious descent into a new structure to her day that filled her with dismay.

Ellie suspected the decision to spike the last two interviews she had secured for *Focus* had its roots in Jerome trying to satisfy Bentley Goodman that his relinquishing of Ellie's talents was justified, rather than a genuine disregard for their worth.

Jed agreed.

'It's pretty dreadful there, El,' he told her. 'If it weren't so awful being out of work, I'd say you were well off out of it.'

Looking at his grim face, the familiar incisive wit now absent, Ellie had no trouble in believing him. What she found hard to take was the fact that Roland had been offered and had accepted the role of managing editor of the group.

'But I thought he was out?' Ellie was incredulous.

'Yeah, but apparently Ian Willoughby over at *Profile* did the deal with Bentley Goodman – he's an old friend of Roland's.'

'But what does it mean?' she asked, totally perplexed.

'It means sod all. Just keeping Roland on board.'

Jobs for the bloody boys. Ellie was livid.

And at the end of the day for all their networking, for

all their power to the girls, what power did WIN and all the other groups really have? As Jed put it, she thought savagely, sod bloody all.

However, Ian Willoughby had surprised her by writing a warm, encouraging letter, asking her to keep him posted of her whereabouts. But no offer of a job.

Ellie was frankly cynical. 'Funny, that,' she told Jed. 'They found one for Roland which has to be next to useless. But nothing for someone who could actually *do* something for the company.'

The features editor of the *Courier* had commissioned an interview with a football hero which he greeted with rapture when she delivered it a week later. Although he said his hands were tied, preventing him from commissioning her more often, he fervently hoped they could come to some arrangement when things got better.

It was a phrase she had come to loathe, along with 'positive' and 'be strong'. The people who urged her to be one or both, she came to realize, were people who had never really had their lives tested.

'What the hell do they think I'm trying to be?' she stormed at Rosie. 'What exactly is "positive"? Being unremittingly cheerful when brown envelopes that you daren't open flop through the letter box? Skipping merrily along the road to the supermarket at the thought of more spaghetti? What is "strong", being able to smile brightly when I hear that the mortgage company want to send someone round to discuss my plans for relinquishing my home to them?'

She began to resent anyone who said it, even though Jed pointed out she was being unreasonable. Even more unreasonable in his view, but for the life of her she couldn't help it, she stopped taking calls from her friends. It was too exhausting to have to be cheerful, pretend all was well, that she was coping. Easier to just fade out of their lives for a while, wait until things picked up.

She was not expecting to hear from Paul. Nor did she. But she missed the comfort and warmth of another body beside her, just knowing she wasn't alone. But lying staring into the darkness a week after she had discovered his relationship with Beth Wickham, she thought of something Louis MacNeice had written:

'Waking at times in the night, she found assurance in his regular breathing, but wondered if it was really worth it, and where the river had flowed away, and where were all the white flowers?'

It was a sobering thought that Paul himself had not been missed.

Ellie heard the knocker on her door and then the buzzer going. She rolled over in bed, willing whoever it was to go away. Her body felt wracked from the shuddering sobs that had engulfed her for the last half hour. She didn't want to see anyone, she doubted she was capable of speech. Her will seemed to be paralysed, as she just lay there, waiting for the caller to give up and go.

There was a pause and then the buzzer went again, an urgent, insistent little ring. Wearily Ellie climbed out of bed, dragged her dressing gown on and padded to the door, through the icy cold flat.

Opening the door, she was faced with the anxious face of the girl who lived in the ground floor flat above her: Gemma Burroughs, heavily pregnant, wearing a turquoise spotted bow in her hair to keep her dusky curls off her face, black leggings, cowboy boots and a huge maternity smock with Madonna's face printed on it, covering the imminent arrival of her first born.

Ellie hardly knew her and for a moment she gazed silently at the worried, prettily plump face gazing back at her.

Gemma rushed into speech.

'Oh, I'm so sorry, I just wanted to make sure you're

all right. Oh dear, you do look poorly, is it flu? Can I do anything?'

Ellie didn't need a mirror to know her face was blotchy, her eyes swollen from crying and her nose red from both the other things put together.

'No, no. I'm fine. Just a . . . just a rotten cold. Sorry, I do look pretty awful. But no, I'm fine, just fine.'

Gemma let out a sigh of relief and gave her an awkward grin, grateful that she hadn't been sent packing or accused of prying.

'It's just that you're not normally here during the day, but you've been around so much the last couple of months, I wanted to make sure you weren't ill or anything. I don't want to interfere, but well, you know . . .'

Her voice trailed off seeing Ellie looking perfectly fit, if red-eyed, answering her own front door.

Ellie was touched by her concern. She hardly knew Gemma or her husband, Bill, beyond smiling greetings if they ran into each other. If she thought about them at all, it was fleeting. Sometimes she caught sight of Gemma's dark curly hair, usually tied on top in a crazy bow, bobbing along in the crowd at Sainsburys. If she happened to leave very early in the morning, she would exchange greetings with Bill, a tall, lean young man, with fair hair and pale blue eyes, who invariably left at dawn, dressed for work in jeans, T-shirt and bomber jacket.

Typical big city neighbours. No social contact. But then, why should they have? Gemma and Bill, a sweet, quiet couple, rarely entertained – or if they did Ellie didn't notice. They both had soft Scottish accents, and clearly money was tight and she was vaguely aware that Gemma didn't work. It was hard to guess just what she'd done before pregnancy forced her to stop. Ellie knew that Bill was in the building trade, and wondered if they were finding London a struggle.

Ellie, on the other hand, had frequently entertained,

worked erratic hours, living the life of any average career girl in the capital, and until three months ago money had not been a problem. No problem at all.

Why should they have anything in common?

Now, exchanging friendly pleasantries with this shy young woman, Ellie felt a surge of gratitude towards her.

In the space of a few months when her spirits had plummeted, her self-esteem had suffered a severe blow and she had begun to believe the world was made up of two sorts of people; those in work who didn't care and those out of work who had no time to care. Yet here was Gemma, a near stranger, caring enough to check on her.

Pure impulse made Ellie ask her if she wanted a coffee and she almost instantly regretted it. What on earth would they talk about?

'Oh, that's so kind of you, but aren't you going to work? Wouldn't that just hold you up?'

'Well, as I've lost my job, that hardly seems to be a problem.' Ellie was surprised at her own frankness.

Gemma grimaced ruefully.

'Oh God, sorry, what lousy luck. I always used to read your column too. I wondered where it had gone. Yes, in which case I'd love some coffee.'

'I'm sorry it's so cold,' Ellie said, leading the way through the chilly flat into the kitchen. 'Come in here, it will soon warm up. When is it due?' Ellie asked, collecting mugs and switching on the percolator and the heat.

Gemma smiled and massaged her swollen stomach.

'Three weeks. I mean if it's not late. They said they would induce it if it went over by more than a week. I suppose it could happen any minute, but Bill wants it to happen at a weekend. Hopes it will, I should say.'

'Why?' grinned Ellie. 'So he won't have to do any shopping?'

Gemma laughed. 'We don't do much of that anyway.

No, it just means he won't miss too many days' pay. He doesn't get paid for the days he doesn't work.'

Ellie put the steaming mug in front of Gemma. 'Is the recession having an effect on his job?' she asked, pouring milk into her cup.

'Well, he hasn't worked since the summer,' Gemma replied, sipping her coffee. Ellie looked puzzled.

'But I thought you said . . . I mean I see him each morning . . . or rather did . . . leaving for work?'

Gemma laughed, comprehension dawning on her face. 'Oh, sorry, you don't understand. Bill's a qualified surveyor. He was made redundant too. Sorry, I thought you knew, but then how could you? There isn't any work, so,' Gemma took a deep breath, 'needs must. I knew I would have to give up work for a while because of this.' She patted her stomach. 'Awful timing, isn't it, but there you are, and we are still delighted we're having him. Just think if Bill had been redundant before I was pregnant, we would never have started a family, would we?

'But then I was made redundant too. Oh, they said it was nothing to do with the baby. But I'm not an idiot. No liabilities on board is what they were after, and it's hard to prove they were discriminating. They said when things picked up they would take me on again. And,' she paused and said with heavy sarcasm, 'any freelance they could push my way they would. Huh! Freelance for a secretary during a recession? Who did they think they were kidding?'

Ellie made a mental note then and there never to assume anything about anyone ever again.

The lean, unmemorable Bill had swallowed his pride and found work on a building site. Gemma was stoically putting a brave face on a very worrying future and she had far more to worry about than Ellie.

Gemma was easy to talk to. Ellie was glad, for after such an emotional start to the day, she still wasn't up to sounding cheerful. But Gemma didn't seem to notice or, if she did, she carefully refrained from saying so, taking the weight of the conversation while Ellie sipped her coffee and let her mind calm down.

'There's no work in Scotland and it seems wimpish to give in and go home. We really want to make a go of it here. We've always been alike, ever since we met. We're both fighters.'

Gemma let her gaze wander around the cosy kitchen, through the tiny patio garden, then back to Ellie.

'It's a lovely flat you have here. So what happened?'

Ellie looked up swiftly, unprepared for the directness of this friendly young woman.

'What do you mean, "what happened"?'

Gemma sighed.

'I mean exactly that. What happened to you? Want to tell me about it?'

The question took Ellie by surprise. Gemma sipped her coffee and waited.

'You might as well,' said Gemma gently. 'You're still in shock, aren't you. Don't worry, I've been there. So has Bill. It's like grief. You're mourning for something that's been taken away. You won't get better until you've unloaded it. And I'm not going to tell all your friends, because firstly I don't know who they are and frankly, I might have more important things to occupy me if Junior decides to make his debut.'

Ellie thought she was extraordinary. Gemma's blunt, realistic approach was like a breath of fresh air. Suddenly she found herself telling this girl, someone she hardly knew, all about *Focus* and being made redundant and how it was a bloody pain in the arse, and how she hadn't been able to move for two days because she had felt so hopelessly paralysed with indecision, and sometimes the fury was greater than the bitterness and every now and then, just when she was beginning to feel positive and back to her own self, something or someone would send her crashing back to square one.

Gemma listened in silence, interjecting the odd question. Genuinely interested.

'And sometimes I feel so disorientated. I used to be so efficient. But I know now it was Lucy, my secretary, making me look efficient. It wasn't me. I suppose I could bear it all, if it weren't for the sudden shutting off.'

She paused and looked at Gemma, wondering if she understood about not being able to get an appointment for her hair when Daniel had always fitted her in. How the renewal note from Blundells had arrived and she could no longer afford to pay another fee.

'Do you know what I mean?' she asked hesitantly.

Gemma nodded calmly, as Ellie went on.

'I used to be able to pull a table at any of four restaurants because the people I took were useful. Then, just to cheer myself up about a week after I got the push, I rang and they put me on a waiting list. Sounds pretentious and stupid now, but it was a body blow at the time.'

Gemma helped herself to more coffee and then leaned across and squeezed Ellie's hand.

'Secretaries don't have those kind of perks, but being laid off was just as bad. I was proud of my job. I was good at it.'

Ellie listened as Gemma related all that had happened to her and it was like someone describing her own circumstances, her own feelings, the misery, the loss, the fear. And the struggle to bring herself to tell anyone what had really happened.

Gemma told her how she took a week to tell Bill the truth and then blurted it out during a row. Ellie confessed that she was running out of people and circumstances to blame, to try and make sense of it all.

'Mmm, I went through that,' Gemma said. 'You know,

why me? Then, why not me? And finally, I can quite see why it was me.'

Ellie found most of Gemma's pronouncements unnerving in their accuracy but comforting in the reassurance that her feelings of rage alternating with humiliation were, after all, quite normal.

'You mean, not being able to understand why, if you've worked hard, been promoted, given it your best shot, you still end up without a job?'

'That's it,' said Gemma. 'Spot on. With no sensible explanation, most people try to find something that makes sense. If you were any good, they would have kept you and got rid of someone who wasn't. So it has to be you. Right?'

'Wrong. Could be anyone.'

Gemma began to tick off on her fingers the myriad reasons why so many people find themselves out in the cold clutching their P45.

'Wrong department at the wrong time. Salary too high. Status too heavy. Last in is not necessarily first out. Near retirement? Then let them stay. Still got a few years to run? Cheaper to let them go. Want an excuse to rid yourself of someone who is awkward, pregnant, too clever by half? What a handy reason. Women suffer from men who think they know more than they do, so what a brilliant way to replace them with someone who understands the fragility of their egos. So who can tell? Cost cutting is no respecter of talent.'

They groaned and exchanged their favourite all-time hate remarks. Gemma decided hers was 'we'll get back to you, a talent like yours', and Ellie, giving it some thought, said hers was 'I can't believe you haven't been snapped up'.

The flat was beginning to warm up. Ellie realized she hadn't laughed for a long time. She even felt better having finally unloaded all the wounded pride she had been harbouring. The hurt, the sheer effort of having to refrain from telling people who once haunted her for her company, what she thought of them.

Even the letter she had got from Liz Smedley on behalf of WIN no longer seemed to be so important. It had arrived a month before, a carefully worded, charming note, saying they had heard from Polly at the last committee meeting how difficult things were for Ellie right now and that they would quite understand if she wanted to stand down for a while as joint chair.

Polly had told them that Beth Wickham was prepared to step into the breach and Ellie was not to think for a moment that she would be leaving them in the lurch.

Bloody, busy, treacherous Polly.

She told Gemma too, about the day she had bumped into Judith. Walking back down Bond Street after a long meeting with the managing director of Prospect Publishing, lost in that half way feeling of not knowing whether to be pleased that the meeting was friendly and honest or sad that there wasn't anything suitable for her, she suddenly saw Judith, emerging from Fenwicks.

'Judith, hey, Judith,' she called, grabbing her by the arm as the other girl seemed to be about to pass her by. Ellie was sure Judith had seen her and was about to ignore her. But ignoring her was too silly for words. They were both in the same boat.

'It's funny,' she told Gemma. 'I always had this faint dislike of her, no, that's not the right word. Perhaps it was because I didn't understand how she operated, but in the end we went and had a coffee together and enquired politely after each other. Jed, that's Jed Bayley, the gossip columnist, used to be her boss, he gives her all the freelance he can, so she keeps going. But she says she's going to New York, to try her luck there.

'But you know, Gemma, not once did she whinge about what a rotten deal she'd had. She just shrugged. She says she always knew the price was no job, but she doesn't regret anything she did, or how she conducted her career. After she'd gone, I thought about her a lot and in spite of myself I admire her. I doubt I'll ever really like her, or be close to her, but she really has a lot of class when it all comes down to it.'

If someone had told Ellie in July that by October, she would be sitting in her kitchen with the girl from the flat upstairs, drinking coffee at mid morning, still wearing her dressing gown, she would have despatched them to a psychiatrist.

She almost laughed. Gemma had been good for her. Polly and Liz and Anne Carmichael suddenly seemed very unimportant. They were laughing at Ellie's description of Polly's face, left stranded in the restaurant, when the door bell rang.

A motorbike messenger was standing there, with a brown wooden box clearly containing a bottle of champagne.

'My, my,' said Gemma, following her to the door, ready to depart. 'Life is getting better all the time.'

Ellie pulled out the card and started to laugh.

'"I'm sure everything will work out splendidly. This is a thankyou from WIN for all your work on their behalf. Keep in touch. Love and hugs. Polly."

'Here,' she said to a bemused Gemma, pressing the bottle with its pink streamers into her arms. 'You have it. Wet the baby's head and tell Bill to let me know the minute you take off for the hospital.'

When Gemma had gone, Ellie dressed, phoned Jed and asked if he fancied buying her a drink later.

'You bet,' he said. 'And Ellie, you don't know how I've been longing for this call. You had me very, very worried. See you later.'

She replaced the phone and sat staring at Polly's white card with its superficial, patronizing message. No two ways about it, Polly regarded her as someone to put on the back burner, someone who really was only valuable as a job title. Redundant again.

Of everything Ellie had learned over the past month, it was that she had not been needed very urgently in any of their lives just for herself. She felt put down and angry. She was still feeling faintly humiliated at the thought that people like Polly could even begin to believe she cared, when the door buzzer went for the third time that day.

The doorway seemed to be filled with a bowl of flowers. Creamy camellias, small white roses, the palest ivory freesias. Ellie gasped and took the exquisite arrangement carefully inside.

'Wired from New York, Miss,' said the smiling delivery man as Ellie signed for them and then pushed the door closed with her foot, carrying the flowers to the glass coffee table.

Paul. It must be Paul. She ripped open the card and read the message. Slowly she sat down and read the message again.

'Your namesake, Eleanor Roosevelt, once said: "No-one can make you feel inferior without your consent".' It was signed simply, 'as ever, Theo Stirling'.

Ellie just stared at the card, not knowing what to think first. How had he found out? Too bewildered, too surprised to take it all in, she read the card again. 'Not without your consent'.

Ellie gazed at the white flowers. So that's where they went, she smiled to herself, the ones that Louis MacNeice had written about. But now they've come back.

She looked at the flowers for a very long while, then for the first time in a over a month, she made some decisions.

'I'm going to get back,' she told herself. 'I'm going to get back with such a vengeance, no-one ever, ever again, will have the power to alter my life without my permission.'

She had spent too long grieving for a chapter in her life that was over. It was time she got on with her life, let the people who loved her back in. Reaching for the phone, she dialled Oliver's number.

'Hey, want a house guest this weekend?'

Whoops of delight emanated from the other end of the phone. 'Tell Jill, I'll be down in time for dinner, Friday. Lots of love.'

She replaced the phone. It was a start. That's all she had asked for.

The heady perfume of Theo's flowers filled the room. It was extraordinary. First Gemma and then Theo. Between them they had given her the courage to face up to the world again.

One a stranger and the other the enemy. The future was beckoning in a very strange way. Ellie wasn't sure she understood anything, except she had taken the first step back on the road to recovery, and now what was she to make of the enemy?

Chapter Sixteen

Ellie spent Friday morning cleaning her flat with an energy and determination that would have left even Amanda, used to Ellie's need for order around her, begging her to slow down. Satisfied that weeks of neglect had now been thoroughly eradicated, she ran a hot, foaming bath and sank gratefully into it, turning the hot tap with her toes to maintain the comforting heat that was easing more than her aching limbs.

After Gemma's extraordinary visit, Ellie had made herself do something that she had never in her life done before. Had never expected to and had never until now had any desire to do. She had finally accepted help. Not financially or materially, but emotionally. This time she had needed her family. Needed the comfort of just being herself and being with people who accepted her for just that.

Suddenly Ellie wanted to go home. Delcourt, Oliver and Jill and their domestic contentment no longer seemed flat and lifeless. With an almost blinding clarity it came to her that to need someone or something has nothing at all to do with becoming dependent on them. Just saying I need you, wasn't so hard after all. What was hard was being strong enough to admit it, to have the courage really, and these days Ellie had needed to plumb the depths of her soul to find the courage just to get out of bed in the morning.

Gemma had taught her all this – laughing, friendly, concerned and so practical and realistic. Ellie had long ago come to believe that people like Gemma had ceased to exist.

It wasn't something Ellie felt very proud of but she was uneasily aware that it wasn't that they had ceased to exist, but that she had ceased to include them in her life. Not deliberately, not consciously. But somewhere along the way to the fast lane, just as Polly had now relegated her to the back of her mind, in her own way Ellie had done the same to people who had touched her life: Amanda, Jill, and when was the last time she had written to or phoned Aunt Belle?

Ellie jabbed angrily at the tap, sending a jet of scalding water into the bath. Cursing, she rapidly twisted it off. No, she wasn't yet ready to confront some of the more uncomfortable facts of her life and nowhere near prepared to include Gemma in the list of people who had deserved, but not received, her attention.

The existence of Gemma rankled more than the others. She had lived upstairs for over a year, was clearly pregnant and not once had Ellie enquired about her or Bill and certainly shown no interest in her. Why? Because, she told herself bitterly, stepping out of the bath and wrapping a soft, warm towel around her, shaking out her wet hair, because she wasn't any use to you and your wonderful, marvellous, unbeatable career.

It was a sobering thought and one that threatened to push her back twenty-four hours since she had sat staring at Theo Stirling's card, and the message that had given her the strength to fight back: no-one can make you feel inferior without your consent.

The Pollys, the Annes, the Pauls of this world had eclipsed real friendship, real involvement. It was not something she wanted to acknowledge too closely, but it *was* strange that it had taken someone like Theo Stirling to find just the right words to put her life back in perspective.

A phone call to Jed had solved that particular mystery. He had met Theo and Debra Carlysle at the premier of

Debra's latest film. Theo had mentioned that he was flying back to New York the next day and somehow, Jed couldn't remember quite how, he had found himself telling Theo that Ellie no longer worked at *Focus*.

'Did you say I had been made redundant?' asked Ellie.

'Well, not exactly,' replied Jed. 'But I had to be honest and say I hadn't heard from you for a week or two and I suppose he figured the rest out. Why? Does it matter?'

Only that Theo would now know she had nothing to threaten him with, no magazine in which to print a profile, no clout to pull a name or two to protect her from the likes of him. As she spoke to Jed, her gaze swivelled round to the bowl of white flowers. A peace offering or a consolation prize?

Neither seemed to matter any more. Deep inside she felt something of the old fighter in her trying to surface, but just for today, just for these few moments, she didn't want to fight anyone at all. Not yet.

And when I do, she thought sadly, there will be nothing but myself with which to fight the world.

Ellie had done some hard thinking in the last twenty-four hours. Redundancy was something that happened to the best of people, the worst of them. It was nothing to be ashamed of; Gemma had convinced her of that. Ellie had, of course, always known it, but sitting in a silent flat, unable to interest anyone in her talent, only too aware that Jed – most definitely not a yes man – and Angus and Rosie and many more had not lost their jobs, she had been assailed by doubts and misgivings about her own competence. But now, although she was still not sure that she was ready to be quite so honest about her predicament, she knew that she would have the courage to admit she had lost her job if someone asked, as Gemma had done. As Theo had obviously done.

'No,' she said into the phone. 'It isn't the redundancy that's the problem any more. It's getting another job.'

Money was now a real problem, but she knew it would be even more critical if something didn't happen soon. Freelancing was hit and miss. Publishers, like everybody else, were still being cautious. The flat might have to go, she could find something cheaper perhaps. Renting. As Gemma had said, a bit of lateral thinking often helped. But with lateral thinking you had to know the end first, and Ellie neither knew or cared to know what that might be. Not yet. Not this weekend.

Dropping the towel into the laundry basket, she walked through to her bedroom where she pulled on some leggings, trainers, a baggy sweat shirt, scraped her still damp hair into a pony tail and packed enough clothes for a long weekend in the country into a Gucci suitcase and zipped it firmly shut.

Lastly she went around locking doors and window frames, turning electricity and heat off and finally moved Theo's flowers to the cooler climate of the kitchen. White flowers. Beautiful, inspiring and the symbol of hope that had come so unexpectedly into her shattered life. Spraying them, she watched the tiny drops of water glistening on the velvet leaves of the roses, poised delicately on the tips of the camellias and freesias. Ellie knew she had never received a more precious gift.

Impulsively she leaned over and plucked one tiny white camellia from the arrangement and, finding a pin in the top drawer of the dresser, clipped it to her sweat shirt. It was a curious adornment for such a casual sweater, but it made her smile. Ellie thought it very appropriate and summed up her life these days to perfection. A very strange one indeed.

Satisfied that she had left things in the kind of order that would be easy to come home to, she let herself out of the flat, ran upstairs to thrust a note through Gemma's door telling her that she was going to Oliver's for a long weekend and, for the first time in weeks, she felt almost at peace with herself as she jumped into her car and thankfully headed for the M3.

Of course Oliver could have opened his hotel anywhere, she mused as she sped down the motorway, but without having to be told she had understood and endorsed his decision to go 'home'.

Every time she left all motorways behind as she threaded her way towards the beautiful West Country coastline, Ellie felt the pressures of London and her problems begin to lift. By the time she drove the last mile through Willetts Green and pulled left into the sweeping gravel drive lined with avenues of silver birch trees and up to the front of the hotel, she was a different person.

For a minute she just sat and soaked up the setting in the rapidly fading light of a chilly autumn's afternoon.

The ivy-clad old Georgian manor house, now Oliver's hotel, sat at the edge of a tranquil lake, beyond which lay the much loved but now threatened wildlife reserve, and was a view which never failed to restore her spirits.

The welcoming sight of chintz-covered armchairs, blazing log fires glimpsed through long lamp-lit windows, with Oliver or Jill always on hand to fuss over weary travellers, had more than once made Ellie understand why so many people found it hard to drag themselves away, back to the grind of city life.

She had never been one of them, so far.

Oliver and Jill's house was a pair of thatched sixteenth century cottages which they had renovated, and it was there that Ellie headed. With boisterous twins and a family life they regarded as priority, it was essential that they did not live and work in the same place. The low-beamed sprawling layout of the cottage suited all their needs, but the stone-flagged kitchen with its open fireplace, latticed windows and deep old sofas, was the heart of their existence.

It was at Delcourt that Ellie, on the few visits she managed, shed her career-girl look along with the dust of the motorway and happily lounged around in the kind of clothes she loved best: leggings, track suits, serviceable boots and an ancient parka which was perfect at that time of the year for long walks along the nearby near-deserted beaches.

Nothing more formal was needed until they walked over to have dinner in the hotel after the twins had finally been persuaded by their parents or Jenny, who was Jill's invaluable right hand, to go to bed. The ritual of eating in the pretty dining room with its Austrian blinds and cushioned wicker chairs was an immoveable feast as far as the Carters were concerned.

'Got to be seen enjoying your own food,' Oliver would explain. 'And you're right there to let the clients see you care about their welfare. Every little helps.'

Sitting outside the cottage as she pulled on the brake and turned off the engine, Ellie gazed back at the familiar outline of the hotel now blurring in the eerie half-light of the early October afternoon, and had never been more certain that she had been right to encourage Oliver to buy the place.

After all, how often did life present you with the opportunity to rebuild a dream? And this had been not just Oliver's dream but hers too.

'Grab it, take it, don't wait,' she had urged Oliver when their former much-missed home, Delcourt, came back on to the market. Conrad Linton, who had bought it and the surrounding land, had finally given up the ghost trying to restore the house and wanted to spend more time with his sons who now lived in Australia. 'You'll never forgive yourself when someone else has seen what potential it has. At least I won't,' she had said, only half teasingly. 'It's perfect for what you and Jill are looking for. You know the area and heaven knows, you know the house.

No-one – except for me – could tell you what needs to be done with it. C'mon, Oliver, remember that game we used to play when we were small? How shall we make it perfect? Well, now's your chance.'

It was all the encouragement Oliver had needed to bid for their former home and to transform it into the exclusive country house hotel it had become. The deal had delighted everyone. Financially Oliver fell short of buying up the surrounding land, but felt confident enough that Linton's love of the countryside would ensure no real threat until he himself could afford to buy the fields that stretched across the boundary, beyond the lake. Even though his two-year hotel management course in Switzerland had equipped him with the mechanics of running such a place, only someone as emotionally linked to the crumbling ruin of a house which had defeated two sets of owners since Stirling Industries had bought it from John Carter could have done it with such loving care.

Where Ellie had opted to come to London, her brother had gone to Switzerland to train, using the rest of the money for his education in subsidizing his two years in Geneva. Like Ellie, he never shirked from hard work, using evenings and weekends to work in bars and restaurants to top up his slender income. And of course he had met Jill, on the same course, with the same aims and to his eternal amazement, the same intention that they should spend the rest of their lives together.

Jill's arrival in Oliver's life had delighted Ellie. Settled in London with a job she loved, and her father married to Alison, she had been concerned about her elder brother arriving back to a lonely life. But Jill, with her elfin face, her shared enthusiasm for starting a hotel with Oliver and plainly so in love, had left Ellie in no doubt that, while she was mystified that Jill had wanted so little for herself, was so content to fall in with Oliver's plans, her brother was a truly lucky – and happy – man.

The only disappointment for all three of them was that their father had not been with them on the day when Oliver and Ellie, together with Jill, had returned for the first time to the house they had left so tearfully ten years before.

'I'm so sorry, Ellie,' Alison had said when she telephoned at the last minute to say John Carter wouldn't be able to make it. 'He's got to finish this painting, but he'll come just as soon as he can – perhaps in a few weeks' time.'

Ellie thought Alison had sounded embarrassed. But although it had dimmed the moment, it hadn't entirely ruined their pleasure.

Even after all this time, as Ellie climbed out of the car, the familiar protective feeling crept around her. She knew that no-one else would be allowed to threaten them again and see them walk so helplessly away.

Ellie had hardly begun pulling her weekend case from the boot of her car when she heard the shrieks of her nephew and niece, followed seconds later by her first sight of them hotly pursued by Jenny, as they rounded the corner of the house and hurled themselves at her.

'I swear you've been feeding them spinach again,' laughed Ellie at Jenny's rueful face while she attempted to disentangle arms and limbs from her neck and waist. 'You two get stronger every time I come here.'

'I'm sitting next to you *all* weekend,' said Chloe, clinging to her aunt's arm and pulling her towards the house.

'No you're not,' objected Miles, pushing his twin away. 'Mum said only for Saturday, I'm having Sunday, you're always trying to . . .'

'Whoa, both of you,' said Ellie, putting down her case. 'Or you won't unpack my suitcase.'

The effect on the bickering children was instantaneous. Not for a minute did they believe Ellie meant to deprive them of the treat, but they weren't going to push their luck. Not when hidden in there somewhere was usually a present, frowned on by their parents, but tolerated provided it ensured reasonably good behaviour while their aunt's visit lasted.

And then there was Oliver, running down the path, concern etched on his face for his young sister and soon she was caught in a fierce hug and subjected to a gentle bullying that brought tears to her eyes.

'Stupid, stupid woman,' he growled. 'I am very angry with you,' and before she could reply, Jill appeared, shooing the twins indoors, flinging her arms around Ellie and joining Oliver in lecturing her.

'We've been frantic. And you wouldn't answer the phone and . . .'

'. . . I'm so sorry, are you okay, what's happened here? . . .'

'. . . And I said to Oliver, if she hasn't phoned by . . .'

'. . . Jill thought I should drive up, but . . .'

Ellie, locked between them, was swept into the house, deposited in an armchair, fussed over and cosseted until in the end she burst into tears, but this time from the sheer relief and joy of being back home.

'Anyone special to be nice to this evening?' asked Ellie, pausing in the doorway.

'I'm nice to all my clients,' said Jill primly, trying to look haughty and failing.

'No. Thank goodness. We're on our own, which is just as well, we're both longing to hear about the awful Jerome, that rat Roland and . . . well . . . anything else.'

'You will,' said Ellie with a grimace and, with Chloe and Miles in attendance, departed for the room which was generally regarded as hers, tucked away at the end of the house with a view out over the cliffs to the sea.

It was strange being here, knowing there was no urgent need to leave, to return to London. Miles and Chloe were showing an uncustomary amount of courtesy which Ellie knew would last just as long as it took to unearth their presents, but it gave her an unexpected pleasure to watch them carefully remove her clothes from her suitcase, trying desperately not to appear too eager. It couldn't last and when Chloe, the quicker of the two, spied the packages an unholy row erupted as they squabbled fiercely over which belonged to whom, all thought of Ellie's unpacking long forgotten.

'I found them, I found them,' shrieked Chloe, holding them above her head as her brother tried ineffectually to grab them.

'Give me them,' he wailed. 'I only want to hold them, not open them, *Ell* . . . eee!'

Groaning inwardly, Ellie pulled the warring twins apart, prised the parcels out of Chloe's hands and threatened both of them with no presents at all if they didn't behave.

Five minutes later, glaring resentfully at each other but in possession of a parcel each, they were summarily removed by Jenny, leaving Ellie alone to undress, while mentally resolving never to underestimate Jill's achievements in life ever again. Stripping off the leggings and trainers, she pulled the sweat shirt over her head and shrieked as the pin from the camellia scraped her shoulder.

Wincing, she undid the clip, looked round for somewhere to place the wilting flower, and decided it would be best pressed between the leaves of her diary. Rooting around in her case, she pulled out the black leather volume – almost as redundant as its owner, she thought ruefully – and flicked through the blank pages, slipping the flower into a small pocket at the back.

Later, changed and with her black cashmere wrap protecting her from the chilly October night, Ellie walked arm in arm with Oliver the short distance to the hotel for dinner, to join Jill who had gone on ahead.

'Have you told Dad about me?' she asked.

'No, not for the moment. I spoke to Alison and she agreed. He'll do what he always does, just clam up. She said she would get him to ring when you get back to London.'

'Is she okay?' asked Ellie anxiously. Like Oliver, she might not feel at ease in her stepmother's company but she cared about her and knew that she would be feeling equally wretched about Ellie losing her job. And Alison had yet to break to their father the threat of Linton's Field being sold to Theo Stirling.

'Practical about it,' replied Oliver. 'Just doesn't want Dad upset – not before his next exhibition. I think she's right, although I'm not sure Jill agrees.'

John Carter had been as pleased with his daughter-in-law as Ellie had been to have her as a sister-in-law, and had been genuinely sorry to miss his son's wedding. An invitation to paint in Spain staying at a friend's villa, he explained, which was impossible to repeat because of the light at that time of the year, clashed with the date for their register office wedding. It was in this, Ellie privately thought, that the coolness which Jill often displayed to her father-in-law had its roots.

Over dinner the chance for Ellie to broach the subject with Jill came up quite unexpectedly while Oliver had gone to take a phone call from Alison.

'I don't dislike him at all,' Jill said frankly. 'As a matter of fact I find him marvellous company; he's so charming and still so attractive. But you know . . .' Her voice trailed off.

'No, go on,' insisted Ellie. 'Know what?'

'Well, has it ever occurred to either of you, that your father is an emotionally irresponsible man? No, I can see it hasn't,' Jill said, taking in Ellie's astounded face.

'Dad? Irresponsible? How can you say that?' said Ellie

in bewilderment. 'He really loves me and Oliver and he'd be lost without Alison and when he speaks about you and the children, honestly, he practically *cries* with love.'

'I know,' said Jill patiently. 'But don't you see, it's all about himself. He is aware only of what we are all doing for him. It never occurs to him to do something for anyone else. He never wonders if you or Oliver are happy, or if Alison is. When was the last time he rang to ask you down to Devon? Or took Alison on holiday?'

'But that's just Dad,' protested Ellie loyally, pushing aside the all-too-vividly recalled disappointment she had felt last time she had rung to arrange a visit. 'He's an artist. He's vague. He forgets, that's all.'

'Hmm,' said Jill. 'Well, maybe. But you'll never find out because you and Oliver keep in touch with him the whole time. You two give out the real love.'

It was true her father never rang her, but then Ellie always phoned him once a week. It had become a habit, and one she had started. Most years she got down to Devon for a couple of visits, sometimes Christmas if Dad didn't have to go abroad to paint. And as for Alison not having a holiday, she went on at least one trip a year with Dad to look after him, if he wasn't staying with friends.

Voicing this aloud, she found her voice fading away. Put like that it did sound as though Alison got a raw deal.

'Well, Dad wouldn't have married her, if he hadn't loved her,' she said almost sulkily.

Jill laughed and spooned some sugar into her coffee.

'Wouldn't he? My dear girl, grow up a bit. Don't you see? He loves Alison because she solves his problems. That's all. She solved Delcourt the first time around . . . all right, all right . . . Aunt Belle never set foot in the place again, but Alison grabbed the one chance she had of getting John, and good luck to her.

'Rent out the rooms or the road was staring John in

the face. She took all the responsibility for converting this into those dreadful bedsits, but really John could have stopped it if he had wanted to. But he didn't, did he?' Jill stopped. Sighed. 'Sorry, love, shouldn't have said it, should I? But Alison would have had your father on any terms. If circumstances had been different, he wouldn't have looked at her twice. Alison offered a way out of all your troubles and he took it.'

Jill paused and looked thoughtfully at her sister-in-law, who was drawing patterns on the snowy white table cloth with the end of a spoon, her cheek resting in the palm of her hand.

Ellie pushed her hand through her hair. Jill was right. Alison, sharp, intelligent, practical, without a fingernail of artistic talent in her body, would not have got a moment's attention from John Carter if she had tried to make herself the centre of his life.

Aunt Belle made no secret of her contempt for Alison's passion for John Carter. Her relationship with her brother-in-law, endured out of loyalty to her dead sister's children, had done nothing to improve her disdain for his reckless disregard for paying bills.

Secretary to the principal of the local art college was one thing, she'd told Alison curtly, wife to an erratic, charming, feckless artist quite another. Particularly since he did not seem to be very concerned where or who he got his money from.

'I might not be what he wanted,' Ellie had heard Alison shout at Aunt Belle when that formidable lady had expressed undisguised scorn at the news of their forth-coming marriage. 'But I promise you, I'm all he'll ever need. And right now he needs me. Not you. That'll do to start with.'

'And finish,' Aunt Belle had shot back bitterly. 'Barbara knew it, almost from the first. Thank God, she never lived to see any of this. I'm not saying my sister didn't love him, but she would have known the truth – but you, you seem prepared to have him at any price. God, you disgust me. And he . . .'

Ellie remembered her aunt's despairing glance around her former home, the grace she remembered, the warmth all gone in a monument to the power of cowboy builders, do-it-yourself and a scandal that wouldn't go away.

Ellie stared fixedly into the distance. The truth? That Dad didn't love Alison? Why should that have upset Aunt Belle so much? That Alison had stood by her father when the Stirlings had wanted him run out of town? That was wrong? How could it be?

He wasn't the first man to have sought comfort where it could be taken. Alison knew – had known from the start – the terms on which she got John Carter.

Ellie knew Jill was right. Always had. It was an uncomfortable feeling. A guilty feeling. She had never discussed her stepmother with her father and she couldn't imagine such a conversation now. And to what purpose?

Instead she said: 'But Alison does love Dad, and as long as she's happy . . .'

'Oh, sure,' Jill said lightly. 'That's all that matters.' But they both knew it wasn't. Seeing Oliver returning, they dropped the subject.

'That,' said Ellie to Jill, discarding her napkin as Oliver sat down, 'was superb. And I think you are truly wicked to make *crème brûlée* so good.'

Jill just smiled serenely.

'Well, we're going to try and make up for the ghastly time you've had with bloody Jerome. And how you can even think about Theo Stirling and our problems at a time like this, defeats me.'

'Well, it hasn't defeated me,' smiled Ellie, hoping her face wasn't betraying her. Think about Theo Stirling? She had done little else, until her own more pressing problems had engulfed her, but back on home ground, picking up the reins of her old life, all the force of the problems facing Oliver came rushing back.

Looking around the pretty hotel, it was hard to believe that in her father's day, it had been divided into what Aunt Belle insisted were flatlets, but locally were referred to as bedsits. Strapped for cash, faced with eviction, John Carter had turned the old manor house into a much needed source of income.

Ellie remembered as a small child coming back from boarding school to find the house a maze of newly erected corridors, the library subdivided into four rooms, thin plasterboard walls an incongruous sight alongside the splendour of Georgian panelling, a carved oak staircase and stone-flagged floors.

'Did it upset you?' asked Jill curiously, as Ellie reminded Oliver of that quite unreal happening in their life.

Ellie wrinkled her nose, trying to remember. 'If it had looked like this in the first place, it might have, but it didn't so no, I don't think it did,' she said slowly. 'I think I was just relieved that for once Dad wasn't hiding from the bailiffs and for the first time ever the wing we went to live in was warm.'

Oliver grunted.

'Didn't last long though, did it?' he said. 'The warmth, I mean. Don't you remember Aunt Belle's rage when Dad spent all the money from the rents on that Lagonda and said we would all just have to wear our coats if it got too cold? Poor Aunt Belle. Can't say I blame her. After all she and Mum had been brought up here. It must have been rotten seeing it all start to crumble, and that Lagonda was a daft thing to buy.'

It was Ellie's turn to laugh.

'That didn't last long either. Just long enough to drive Aunt Belle to the station and me back to school. Thank God for Alison.'

Their reminiscences were brought to a halt by Jill who, Ellie noticed, had not looked all that amused by these revelations.

'Sorry, Jill, boring for you.'

'No, just sad, really. Quite a character, your father. However, I would hate to see Delcourt move out of Oliver's hands, just because Stirling wants a strip of land for God knows what, wouldn't you?'

She didn't need an answer. Oliver's face was grim.

'Although he clearly isn't going to give in without a fight,' he said, draining his coffee. 'But then neither are we. And you still haven't told us your full story, Ellie.'

It seemed so long ago that all this had started but it was barely a little over three months, and a month since Ellie had last discussed it all with Oliver and Jill. So much had happened. She hardly knew where to begin.

But begin she did. An hour slid by before she finished by telling them of the extraordinary wall of silence surrounding Theo Stirling, with the exception of the husky-voiced woman who she was convinced was Lady Caroline Montgomery, even if she was pretending not to be.

'The only one who is on record as feeling bitter towards him. Also the kind of information she's got could only come from someone who had got close to him. And she knew all those people well enough to feel confident they would back what she said.

'I can't make him out though,' continued Ellie, stirring her coffee. 'If you were to meet him, he'd be charming and courteous, with a marvellous sense of humour. But then when I saw him at his office, I said something that he disliked and he was as hard as nails, totally unrelenting, indifferent . . .' Her voice trailed off.

'Oh, ho,' said Jill, raising an eyebrow. 'Methinks you are not indifferent to him either.'

'Oh, honestly, Jill, you do talk such rubbish some-times,' muttered Ellie, crossly aware that she was blushing. 'Getting those phone calls was a lucky break. Or it seemed like it at the time. But now I have nowhere to use the information, so for the moment until I can come about again, I'll have to think of some other threat to use against him. Any ideas?'

Her remark was lightly delivered, and she didn't catch the uncertain look that passed between her brother and his wife.

Oliver frowned and stirred his second cup of coffee, looking hesitantly at his sister. He could tell, from the dark circles under her eyes and the tired tone of her voice, that she had been through the mill.

'What is it?' Ellie asked, seeing him looking at her, as though he didn't quite know her. 'Why are you looking at me like that?'

Abruptly he replaced his coffee cup in the saucer. Something about her seemed to make up his mind for him and leaning forward, he began speaking, carefully, as though fearful that he might say something to upset her.

'I've been thinking, Ellie. Suppose the site is to be used for building a factory of some sort. Although it might provide work locally, it's too far away from bus routes and train stations to make it a serious option for anyone without a car. I'm willing to bet that this community would hate to see a wildlife reserve being wiped out for very few jobs. What if we were to ask Joe McPhee if he would support a campaign preventing the land being used for anything else?'

Ellie leaned forward eagerly at the mention of Joe's name. Her first job on the local paper before she had left for London had been working alongside Joe, then deputy editor and now editor.

'Oliver, that's a superb idea. I was going to drop in to see him anyway, I'll ring him tomorrow.'

'Even better,' grinned Oliver, who was imbued with the same fighting spirit as his younger sister, 'he's joining us for a drink later. Couldn't make dinner – and besides we wanted you to ourselves on your first evening – but he's sworn to secrecy and thinks it would make a first-class story, not to mention a real environmental campaign that would get attention.'

Ellie looked admiringly at her brother and felt a pang of conscience. Instead of wrestling with her confused feelings for Theo Stirling and drowning in self pity, she should have been using that energy to do something positive . . . no, meaningless word, stupid word. Something . . . constructive. That was it.

'I'm pretty confident,' Oliver was saying, 'that unless you or I mention the name Stirling, no-one at this stage will know he's even involved. All we need say is that we have had it confirmed that redevelopment of the land is on the cards.'

'I thought you said Stirling Industries used to employ dozens of local people,' interjected Jill.

'They did,' said her husband. 'But that was a long time ago and once the company moved on to make its head-quarters in London, apart from the Stirling family being known around here, no-one actually worked for them any more who would remember all that stuff about Dad unless they are reminded.'

'All that's left now,' added Ellie, 'is the house Theo's grandfather bought all those years ago when he started the company down here. I'm not even sure if anyone goes there any more, are you, Oliver?'

Oliver signalled for the head waiter and asked him to let him know when Joe McPhee arrived.

'It's still owned by them but it's been let out a lot. Americans on short term tours of duty wanting something uniquely English, Japanese businessmen, that kind of thing. But it's been empty for a few months now.'

Any more that he knew on the subject was left unsaid when the head waiter came to tell Oliver in a low voice that Mr McPhee was waiting in the lounge. Led by Ellie, they went out to greet him.

'Joe, how lovely to see you,' exclaimed Ellie, kissing the short, grey-haired man on both cheeks.

'You wouldn't like to do that again,' he joked. 'This time so the whole lounge can see.'

'Now you see why I had to leave him,' sighed Ellie. 'The mad passion I felt for him couldn't be contained in such a small office.'

Jill summoned more coffee and brandy and, after enquiries about mutual friends, it was Joe who leaned over and squeezed Ellie's hand.

'No use pretending I don't know, because I do. And if I could afford you I would offer you your old job back tomorrow, even though I know you would say no.'

Ellie was touched. 'Thanks, Joe. But I'd be such a nuisance. I've become even bossier, if that's possible.'

He smiled disbelievingly. 'Well, at least you can turn all that energy to good use. I've been hard at work getting some action going.'

All three of them looked expectantly at him.

'I've asked Sandy Barlow at the local radio station to squeeze you in for an interview on his lunchtime news roundup tomorrow.'

'Brilliant, Joe,' said Oliver, while Jill looked delightedly at Ellie.

'But I think you should do the interview, lassie,' Joe said bluntly, as though he was expecting her to object. 'You wouldn't have to fake your commitment – and I take it you do still feel a strong commitment to the old place?'

Ellie looked squarely at him. She knew Joe was acutely aware just how far she had gone since the days when she'd trailed round the county trying to elevate local news to the excitement level of national papers. What pained her was suddenly realizing why Oliver had looked so oddly at her and why Joe was being so defensive.

These good, kind, lovely people had felt nervous about asking for her help. They had not been at all confident that the comfort and warmth, which she had taken for granted would be waiting for her back here in Willetts Green, would be forthcoming from her. Just how grand and superior had she become? What kind of person did they think she was? She didn't want to confront the answer at all.

She simply nodded at Joe.

'You don't even need to ask, Joe. It's the same as it ever was, only deeper. And if Oliver agrees, I'll give it my best shot.'

Joe looked relieved, but just grunted and launched into the strategy he wanted her to adopt.

'Just tell them about your childhood memories of the place, how you both have retained roots here, how dreadful it would be to desecrate the countryside. Then emphasize that you hope any would-be developer will stop and think about how irresponsible such a move would be – and how the local paper is supporting any move to prevent it.'

Delighted with this contribution from Joe, who, it must be said, could very shrewdly see a circulation-boosting story in the offing, they parted company, feeling more optimistic than they had for a long while.

'And I must brush up on a few notes,' said Ellie. 'I don't mind asking questions, it's having to answer them that terrifies me.'

When she had been going through Theo's press cuttings from the *Focus* library, Ellie remembered reading that shares in his UK company were stable. The British end of the company, said the stock market analysts, ran smoothly and profitably and was weathering the recession as a direct result of shrewd and careful management.

What else had it said? Back in her room, having agreed

to be at the local radio station by eleven thirty the following morning, and sitting propped up in a mound of white lace pillows, she searched quickly through the photocopies of the file that had become a permanent fixture on her desk and which she had unearthed that very morning from the boxes in the spare room.

Dated over five years before, the one she was searching for had been written by the financial correspondent of an upmarket Sunday newspaper.

'It will obviously relieve the tense situation created by the sudden and largely unexplained resignation of the five senior executives of Stirling Industries in the US, that Robert Stirling has appointed his son Theo to head up the US operation and to restore confidence in the company in a shaky market.'

The voice of Matt G. Harksey came floating back. 'Forced to say I had resigned . . . avoiding a scandal . . . incompetent Stirling . . .' There was no denying the facts, they were all there.

'Winchester- and Oxford-educated Stirling is no stranger to American hard-nosed business methods or boardroom battles,' Ellie read on, 'having started his working life in disagreement with his own father.'

That Ellie found surprising. The accepted view of Stirling senior and his heir was that of a closely united duo, but clearly this hadn't always been the case. She smothered a yawn and read on.

'It is no secret that Stirling junior was not keen to join the family firm, which was founded by his grandfather just after the Second World War. But in a surprising volte-face shortly after leaving Harvard Business School, it was announced that he would be joining his father after all in one of the fastest-rising property companies in the UK, rumoured at the time to have narrowly avoided disaster when a rival company had beaten them to a lucrative contract they had thought was in the bag.'

Her heart missed a beat. No other details had been included. No names, no dates. She let out her breath. If Jed read these cuttings, he would be none the wiser. And it was all so long ago.

'Having successfully masterminded the expansion of the company from its orignal home base in Dorset to London and New York, Theo Stirling now finds himself based indefinitely in the States, attempting to restore the financial security of the company.'

Since then, Ellie knew, his visits to London had been brief and infrequent. Good. Less chance for him to interrupt their campaign.

Joe calculated that the planning committee would hold fire on a decision until Conrad Linton presented them with his final application. They could then oppose it. Local support could help stall a decision long enough for Conrad to get bored with his plans being frustrated and sell to Oliver, to rid himself of an unprofitable problem.

So given that it was now October, Linton wasn't due back until early in the New Year . . . Ellie paused. For the first time it occurred to her that they really didn't have much time if they were to capture the imagination and support of the county.

They? Slowly she lowered the sheaf of cuttings and knew that at some point that evening, during the hours spent with her brother and her old friend and colleague Joe McPhee, she had slipped over the edge from regarding herself as an outsider, back to being very much one of them. Weeks ago the thought would have horrified her. Now it gave her comfort and intensified her desire to fight not just every inch of the way for them, but until she'd won.

She turned her attention back to the cuttings and her strategy for the next day.

For those who remembered the strange goings-on between John Carter and Robert Stirling it was, in that small close-knit community, in the way of small villages that resent outside meddling, a subject that commanded a discreet silence.

Until Theo Stirling damn well started to interfere again, Ellie thought furiously.

Memories of the first night she had encountered Theo again came flooding back. He had warned her to stay out of the arena. He had told her she would cause untold damage.

She do the damage? Of all the arrogant assumptions. It was Stirling who was the public figure, not Oliver. Stirling who would attract just the sort of gossip and speculation that she and Oliver had, for their father's sake, so successfully avoided. Damn the man, she thought coldly. And any thought of Theo Stirling's ability to confuse her emotions was wiped away by the more pressing need to put a stop to him attracting attention to the Carter family before it became public knowledge that he was once again trying to disrupt their lives.

She found it comforting, after an evening back in the centre of family life, to know that she wasn't alone in fighting to keep Theo Stirling off their backs.

Reaching out, she pressed the switch on the bedside lamp and as she lay back on the pillows, enjoying the stillness of the night, a slow smile spread across her face. She hadn't thought about *Focus* once, not once.

'You're winning,' she whispered happily. 'You're winning,' and with that she closed her eyes and for the first time for a long while she fell into a quiet, peaceful sleep.

Chapter Seventeen

The interview was not what Ellie, or indeed Joe McPhee, had expected.

Sandy Barlow, bright and breezy with headphones clamped on to his shock of ginger hair, had greeted Ellie with a silent wave as she was ushered into the sound-proofed studio where the midday news programme was already well under way.

A well known pop star was just vacating the studio, having spent ten minutes lavishly promoting his latest record and a concert in a nearby town, and swept past Ellie, bringing in his wake an entourage of minders which said much for his bank balance and even more about his ego. Ellie smiled her agreement as the producer rolled his eyes in disbelief and nodded her assent as he mimed to her if she wanted a carton of water.

She waited silently as Sandy, arms waving as though he had a visible audience, and clearly in his element, cautioned drivers to avoid roadworks in the area and exhorted all and sundry to be sure to come and see him open a local supermarket later in the week.

'After this next record, I'm going to be talking to local girl made good in the big city, journalist Eleanor Carter. Eleanor, who is now based in London, is home for the weekend with a story that is a reminder to all of us that home is where the heart is.'

After which he cued in Paul Simon singing 'Homeward Bound', pulled his headphones round his neck and switched his microphone off so that he could chat to a by now extremely nervous Ellie.

'So when are you going to feature me in *Focus*?' he asked cheerily as he glanced through the notes in front of him.

Ellie swallowed hard. Telling friends she was redundant was one thing; announcing it on local radio quite another.

'I . . . er . . . um. I don't work for *Focus* any more,' she told him.

Sandy Barlow looked puzzled and ran his eye down his notes. Ellie intercepted the next question.

'I parted company with them three months ago.'

'Oh, I see, where are you now?'

Ellie could hear Paul Simon: 'I need someone to comfort me-ee, Homeward Bound, I wish I wa . . . as . . .' She took a deep breath.

'Nowhere. I mean I freelance.'

Gemma's voice came back to her. 'Nothing to be ashamed of, could happen to anyone.'

She cleared her throat. Her voice held a note of defiance.

'Actually I was made redundant.'

Sandy whistled softly. Ellie waited for the astonishment. It didn't come. She could hear Paul Simon bringing the beautiful ballad to a close.

Too concerned with the record and cueing Ellie in, Sandy had time only to look sympathetic, before moving briskly on.

'Oh, that's tough. Poor you. Now, I'll start by asking you about the threat to . . . where is it? Oh yes, Willetts Green, then take you on to urging support for a local campaign to prevent the land being misused.'

Ellie thought he must have misunderstood and then with a wave of relief sweeping over her, realized she'd done it. She'd said it, and nothing dreadful had happened. Nothing at all. Sandy Barlow was racing on.

'Then we'll break for a record, after which you can take some calls . . .'

'*Calls!*' whispered Ellie, aghast. 'What calls?'

'You wait,' Sandy grinned. 'The airwaves will be jammed. Just pick up those headphones when I tell you . . . no need to worry, I'll guide you through it . . .' He had started to replace his headphones and, flicking his microphone back into life as the song faded away, continued his lively patter.

'That was Paul Simon and this is Eleanor Carter, star profile writer, formerly with award-winning *Focus* magazine, now spreading her talent around as a freelance writer, who has returned briefly to her home in Willetts Green with some disquieting news. Good morning, Eleanor, nice to have you with us. Tell me . . .'

And they were away.

Clearly, calmly, Ellie described the pleasure that would be removed from the lives of so many people not just in the area but nationally if Linton's Field was redeveloped. With a knowledge of the environment she was, until that moment, unaware that she possessed, she talked fluently, passionately about the need for protecting wildlife and areas of widely acclaimed beauty to give ordinary working people a breathing space, somewhere to find a sense of peace and calm in their stressful lives.

'It's also so wrong, so very wrong, that the livelihood of people like my brother and his wife should be so threatened and maybe even sacrificed on the altar of someone else's ambitions. I'm sure that the people who are bidding for this land would not want to redevelop it if they were aware of just how much damage they would do. And for what?

'We live in tough times, the recession has caused lots of hardship already. Homes have been lost, families split up. Savings that were meant to cushion the elderly from the financial burden of paying for basic living expenses are dwindling as prices spiral and resources dry up. So many people have been made redundant and no-one who has gone through it would wish it on anyone. The management who make these decisions rarely suffer as much as the foot soldiers further down the line.'

If it occurred to her that Sandy Barlow had gone very quiet and that no further questions were being put to her, Ellie didn't care. Her voice left no-one in doubt that these were no mere platitudes being voiced by a successful career woman doing her bit. Ellie, with a conviction and passion born of the misery of the last few weeks, was unstoppable. She hadn't noticed the urgent exchange, the silent agreement between the producer and Sandy to let her just talk.

'When you are out of work, no-one wants to know. You face four walls each day and hesitate to spend money because you don't know what the future holds. So when I hear of quite unnecessary acts that would inflict even more bleakness on our lives, I can't just stand back and say nothing. Do nothing. This is not just for my family, but for anyone who has worked hard and through no fault of their own become a victim of someone else's decision about their lives.'

For the first time she noticed Sandy's signal and stopped abruptly, looking apologetic.

'Sorry,' she mouthed as the commercial break took over. To her bewilderment, the producer raced through the door and clasped Ellie's shoulders in delight.

'Marvellous, bloody marvellous. Keep it going. The lines are jammed. But not just about your campaign.'

Sandy, beaming from ear to ear, blew Ellie a kiss. 'Brilliant. Wouldn't be surprised if we don't sell this to the national networks.' Ellie was utterly dumbfounded. What were they going on about? She soon found out.

'Hello, Maurice,' Sandy greeted the first caller. 'What's your question for Eleanor Carter?'

Maurice was obviously nervous, a first-time caller with

a middle-aged voice, nothing to betray anything else about him.

'I haven't got a question, I just want to say, I was made redundant a year ago and frankly I've never even thought about saving any land, but when I heard her . . . Miss Carter . . . I just felt she was talking about me.'

Ellie held her breath. Who was he? Did she know him?

'It's bad enough not knowing if you will ever work again, trying to pretend you're not redundant, that you *chose* to go. Stupid, isn't it? But one has one's pride, and I realize it has been walking or just sitting gazing out over undisturbed countryside that has kept me sane,' he went on. 'Knowing that round here there are a few isolated areas where you can just get away from it all. I've never heard of Linton's Field but I'll campaign for that young lady any time. Sorry, boring old bugger I know, just wanted to say it,' and he rang off.

Ellie's eyes flew to meet Sandy Barlow's. She didn't know Maurice at all. He just felt he knew her, felt the same. Sandy looked jubilant.

Call after call came, from people who had lost jobs, who asked Ellie's advice, who wanted just to share their fears with someone who understood. Finally the question came that Ellie had been dreading, not knowing how she would cope.

'Josie from Bourne Green on the line,' intoned Sandy. 'What's your question, Josie?'

Josie sounded defensive and aggressive and was clearly steamed up.

'I think your guest has got a right bloody cheek. What does she know of the misery of being unemployed?' she burst out. 'She's a well-known journalist. I read her magazine. She has choices in life. I have none. I was made redundant a year ago and I scrape around for work.

There's not a lot of that for graphic artists in London and none at all around here. Just jumping on the bandwagon to get sympathy for her campaign is cynical. What do you know, Miss Carter, about the shock of having your job taken away? Go on, just tell us that, then we might believe your campaign.'

Ellie licked her lips, and looked helplessly at Sandy. He stared back, offering no help, no intervention.

'Josie,' she began. 'I do understand. I understand more than you think I do. You see . . .' She stopped. The gulf was wide, she wasn't sure she had the courage to leap. And then she thought of Denton, and Judith, Gemma and Bill, and today, all the other people, like Maurice, who had occupied her life for the last half hour.

'You see, Josie, like you I don't have that many choices, because last August I too was made redundant. I know what it is to feel scared at night, to sit staring in disbelief out of the window. Like you, I've been there, Josie, every last, frightening, resentful, angry, fearful inch of the journey from security to not having a clue what's going to happen next. I'm out there too, Josie. We may have different jobs, we may not even have anything else in common, but believe me, Josie, you, me and every other man or woman who has lost their job, have one thing to share and instead of berating each other we should become allies, and start to make it easier not to be ashamed of it.'

Ellie paused, looking uncertainly at Sandy and then at the producer through the glass window in the control box. They were both mouthing and gesticulating with their hands, urging her on.

'Angry, yes – but just for a while. I'm just starting down the road to recovery, Josie. No, not a job, but coming to terms with myself and determined to do whatever little I can to stop people like me and you, and my brother and anyone else who has called in this morning, being hurt any further.'

'Tell me how, Ellie,' broke in Sandy carefully. 'How can you do that?'

Ellie wasn't fooled. Even in the midst of such an out-pouring of honesty, she knew, as a journalist, that she was saying not what he had expected to hear, but something he could never have hoped for.

Too late to worry about that.

'How, Sandy? Well, I'm going to try to encourage people in jobs to treat people who haven't got one with a great deal more courtesy. Return a phone call, answer a letter, keep them in mind for when a job might come up, maybe a drink, lunch every now and then. Not much is it? But when you are abruptly left to cope alone, it can mean the difference between sinking into depression and keeping your spirits up.'

There. She'd done it. Sandy silently applauded her. Josie had gone off the line.

Ten minutes later Ellie left the studio, having been shrewd enough to lift the mood of the programme to end on a positive note by exchanging quips with a crusty old Colonel who'd phoned. She'd made sure to give Joe McPhee's paper a good plug and urged anyone who wanted to save Linton's Field to write to her via Joe so that the campaign could start in earnest.

But as she emerged to meet the ecstatic producer, she was cynical enough to know that their joy had its roots as much in getting the kind of drama they needed and rarely found on local radio as in pleasure in her contribution.

'You don't want to come back next Saturday?' he half joked. 'Great stuff. You'll have them linking arms across the road to stop anyone touching the place. You really meant it, too, didn't you?'

'I do mean it,' said Ellie. 'And I'd like to come back

if we need to whip up some more support.'

'No problem. Delighted. You've got a good voice for this kind of thing,' with which he signalled for his PA to show Ellie out of the tiny building.

Chapter Eighteen

Ellie reached her flat late on Monday evening. She heard the phone ringing as she opened the door, dropped her case and ran to answer it.

Joe McPhee was brisk but Ellie could tell he was trying hard to sound quite cool.

'TVW, lassie. Want an interview. I said we could probably squeeze it in. It's for "PrimeMovers", goes out tomorrow, early evening.'

Ellie knew the programme. It was regarded as the sounding voice for the West Country, politically influential, socially significant.

'Wow, Joe,' she laughed. 'Go on, admit it, you're impressed. Squeeze them in indeed.'

Joe allowed himself a chuckle. 'But the real point is, can you get back to do it?'

Ellie hadn't thought of that. But after Saturday's broadcast, Joe had been fielding enquiries all day from the networks for Ellie to talk to them. Meeting all their requests had delayed her planned departure but on the drive back to London, having completed two phone interviews for radio stations covering the Willetts Green area, and agreeing to write a piece for Joe's paper, she had committed herself to do whatever it took to make the campaign a success.

Somewhere she knew that she was feeling alive for the first time in weeks. That the adrenalin was beginning to pound, the excitement of being back in the centre of things beginning to work its old magic.

Neither of them mentioned it, but Ellie and Joe were

both aware that while Linton's Field was a local issue and bound to attract attention, outside the area there was no arguing that it was Ellie herself and her moving interview with Sandy that had the media people clamouring for her to talk to them. Such a frank admission of her feelings, the sincerity and the conviction of her views, had sent them racing to sign her up.

So what, she shrugged to herself. If I can talk about the campaign and get them interested in that, what does it matter if I have to bare my soul a bit? Who cares?

'Of course I'll come down. It's live, isn't it? What time do they want me there?'

Joe sketched in the details and agreed to meet her at the *Recorder* offices at about five on the following afternoon. He would go with Ellie to the studios for a live broadcast at seven.

When she'd replaced the receiver she flicked the playback button on her answer machine. Rosie reminding her about dinner on Wednesday – damn, she would have to cancel – Jed, just to say hi, Paul from New York wanting to know where she was, and, most intriguingly, Ian Willoughby – would she call him?

Would she? First thing in the morning.

Rapidly she flicked through the post that had arrived and with the exception of a buff-coloured envelope, the rest looked like bills. Ellie threw them on one side, intending to face the realities of living in London after she had eaten and made some coffee.

The flat was cold and with a groan of annoyance she remembered that, in the frenzy of clearing and cleaning on Friday, she had blitzed the fridge. She knew without looking that all the cupboards were bare. Frowning, she glanced at the clock. Ten to ten. The deli would still be open. Switching on the heat, Ellie grabbed her purse and took off for the all-purpose late-night delicatessen, a five-minute walk away around the corner in the Fulham Road.

Half an hour later, clutching with both arms a bag stocked with enough provisions to keep her going until she left again for Dorset she hurried back to her flat. And then she stopped in alarm.

Outside Ellie's flat an ambulance had pulled up; the doors were open and so too was the door to the ground floor flat. Gemma's flat.

Gemma! Ellie broke into a run and, hastily leaving her groceries leaning against the gate, took the stone steps two at a time.

The door to Gemma's flat was ajar.

'Gemma? Gemma? It's me, Ellie. Bill, are you there?'

Without waiting, Ellie pushed open the door to find a white-faced Gemma, sitting in an armchair, panting and clutching the arm of a reassuring-looking ambulance man.

Seeing Ellie in the doorway, Gemma tried to laugh but almost immediately began to pant, her face fierce with concentrating on what was clearly a contraction.

Ellie rushed over to her. 'I'm a neighbour, a friend,' she explained to the men. 'Is it the baby? But it's not due.'

One of the men smiled while the other timed the contractions.

''Fraid babies haven't got much sense of timing, this one's in a hurry.'

'Gemma, can I do anything?' Ellie asked, taking the scowling young woman's free hand. 'Where's Bill?'

Breathing fast, her forehead covered in perspiration, Gemma smiled weakly at Ellie and began to force out the words between gasps.

'He's in Middlesbrough. On his way back. Interview. Never expected this.'

'C'mon, young lady, we've got time to get you there,' said the officer holding her hand.

Gemma was helped to her feet, Ellie grabbed her coat and wrapped it around her. 'Don't worry, Gem, you'll be fine,' she said, trying not to sound panicky. 'Just get going. I'll lock up. Is there anybody I should tell?'

Gemma just shook her head. 'No, no-one. My mother's in Glasgow, she was coming down next week. Bill will come straight to the hospital. I've scribbled a note. Ellie . . . ?'

Gemma's face was very white, her voice little more than a whisper. 'Ellie, I'm scared . . .'

Ellie, quickly switching off fires and lights, took one look at her neighbour. Then she ran into the kitchen. 'Don't be scared, Gemma,' she called, hastily running an eye over the tiny room. Everything okay there.

'Don't be frightened,' she ordered, as she ran past her to close a window. 'Nothing to worry about. I'm coming with you. Shut up and just get going. Of course I'm coming.'

Gemma tried to laugh as she moved slowly, hugely down the steps. Ellie slammed the door after them, locked it and climbed into the ambulance after Gemma for the expected twenty-minute drive, blue light flashing, to St Rupert's, which was expecting Gemma as an emergency admission. The ambulance drive was achieved in only fifteen minutes, during which time Gemma had regular contractions. After that the machinery of the hospital took over.

Ellie clutched Gemma's hand, reassuring her, and told her that even if the baby was born in an ambulance, so too had been the Queen Mother and she'd done all right.

'Oh Ellie, trust you to think of that,' gasped Gemma, as the doors opened and a young doctor leapt in, rapidly but calmly assessing Gemma's advanced stage of labour.

Gently lifting her into a wheelchair, a porter under

directions from the doctor began wheeling her down corridors, past outpatients and into a lift. Ellie raced to keep up, holding Gemma's hastily prepared bag.

Ten forty-five. Less than an hour since she had arrived home. Where was Bill? Please let him get here on time, prayed Ellie, temporarily abandoned as Gemma was wheeled straight into the delivery room.

'Are you Ellie?' called a nurse. Ellie spun round and started towards her. 'C'mon, buck up, Mrs Burroughs wants you with her. Don't look so alarmed. Nothing will happen just yet, but I gather her husband is driving down from Middlesbrough.'

Ellie hesitated. The nurse said kindly, 'She needs a friend.'

Ellie took the green gown and cap that was handed to her, threw her mac on to the nearest chair, struggled into the protective clothing and followed the nurse through some swing doors.

Gemma was lying on the delivery table, looking very young and vulnerable. Twisting her head, she saw Ellie and smiled with relief.

'Listen, kid. You don't have to look, just scream with me.'

The next two hours seemed like two days. The staff were kind and efficient. Ellie more than once wished she had taken more interest in the birth of Chloe and Miles.

At five to midnight, Ellie's back and arms were aching from massaging Gemma's back and she was convinced they would never recover from the bruising that Gemma, clutching tight, had inflicted every time a contraction proved too much for her.

'That's right, Mrs Burroughs,' said a young doctor with unremitting good humour even at that time of the morning. 'Your friend can take it.'

Ellie eyed him with hostility. She would have killed for a cup of tea.

At one o'clock Gemma was exhausted, and past conversation. Ellie was still telling her it wouldn't be long now, sounding less convinced every time she said it. Where the hell was Bill?

At five to two Ellie ventured to suggest that maybe Gemma shouldn't be so keen to have this baby naturally and was rewarded with another shriek and a grip that would have put a Sumo wrestler to shame. Ellie gritted her teeth and assured Gemma that she was fine.

Just when Ellie was about to suggest that after three hours of this agony surely modern science could find some way to hurry things along, there was a burst of activity. The young doctor, two nurses and a midwife all appeared at once.

Tears started to roll down Gemma's cheeks. 'Bill. I wanted him here. Ellie ... where *is* he? Oh God, Ellie ...'

Ellie looked helplessly at the young girl, about to bring a child into the world, and the one person she needed most not with her.

'I'm here, Gemma,' she whispered clutching her hand. 'I'm here.'

And then there were urgent instructions. Push. Wait. Nearly there. Good girl. Ellie thought Gemma would never make it.

Behind her she heard doors swinging open and then she was being propelled unceremoniously aside and then, there was, oh the relief, there was Bill. Hugging his wife, whispering, soothing, holding her hand. Gently smoothing her hair from her face and Ellie, clutching her own throbbing hand, stood back, forgotten and grateful that she was.

Slowly she backed out of the room, out into the cool corridor. This wasn't her moment, it was Gemma and Bill's. Leaning her head against the marble wall, she closed her eyes and sank slowly down to the floor and waited.

It was two thirty in the morning. She had been up since dawn, been interviewed twice on the radio, once by a reporter from a county newspaper, driven back to London, arranged a television appearance and attended the birth of a baby.

As her life went these days, Ellie no longer tried to understand how she had got caught up with so much. The struggle to make sense of it, sitting wearily in a hospital corridor, made no sense at all.

'Ellie, Ellie?' She looked up, startled. It was the young doctor. 'Mrs Burroughs is fine, so is her daughter. She'd like to see you.'

Ellie gazed blankly at him. Daughter? What daughter? Oh goodness, *that* daughter. Scrambling to her feet, she followed him back into the delivery room, where Gemma, elated but exhausted, was clutching a tiny bundle and Bill, looking haggard and desperately happy, was leaning on the edge of the delivery table, not quite able to take in he was now a father.

'Hi,' said Gemma. 'Say hello to Amy.'

Ellie, grinning like a Cheshire cat, peered gingerly at the red-faced baby, sucking her mouth into little mewing shapes, her eyes tightly shut, her hair, black and wispy in flat, moist little curls, utterly indifferent to such awed people around her.

Stooping, she kissed Gemma and hugged Bill and then gently, very gently, ran a finger along the infant's cheek.

'Hi, glamour puss,' she said softly. 'I'm Ellie.'

'No,' said Gemma. 'No, you're not just Ellie. You're my very dear friend, Ellie.'

The streets were deserted at four in the morning as Ellie made her way back along the Fulham Road.

The young doctor who had delivered Amy Burroughs

had offered her a lift but, wide awake and knowing she would never sleep, she had made him drop her near South Kensington, so that she could walk the rest of the way.

Once, she told herself, as she turned into the road leading to her flat, you thought you lived a full and active life. But the strange thing is that until last summer, you didn't know what life was about.

As she let herself into the flat, picking up the groceries that were still propped by the gate, she caught sight of her reflection in the mirror. Her hair dishevelled, no make-up, and dressed in a sweat shirt, trainers and track-suit bottoms, she found it hard to believe that this was the same girl who, only a few weeks before, had her life under control, her wardrobe worked out and her schedule planned weeks ahead.

And here she was, in the small hours, looking bedraggled, daily faced with the choice of eating or paying the mortgage and the only thing she knew for certain was that later that day she was going to be interviewed on television. She just prayed she wouldn't fall asleep.

The thought made her laugh and even funnier was that if Theo Stirling could see her now, he would laugh himself sick that he ever took her threats to damage him with any seriousness at all.

For some curious reason, that thought suddenly didn't amuse her at all.

Chapter Nineteen

'You're not serious? She's going into court?'

Ellie listened in amazement as Alistair Bell confirmed the contents of the letter she was holding in her hand. Kathryn Renshaw meant business. Kathryn Renshaw, ex-wife of the British ambassador to France, wanted her day in court and she was clearly going to get it.

'Oh, sheer spite. But then, she's an accomplished actress and will probably win. Sorry, Ellie, I have been trying to contact you to tell you.' Alistair paused and then went on in a hesitant voice. 'You left in such a hurry, I didn't have time to see you. And then Jed said you had gone to ground for a while.'

'Bloody hell,' Ellie said slowly. 'I thought this was one that might go away. I mean it just isn't libel, is it? Sorry, Alistair, what did you say?'

There was a relieved laugh from the other end of the phone.

'Nothing. I said we all miss you, and yes, it isn't libel, but then we never did think it was. The hearing is in January. I'm afraid you've got to be there.'

Just as well he couldn't see her face, Ellie thought, he might have wondered – well, perhaps he wouldn't – why she was smiling so cynically.

After all, where was she likely to be the way things were going? Cardboard city beckoned, she thought gloomily. But instead she assured Alistair that she would not fail him, arranged to see him nearer the time to give a statement and to meet their QC, and then rang off.

Kathryn Renshaw was just a shrill, self-centred woman

and John Carpenter Renshaw must have been deranged to have left his first wife in order to marry her. Ellie's feelings on the subject were unequivocal. A rich bitch, pleading poverty and outrage and frustratingly likely to be awarded enough to make her even richer and even hungrier to get someone else into court to complain about.

Picking up the rest of the post, she crammed Alistair's letter and the copy of the high court writ in which she was named as co-defendant in the action being brought by Renshaw, back into the buff envelope.

The other letters were, as Ellie had thought, just bills and she didn't want to study them too closely. Nor could she bring herself to examine her finances. Dark winter days were not conducive to re-energizing yourself at the best of times. But like it or not, she would have to get something to do, otherwise what would become of the flat?

That too was a thought relegated to the back of her mind as she addressed herself to the more pressing need of keeping awake, what to wear and getting herself back to Dorset by five o'clock to be interviewed on TVW.

Bill Burroughs had arrived back from the hospital an hour or two after Ellie and seeing her light had tapped on the door.

'Well,' she laughed, standing aside to let him in, taking in his happy but exhausted face. 'At least I can give you black coffee, I'm not sure even you can face anything stronger at this time of the morning. So, how are the women in your life?'

In the two years he and Gemma had lived upstairs, Ellie had never really studied Bill very closely, and she could tell that the same thought had crossed his mind.

Dressed in a suit, albeit crumpled, and unshaven, he didn't look much like the man she had frequently smiled good morning to when they had left for work at the same time, when he'd been in jeans and bomber jacket. Nor was she expecting him to be such hard going to talk to. Gemma must love him very much, Ellie decided.

'It was just so marvellous of you to stay with Gem,' Bill said with a shy grin. 'It wasn't meant to happen until next week, and then this interview came up.' He spread his hands in a helpless gesture, clearly guilt-stricken at what he had decided was a mistaken set of priorities. 'I should have been here, she was so brave.'

'And Gemma, quite rightly, made you go,' Ellie interrupted briskly, pouring some freshly brewed coffee and turning back to the fridge to get some eggs. 'Now while you extol the virtues of Gemma and the beautiful Amy, I'm going to make you some breakfast. Rubbish,' she said ignoring his protests. 'I don't suppose you've eaten since lunchtime yesterday – I know I haven't and I'm starving. And you can also tell me how come you were still driving from Middlesbrough at that time of the morning?'

'Oh, that's easy,' he said, slipping his jacket off and loosening his tie. 'The interview wasn't until five o'clock, the guy kept me waiting an hour – an hour to tell me he'd let me know if I was on the short list – and the guy that was going to give me a lift back to London got caught up in some meeting that went on for hours. I kept ringing the flat but there was no answer and I was really frantic. When I got there and found Gem's note ... Ellie, you don't know what a relief it was when I heard you were with her. I mean ... well, I don't really know you very well, and you didn't seem to me to be ...' He broke off, embarrassed.

'You mean I didn't seem to be the kind of person who could hold Gemma's hand in a crisis,' she finished drily. 'Don't worry, I didn't think I was either. However, I've surprised myself quite a bit since I lost my job.'

She began tucking bread into the toaster, cracking eggs

into a bowl and whipping the mixture into a bubbling, yellow froth.

'Anyway,' she said, pouring the contents of the bowl into a saucepan and beginning to stir with a wooden spoon, 'I'm sorry about the interview. Dragging all that way. Anything else lined up?'

Bill smothered a yawn, the memory of a not very successful interview, which had almost made him miss the birth of his daughter, being readily eclipsed by the sheer wonderment of becoming a parent.

'Oh, sod it,' he said easily. 'My wife and daughter are all that matter. We'll get by. How about you? Any luck, yet?'

And so the sophisticated career girl, redundant, and the good-natured but unemployed quantity surveyor sat down to breakfast together and exchanged news like old friends and the neighbours they had wasted two years becoming.

Just after seven o'clock, having demolished most of the scrambled eggs, toast and coffee, and told her many times he and Gemma were indebted to her forever, Bill departed to get a couple of hours' sleep before returning to the hospital.

After he'd gone, Ellie cleared away and wasn't at all surprised that Gemma thought the world of him. He was a straightforward, direct man, not given to charming speeches but, like Gemma, he wasn't going to let a jobless existence get in the way of getting on with life.

Who would have thought that in spite of the high profile crowd she had been running around with, it would take the Burroughs to be the most inspirational?

'Such news, my child,' whispered Jed theatrically when she called him later. 'No, not telling you unless you promise to come out to dinner with me and,' there was an infinitesimal pause, 'Ashley.'

'Love to when I get back. But . . . er . . . Ashley? Is he back?'

Jed sighed. 'Yes and no, and I'm not sure that I should even be encouraging him, but you know him, Ellie. It always was one of those relationships that was heading for the rocks before we had even set sail.'

It was a sore subject between Jed and Ellie, who could never understand why her friend remained loyal to the capricious designer who had yet to demonstrate his loyalty to anyone other than himself. Even Jed found it difficult to explain; the best he could offer was that it stopped him getting tied down.

'Anyway, all that nonsense about playing the field has been curtailed, duck,' he said. 'Too many good friends meeting the Old Reaper before they should. Ashley understands that.'

Ellie wasn't sure that Ashley understood it at all, but he had a curious hold on Jed's feelings. But his habit of reappearing and taking up where he had left off, just when she believed Jed was learning to live without him – and happily too – was a source of irritation to her. The way Jed just accepted it, never tried to assert himself. Just put up with erratic moods, unreasonable emotional burdens. She stopped. Christ, she could talk. Didn't that sound just like her own relationship with Paul? When she'd finished her call to Jed, she wandered into her sitting room. Kneeling down she lit the gas log fire and leaned back against the sofa.

Although she found it difficult to admit, Ellie had been deeply hurt by Paul's defection, the way he had just taken off when she needed support. The TV film could have waited, they both knew that, he had turned down such offers before. No message of support, comfort, love had come when he must have known, did know, yes, absolutely *did* know, that she was on her own at the flat, feeling desolate.

And then Beth Wickham. *Beth Wickham.* Bloody old slag, Ellie thought viciously, punching the cushion she was hugging to her as she sat watching the flames lick up the chimney. Wasn't there anything belonging to her that Beth Wickham didn't want? Her place chairing WIN, her boyfriend?

And now, the message on her machine from New York from Paul. Where are you? She wasn't fooled. Paul, like Polly, kept all his options open.

'This won't do,' she told herself, rising to her feet and heading for the bedroom, in a half-hearted attempt to get organized for the trip back to Dorset. Thinking about Paul did nothing for her self esteem. What was it Theo Stirling had said: 'No-one can make you feel inferior without your consent.'

Well, she announced, looking at her haggard reflection in the mirror, taking in the unkempt hair and the red eyes, better stop giving the world permission. God, what a sight. Peering forward she pulled down the corner of her eye, not really knowing what to expect, but that's what they did in films when they were nearly dead on their feet, didn't they?

Then she examined her jawline, pulling it this way and that. Would she ever consider a lift? Mmm. Sticking her tongue out, she rolled her eyes, recalling that a magazine article somewhere had said it worked wonders for the muscles in that area. Perhaps, she thought, leaning forward, pressing her elbows either side of her breasts to examine her cleavage, it would do wonders here. Sighing, she decided that a life of stress and strain and weight loss wasn't helping. Why did it always go first from the bust?

She stopped and sank her chin into her hands. God, you're really losing your marbles, she decided. Or so tired you don't know what to do next.

An hour tossing and turning on her bed had failed to send her to sleep. Her mind was too full of the events of the last twenty-four hours and finally, not wanting to risk driving, she decided to catch the two o'clock train to Dorset.

Before she left she put a call through to Joe McPhee and learned from his secretary that he was locked in an editorial conference.

Dialling the hotel, she caught Oliver as he was about to leave to walk back to the house, and arranged to stay the night with him after the TV broadcast. They were, he said, poised with the video to record it and all of their friends had been alerted.

Protesting that she was likely to fall into a gentle slumber, and that she could barely remember her name let alone what she was supposed to say, Ellie felt an even greater need not to let them all down. They were so loyal, so confident that she would be brilliant.

'And Ellie,' Oliver finished, 'I've told Pa.'

She moved the phone to her other ear, wincing.

'Told him what? About the land or me?'

'Both,' said Oliver. His voice sounded strained.

She wasn't surprised. She began to draw circles with her toes on the carpet.

'What did he say? How did he take it?'

'Oh God, El, I don't know. I'll tell you later. It isn't worth going into it. It's just that TVW covers Devon and he was bound to see it. I didn't want him to hear it from you on television.'

Oliver sounded really cut up and she knew her father had taken it badly. Don't, she admonished herself, don't let it worry you, not yet, not now. Later, maybe. But not now.

Ellie had been delaying confrontation over so many things it was becoming second nature. 'Deal with it when you feel strong enough,' was Gemma's advice. 'If it's going to upset you, delay it. Start loving yourself a little, spoil yourself.'

Grimly Ellie tried to apply the maxim to herself, but she failed miserably. Her father's distress had always had the power to slay her and Oliver. Some things never changed.

Before she left she raced round to the high street and bought a bouquet of freesias and white carnations from the stall outside the deli, and in the gift shop next door a miniature T-shirt in sky blue that would just match Amy Burroughs' sleepy eyes, which carried the legend 'A Star is Born'.

While she didn't begrudge Gemma and Amy a second, shopping had taken longer than expected. Instead of having all the time in the world, it was now fast approaching one o'clock. The train left at two and Waterloo was half an hour away.

Really, she must be mad, Ellie decided as she flew around her small flat for the second time in two days, securing it before she left. She hadn't stopped for three days. Not even in her most frantic moments at *Focus* had she been up against such pressure. And not earning a penny of money either. The letter from the bank manager was stuffed into one of the kitchen drawers; Ellie knew what it said without opening it. It said that she was going to have to do another piece for the show biz page of the *Strumpet*, the nickname she had for the *Daily News*.

Meanwhile, she concluded that people on the campaign trail who have recently been made redundant should not make television appearances unless they were brave enough to wear scarlet, and defiantly she pulled from the wardrobe the suit that Theo had given her. Holding it against her body, she surveyed herself in the mirror. Perfect. Theo was still in New York, unlikely to hear about her television appearance; she didn't know whether to be sad or glad. In the end glad won, and she zipped the suit into a plastic cover and threw it over the Gucci holdall already packed on her bed.

As she propped the flowers and the extravagantly wrapped present for Amy outside Bill's door for him to take to the hospital later, she convinced herself that she had taken the right attitude. Much as she would have relished the idea of letting Theo Stirling see she might well be down, but out she had yet to encounter, Ellie had to admit that there seemed to be something ethically quite wrong about going into battle wearing the armour provided by the opposition.

The television station was housed in a chrome-and-glass, triple-storey building, and was not the crowded hive of activity Ellie had imagined.

Joe McPhee, tracked down by Oliver, had picked her up from the train station and on the short drive to TVW he had brought her up to date with events as they had been unfolding in Willetts Green.

'Seems to me, lassie, that you've got two campaigns on your hands and that's no bad thing. I'm not one for praise, as you know, but it took courage to do what you did. I always knew you had it, but sometimes it got drowned in all that family pride. Oliver's got it and your mother had it.'

'And Dad too,' said Ellie absently.

She didn't notice the hesitation or the way Joe said a bit too readily, 'Aye, yes, and John too.'

They were met by a flustered production assistant who introduced herself as Maria Cheriton, ordered everyone about, and kept telling Ellie that Taylor Carnforth, the anchorman, was an absolute love, a real poppet. Nothing to worry about.

As the absolute love and real poppet chose that moment to storm past them roaring for the heads of the researchers on individual plates, Ellie could only marvel at how Maria loyally maintained that he really needed a break, poor lamb.

Joe was ushered into the hospitality room and Ellie was taken off to be made up. Her outfit was whisked away to be pressed. After two months of near neglect, Ellie felt awkward about having her face made up so expertly by a chatty girl called Jillie, and kept making excuses for her dry skin and lacklustre hair.

Jillie looked at her in amazement. 'Honestly, you'll look great when I've finished. You should see what I have to do to half the presenters to make them look half way presentable. They'd kill for your skin.'

Ellie didn't really believe her, but she was grateful that she hadn't been made to feel a real challenge to Jillie's entire talent.

'Now a quick run through with Letty Brereton, the producer – not Taylor, I'm afraid,' apologized Maria, collecting Ellie half an hour later. 'Poor love, he's had the most awful day. Awful cold coming, I think.'

'Awful come down, more like,' breathed Jillie. 'He's such a prat. Snorting far too much. You'll have him eating out of your hand if you just tell him he's better than Brook Wetherby.'

Ellie knew she would have no trouble at all telling anyone they were more talented than Brook Wetherby but all the same, after nearly thirty-six hours without sleep, she would much rather someone massage her frail ego than cope with a coke-addicted presenter on her first TV appearance.

Following Maria through the maze of corridors and finally through double swing doors into the studio, Ellie stepped across layers of cable, ducking under TV monitors until ahead of her, past some silent technicians, she saw a blaze of lights and a set that reminded her of a rather dated nightclub.

'Taylor always sits on the right of the set, his guest on the left,' explained Maria, ushering her across the set to where Letty, headphones clamped on firmly, was issuing instructions into a small microphone angled in front of her mouth. Letty waved a silent acknowledgement to Ellie, taking her arm to keep her from moving on while she finished the conversation.

'Hi,' she said, pulling the headphones off. 'Glad you could make it. Great interview with Sandy Barlow.'

As she spoke she was guiding Ellie to the edge of the set. Peering round the corner, Ellie could see the studio audience already in place and hear the floor manager welcoming them, joking about their role in the forthcoming drama.

'Now, Taylor *will* be with us in a moment,' said Letty, looking pointedly at Maria and as the other woman scuttled away to verify this, Letty turned her attention to Ellie.

Somewhere in her late thirties, Letty was taller than Ellie, slender as a beanpole, with short spiky hair and glasses that were both owlish and splendidly eccentric. Ellie wasn't sure why, but she instantly liked her.

Letty, studying her running order, seemed to have eyes and ears everywhere. 'The programme is for forty-five minutes. You will be first on for about fifteen minutes ... *Charlie!* Taylor's cues are meant to be in the studio, not in the car park ... right ... but we would like you to stay put for the rest of the programme because at the end there is a general discussion ... Maria, where *is* Taylor?

'Bart Fellowes is on after the first break,' she went on, turning back to Ellie, who recognized the name of an actor currently promoting his latest film. 'Then there's a ten-minute slice of Jonquil Adams on film talking to that historian, Charles Peterhouse, and then by that time Clive O'Connell Moore will have joined us to talk about his fight to get his book published.'

Ellie looked swiftly up at her. 'I know,' smiled Letty. 'I used your interview for background notes. Good stuff.

Now your bit. Taylor will ask you about how you came to be made redundant, then the immediate problems followed by the emotional level you have to cope with. Then . . .'

Ellie froze. This isn't what she had agreed to. There had been a terrible mistake.

'Letty, I'm sorry,' she interrupted. 'I thought we were talking about the campaign for Linton's Field. We are going to talk about that, aren't we? I mean, I don't mind about saying I'm out of work, but the whole point about this is, it's my brother who will be out of work if that damn field is sold to a property developer.'

Letty argued that Ellie's redundancy was more interesting. Ellie countered by insisting it was a personal decision for her, not a public issue, which the campaign was. Conceding she had a point, Letty pressed Ellie to try and understand that she had to have a riveting programme, one that would have the viewers writing in, that would get the ratings up. A campaign about a conservation area wouldn't do that.

Ellie stuck to her guns. The room was hot, her make-up felt like a pound and a half of Plasticine. The lack of sleep was beginning to tell and here she was, minutes away from transmission, arguing about her role in all this.

Letty looked straight at her and sighed. Ellie's unwavering gaze had settled it.

'Bugger it,' she said baldly. 'Yes, okay. I thought I might get away with it. But I can see it isn't worth struggling about it.'

Waves of relief flooded over Ellie. 'I promise you faithfully I'll make it interesting,' she assured the disappointed Letty. 'I won't let you down.'

Minutes later, Ellie was fitted with a radio mike by the sound man, and Taylor Carnforth strode on to the set, sniffing and wiping his nose with a large white handkerchief. Close to, his face was grey, his eyes a paler blue than Ellie remembered and the fine lines around his eyes were nothing compared to the deeper recesses of those around his mouth.

'My dear,' he smiled, showing perfectly even white teeth. 'I read your interview with Brook Wetherby. You were far too kind. He's really rather passé now, isn't he?'

After which he ignored her, contenting himself with calling for make-up, the cue boards to be brought nearer and plaintively telling wardrobe that he knew he was right, grey was simply not his colour.

Ellie watched in fascination, wondering if he would ever get round to the job in hand. The hands on the studio clock crept up to five to seven. Letty was whispering to Taylor, who seemed bored, as he glanced indifferently at Ellie and then with a shrug, ran his eye down a set of questions Letty thrust into his hand.

Left alone for the last few seconds of the countdown, Ellie felt only a dry mouth, clammy hands and a deep longing to be anywhere other than where she was.

Too late. Out of the corner of her eye, she saw Joe, hands thrust into his pockets, smiling encouragingly at her. She smiled nervously back. The cue music came up, the credits rolled. Taylor was adjusting his tie, his trousers, his cuffs. And then the red light on top of the camera flashed and he moved smoothly into his opening comments.

'. . . Eleanor Carter.'

Someone pushed her urgently, but gently, in the small of her back. The lights blinded her. Her face felt as though every muscle was locked terminally into place.

Afterwards she remembered nothing of the walk from the wings, out across the studio floor, the audience, urged on by the floor manager, politely clapping, Taylor standing with his hand out. Up one step, Taylor kissing her on both cheeks and waiting until she had seated herself in the left-hand chair, before sitting down opposite her, his best profile to the camera.

'Welcome, Ellie. Nice to see you again. What an extraordinary thing for you to be doing. There must be something more to all this than just an ambition to save some land?'

For one horrifying moment Ellie couldn't think what on earth that could possibly be. Crossing her long, slender legs encased in sheer black tights, she could only smile at him. And then, miraculously, the words came, just as they had with Sandy Barlow.

Taylor, for all his affectations and his tantrums, proved to be a competent and well-prepared interviewer, moving skilfully across a range of questions, until Ellie forgot that thousands of people would be watching her and pushed the campaign message to the hilt.

Fifteen minutes passed in a flash and, as Taylor thanked her and asked her to stay with them, she leaned back in relief and caught Joe's eye. He was standing behind a camera, clenching both hands jubilantly above his head.

Then Bart strode on, kissing Ellie on both cheeks although he'd never laid eyes on her before. Jonquil's film ran after the break and then she saw Clive O'Connell Moore being led on to the set by Letty, waiting to be cued.

'I am pleased to welcome Clive O'Connell Moore to PrimeMovers,' and the controversial author joined them, shaking Ellie by the hand and paying her a graceful compliment as he took the seat next to Taylor.

Listening to someone else interviewing Clive aroused all Ellie's professional instincts. She envied some of Taylor's questions, the way he stubbornly kept Clive to the point. She also admired Clive's courtesy and lack of anger at even the most pointed questions, and found herself enjoying the exchanges between the two men.

'And you don't think that publishing your book,

revealing such lapses in the way the government has handled the economy, is going to damage it irreparably?'

Clive leaned forward and said firmly:

'No, I don't. How can anyone say that when there are so many people in this country irreparably damaged by the way this government is handling the economy? Hundreds of people out of work. People who have a contribution to make. People like,' he paused and looked at Ellie, who felt a trickle of fear down her spine, 'Well, people who don't deserve to be.'

Ellie glanced at Letty, who was quite blatantly holding crossed fingers above her head and pleading with Ellie.

'I hope by that you mean me?' she found herself saying smoothly.

'If you mean, "don't deserve to be", I most certainly do,' smiled Clive.

Taylor allowed them to enjoy a brief exchange, Ellie saying that it was not the most difficult problem in the world.

'Compared to homelessness, illness and most of all the loss of someone dear to you, it finds its rightful place. But because it affects so many people, it is an issue that should be addressed so much more honestly. Whether or not it is a problem that this government, another government or worldwide government could or could not have avoided, is almost immaterial.

'Like some social disease, people avoid the subject. So many people are ashamed of having lost their jobs. It's that aspect of it that concerns me. You feel such a failure when you're made redundant, even if you know it isn't your fault. And it isn't. The failure belongs to this government.'

Bart Fellowes, quietly seething that the best clip from his film had been overshadowed by this writer and bloody journalist, decided to drag attention back to himself.

'I thought what Ellie was saying earlier about having

somewhere to go to think, is important. Much more important than a job. I mean in some ways,' he hastily amended as he saw Ellie's shocked face. 'I myself do all I can to help the unemployed. They get reduced prices to my shows.'

Ellie thought she would never keep a straight face. 'I am delighted to hear it, Bart,' she said solemnly. 'I had no idea you were so interested in unemployment and conservation.'

'Oh yes,' said Bart, preening. 'Greatly interested. I'm a very green person.'

'Well, that's marvellous,' said Ellie. 'I know Joe McPhee, who is organizing our campaign, will be thrilled to know that especially as you're currently appearing down here. Perhaps we can persuade you to lend us your support.'

Bloody woman, Bart thought savagely. Boxed him in. Oh well, the publicity will be worth it.

'Surely,' he said expansively. 'Look forward to it.'

The credits rolled, the audience applauded wildly and Taylor looked pleased. Ellie thought she would drop where she sat.

Joe came over and hugged her. 'C'mon, let's have a drink with Letty and then I'll drive you home.'

'Perhaps you'd let me do that,' said a voice behind her. Ellie turned and found Clive O'Connell Moore gazing at her. 'You were very good. I'm driving back to London tonight, I'd be happy to take you.'

Letty came striding over. 'You can drive Ellie anywhere she wants to go, but not until you've all had a drink and not until I've had a private word with her.'

Longing only to lie down somewhere and sleep for a week, Ellie moved over to make room for Letty on the sofa.

She didn't waste any time.

'Would you be interested in a job? Here. Jonquil is on

leave for three months. We need a temporary replacement. Someone who can interview *and* knows the area backwards. The MD was watching you. We think you'd be great. What do you say?'

'Ellie? Ellie . . . Oh my God, someone get some water. Ellie? Ellie? Are you all right?'

Clive O'Connell Moore, Joe McPhee and Taylor all came running back, leaving Bart signing autographs, to find Ellie crumpled on the sofa.

'She's fainted. My goodness, she's passed out,' cried Maria.

Somewhere in the mists of unconsciousness and a babble of voices, Ellie heard the amused voice of Clive saying:

'Fainted? Nonsense. I think you'll find she's simply fallen asleep.'

Chapter Twenty

What could she say?

The embarrassment of falling sound asleep in the middle of being offered the best, the only, chance of employment in the last three months was going to haunt Ellie for some time. So too was the memory of being woken after a minute or two by Joe McPhee and finding a quartet of anxious faces peering down at her.

'I'm so sorry,' she stammered, struggling to sit up as several pairs of hands anxiously pushed her back again. She knew she was gabbling, but she simply had to explain.

'It's just that I've been up for nearly thirty-six hours, and there was no time to sleep, because the girl upstairs was rushed off to have her baby, and I had to stay with her until her husband arrived. And then when I got back there was this writ waiting for me . . .'

She stopped, seeing bewilderment on their faces at this incomprehensible explanation for her exhaustion.

'Well, it was all a bit much,' she finished lamely. 'I'm fine, I just need a night's sleep. Honestly.'

While Joe, Letty, Taylor and Bart seemed relieved that it was nothing more serious than lack of sleep, only Clive O'Connell Moore seemed to find it amusing. Sitting down beside her, he pulled her arm comfortingly through his, stroking her hand, in a way that Ellie would not have described as avuncular.

Nor would Joe McPhee or Letty. Bart Fellowes, having run out of fans, had rejoined them, irrationally annoyed that this blonde nobody seemed to be commanding centre stage again. He was inclined to suggest that she wised up a bit if she wanted to be in show biz and was almost on the point of offering her some of the exotic substance he had in his back pocket when he was stopped by a frown from Taylor, and thought the better of it.

No point in wasting it, he decided. Taylor was more useful to him anyway. Besides, this author bloke was trying to score in another direction, and the blonde did seem to be rallying and listening to what he was saying.

'Did it myself once,' Clive said, as the flustered Maria rushed a cup of steaming black coffee back to where Ellie was now sitting upright and looking more alert, if very pale. 'After working through the night to meet a deadline, I had to go up to Manchester for an interview and then back to give a speech at a dinner being held at the Dorchester. Fell asleep as they were proposing a vote of thanks to me. Started snoring too.'

Ellie stiffened and looked around in alarm, pulling her arm away from Clive's.

'I didn't . . . I mean . . . I wasn't . . . ?'

Clive folded his arms across his chest and looked innocently up to the ceiling.

'No, not snoring, precisely. But you talked a lot.'

Ellie looked uneasily at the group, and then back to Clive as he went remorselessly on.

'I think you said – now what was it? Oh yes, you said, I would love to have dinner with Clive. Yes, come to think of it, that's exactly what you said.'

Joe intervened. 'He's pulling your leg, lassie, but I think food is not a bad idea and then we'll see about getting you home.'

Letty got up and began to help Ellie to her feet.

'I'll call you tomorrow, can I reach you at your brother's house?'

Ellie straightened her skirt and nodded. 'Letty, did I hear you correctly, before I decided to nod off? Did you . . . ?'

The small knot of interested bystanders were beginning to move away. Letty collected her clipboard and shook her head sadly.

'Must be losing my grip. I don't usually get that reaction when I offer someone a job.'

Disbelief mingled with delight was written on Ellie's face.

'You did? Oh, you *did*? That's brilliant . . . Er . . . what was it?'

Letty laughed. 'This is bizarre. Let's talk about it properly tomorrow. But basically Jonquil is about to have her baby, she wants three months off and we want a good stand-in, who knows the area and is a bloody good journalist.'

She watched Ellie's excited face and laughed.

'Don't look so excited. It's an eight-minute slot, and the money is lousy. You couldn't live on it.'

The chance was too fantastic to miss. Ellie didn't care if it went out at three in the morning for a mere ten seconds. It was a job and she'd worry about the money later. It was something to do. And it was something very challenging to do.

Eagerly she took Letty's hand and shook it fervently.

'You don't have to ring me tomorrow, I'll do it. I've never done television before, but I learn fast and I'm sure I can handle it and . . .'

'Hey, hold it,' Letty protested. 'Go and get some sleep. Take up Clive's offer to drive you home, or at least to have a meal. Call me from wherever you are tomorrow. And, Ellie . . .'

Barely able to contain her excitement, Ellie paused, as she was about to set off after Joe and Clive.

'The suit's great, but it's not right for Jonquil's spot. Something a little less powerful, okay? We'll have to talk image as well. Will you mind?'

It was the last thing Ellie had even considered. If only

Letty knew the truth of it. Image. *What* image? Out of work, about to lose her flat, sorely in need of money. Did she *mind*? She couldn't wait.

'Don't worry,' she smiled at Letty. 'The real me couldn't afford Oxfam at the moment. This outfit was given to me.' And, promising to call Letty first thing next day, she departed knowing that she had bent the truth just a bit, but what the hell.

In the foyer Joe was waiting for her with Clive, both men rising to their feet as she approached.

'Sorry,' she said sheepishly. 'What a thing to do. And I am starving.'

Ellie still looked hollow-eyed and rather pale, but the news that she had been given a tentative shove on to the first rung of the ladder that might, just might, pull her life back together again, had brought a long-vanished sparkle back into her eyes.

Both men spoke at once. Joe was all for rushing her straight over to Oliver's, Clive for going to dinner. In the end they compromised and all three drove to her brother's house where they were greeted like homecoming heroes.

It could not be said that Ellie was the most invigorating companion and long before the others had finished eating, she excused herself and walked over to the house to go to bed.

Clive and Joe both rose as she left the table; Clive, having accepted Oliver's invitation to stay in the guest room, said he would drive back to town with Ellie next day.

'Which seems to me to be the only way to get you on your own,' he whispered as he kissed her cheek and looked in mock dismay as Ellie told him primly to behave himself.

The exchange wasn't lost on Jill, who raised her eyebrows at her sister-in-law as she hugged her goodnight.

'V-e-ry nice,' she murmured. 'But maybe you should lock your door.'

'Spoilsport,' murmured Ellie and waved a cheery hand at Joe, promising to call in on him next day when she'd settled the details of her new job with Letty and before she left for London.

It was a sharp, cold night. Clouds scudded across the moon as Oliver walked her across to the house. So much had happened since they'd last spoken only a few hours before that Ellie had almost forgotten the conversation Oliver had had with their father.

'Grim, was it?' she asked, looking anxiously at him.

He nodded silently. 'Ellie, what *is* it with him? He just gets so angry, so upset about everything. I was telling him all kinds of stuff in the end that wasn't true, just to calm him down. It's like dealing with Miles sometimes.'

Frankly Ellie wasn't as surprised as her brother. After all, when she and Oliver had been told of the awful accusations levelled against John Carter by Robert and Theo Stirling, all those years ago, they would have moved mountains, if he had let them, to clear his name.

Why shouldn't he be angry hearing that she had lost her job?

'Angry because you've lost your job? You must be joking. That, El, was dismissed with: "Oh, dear, poor, poor Ellie. You must get her to ring me. How awful."'

Ellie was shocked.

'Is that *all* he said? Didn't he care? Wasn't he interested?'

Oliver shook his head. 'Not in the way I care, or Jill does. Furious on your behalf, outraged that you could have been treated like that. No, not like that, just sad for you. It was the campaign that set him off. Honestly, El, he just kept shouting that we didn't know what we were doing. To stop it at once. That the hotel could surely survive a few buildings being built opposite it, I just couldn't get a word in.'

'Pa said all that?' she gasped.

Oliver's fury and distress were evident. 'He just doesn't want us to have anything to do with Stirling, at any price. Oh God, I know it sounds unreasonable of me, because he was so hurt by it all, but Ellie, I can't stand by and watch Stirling knock my life for six, just because some prime land is on the market. I simply can't. And anyway Jill would have a fit. Pa doesn't seem to realize that there are other people involved. If it was Oldburns on their own I would still have to do this.'

This was madness, thought Ellie. Oliver was right, there were other people to consider, other people's feelings to take into account.

'Didn't you explain that we were keeping his name out of it?' she asked as Oliver, seething with frustration, kicked a stone hard into a clump of bushes. 'I mean I can quite see that he's afraid all that rubbish will be dragged up again, but we've started the ball rolling now, how on earth can we stop it? He must see that.

'And anyway,' she added indignantly, 'why the bloody hell should Theo Stirling, oozing charm and treachery, be allowed to take what he wants, when he wants? I won't have it.'

On another occasion Oliver might have voiced the fleeting suspicion he had harboured for many weeks, that Ellie was as much set on getting even with Stirling for entirely personal reasons as on protecting his land, but, wound up with his father's fury, he let it go.

They reached the house, where he left his sister to walk back to join the others to finish dinner, telling Ellie not to worry too much. They would talk in the morning.

Ellie doubted she was capable of ever speaking again as she finally, gratefully and groaning with pleasure, fell into bed, squirming almost painfully under the soft cotton quilt with the delight of knowing she could give herself up to uninterrupted sleep.

Her last waking thought, however, was not what she would say to her father but that there was no doubt about it, Clive O'Connell Moore obviously fancied her rotten. Then she fell into a deep, dreamless sleep.

A sleep that lasted undisturbed until the early hours of the morning when she felt the bedclothes being stealthily pulled back and a shadowy figure began to climb carefully in beside her.

Drugged with sleep, Ellie twisted over, fright mingled with disbelief. He wouldn't . . . ?

'Are you mad?' she whispered fiercely, sitting up, her eyes becoming accustomed to the gloom.

'Shh,' said a small voice as the tousled, curly-headed figure of Chloe snuggled down beside her with a contented giggle.

'I knew you were here,' she whispered in a pleased voice, putting icy cold feet against Ellie's legs. 'Won't Miles be cross that he stayed asleep?'

'*Chloe,*' Ellie groaned, pulling the little girl into a warm cuddle. 'You are a wretch. Now sleep. Instantly.'

Ellie tried to sound severe, but in the dark she was cracking up with mirth and, she had to admit, something perilously close to disappointment.

Chapter Twenty-one

The interview with Letty went without a hitch. They met in her tiny office on the third floor where files, photographs and scripts jostled with each other for space on a desk that virtually filled the room. Letty had asked Jonquil Adams to join them out of courtesy, as she explained to Ellie, since this was Jonquil's slot on the programme.

Jonquil, pregnant, pretty and peremptory, greeted Ellie with a sharp look and the information that she had only a few minutes, so could they please get on? She then emphasized many times that she would be returning to work not a day before or a day after 1 February.

'I would be back sooner,' she explained. 'Only Jules, my partner, is very anxious that before I do, the bonding process is complete. But,' she said, throwing a haughty look at the indifferent Letty, 'if this company had any sense of what is due to women, they would have found some way to facilitate my child's needs and my own desire to return to work immediately, and none of this disruption would have been necessary.'

Ellie thought she was dreadful.

Jonquil, who clearly retained a firm grip on her job because of her olive skin and perfectly proportioned features, not to mention a ferocious ambition that deterred most people from even attempting to usurp her, was making certain that Ellie understood many things. Chief amongst which was that any ambition Ellie had for a more permanent arrangement with TVW was pointless and that the content of her spot should remain in accordance with the style and standard laid down by Jonquil herself.

'It is my ability to listen and draw people out that is the hallmark of my interviewing technique,' she said, firmly oblivious to the fact that in a ten-minute meeting, she had yet to relinquish the floor. 'Remember,' she emphasized, 'no-one is interested in you.'

Having made it plain that she expected Ellie to pose questions out of view of the camera and make as little impact on it as continuity would allow, Jonquil turned her attention to off-camera conditions. Letty listened to this parade of demands with a bored expression and made no attempt to intervene.

After a couple more points, which included all invitations and 'extras' to be passed on to her at her home, Jonquil pulled herself to her feet and announced she simply had to fly, one of the nationals was interviewing her about being a working mother.

'But she isn't, not yet, anyway,' Ellie said to Letty as they watched Jonquil walk away as briskly as nearly nine months of pregnancy permitted.

'No, but then Jonquil would never allow a small thing like that to come between her and a headline. Now, let's start with how we are going to approach this.'

'But I thought, I mean Jonquil said it was to be in the style that she's set.'

Letty looked at Ellie over her glasses, removed them, folded them and tapped them thoughtfully against her teeth.

'Let me put some questions to you, my dear. First, who produces this programme? Good. Are we talking about an eight-minute slot on a regional programme once a week, or "Panorama"? Excellent. And finally – and take your time about this – who wouldn't recognize the ability to listen if it was ten feet high, and driving recklessly in the wrong direction along the central reservation of the

M3? You catch on fast. Now let's get down to business.'

And they did. For over an hour, Letty took Ellie through tapes of Jonquil's interviews. At first Ellie was blinded by the sheer speed and numbers of the tapes, but gradually she grew uncomfortably aware that Jonquil's standards were abysmal, relying on beautiful, soulful camera shots of her in a variety of moods to give weight to her particular slot.

Letty studied the screen without comment. Half way through, Ellie stole a sideways glance at her, trying to compose some remarks that would be constructive without being untrue.

'Don't bother,' Letty said with a sigh, reading her thoughts. 'Bloody awful, isn't it? Problem is the camera likes her and for some reason so do the viewers.'

This wasn't going to be as easy as it appeared, thought Ellie grimly. Finally when Letty switched the video off she said:

'Perhaps if while I was doing it, we could emphasize more of a difference between the main show and this slot, it wouldn't be quite so much of a hassle for Jonquil when she returns. I mean, if that style is her particular trademark, it might be better if I did something quite different.'

'Like what?'

'Well, supposing this bit offered a complete contrast to the glamour of Taylor's interviews with actors, authors, models. What if I took an issue each week and interviewed real people caught up in it?'

'Is that what you'd like to do?'

Ellie nodded.

'I'd feel comfortable with that. I know I could handle interviews with the Good and the Great, but I can't see the point of that if Taylor is already doing it. And,' she added honestly, 'he does it well. If I have any criticism of Jonquil's tapes it's that it seems to be just more of the same. There isn't any contrast between the two.

'These days I feel more in tune with people who have to grapple with all that life throws at them rather than the favoured few and I genuinely believe it would have a response, a strong response from viewers.'

She waited, giving Letty time to consider all she had said, but finally Letty shook her head.

'Wouldn't work. It would sound like one long whinge. Real people are usually forgettable. If they weren't everyone would have them on, a lot cheaper too. But I tell you what would work,' she went on, seeing Ellie preparing to disagree. 'What if you acted as advocate for someone with a problem and took it to the right people to get some answers? The problem must be local but the answer can come right from the heart of Westminster if necessary. All on film, it can be done anywhere. Saves money too. We haven't got to keep dragging people down from London or Manchester or wherever they happen to be located. What do you think?'

Short of removing her clothes in public, the last three months had left Ellie in no mood to argue her way out of a job. She assured Letty it was a brilliant idea. For the next hour they thrashed out the details, parting with an action plan for both of them: Ellie was to come up with some key issues ready to begin work the following week, and Letty was to plug the new spot on the next edition of 'PrimeMovers', to get the letters coming in.

'And you were going to mention um . . . image?' Ellie reminded the producer as they walked towards the reception area. Unlike the previous evening, there was now a constant stream of activity: messengers arriving, girls with clipboards trying to locate programme guests, office workers impatiently pressing the lift buttons. The bank of monitors above the reception desk was soundlessly transmitting not only TVW but the network lunchtime news bulletins.

Ellie thought it was bliss.

And now she was part of it. Not a very big part. But she had somewhere to call in to, somewhere to fit in. As long as she looked the part. She looked anxiously at Letty, who took in the black cashmere polo neck sweater worn over a knee-skimming houndstooth check skirt, black velvet tights, flat black pumps.

Ellie's blonde hair was pinned back in a slim velvet bow at the nape of her neck and she carried a black silk parka, which she pulled on as she spoke. A night's sleep had restored her customary energy.

'Image?' smiled Letty. 'Your image looks just fine to me.'

'Let's hope it does to the viewers,' Ellie laughed and, confirming that they would see each other the following Monday, they parted company, Letty to tell the MD that Jonquil was going to be fit to be tied and to watch out for the squalls and Ellie to try and remember how long ago it was when she had earned so little.

Later that afternoon, with Jill and the twins waving her goodbye, she headed back to London installed in the passenger seat of Clive's Aston Martin DB6. So much had taken place in such a short space of time that Ellie was glad of the chance to sort out how she could best cope with working in Dorset while being stationed in London.

Joe McPhee was keen to generate more local activity for a campaign that he had thrown his newspaper's weight behind, but nevertheless they both knew they had to tread warily. No-one, least of all Ellie, had expected such a swift turn of events.

Ellie as a local reporter, albeit on TV, stood in danger of being thought cynically exploitative if she was seen pushing the campaign too much, and even Oliver had warned her of the danger.

'You've done more than anyone could have asked,' he'd said warmly, as they sat in his office at the hotel having coffee, while Jill took Clive on a tour of the hotel. 'Now you've got to think of yourself. Don't risk losing this chance. Anyway, when Miles and Chloe find out you're on TV they will be impossible to handle. The idea that you might *not* be on TV will make them a living nightmare. So if you have any regard for me and Jill and our sanity, just think of yourself.'

Ellie had then set off to liaise with Joe.

Joe was totally in agreement with Oliver, but he had shrewdly guessed that if the campaign were to become a personality cult – which having Ellie so strongly in evidence it undoubtedly would – it could easily backfire. Public sympathy would be on their side if the campaign was a genuine local issue, not one of ownership.

'I'll get together with Oliver and organize the next stage,' he told her. 'I don't think you can handle any more radio or TV interviews if they come up, or newspapers either. But it's imperative that we have a proper public meeting and whip an official protest into the planning office. They always drag their feet, but who knows if Linton won't suddenly turn up and get the ball rolling.'

'Do you think he might?' asked Ellie nervously.

Joe shrugged.

'We'll find a way around it,' he said philosophically, as they made their way to the Jollife Arms next to the *Recorder* offices for a quick lunch. 'In fact, do you remember that woman who rang you on the programme, Josie Fallon?'

'Gosh, do I?' Ellie grimaced, following him to the bar. 'She was so angry, I could feel the fumes down the wire. But how do you know she's called Fallon?'

'She rang me on Monday. Asked if there was anything she could do to help with the campaign.'

Ellie gaped at him.

'You're kidding? She rang?'

'For sure, she did. Anyway, it turns out that her

husband died a couple of years back and he used to work with me on the old *Sentinel* in Glasgow – oh, years back. It was hearing you say my name that prompted her to ring.'

'Aha. So it wasn't me,' Ellie giggled. 'An old flame, eh, Joe?'

Joe tried to look fierce and failed.

'Nothing of the sort. But she was always one for speaking her mind, I do remember that. Anyway, she's coming over to see me and maybe she can be inveigled into helping. Just like old times, Ellie,' he laughed, carrying their drinks to a corner table.

Ellie looked around the crowded lunchtime bar. In her day it had been rather shabby and boasted nothing more than crisps and nuts to go with a shandy. Now it had red plush seats, cosy booths, and while it thankfully had not yet allowed wall-to-wall muzak, it did do bar snacks which Joe assured her was a godsend, what with all those poncy wine bars springing up all over the place.

'It's been a long time, Joe,' she sighed, remembering the quick after-work drinks she used to have here with the crowd from the *Recorder* before going back to her bedsit in the town for beans on toast. 'I've come full circle, haven't I? Who would have thought it?'

Joe smiled gently at her. He'd known her parents, remembered when she was born, and the horrific car crash that had killed her mother. He'd been in his twenties then. Willetts Green was merely a brief stop en route to Fleet Street. But then he'd met Fay and the boys had come along and suddenly Fleet Street didn't seem so important.

It still hurt. One day a happy family man, outings, a job that absorbed him and the next, his wife had fallen in love with someone else and within a year it was all over. Joe had been left in the house in Sidlow, twenty minutes' drive from the office. And his sons were fifty miles away in Bournemouth, with their mother and the man who had stolen them all away. That's why he couldn't remember all the details of John Carter's problems, all that business with Stirling; he'd been grappling with enough of his own problems to last a lifetime.

But he did remember Ellie's mother. In looks Oliver favoured her, Ellie did not. Tall, but dark, green eyes and a warmth that had kept John Carter entranced all through their marriage and near enough destroyed him when she died.

But Ellie had got the charm. Such charm and dignity. She would never have let Delcourt slide into such disarray.

Memories of Barbara Carter, wheeling the baby Ellie and toddler Oliver through the village on warm summer days, in that big upright pram, came flooding back as he watched the girl beside him. The enthusiasm and energy with which Barbara Carter, and indeed her sister Belle, had always embraced village life, meant Delcourt with its straggling gardens and apple orchards was willingly handed over for fetes and fairs and Barbara herself had been a tireless organizer.

Somehow Oliver and Ellie fitted into all of this and the village grew used to John Carter always forgetting the days he was meant to be helping at one of the village activities, or off painting along the cliff paths on the mornings when he should have been caring for Oliver. Then Barbara could be glimpsed tearing through the village with no option but to take Oliver with her in the back of the old Ford on her way to teach at the local art school, which everyone knew was how they kept the wolf from the door.

In Ellie, Joe saw the same reserves of strength, the same fierce pride that in spite of the dazzling life she had been leading in London, he knew – as Oliver and Jill had always known – was still there. Just like her mother.

'Not quite, lassie,' he said, smiling at her downcast face. 'You've just come back to get your breath, that's all. Just to make sure the roots are firmly in place. Otherwise how else can you measure success, if you don't make sure that the starting point hasn't been moved?'

Ellie was silent. The one thing she had dreaded had happened. She was back at the beginning. A local reporter, lunching with Joe in the pub that had been 'their' pub all those years ago, trying to make her way back in the world.

Well, not quite. This time she had a flat to go to. Friends to call. Not the ones that belonged to her old life, except for Rosie and Jed, but Gemma and Bill. Now there was Letty and probably Clive too.

Clive was a strange person. A tall, amusing, attractive – what? Rogue, Ellie decided with a chuckle.

He was nearly forty, divorced, with two teenage children who occupied most of his weekends and with whom he was quite openly besotted. She knew all that from when she'd interviewed him. He was also clever, cynical, a fashionable name, with a casual disregard for convention and perfectly capable of being blunt to the point of rudeness if he disliked someone or something.

She liked him. Liked his easy-going manners, and the directness of going for what he wanted.

At the moment, driving a shade too fast back up the M3, holding Ellie's hand on his knee, it didn't take a genius to work out what he wanted this time.

I'm going to enjoy this, she decided. It will take my mind off the bank manager's still-unopened letter, the phone call to the *Strumpet*, and the problem of how to exist on the pittance that TVW had offered.

Good heavens, life was getting better all the time, as Gemma would say. It would also take her mind off the feckless Paul and . . . well, anyone else really.

*

Arranging to meet her at eight, sighing that he would endure Jed and Ashley's company but only because those appeared to be the only terms on which he could see her, Clive dropped Ellie at St Rupert's. There she had found Gemma, impatient to get home to Bill, cuddling her daughter who she pronounced was living up to the slogan on her T-shirt, and was longing to hear all Ellie's news.

Ellie thought she still looked shattered and cringed with Gemma when she gingerly moved her position in bed. Through gritted teeth, Gemma confessed that childbirth was nothing to enduring the stitches, which made sitting a nightmare.

However, Gemma shrieked even more loudly when Ellie told her about the TV job. This disturbed Amy, who woke up protesting indignantly and had to be lulled back to sleep, while her mother and Ellie looked guiltily around at the other mothers in the ward.

'It's a start and you were right, Gem, once you start sharing your experience with people in the same boat, it gets easier to bear.'

Gemma smiled smugly.

'I might become an agony aunt when Amy is older. I just love dispensing advice. I can see it now – Gemma's Gems of Wisdom. What do you think?'

'I think,' said Ellie, gathering up her bag and suitcase and hugging Gemma, 'that it's the worst headline ever, and the only little gem you've got is that one.'

'Okay, Star,' Gemma teased. 'But watch this space, I'm planning a comeback, some time, some way.'

Ellie waved and caught a cab the rest of the way home.

It was strange not to come back to a litany of plaintive messages from Paul and to be getting ready to go out with someone else.

This time, she told herself as she unpacked her overnight case and hung her red suit back in the wardrobe, no complications. Don't allow anyone to put you down,

277

expect you to be there for them, expect you to fit into their lives.

Just remember what Theo says: 'Not without your consent . . .' She unpacked her make-up bag, deposited the scripts that Letty had given her to study on her bedside table and was about to put the black leather diary into her top drawer when she stopped. Inside the back pocket she found the white camellia. Flat, crinkled but intact. Holding it carefully in the palm of her hand, Ellie studied it for a long while as she sat on the edge of her bed.

What a strange man. Obstinate, ruthless and influential.

She should still be afraid of him. But she was now simply angry. Where others exerted themselves to be part of his life, she simply wanted him out of hers.

Turning the camellia carefully over in her hand, she stroked the wrinkled leaves and tried to understand how someone so prepared to disregard the needs and the lives of other people could be sensitive and thoughtful enough to arrange such a gesture. It was done to disarm her, of that there was no doubt. A deliberate attempt to make her back off. But even if she had, he must surely know that Oliver would have carried on the fight?

After wrestling with this tangled thinking for several minutes, Ellie had to admit she was no nearer understanding such a complex man. So many people had remained loyal to him when she had tried to confirm her belief that he was ruthless. All, of course, except Caroline Montgomery.

The buff folder that had remained closed for the last three months was once again locked away in the files she had brought home with her from *Focus*. Many times she had been tempted to throw it away, because now she had nowhere to use it, her one weapon removed from her. So why did she find that fact was like a weight removed from her mind, rather than a source of irritation?

The problem with you, my girl, is that you got yourself too close to him, became too aware of the charm. After all, what kind of man is it who can be heavily involved with a woman like Debra Carlysle and at the same time send white flowers to another? A professional charmer and a seducer of stupid women, she thought wryly.

She was still holding the camellia, although the way she was loading it with so much significance could not be good for her. It was only a white camellia. He probably didn't even know what kind of flowers he'd sent. Like her suit, his secretary had clearly been despatched to arrange the whole thing. Oh, just chuck it, she said impatiently, swinging herself off her bed, and walked over to the corner and dropped it into the waste paper basket.

After which she made coffee, then rang Jed and said she would meet him and Ashley at a favourite bistro in King's Road. She dialled Rosie's number and persuaded her to come too, saying she wanted them all to meet Clive. Then she phoned Amanda, told her she had met the most divine man and yes, she was sure she would now have the courage to jettison all thoughts of Paul from her life.

She didn't even mind when Amanda said she would believe it when she heard it.

Taking her coffee, Ellie went back to her bedroom, slipped on a pair of black trousers, pulled a white cable-knit cotton sweater over them, piled her hair into a coil on top of her head and with a cursory glance in the mirror, whirled out, closing the door behind her.

Seconds later, she opened it again, walked quickly to the waste paper basket, gently extricated the camellia and placed it carefully between the leaves of a book of Louis MacNeice's poems.

Then avoiding her reflection in the mirror, Ellie shot out of the house to a welcome reunion with Jed and Rosie and to hear exactly what this amazing news was that the gossip columnist had promised to impart.

Outside she ran into Bill returning from the hospital and, on a high that she hadn't felt for months, Ellie insisted that he joined them for supper. He looked a bit bemused, but finally gave in, when Ellie pointed out that Gemma would expect him to keep his strength up and that this was a night when she wanted all her friends around her.

The bistro was packed. Jed and Ashley were already there, and they promptly appropriated another chair for Bill. Ellie guessed they had been rowing, but this was not a night for soul-searching. This was the night that Ellie was re-entering the world of the workers – not with a buzz of excitement that would have the phones ringing, and not in the most lavish place. But somehow it was very appropriate.

The checked tablecloths, the black and white photographs of the owner with every celebrated name that he claimed had dined there, cluttered every inch of space on the walls, the chalked-up menu and the screaming oaths that emanated from the kitchen from the temperamental Italian chef all contributed to the air of delightful craziness, which suited her mood.

Rosie's arrival was the signal for more wine and cheers. Amy's health was drunk. And Bill's. A great deal of teasing went on as the hour dragged by to nine o'clock and there was no sign of Clive.

Curiously, Ellie felt very confident that he would come. There was something she instinctively sensed about him that she never had with Paul. He was too blunt, too uncomplicated to play games.

And then he came through the door, searching the room for their table, and Ellie just gazed at him, helpless with laughter. Pushing his way through the crowded room, he was carrying the biggest, most vulgar, over-dressed, heart-shaped box of chocolates, which must have taken a lot of nerve to buy.

'I knew the competition would be severe. I wanted to improve my chances,' he said gravely, presenting them to her and kissing her on both cheeks.

It could not be said that any of them did justice to the food that evening, but a gratifying amount of champagne flowed and the conversation with it.

Clive clearly loved an audience. Rosie, gentle-natured and not easily won over, provided him with a flattering degree of hysteria at almost everything he said. Jed extracted from him two very indiscreet stories, Ashley got quietly drunk and Bill, to Clive's evident delight, had read his last two books and was immediately promised a signed copy of the current controversial tome.

The revelry almost put into the shade Jed's news that Ian Willoughby had been appointed Editorial Director of Goodman Coopers Publishing, Dixie had been promoted to Bentley Goodman's secretary, the bimbo Sonya Harvey-Lloyd who had plagued Rosie's life for four months had become Jerome's personal secretary and Jerome Strachan was being kept on a tight rein, furious that once again he was reporting to his old boss.

'The interesting thing is, El,' said Jed, undercover of shrieks of laughter as Clive regaled Rosie, Bill and Ashley with the story of Ellie slumbering on the set of 'Prime Movers', 'I casually mentioned that I was seeing you, and Ian said, "I expect to be doing that myself before long."'

'Maybe the freelance scene is easing a bit,' Ellie replied. 'I had a note from him today asking me to call.'

Jed was regarding her with a satisfied smile.

'What's the matter?' she asked, sitting contentedly back against the cushioned back rest, enjoying Clive seducing all her friends.

'Just good to see you again,' Jed said. 'Good to see you looking happy. I mean I might be your best friend, but I knew I couldn't take that haunted look out of your eyes. I like Clive . . . and Bill.'

'And you'll love Gemma. And Amy. I bet you'll like Letty too. And you know you've never met Joe McPhee, have you?'

Ellie was very tipsy, and very happy. Jed laughed and told her so.

'Probably,' she said, trying to sound sober. She looked around the table and remembered another night when she had dined out: Polly Lambton's dinner party. The night Warren had fallen asleep and Beth Wickham had got her claws into Paul. The night Polly had made them all toast her because it was the day she had finally made it. But made what?

Made life that bit easier for Polly and anyone else who found her useful. Or rather her title. The Eleanor Carter Interview.

Eleanor Carter, she recited in her head. Eleanor Carter, joint chair of WIN. Eleanor Carter, who will be delighted to attend, come to, help with. Miss Carter will be available for anyone, anytime, anywhere. And where had it got her?

Ellie started to feel drowsy. Clive leaned over and said solemnly, 'You've tried that trick once. You are a fake, not an original at all.'

Laughter lit Ellie's eyes. He was nice. So were they all. The night she had dined at Polly's had been lavish, lush and loaded with style. It was all so long ago, like another lifetime and another world. And suddenly she absolutely knew that the world she had struggled to re-enter, to get back on terms with was, for her, over. She never wanted to go back. This was where she belonged, comfortable, at ease, relaxed and being exactly who she was. Ellie Carter.

An hour later they reluctantly found themselves being ushered out by two polite but yawning waiters and the owner, who was torn between annoyance at being kept from his bed, and delight at the size of the bill they had just settled. Jed and Ashley flagged down a cab and bundled Rosie inside, leaving Ellie to walk back arm in arm with Clive and Bill, feeling drunk with relief that after so long she was, please God, emerging from that awful bleak winter.

That night she slept with Clive O'Connell Moore for the first time and could only agree with the old Woody Allen joke, that it was the best fun she'd had in a long, long time, without actually laughing.

Chapter Twenty-two

'I think Ellie needs to stop and think a bit.'

Jed dragged his eyes away from the sight of Ellie and Clive, racing around the back lawn of the cottage, Miles and Chloe screaming encouragement, trying to stop their bonfire petering out by piling it high with brushwood.

Helpless shrieks of laughter drifted across to where Jill, Jed and Ashley lounged in the drawing room of the cottage, where the shuttered latticed glass doors led on to a small terrace. This gave them an uninterrupted view of the walled garden where it stretched down to meet the boundary of the heavily disputed Linton's Field.

Jill lowered her cup and looked quizzically at him. 'Don't you?' she repeated.

He looked up at her as she rose to refill his cup and shook his head.

'I hope,' he said with a note of alarm, 'that you are not asking me to tell her?'

'Lord, no,' said Jill. 'Just a comment really. Stupid of me in many ways. But she seems to be ricocheting from one set of emotions to another and I just don't want it to end in tears.'

Ashley stirred in the armchair where he had been sleeping off the effects of Sunday lunch, stretched, yawned and told them they ought to be grateful that she wasn't still with that ghastly little prick who'd ruined every evening they had ever spent together.

'Never, *never*, have I met anyone so spoilt as Paul D'Erlanger,' he complained, not noticing the effort with which Jill controlled her face or the uneasy glance that Jed flicked at her.

'Much better off with an older man and one who makes her laugh,' continued Ashley lazily, blissfully unaware that in the Carter household where Jed was regarded as family, he was often talked of in much the same vein. 'I must say I do like amusing people. Can't stand intense personalities.'

Not for a moment did Jill doubt it was the more attractive of the two characteristics but it still didn't stop her thinking that her sister-in-law was not so much laughing with joy, but screaming with relief.

'Yes, I'm sure you're right. Oh Lord . . . *Miles. Miles.* Put that back in the bucket. Yes. Right now. Excuse me,' she said, opening the doors and striding off down the garden to help her small son replace the contents of the bucket he had just unearthed.

It was nearly December. The blue smoke from the bonfire swirled into the deepening mist of the afternoon, the sharp, raw day closing rapidly and a three-hour drive back to London lay ahead of them. These days Ellie seemed increasingly reluctant to leave. But as Jill disappeared, Jed jumped to his feet and called after her.

'Jill, tell them to buck up. We'll have to get a move on. Ashley needs to be back in town by eight.'

They watched her as she reached the group, saw Clive swing an arm around her waist and playfully pretend to throw her into the pile of brushwood. Ellie, in an old pair of jeans, green wellies and a multicoloured sweater, rushed to her aid and all three fell into a heap on the ground with the twins hurling themselves on top.

'You would think, wouldn't you,' remarked Jed carefully to Oliver who had just joined them, 'that she had been involved with Clive for at least six years instead of just six weeks?'

*

The relationship that Ellie embarked on with Clive so easily, so readily, was what Gemma soon dubbed not so much a love affair as a laugh affair.

Ellie herself would not have ventured to put a name to it, but never had she found herself caught up with a man so intent on filling every day as though it was one to remember for ever, not considered complete unless you finally closed your eyes, mourning its passing but embracing the thought of the next.

Two days after she met him again on 'PrimeMovers', Ellie decided he was probably mad, but so gloriously, magnificently mad that she felt it her duty to behave as one would towards a lunatic and humour him.

He took her rowing in mid-winter on the lake in Battersea Park, ignoring her protests that she would freeze, simply recommending that she tried to think hot. At five o'clock on the rawest, foggiest November morning she could recall, he dragged her from her warm bed and marched her off to help a friend on his antique stall in Brick Lane. Collecting her for breakfast in Fulham in his Aston Martin, she ended up having lunch in Calais.

The sex was great too. No, not just great, she decided, but a discovery about herself, about her confidence, which filled her with pleasure and astonishment.

Paul had at first made her feel gratitude to him for wanting her, then naive because she rarely satisfied his demands and finally frigid when reluctance replaced desire when he took her to bed.

Perhaps she had been too tipsy, too happy to worry about nerves or shyness or fear of failing Clive the night they had tumbled into her bed, having waved Bill Burroughs into his flat. With Clive there had been no point in pretending that they had anything else in mind.

'Stand still, woman,' he'd ordered as she began to pull at the buttons on his shirt. 'What a greedy little girl you are. Didn't your teachers ever tell you, ladies first?'

And he meant it. In every way. And when he finally, skilfully, stroked and kissed and teased her to the point where she understood wholly and without reservation that the word rapture had been much misused and almost outraged that he should keep her waiting, she told him so quite forcibly.

And he had laughed and kissed her, telling her that everything comes to those who wait. Then, with an intensity that made her gasp, he triggered the explosion of pleasure, leaving her sweating, sated and elated with the strangest feeling that she had been travelling for a very long time and all the signposts, until now, had been deliberately misleading. His own climax followed swiftly and when they lay tangled up in arms, legs, sheets and the remains of the Bollinger that had, at the height of their passion, gently tipped over oozing on to the sheets, she had smiled sleepily up at him.

'Who said I haven't got any manners?' she asked with a drowsy chuckle. 'Thank you for having me.'

'Not at all,' he said politely, wrapping her in his arms. 'Thank you for coming.'

The first of Ellie's reports for 'PrimeMovers', on the need for a hostel for homeless teenagers, brought a respectable number of viewers' letters into Letty Brereton's office and the second, on the lack of support available for the families of drug addicts, got a mention in the national press. But the third, on the damaging effects of redundancy on family life, forced Letty to hire a temp to deal with the avalanche of letters that arrived.

By the time she had completed her fourth week on the programme commuting between London and Dorset, Ellie had been lunched by Ian Willoughby and had done a deal with him that she knew was, in these straitened times, almost beyond belief.

They lunched in the Horse Guards Hotel where Ian

was clearly a welcome and familiar client and where it was unlikely that they would be observed.

'For my protection, not yours,' he assured her as he greeted her in the wide, carpeted foyer. 'If you say no to what I'm going to suggest, then I won't have to suffer the humiliation of Bentley Goodman knowing I've been turned down.'

There was no way she couldn't like him. Ellie had been curious about him ever since he had written to her in the first awful weeks of her unemployment and, urged on by Jed, she had telephoned him on hearing that the once-editor of their chief rival, *Profile*, and Jerome Strachan's former boss, had now been appointed editorial director of the whole of Goodman Coopers Publishing. Ian Willoughby hadn't been around to take her call, but shored up by her new-found confidence and belief in herself, Ellie had simply written him a note saying she had been in touch.

His phone call came the day after she had posted the letter and lunch had been arranged for the following week.

Ellie had dressed carefully for the occasion but where once she would have raided her wardrobe for something that would get results based on drop dead glamour, she no longer felt at ease in power suits and executive chic. A cornflower blue silk shirt with a much cherished navy cashmere man's cardigan over it was the simple but uncluttered style she enjoyed these days.

Ian Willoughby thought she looked sexier than ever, but he was too shrewd a man to tell her so, certainly not over a business lunch. And, he reflected as she listened carefully with those serious grey eyes and her head tilted just a little to the side, there must be a man telling her that anyway. She had that look about her.

He didn't waste any time. Roland was now managing director of the company and too engrossed in the problems of Goodman Coopers worldwide to pay enough attention to the editorial quality of their publications. Hence Ian had been lured away from *Profile* to take over editorial control of the entire group.

Ellie listened carefully. All editors, including Jerome, had to report directly to him for final approval of each issue and all their future plans were forwarded to him before they could be implemented.

'I hope it won't be more than a short-term operation, but one or two of the editors are more talented than experienced and still have to learn that it's as much a question of addressing their minds to budgets and quality, gauging the public's mood, as producing brilliant ideas,' he explained. 'Also, I think there is a blurring of identities going on within the group.'

He paused while a hovering waiter poured more wine into his glass. Ellie signalled briefly that she would stick to mineral water. Ian waited until the performance was complete before he went on.

'For example, *Pace*, which is essentially young, trendy and for the under twenty-fives, is being overburdened with political issues. That's fine in itself, but you can't avoid the fact that that age group deeply resent political influence or what is perceived as political influence, so they are turning to other publications.'

Ian's tone was hard to analyse. Ellie had been in the business long enough to recognize that a senior management figure talking with such considered tact to a writer was undoubtedly putting a gloss on a problem causing the company concern.

'*Focus*,' he continued, studying his wine glass, 'on the other hand, has perhaps gone too far the other way and is becoming rather lightweight. We all think very highly of Jerome, but during these early days, all editors need support and that is what I am here for.'

To her credit, Ellie didn't actually sling her napkin into

the air and scream with pleasure. Boy wonder wasn't so wonderful after all. Instead she remained impassive. What had all this to do with her?

Reading her thoughts, Ian smiled and said, 'Now how can I put this? Let me see. I know your departure from *Focus* was not under the most pleasant conditions, I know Jerome was deeply upset at some of the more difficult decisions he had to make . . .'

Ellie had had enough. She had not gone through months of unalleviated misery, brought on by the foolish, spiteful behaviour of an inexperienced editor, only to have to sit silently while his actions were endowed with a compassion she knew was wholly absent. Carefully she pressed her napkin to her mouth. Slowly she placed it beside her plate and fixed Ian with a level gaze.

'Ian, I truly appreciate this gesture – inviting me here. I am enjoying your company and nor have I forgotten that you troubled to write a note to me when I couldn't get arrested, let alone get a job. But please,' she went on, 'you must see that my view of Jerome is not yours. I'm afraid I would be less than honest with you if I sat here allowing you to believe that I shared it. Do you think, since I am being honest with you, that you could be just as honest with me and put me in the picture? Why am I here?'

Ian looked squarely at her for about ten seconds.

'Would you like your old job back?'

It was blunt. To the point. Ellie felt as though someone had delivered an electric shock.

She didn't hesitate.

'No thank you, Ian. No . . . let me finish. Thank you for making the offer, but you see . . .'

She stopped. How could she make him understand that she had come a long way since the day she sat in Green Park facing a future that filled her with terror? So much had happened, so many things had been revealed to her.

Not just about the way she lived, but about who she was and more important, how to hang on to being what she was.

What was it Theo had said? 'Not without your consent.'

Going back to *Focus*, the one thing she had dreamed about for that first month, now didn't seem terribly necessary to her.

Ian was quietly waiting for her to explain. He didn't, Ellie noticed fleetingly, seem all that surprised by her answer. But she surprised herself next. The fury and contempt that had filled her for Jerome Strachan's pettiness had sustained her on many a night when she had mentally rehearsed this speech for just such a moment. Suddenly it all seemed so petty and small and undignified. Perhaps more to the point, the Jeromes of the world were no longer that important to her.

She found herself describing to Ian what she wanted now and as she spoke it all began to fall into place. When had she changed, at what point over the last four months had she decided this was what she wanted? But even as she spoke she knew she hadn't changed, she had just resumed being herself.

'You see, that kind of interview, glitzy, glamorous and preoccupied with the fast lane of life, is wonderful to read and I lap it up. But I don't particularly want to do that any more. You learn that not everyone in the world cares about the workings of the minds of the Rich and Famous and the Good and the Great, not when they have lives to lead and ambitions to achieve in the real world. It's great escapist stuff. I adore Jed's column. I can't get enough of Rosie's fashion pictures. Even Paul's travel pieces are fascinating.'

Paul's name had just slipped out. Easily, no pangs, no lurching of the heart. How strange.

'But I want to try more analytical journalism now. I

don't want to record the thoughts of anyone, I want to be able to judge their performance, to be able to push them into knowing that they should put their money where their mouth is. I want to interview people who matter in a way that will make them accountable for their actions.

'Oh, don't look like that. I'm not going to bullshit about not needing work. I do. I can just about get by with the report I do for "PrimeMovers", provided I back it with some regular freelance work. It's just that I now only want to live my life – as far as possible – the way I want to live. I don't think going back – in any sense of the word – would achieve that.'

She stopped. Ian stretched out his hand and closed it over hers.

'Good girl,' he said gently. 'You haven't disappointed me at all.'

'What?'

'I meant what I said. *Focus* could do with the weight of your writing, but I should have known you wouldn't stand still.'

He sighed and signalled to the waiter for more coffee.

'But if you think I'm giving up there, my girl, you don't know your man.'

Nor did she. They left the restaurant an hour later, Ian to report back to Roland that Ellie would be resuming her relationship with *Focus* as from the first week in December, but not, he emphasized, resuming her job.

Ellie on the other hand had walked nearly half way to Lambeth Bridge before she realized what she was doing. Barely able to stop laughing, she turned round and ran all the way to Clive's flat overlooking the Thames at Westminster to tell him her amazing news.

'Why not?' he said, whirling her around the room and swinging her off her feet. 'It's only when you don't want something that you can state your terms and usually get them. Sod's law. When you wanted a job you couldn't get one working twice as hard for half the dough, and now look at you.'

Ellie hugged herself, hugged a grinning Clive, whooping with delight.

'Freelance contract for a year, one interview a fortnight and I can work from home or the office, whichever fits in with TVW. The money is ludicrous,' she said, excitedly following him into the drawing room and watching him clear a space on one of the sofas, piled high with books, newspapers and for some reason one of his teenage sons' guitar and trainers, so that she could sit down. 'It's nearly as much as I was getting before for doing three times the work.

'Clive, what is this?' she asked, suddenly pulling a high-heeled shoe from underneath her.

He looked blank and then delighted.

'Oh, good girl, that's where it went.'

Ellie felt an odd sensation in her stomach. It most certainly wasn't her shoe. She tried to make light of it, but Clive was openly laughing.

'It's Joanne's,' he said. 'You know, Joanne, as in mother of my children.'

Ellie blushed. How stupid. So used to Paul's infidelities, she had automatically assumed Clive would be the same. Or had she?

No, of course not. Once he had been, he'd told her that. To be honest, he had said, twice. Twice unfaithful to his wife and while she forgave the first one, she couldn't cope with the second and had slung him out.

'Sorry, I wasn't prying or anything,' she mumbled, knowing that's exactly what it sounded like. 'It was just sticking into me.'

And then Clive sat down and took her hands and said seriously, not since Joanne had he felt so at ease with someone, or had felt like laughing, and while he had resented any questions about his wife and children from the girl who broke up his marriage and who he had instantly lost all interest in, he didn't dislike them in the least coming from Ellie.

'You've been so good for me,' he said, stroking her face. 'I think if you hadn't come along, I would have given up the human race for ever, having failed me so many times. My own fault of course,' he went on, perching his huge frame on the arm of the sofa, running both hands distractedly through his shock of grey hair. 'I'm an undisciplined man. I've learned that. Joanne had a lot to put up with, but I was so stupid, I thought she was trying to restrain me. Do you know what it's like to suddenly find everyone wants to ask you to their parties, their homes, to give you things because you've got a bit of a name? It's not you they want, it's the fame they enjoy. Unfortunately,' he said, getting up and walking to the window to gaze out over the churning grey water of the river, 'I was seduced by it all. And the life and . . .' He paused, adding softly, 'And the women.'

Ellie just let him talk. He was unpredictable. Sometimes he just behaved like a wild young boy instead of the mature man of forty that he was. At other times, he talked with an insight and passion and an understanding of the world made Ellie hold her breath in case he heard it and stopped.

Now she knew him well enough to know that he needed space to unload all the guilt and remorse that he had piled up over the last five years. She knew that whatever the future held for them, one thing was certain; she owed him a debt, and if listening to him and just being there could repay some of it, then it was her privilege to do so.

Now was such a time.

They had known each other for a mere few weeks and were openly enjoying what Clive called being 'in crazy' with each other. Ellie was in no doubt at all about the place she occupied in his life. But the pivot of his life was his sons, Callum and Sean, barely into their teens, who she could see from photographs were clones of their father. That he missed their daily presence was beyond doubt.

Knowing Oliver's devotion to the twins, she did not find it at all difficult to understand. What she found a little more complex to grasp was his relationship with Joanne. It was love, it was hate. It was pride and it was fury. His wild Irish temperament and her cool English reserve had been both the attraction and the destruction of their marriage. And yet, she was there. Referred to frequently, accused often and praised overwhelmingly, particularly if he was drunk and always after he had dropped the boys home after a weekend visit.

Ellie wasn't the first woman who had instinctively wanted to organize Clive's life, but she was rare in that she refrained from doing so. Having elected to live in a beautiful penthouse apartment with a view clear upriver to St Paul's and downstream to Fulham, Clive had thereafter abandoned any pretence that he knew how to run a home.

It was no secret that he had made a small fortune out of his books, two of which were bestsellers and the recent one likely to make him a tax exile. But he was as generous with his money as he was with his feelings and Ellie knew why women adored him but why he was the despair of his accountant.

If his sons saw nothing wrong with the eccentricities of his lifestyle, he said to Ellie as he investigated the contents of a fridge that was frequently a tribute to fast food, milkshakes and Bollinger, he didn't see why anyone else should complain.

Indeed not. So she turned a blind eye to the chaos he lived in, and revelled in his company. The pair of them even managed to treat Jed's mischievous story as a wonderful joke.

The furore about Clive's book was still going strong and Jed had published in his column that Ellie and Clive were now an item around town. He had called her a TV personality, which had resulted in an immediate missive being despatched by Jonquil to Letty, wondering if Ellie had misunderstood and urging her to emphasize to the 'stand-in' that the job was only for three months – for Ellie's own sake, Jonquil ended, with a concern that fooled no-one, least of all Letty.

The reaction from Clive's ex-wife had seemed to give him particular satisfaction when Joanne, in a voice that would have frozen the Sahara, promptly phoned demanding an increase in maintenance.

John Carter, however, when Ellie had called him to say she was now employed, simply said vaguely that he was glad she was enjoying herself and pleased that she was back at work. He wasn't quite so amused to hear that the campaign to secure Linton's Field was still a matter of priority for his children.

Clive listened to Ellie's end of the conversation as he lay in her bed and watched her pacing furiously up and down when she finally replaced the receiver.

'Now,' he said, pouring the last of the Bollinger into his glass and handing it to her, 'while I think you look magnificent in a temper and it is definitely very erotic watching you march up and down in that thing,' he indicated the battered T-shirt that Ellie was wearing, 'it might be beneficial to both your temper and my nerves if you told me what all this is about.'

She was very tempted. 'Oh, nothing, really. He just hates a fuss and me being on TV is getting to him.'

Clive looked at her thoughtfully.

'Little liar,' he said easily. 'Maybe when you know me better you'll tell me the truth.'

'Honestly, I do know you and that is the truth.'

'Well, in which case,' he said, stretching out and pulling her to him, 'if you know me so well, you must know that I need constant attention and it has been sadly lacking so far this evening.'

Chapter Twenty-three

Theo Stirling telephoned Ellie on the same day that Letty asked her to stand in for Taylor, who had gone down with flu.

Of the two Ellie was more panic-stricken about meeting Theo Stirling than hosting a chat show for TVW, which Letty was confident she could handle.

'Don't worry, we've actually got a filmed interview that Taylor did with the Chancellor yesterday, so that will occupy the first slot, which means you'll only have to cope with two interviews live.'

The names Letty had lined up were familiar. One was a retired general whose memoirs were about to be published and whose political views were somewhere to the right of Genghis Khan. The other was the brilliant film director, Max Culver, whom Ellie had once interviewed. She noted drily that he had directed Debra Carlysle's most successful film and was currently about to start directing her in another.

'Do you still want a report?' asked Ellie, with no clear idea how that could be fitted in as well as getting her copy to *Focus* on time.

'We'll give it a miss,' Letty decided. 'Taylor's on film so we can afford to lose it for this week. Just get down here as fast as you can.'

That was the least of Ellie's problems. She had planned to stay on after her own filming was complete because Joe and Oliver were holding the first public meeting for the campaign, but it was hearing that Theo would be ensconced in his former home for the weekend that threw her.

She deliberated about returning the call for a full two hours and then rang and asked for Roger Nelson.

'I'm afraid Mr Nelson no longer works here,' came a crisp voice. 'Can anyone else help?'

Ellie was startled and asked if Ann Winterman was available.

After a few minutes Ann Winterman came on the line.

'Roger left the company a couple of months ago,' she said carefully. 'No, I'm afraid I don't know where he's gone.' Her voice was cautious, her tone not conducive to further enquiries. 'Can I help you instead?'

'Yes, of course,' said Ellie politely. 'I'm returning Mr Stirling's call.'

There was a pause. Ann Winterman sounded puzzled. 'Mr Stirling's call?'

Now it was Ellie's turn to feel uneasy. 'Yes, I have a note here. He called at nine a.m. this morning.'

'Just a moment, Miss Carter, I'll check his office.'

Ellie waited and in less than a minute Ann Winterman was back on the line, sounding just a little irritated.

'He asked if you would be kind enough to hold while he finishes another call. I apologize for not knowing about his phone call, I gather he dialled the number direct himself.'

The delay had given Ellie extra time to remain calm when Theo finally came on the line. If it flickered through her mind that she had long ceased to be afraid of him, she did not allow the thought to trouble her.

'Why?' she asked him, her mind careering over all the possible reasons he would need to talk to her, let alone join her for a drink.

'Why not? I hear you're making quite an impact down there.'

'I'm not sure I agree with you, but if I am, does that mean that I might be useful to you in some way?'

There was an infinitesimal pause.

'Unfair, Eleanor, and not worthy of a good opponent. When have I ever suggested you might be useful to me?'

'Then why?'

'I suppose because I still believe that making such an issue about Linton's Field is unwise, and that you are travelling a road that can only cause misery to a lot of people who are not involved in any of this.'

'You seem to be remarkably well informed about the roads I choose to travel,' Ellie retorted. 'What makes you think I'm travelling anywhere that would involve you?'

'Because you're the one who is involving me. I don't ring anyone about you.'

She felt uneasy. It had been a good five months since she had made all those phone calls, but she knew without even having to ask that her arrival back at *Focus*, coupled with the campaign locally, had made her appear once again a formidable opponent.

She found she enjoyed the idea more than was decent. But trying to compose a sensible sentence to convince him that she meant business without sounding petulant and childishly rude proved a little trickier. Somehow, in direct confrontation with this man, her intended elegant speeches and coolly delivered criticism emerged closely resembling the ill-tempered rantings of a foot-stamping brat.

For once she said nothing. Clive, she was convinced, would be ashamed of her.

'Look, this is my private number,' Theo was saying. 'I'll be there all weekend. I said once before and I meant it, if you want to talk, just phone me.'

And then he rang off, leaving Ellie at a loss to know what to make of him, curious about why the loyal Roger Nelson no longer worked there and even more curious to notice that she had hastily scribbled down his number.

The possibility of cancelling the campaign meeting occurred to her, but Joe was more bullish when she rang his office.

'What can he do? Storm the meeting? He won't do that. It's not his style. And anyway, it's not in his interests to appear the ogre once again. So far his name is still not in the arena.'

Joe was right. She was panicking unnecessarily. She'd make a lousy general, she thought ruefully. In full retreat as soon as the enemy appeared on the horizon.

Although that was not the case with Jerome Strachan. Thus far Ellie had had only one meeting with him and that in Ian's office. Jerome had greeted her with a bluffness that didn't deceive her, but mindful of Ian's unvoiced hope that she was above openly enjoying his discomfort, she shook her old boss's hand and, taking a leaf from Jonquil's book, suggested they got straight down to work.

To her delight Lucy had been asked to give Ellie what assistance she might need and her old office, now occupied part-time by another contract writer, was made available for her use on the days when she needed to be in the office.

Now she rang Lucy and told her that she would not be in until Tuesday, and casually asked if Theo Stirling had got her number from her.

'Not from me, Ellie,' said Lucy. 'No-one's asked.'

'Lucy,' Ellie said suddenly. 'Can you find out for me – very discreetly – where a man called Roger Nelson is now working? He used to be Theo Stirling's first lieutenant but he's moved on. Don't let Stirling's aides know you want it. Ring their accounts office, say you're the Inland Revenue just wanting to forward some papers – that might be a better starting point. By the way, did you ever hear from that woman who used to phone without leaving her name?'

'No, not that I know of. Anyway, I always thought she was a nutter,' said the matter-of-fact Lucy. 'I shouldn't give her a thought.'

The clock above the dresser reminded Ellie that she had about forty minutes before she had to be on the train to Dorset. She didn't want to think about that woman at all. But how odd that Theo Stirling should ring, and who had given him the number? She was, after all, ex-directory. And why had Roger Nelson left him? He had seemed so loyal.

Leaving a message for Clive, who was taking his sons to Ireland for a week to see their grandparents, she headed for the West Country and the hot seat of 'PrimeMovers'.

'Today "PrimeMovers", tomorrow "Insiders",' crowed Oliver when Ellie finally arrived back at the cottage after the programme had gone out. 'Eat your heart out, Brook Wetherby. We've taped the lot. You were great. God help you when Jonquil gets to you, or Taylor, come to that.'

Exhausted, Ellie fell into one of the armchairs by the fire. 'Oh, very kind of you, but I need to feel a lot stronger before I hear another word. I thought I would die laughing when General Brigstock said he would only answer my questions after he knew my views on corporal punishment.'

Oliver shook with laughter. 'Honestly, Ellie, fancy saying only for insensitive property developers.'

Jill came flying in, having managed to get rid of the umpteenth call from friends who had watched the programme and wanted to let Ellie know how much they enjoyed it.

'I like that Max Culver,' she said. 'Dead dishy. Does he know you-know-who?'

Taking this as a reference to Theo, Ellie nodded. 'Staying with him for the weekend. Often does, apparently.'

'Well, he certainly knows the area well enough,'

remarked Jill, handing Ellie a drink. 'Nice touch that, making a movie director talk about solitary walks and time to think. I noticed you managed to get in that you too loved Willetts Bay Beach. Hoping to run into him?

'Which reminds me,' she said, ducking to avoid the cushion Ellie threw at her, 'the twins are now clamouring to be taken for a walk tomorrow on your favourite stretch of beach, convinced you're more famous than Madonna.'

Back down to earth after an evening of fame, Ellie was only too willing to take Chloe and Miles for a walk, giving their parents a well-earned, rare break on Saturday afternoon.

Straight after lunch next day, she went in search of the children. Minutes later, warmly wrapped up in parkas and wellingtons with the twins arguing about who was to carry the bright red frisbee they had insisted on taking, all three set off for the nearby Willetts Bay, which had just enough clusters of rocks and inlets to make an adventure out of their walk.

Ellie was uneasily aware that, caught up in a whole new way of life dashing between London and Dorset, she wasn't getting all the exercise she should be. Her intentions were always of the best. Hardly a day went by when, if she was in London, she thought of rejoining Blundells or, if she was in Willetts Green, she convinced herself that a regular run on the beach in the early morning was exactly what was needed to keep her fit.

But after an hour racing around with Chloe and Miles, who would exhaust a marathon runner, she decided scaling a mountain twice a day wouldn't be enough to keep pace with those two. Breathless from an energetic game of 'It' and having diffused several quarrels on the subject of cheating, she marched them firmly to the shelter of a rock. She then produced some cartons of fruit juice from the pockets of her jacket and ordered them both to sit down and keep quiet for at least ten minutes.

After five they were on their feet.

'Okay, but no further than the first line of rocks,' Ellie said, pointing to a cluster twenty yards from where she was perched, well clear of the grey curling waves that were crashing on to the shore, dragging grey fingers of foam back to meet the next swell of the tide. They didn't need a second bidding and raced off on to the sand.

Gathering her jacket tightly around her, Ellie sat on the top of a rock where she could see them playing, hugging her knees under her chin, savouring the salty air and the sharp wind that had whipped her hair out of its pony tail, making her face damp with salt spray.

For once Miles and Chloe seemed to be in perfect accord with each other, digging furiously in the soft sand for treasure, and Ellie grabbed the chance to relax and let her mind wander. The meeting that morning had not been as well attended as she had hoped. She had prepared herself to be sympathetic to Oliver and Joe McPhee, but to her surprise neither seemed daunted by the fact that only about twenty people had turned up.

To her amazement a middle-aged man and his wife, who had been sitting together at the back of the hall, sought her out after the meeting and Ellie had the oddest idea that she knew him.

He was grey-haired, with a wispy beard and twinkling blue eyes, yet she just couldn't place him. His wife, a plump motherly-looking woman, was smiling anxiously at Ellie as her husband extended his hand to her.

'You probably don't remember me at all,' he said courteously. 'My name is Maurice Middleton. I heard you on the radio.'

Ellie smiled in delight. Maurice. Of course. She greeted him and his wife warmly and was really not that surprised to see him.

'Just wanted to do our bit,' he said. 'Let us know when

you're having the march down the high street, won't you?'

Ellie introduced him to Oliver and Joe, and was inwardly delighted when she heard them invite Maurice to come up to Delcourt for a strategy meeting.

Josie Fallon, Ellie noticed, was another supporter and she was a surprise. Much younger than Ellie had expected, she was also much more attractive. Ellie had visualized a middle-aged woman and for some reason she had imagined her to be a bit common.

Josie was none of those things. Forceful, yes. And as Joe said, not slow to speak her mind, but at around five feet two with only a smattering of grey in her dark bob of hair, she had arrived wearing a tweed hacking jacket over jeans and a Black Watch tartan scarf slung loosely around her neck.

Close to, she betrayed signs that her fortieth birthday was some way behind her, but she had an energy and vitality that proclaimed a much younger woman. Clearly her relationship with Joe went back a long time and it was not really surprising to hear that she was joining him and his son for lunch.

It could not be said that she actually apologized to Ellie for being so brisk – well, rude – to her on Sandy Barlow's programme, but just appeared to take it for granted that Ellie had been the author of her own misfortune and that she had to expect these things being in the public eye.

In fact Ellie was finding the public eye just a bit too intrusive and fame, no matter how local, was still unnerving for her.

As they walked back along the village high street towards their cars, Oliver, Ellie and Jill to head for Delcourt, Joe for a lunch date with his younger son (must be a weekend for sons, thought Ellie, wondering how Clive was getting on with his two in Dublin), Joe was remarkably cheerful.

'Considering there is no immediate decision going to be made, I think it's a good barometer for what interest there will be when the danger day draws close.' He gave her a hug. 'Have faith, lassie. And I think I'll leave you here, looks like a couple of fans approaching,' and he disappeared with a huge grin on his face as Ellie, scarlet with embarrassment, signed two autograph books proffered to her by a couple of giggling schoolgirls.

At that point, sitting snugly on her rock gazing out to sea, Ellie's gentle meanderings over her new busy life were brought to a halt. Miles chose that moment to come running back asking for his frisbee. Ellie threw it to him and settled back against the rock, pulling up the hood of her parka.

It was so comfortable there. Cold, but comfortable. She squinted up at the sky, decided that she could risk ten more minutes before the rain came on and wriggled her back against the unyielding rock to a more agreeable position.

No longer was she haunted by her old life. Hadn't been for weeks, so what was it that had made her say yes to Ian Willoughby's offer?

'I'd say you're trying to prove a point – that no-one but you thinks is necessary,' Gemma had told her.

Dumping the sleeping Amy into Ellie's lap, she'd begun collecting up bottles and nappies and carting them away to her cluttered kitchen.

'Perhaps you need to get it out of your system, lay the ghost,' she'd said, returning with steaming mugs of coffee.

Amy had stirred in Ellie's arms and she'd moved the sleeping child to her shoulder, gently rocking her until she settled.

'Maybe I do. But I think it has more to do with wanting to be able to prove it wasn't me that was at fault, it was Jerome's misjudgement. But you know, Gem,' she'd said, carefully replacing her coffee on the table and squinting down at the now peaceful baby on her shoulder, 'it's also got so much more to do with not having to rely on any one person or organization ever again.'

Gemma had looked mockingly at her.

'Knock it off, Ellie, you want to score a point – and,' she'd said, removing her daughter from Ellie's shoulder and laying her gently in the wicker basket by her feet, 'I can't say I blame you. Don't keep thinking you've got to behave like a saint the whole time, just because they behaved like monsters.'

Gemma's frank appraisal of her motives made Ellie grin and she let her mind wander to Clive.

Clive, who had invaded her life, brought her alive again, who made her laugh and openly adored her, and who had given her the courage to be herself, now occupied a special place in her heart. And she loved him.

Loved him, yes, how could she not? Clive, who had taught her to enjoy sex, to cease burdening it with commitment and forever, who had loved her for herself?

She was certain he loved her too. He said so often. She hadn't even tried to tidy him up, but that only made him laugh delightedly, and when he rang – as he had done twice in the six weeks she had known him – to cancel an outing because his sons had asked to see him, she had envied them, but only because her own father would not have put her first.

The one thing she had noticed was that Clive never said he loved her when they were in bed.

But then nor had she.

It occurred to her as she idly watched the twins, arguing over a pile of shells on a mountain of sand which Ellie could hear Miles shrieking was a space station, that for two people having such fun, so completely at ease with each other, who both made a living out of writing, they were being awfully cautious with words. It was as far as she got. Quite how she knew something was wrong, she was never afterwards able to say.

She hadn't taken her eyes from the children for a moment. She had been carefully monitoring the activities of a large dog of indeterminate breed who was circling them, moving nearer, its owner having little success in calling it to heel.

Bored with digging, Miles had started throwing the frisbee. The dog moved like a fox towards the child. Ellie was instantly on her feet calling a warning as she saw the dog pounce on the frisbee, wrenching it from Miles, grasp and race with it towards the sea, Miles in hot pursuit.

'Miles, Miles!' she shouted. 'Leave it, come back. Chloe, get back!'

She was scrambling down the rocks, hair flying, streaking across the beach, as Miles, suddenly aware of the danger he was in, stood rooted, frozen with fright as the waves crashed around him, and the dog, having lost the frisbee, turned its attention to the child.

Paws up, body twisting, it hurled itself at the terrified boy, sinking its teeth into his sleeve, pulling him backwards into the pounding waves.

Dimly aware that Chloe was safe, if petrified, and being held by the woman owner of the dog, Ellie was already pulling off her parka, no thought for anything but Miles. Blinded by salt spray and the wind, she plunged into the foam and grabbed the small boy, pushing him clear of the dog and the waves, using her own body to shield him from the howling animal.

'Move, Miles, move,' she yelled above the noise of the waves as the dog turned its attention to Ellie.

A swift glance over her shoulder was all Ellie had time for. Miles was now on the safety of the sand with nothing more than a fright and wet jeans to cope with as the dog leapt up at her, sending her plunging with shuddering force under the next wave, which crashed in a swollen rage on the shore and sent her sprawling.

Her hands frozen, her face numb, she rolled helplessly, defenceless against the next roaring wave, as it gathered force to swamp her, and swiftly engulfed her in a powerful shock of weight which knocked her almost senseless.

She felt rather than saw a strong arm grab her around the waist and haul her firmly back on to the beach. The shrieks from the dog's owner finally penetrated the ears of the uncontrolled animal and he ran off as Ellie sank to her knees, waves of nausea washing over her. She was aware of the man's figure crouching beside her, asking her if she was all right, heard him calmly reassure the twins and curtly tell the dog owner that her help wasn't needed and she'd be better employed keeping her dog under control.

'Okay, sit still and don't move,' an unbelievably familiar voice told the now silent children, as the dog's owner feebly protested that the animal was only playing before obeying the icy command of the man who had appeared from nowhere, and moved away.

'You'll feel better in a minute,' said the same voice, pushing her head between her knees as her whole body convulsed. 'Gently, take it easy.'

Opening her eyes, Ellie raised her head slowly, taking in the man's jeans tucked into green wellingtons, drenched to the waist. Her eyes travelled upwards to a dark blue guernsey sweater over a blue denim shirt, which was unable to disguise lean shoulders, and a tanned neck and face.

'What are you doing here?' she asked weakly, gazing straight into Theo Stirling's face.

'I came to find you,' he said, holding her shaking body against his side. 'I wanted to talk to you and you very obligingly dropped several clues on television last night where you might be. I had just parked at the top of the cliff when I saw you had decided to take a dip.'

'Miles?' she croaked through clenched, chattering teeth. 'Is he okay?'

'Take a look for yourself,' Theo said calmly, indicating behind her to where Chloe and Miles were already beginning an argument about whose fault it all was. 'I assume they're Oliver's children. Frankly, you're the one who's come off the worst,' remarked Theo as she nodded silently.

Helping Ellie to her feet and without consulting her he began to pull her sweater and shirt off.

'What are you doing?' she protested.

'There's no point in putting a perfectly dry jacket on over these sopping clothes,' he said, apparently oblivious to the fact that she was wearing only the skimpiest of lacy bras.

'You do make a habit of this, don't you?' he said, half laughing as he draped her jacket around her and then, retrieving his hastily discarded Barbour from the sand where he had dropped it in his race to pull her from the sea, put that on top. 'Unfortunately I don't happen to have a wardrobe of clothes around me to come to your rescue this time,' he apologized, still holding her around the waist to steady her.

If she hadn't felt so ill, Ellie knew she would have been crippled with embarrassment. As it was, all she had was an overwhelming desire to stay in the safety of his arms.

'Thank you,' she whispered, her teeth chattering uncontrollably. 'I must get the children home ... get some dry clothes, you're drenched. You must be frozen as well.'

'To the bone. C'mon, I'll take you, we'll be there in five minutes. Okay, you two,' he said cheerfully to the twins. 'Bet you can't get to the top without a carry ...'

'Course we can,' they said scornfully and set off ahead of Theo, who took Ellie's hand and guided her carefully up the cliff path to where he had parked his Range Rover, and home.

Chapter Twenty-four

Oliver, when he and Jill returned and heard about the afternoon's adventure, was inclined to phone the police and have the dog's owner prosecuted.

'Not much point,' argued Ellie, sitting in a dressing gown in the kitchen, sipping hot chocolate. 'When it comes down to it, the dog didn't bite Miles or me, just managed to get us both soaking wet. Anyway, I blame myself. I shouldn't have let them move a yard from me.'

'Oh, rubbish,' said Jill. 'I would have done the same, and I'm their mother. You can't keep them strapped to your side. There are so few things that small children can do these days that we once took for granted, and playing twenty yards from you on the beach is one of the rare freedoms they can enjoy. You seem to forget you were there in seconds. More to the point, they are so young they've forgotten it already. You're the one who's going to have the nightmare.'

'Well, actually,' said Oliver wryly, 'we're all in a bit of a fix because I at least am now indebted to the man we're pledged to see off.'

The three of them exchanged silent glances. It was Jill who spoke first, Oliver and Ellie looking so like her own twins that she almost laughed at the consternation on their faces.

'Sorry,' she said practically. 'It has to be done even if he is the enemy, and I genuinely *do* want to thank him for coming to your rescue. And you do as well, don't you, Oliver?'

'You know I do,' he said. 'Did you say he was going

up to his house, Ellie? We could drive over now.'

Ellie nodded. 'Shall I come with you?'

'No, you need to get warmed up and have a rest. I'll tell Jenny to chain the twins to the wall until we get back, and I'm only half joking,' said Oliver as he unhitched his coat from behind the door, handing Jill hers. So they went off to be grateful to a man they were far from feeling well disposed towards.

Ellie was relieved to have been spared that. Leaning back on the mountain of cushions, she closed her eyes and with little hope that she could sort out the jumble in her head, tried to make some sense of her feelings.

A hot bath and Jill's ever practical approach to dramas had done much to calm her jangled nerves, but the day's events had done little to give her peace of mind.

If only she didn't feel so uneasy every time she met him, Ellie told herself, it would be so much easier to see him for what he was. Childhood memories could still unnerve her. Adolescent recollections of days without a proper meal, days when villagers walked by awkwardly avoiding her and Oliver. Frightening memories of the days when the Stirling family held the Carter family's fragile destiny in their callous hands.

And then she thought of Alison. Alison, who of all of them had remained calm in the face of disaster, gathered their pitiful resources, their broken spirits and shown them a way out.

Alison. How strange. Her thoughts wandered on.

Being charming is just second nature to him. He's so used to it, he must turn it on like a tap. And now they were indebted to him for helping her out of a real dilemma.

In the Range Rover on the short drive home, Theo had made no attempt to talk to her, just firmly but cheerfully insisting the twins wore seat belts and smothering a laugh when Chloe told him that she could undress herself.

'That's very clever of you,' he replied dutifully as he manoeuvred the sturdy vehicle around a sharp bend in the country lane. 'You must be very grown up.'

'Well, I am,' she said. 'More than Ellie, 'cos you had to help her, didn't he, Miles?'

'*Chloe!*' admonished Ellie, seeing the undisguised mirth on Theo's face, and was thankful that at that moment the house came into sight.

As she climbed out of the jeep and the twins stormed ahead, shrieking to Jenny to guess what had happened, she turned to Theo and tried to say something that sounded grateful.

'Go on in,' he said with such concern she almost burst into tears. 'I'll telephone later to see how you are.'

Lifting a hand she held it out to him, but instead of taking it he reached out and without a word pulled her towards him, kissing her briefly on her forehead, then turned her round and pushed her gently towards the house.

If he would just tell me why he wants the land so badly, Ellie thought, and why they blamed Dad for something he didn't do, maybe I could understand his motives. He's so complex. So unpredictable.

That's all he is, she told herself firmly. He's not like Clive. Warm and generous and as uncomplicated as a child.

Really, she chided herself, I must be going dotty. A deliriously happy few weeks with Clive, a career that had miraculously resurrected itself. Quit while you're ahead. Phone Clive in Dublin. A quick chat would put her feet firmly back on the ground and rid herself once and for all of a fantasy. Good heavens, she must have been more stunned by that wave than she'd thought.

The woman with a soft Irish lilt who answered the phone told her Clive and the family were not yet back. To try at around seven.

Ellie sighed and replaced the phone. But just that short phone call had made her aware again of Clive and she tried to picture him laughing uproariously with his sons, striding over the fields but for some reason she just couldn't get him into focus.

Yawning, she curled up on the sofa and laughed to herself. Well, of course you can't picture him striding over the hills, there aren't any in the centre of Dublin . . . and the next thing she knew was waking with a start to hear Oliver and Jill returning.

'Not there,' said Oliver briefly, removing his coat. 'Some sort of house party going on, I think. Jill said she could swear the redhead who swept up after us was Debra Carlysle.'

Ellie couldn't understand why the information did nothing for her already gloomy spirits.

'Anyway, Jill discovered the housekeeper and left a message for Theo to say that we had called to say thank you and that we are very grateful to him for coming to your aid. Oh God,' he said, looking at the clock. 'It's not six thirty already, is it? Must dash, my guests await me.'

Within twenty minutes, both Oliver and Jill had departed for the hotel where they were hosting a small drinks party before dining with Gregory Merton, the local MP, Joe McPhee, and the very distinguished historian that Jonquil had interviewed on 'PrimeMovers' when Ellie had made her first appearance as a guest.

It was meant to be a social occasion, a small dinner party with their wives, but Ellie knew that Oliver and Joe were quietly whipping up influential support for their campaign and the presence of Josie Fallon confirmed it. After Ellie's very competent handling of 'PrimeMovers' the night before, they had all agreed that it would look like a pressure group if she was included.

She stuck her tongue out at her brother. 'And to think I spent all day looking after your children . . .'

'. . . Is that what you call it?' he scoffed.

'. . . and all I'm getting is beans on toast on my own. Miserable lot,' she grumbled.

After they had gone she strolled through to the kitchen to investigate the possibility of something more exotic than baked beans, and on impulse decided to try to ring Clive again in Ireland. She wanted to tell him how hard she had to tried to visualize him climbing mountains in O'Connell Street and was smiling as she asked if he was there.

'I'm afraid not,' said the same voice. 'He's out at the airport collecting Joanne.'

Ellie knew she was being unreasonable, but she stiffened.

'Joanne?'

'Yes. She wasn't sure she'd be able to make it, but she rang to say she could, now isn't that delightful?'

'Delightful,' agreed Ellie. 'No, no message. I'm just a friend from London.'

Now why wasn't she angry? Hurt? Oh, don't be so stupid. Well, what about deceived? No, not Clive. Then what?

Why aren't you falling about in a heap, like you were when you found out about Beth Wickham?

No idea, except I think he's so lovely that I hope he has a smashing weekend. But deep in her heart she knew the reason she wasn't falling about was that the unspoken words between her and Clive were all too obvious. Still, she couldn't help feeling just a little put out and just a little bit sorry for herself.

Poor Ellie, still looking for love in all the wrong places.

When the phone rang, she half hoped it would be Clive so that she could tell him what an idiot she was being. But when Jenny put her head around the door, it wasn't Clive on the phone, but a Mr Stirling.

'He wanted to speak to Oliver or Jill. But I said only

you were here. So he said that you would do.'

'He said that, did he?' snapped Ellie. Charming, she thought acidly, but nevertheless went and picked up the extension. 'I'm sorry my brother and sister-in-law are dining at the hotel,' she said. 'I know they want to thank you personally for helping me, but I gather you'll make do with me.'

'That of course would be an unexpected pleasure,' he laughed. 'Well, you sound as though you've recovered – so will you come and join us for dinner tonight?'

'Us?' said Ellie, mentally reviewing the clothes she had brought with her.

'Just a few house guests. Unfortunately, they all seem to be quite fond of me, which I realize can hardly recommend them to you, but I'm sure you could over-look it.'

'I'm not prejudiced by anyone's lack of judgement,' she said lightly. 'Just not sure what dining with you and your friends would achieve.'

'It might save you the trouble of having to ring so many of them to find out what I'm like,' came the reply.

She swallowed hard. Impossible to have hoped her enquiries wouldn't have reached his ears. 'Oh, I know that already,' she replied, trying to sound unperturbed. 'However, my job requires that I at least try to find some-one who will disagree with me.'

'There you are then,' Theo said, unmoved. 'I'm provid-ing you with plenty of raw material to work on. You can hardly refuse.'

Her mind flew to Clive with his family in Dublin. What would he say? She knew without even asking.

'Stop looking for a purpose behind everything. Do what your spirit tells you to do.'

So what was stopping her accepting Theo's invitation?

Her common sense told Ellie he was ruthless. Her prac-tical nature said that she should politely refuse and replace the phone. Her head reliably told her she was being ridiculous.

'Very well then,' she heard herself say. 'Why not?'

'I'll send my car over for you,' he said, ignoring her protests. 'I don't think you should be driving over here on your own and especially not after the day you've had,' with which he bade her goodbye, giving her thirty minutes in which to get ready.

It wasn't hard to understand why he had become so powerful, she thought as she ran upstairs to tell Jenny she would be going out. He simply never took no for an answer and just assumed that what he said would be obeyed.

Her make-up took less than ten minutes, her hair, freshly shampooed earlier, was swept up into a loose chignon, secured by two diamanté combs. Rummaging through her clothes she pulled out a black crepe camisole top, letting it fall straight over a full length matching skirt that was split at the front from just above the knee to the ground.

Grabbing the phone as she sprayed herself with Paloma Picasso, she managed to get through to Jill, who was only too grateful to be given a breather from the bumptious MP.

'Goodness me,' Jill giggled down the phone. 'Dining with the enemy, eh?'

'I just thought it might help,' said Ellie lamely, wondering who she was fooling. 'And I bet he's offering more than baked beans and . . . well, it seemed rude to refuse, after today.'

'I quite agree,' said Jill. 'Do let him know that I will take the first opportunity to thank him personally, it's just that he's so elusive. And Ellie . . .'

'Yes?'

'You will be careful, won't you?'

Advice, Ellie thought as she sat in the back of the

white Mercedes that Theo had sent for her, that it was sweet of Jill to offer, but unnecessary. She had got Theo's measure.

The house, unseen from the road, lay at the end of a long, curved drive, approached through trees which gave way to a vast lawn that fronted the entire length of the grey-stone house.

Unless you actually saw someone drive in from the road, almost quarter of a mile away, how would you know anyone was here?

Once or twice when Ellie and Oliver were small, they had crept up the drive to explore, but had decided that it was too imposing and unfriendly to be of interest, preferring the more comfortable chaos of the old manor that was their home.

It was too dark for Ellie to decide whether the house still felt like that, but with lights blazing and the drive lined with cars her heart sank and she could remember very clearly the day she had run, heart pounding, as fast as her seven-year-old legs would carry her, down the drive, terrified that at any second a powerful voice would boom out asking her just what she thought she was doing.

The stolen milk from the doorstep had been icy cold and slippery in her hands.

Oliver had been running ahead, clutching another illicit bottle, twisting his head to make sure his little sister was still behind. 'C'mon Ellie, quick, quick,' he had urged her and he had grabbed her hand and pushed her into the bushes only seconds before a large black car swept past, allowing them their one and only glimpse of Robert Stirling at the wheel.

Silly children, she thought. Even sillier adults. What on earth are you doing here?

For all her composure as a journalist, Ellie still loathed walking into a crowded room on her own, unless she knew people already there. And with the first flush of confidence that she had felt accepting Theo's invitation now fading fast, she regretted having come.

Tonight, however, she was spared the ordeal of a lone entrance. As she alighted from the car and mounted the steps to the door, it was opened almost instantly by the ever discreet Joseph, who greeted her like a familiar visitor with a cordial good evening.

'Nice to see you again, Miss Carter,' he said, handing her wrap to a younger man who disappeared with it across the stone-flagged hall to what appeared to be a cloakroom. 'Mr Stirling asked me to let him know when you arrived. If you'll just come with me.'

'No need, Joseph.' She heard Theo's voice and turned to see him closing double mahogany doors behind him, which immediately drowned out the light babble of voices coming from the other side.

'Good evening, Eleanor,' he said, taking her arm. 'You look quite beautiful – as indeed I knew you would. Although I was, of course, quite taken with the wellingtons and the parka – or lack of them,' he added wickedly.

Recognizing the light flirtation for what it was and knowing it was not meant to be taken seriously, Ellie simply laughed.

'I think I prefer to know you have a wardrobe that I can help myself to should the need arise,' she smiled, making a mental note that dinner jackets always made men look good, not just on him.

'Do you always travel with your staff?' she asked as Joseph discreetly withdrew.

'Absolutely. Joseph has got it into his head that I can't do without him and I'm too much in awe of him to tell him he's right. And much as I would like you to myself,' he smiled, 'I must introduce you to everyone else.'

Oh, just enjoy it, Carter, she told herself. What's the harm in liking a little flattery, no matter how insincerely intended? But even so, she felt the fact that he held her hand leading her into the room was a proprietary gesture that she could have done without.

'My dear, how marvellous to see you again,' said Lady Montrose, bustling across the room. 'You were superb on the television last night. I knew you were committed to the environment but I said to Theo, now there's a girl . . .'

Her voice tailed off as Theo cut in with, 'Absolutely, Sally, you can talk environment and rainforests with Eleanor to your heart's content later on.'

Lady Montrose waved impatient hands at him. 'Don't be so bossy, Eleanor may well want to talk about it now.'

'No she doesn't,' he said firmly. 'She wants to meet everyone else first, don't you?'

Theo then proceeded to introduce her to his other guests who included the managing director of his UK company, a silver-haired man in his fifties, with his elegantly gowned wife, who must have been in her fifties but looked forty.

They greeted Ellie warmly, the wife asking her in a whisper if the item in Jed's column about the Prime Minister was true and was Taylor Carnforth really a coke freak?

'Don't know about Taylor,' Ellie lied, 'but I think Jed's stuff must be true. At least he hasn't had a writ yet.'

Theo's closest friend Jack Ferguson, who was also his lawyer, and his tawny-haired wife Maggie were introduced next, Ellie instantly liking the pretty, obviously down-to-earth young woman who she guessed was probably in her early thirties.

'Got to see Carlysle's face when she sees this,' Ellie heard her say gleefully to her husband as she moved out of earshot to be introduced to Sarah Montrose's husband, Sir Findlay, who was as retiring as his wife was gregarious and made rare appearances at social functions.

'Theo is an exception, because he won't take no for an answer,' he said grumpily.

'And because he'll play poker with you till dawn,' interjected Lady Sarah as her husband made an unconvincing attempt to look angry.

Ellie thought they were delightful.

Five minutes later, all introductions complete, Ellie was deep in conversation with Max Culver, who was teasing her about sneaking off to the beach without him, when Debra Carlysle herself swept dramatically into the room.

Swathed in a figure-moulding turquoise silk dress, her mane of red hair cascading around her bare shoulders, she paused for just a fraction of a second framed in the doorway and then moved slinkily towards Theo in a cloud of perfume that lingered in her wake.

As an entrance it was unbeatable.

'Perfect timing,' giggled the irrepressible Maggie into Ellie's ear. 'She was probably waiting on the landing until Joseph tipped her the wink, everyone else was here. But just clock the rocks, will you?'

Ellie desperately wanted to laugh at the description of the diamonds hanging from Debra's ears, and trailing around her throat, but managed to remain poker-faced while Theo waited as Debra gushingly greeted his most intimate friends.

'You remember Eleanor, of course,' he said as they approached her and it wasn't lost on Ellie that his hand was placed lightly around Debra's slender waist.

'Do I, darling? If you say so, I'm *so* bad with faces. Sweet little dress,' murmured Debra condescendingly, her eyes already gazing in a bored fashion over Ellie's shoulder to her director.

'Darling Max,' she said, kissing him on both cheeks. 'Are you enjoying yourself? I'm sorry, did you say something?' she asked sharply, turning back to Eleanor, aware that Jack and Maggie were having trouble with sudden coughs having heard Ellie say quite distinctly: 'Well, he was.'

'Er . . . a drink, Debra,' said Theo hastily, the remark having not been lost on him either. 'Come and talk to Jeremy. He was asking me this afternoon about the progress the film is making.'

'Yes, but I bet he won't tell her what Jeremy was asking,' said Maggie mischievously as they moved away. 'How soon she was going to Paris so that he can get Theo's attention.'

'Why? Does she distract him that much?' asked Ellie, amused.

'Don't think so,' said Maggie candidly. 'But you can't tell with Theo, can you?'

'I wouldn't know,' smiled Ellie and asked Maggie how many children she had.

It should not have been so surprising to Ellie that dinner served in a very formal dining room was not the formidable affair she had been expecting.

Theo's closest friends were relaxed and entertaining, his staff discreet, the food ambrosial and Theo himself had somehow reverted to the man she had chatted so easily with in her small kitchen in Fulham. The memory of the tough, uncompromising, unfeeling man she had encountered in his office was difficult to recall.

A charming and attentive host, he made what Ellie knew to be an exacting task a seemingly effortless exercise, ensuring that his guests' every need was met instantly. Jokes and light-hearted banter eclipsed the formality of the setting which was, like his London apartment, a wonderful mixture of classic elegance and stylish charm.

'Interview me,' Jack pleaded when Ellie, seated between him and Max, told him only a handful of interviewees had ever interested her personally.

'I wouldn't mind getting you interested in me,' he said,

ducking as Maggie shrieked 'swine' and threw her napkin at him.

'I'd probably run off with you,' Ellie teased him and looked up to find Theo watching her over the rim of his glass.

His eyes held hers and then slowly, very slowly he smiled at her with a degree of intimacy that couldn't be mistaken. For a very brief moment, Ellie felt as though she had been caught in a bright light. She smiled back, an exchange that was not lost on Debra, sitting as close to her host as her chair would allow.

'Be careful, Jack,' the actress drawled. 'Theo says Eleanor is after all his secrets – none of us are to be spared. We must all be charming to her and then she will only write nice things, is that not so, Theo?' and the accompanying laugh was as artificial as her eyelashes as she reached out and closed her hand over his.

Ellie, aware of the silence that now hung over the table, flushed at the obvious insult but knew there was just enough truth in it to hurt.

What a fool she had been, being lulled by all of this, his friends briefed to be utterly charming to her, to disarm her. Just as he had intended she would be. She suddenly wanted nothing more than to be on her own, to never meet Theo Stirling again.

Pride made her drag her eyes away from the bracelet she had been adjusting on her arm. Pride made her meet his gaze with a cool look and pride made her slowly smile at Jack and Maggie, who were looking so outraged she wondered if two such civilized people could between them be every bit as murderous as they seemed.

And why not, after Debra had so bitchily exposed them all for the hypocrites they were?

Before Ellie could speak she heard Lady Montrose's carefully controlled voice from the far end of the table.

'Personally, I find the press as useful as they find me,'

she said calmly, earning a surprised look from Ellie. 'As indeed so many in your own profession do, Debra. After all, why pay out all that money for Gavin to attract their attention? Doesn't make sense. Don't you agree, Max?' she said, turning to the director who she had just persuaded to make a short promotional film on her favourite theme.

'Which reminds me,' she went on remorselessly, ignoring Debra's furious retort that Gavin was paid to keep the press from hounding her, not to intrude on her privacy. 'Eleanor, what can I do to help you with this campaign I hear you're involved in? Now move over, Jack, I want to talk to Eleanor.'

With which she swept from her place at the table to join Ellie, leaving Debra rolling her eyes theatrically saying, 'How very droll,' to a totally unsmiling and silent Theo.

'Perhaps we could have coffee in the drawing room,' said Theo, also rising. 'And Max has a surprise, an advance showing of Debra's next film on video.'

A general chorus of 'marvellous' and 'how exciting' was the perfect cover Ellie needed as she excused herself to Lady Montrose.

'I'm afraid I must leave,' said Ellie quietly as everyone moved towards the door, not wanting to look at Theo. 'It's been quite a day. Thank you for . . .'

'Not yet,' Theo said, curtly interrupting her. 'I want to talk to you, then I'll drive you home.'

'I don't think we have anything to say and Oliver can send a car for me . . .'

'On the contrary, I think there is a lot to be said and I will drive you home.'

'What about your guests? And Debra's film. Surely . . . ?'

'For heaven's sake, Eleanor, just do as I say,' he said with such anger in his voice, she visibly stiffened. His expression didn't change, but his eyes and tone did.

For a brief second she looked at him in a way that did nothing to disguise her anger at being so addressed. He dug his hands impatiently into his pockets and shrugged.

'Please?' he said, in quite a different voice.

Chapter Twenty-five

You don't have to do this, Ellie told herself as she waited for Theo to join her. I mean, why don't you just get up and go? You owe him nothing.

But even as she remonstrated with herself, she knew that a combination of curiosity and anger was proving a stronger argument for staying and that eminently more potent mixture was going to see her through the next few minutes.

And minutes are all he is going to get, she fumed.

She glanced around the room into which Theo had silently escorted her a few minutes earlier, across the stone-flagged hallway and along a small passage to what was obviously the library.

Her departure had gone unnoticed since they were all converging back into the drawing room, where Joseph's young assistant had already set the video, to watch Debra's latest movie.

'Wait here, I won't keep you long,' had been Theo's terse, unsmiling comment as he closed the doors behind her. Ellie was left alone in a book-lined room with a log fire blazing comfortingly in an open fireplace. Long crimson velvet curtains were drawn across the mullioned windows, low table lamps cast a warm glow across the silent room.

Ellie crossed to the fireplace and sat down on a velvet stool, leaning back against a deep, winged chair. She could feel the warmth and movement of the fire beginning to calm and soothe her anger, the wind whistling through the open cavity blowing the smoke in wild swirls up into the darkness. The contrast between this restful, still room, cocooned from the world, and the difficult scene she had left behind was welcome.

Debra's sharply aimed barb had found its target. In a more reasonable moment, Ellie would have found no difficulty in shrugging it off as the ill-mannered comment it undoubtedly was.

However, Jill's warning came back to her, making Ellie groan. You fool, she harangued herself, wrapping her arms round her knees, rocking to and fro, and you thought you knew better? You fell for the charm, the physical magnetism that someone like Theo Stirling dispenses and uses with the ease of a man born to get what he wants. He only had to crook his finger and you came running, she jeered at herself. It was hard to choose which offended her the most: that she had been such a pushover, or that he had known she would be?

Being angry did not eclipse total common sense, although it began to dawn on her that these days, where men were concerned, she was giving a highly persuasive performance that she was utterly bereft of anything of the kind. The idea unsettled her. And so did sitting so close to the fire, which was of course the reason her face suddenly felt flushed and obviously had nothing to do with how she felt about herself. Of course not.

She was rising from her position in front of the fire to find a psychologically more advantageous one – such as safely home at Delcourt or Fulham – when the door opened so softly that Theo was in the room before she could move.

Ellie looked up with a start, hearing the click as he closed the door behind him.

'No, don't get up,' Theo told her, as he crossed the room. 'Joseph will have coffee and brandy sent in here. But it would help if you stopped glaring at me. You really can be very frightening, you know.'

She knew it was absurd, that it was a comment designed to disarm her. She also knew that never again would she be lured into such a defenceless position by a man so practised in the art of seduction. She had to fight to stop herself smiling. She managed instead a very creditable display of cold displeasure.

She gazed up at him. 'I might appear to you to be – frightening, but then I can only appear to be so if you have something to be frightened about.'

He studied her thoughtfully and was spared the necessity of replying by the arrival of Joseph with a tray of coffee. Setting it down, Joseph then poured brandy into two warmed glasses and silently brought the tray to Ellie. She was about to refuse but seeing Theo – who had clearly remembered she disliked it – about to do so on her behalf, she promptly decided the thing she most wanted in the world was brandy and, smiling sweetly at Joseph, removed one glass from the tray.

After the manservant had gone, she half expected Theo to sit in the winged chair just to disarm her even further and sliding off the stool, she carefully removed herself to a safe distance. Instead he strolled over to the fireplace and dropped down on the rug in the space she had vacated directly opposite.

'I hope that you drink every last drop of that brandy,' he said pleasantly. 'And I'm going to keep you company until you have even if it takes all night. And if it makes you feel ill, it serves you right,' with which he leaned back against the winged chair, his elbow on the seat, the other with his hand cradling his brandy resting on his raised knee. He smiled expectantly at her.

Without taking her eyes from his, Ellie deliberately lifted the glass and managed to swallow a respectable quantity without a change in her expression.

'I think,' she lied, slowly lowering the glass, 'like most things you surround yourself with, it's the best I've tasted.

I don't think you'll be sitting here all night.' With which she matched his smile, just hoping she wouldn't actually be sick.

He looked as though he was trying not to laugh and, oh damn him, Ellie groaned as she fought to control her features, it really was absurd. Two grown people waging war over a glass of brandy.

His reserve broke first. 'Eleanor, you are wonderful,' he laughed as she broke into a grin. 'I wish you liked me instead of wanting to fight me.'

'I don't want to fight you,' she answered quietly. 'I just want you to . . .'

'What?' he prompted gently.

Ellie studied the contents of her glass. She suddenly wasn't sure of anything, searching for the right words. She was going to say, I just want you to get out of my life, I just want you to leave us in peace. She looked at his face; his expression was puzzled, serious, waiting.

She took a deep breath. It all came out in a rush, the anger, the misery, the confusion. 'Why do you want that land, it's Oliver's home you're damaging? Why do you keep insulting me? Why do you want to use me like this . . . like tonight? Just tell me why? What have we . . . I . . . any of us, ever done to you?'

'Oh, Eleanor,' he said with a crooked smile. 'You look just like you did when you were fifteen and I found you in the garden. Ready to fight the world. You haven't changed.'

'Of course I have,' she cried. 'I want answers just like I did then, only now I'm determined to get them. Tell me. Please just *tell* me!'

The silence hung heavily between them. He looked down at his glass, frowning, and she waited, totally lost now, nothing else to say. Finally he raised his head and looked steadily at her.

'Tell me, why were you at the house that day?' he asked abruptly.

'What . . . ? That day . . . ? I . . . I was looking for something. Something that was quite personal to me . . . daft really,' she said as he signalled to her to go on. 'My mother fixed it above my bedroom door when I was a baby . . . a silver horseshoe, not very big, but it had my name on it and her name and . . . well, I don't remember her, she died in a road accident before I was two. It was just something I used to find comforting.

'I thought I might be in time to take it, but then you appeared, shouting and ordering me off the land, and I just went. You were, er . . . pretty frightening,' she ended sardonically.

'Didn't you have anything else to remember her by?' Theo asked, surprised.

'Well, no. The house belonged to my mother's family. But Dad was always hard up and it was a barn of a place, so when she died everything except her wedding ring and engagement ring was sold to raise money.'

Ellie was puzzled that his face had become hard and inwardly she just shrugged. A man like Theo, with his parents still alive, with all his money, wouldn't understand that being sentimental isn't a luxury every family can afford. They were poles apart; there was an unbridgeable gulf that was getting wider by the day. Sadly she turned and gazed into the fire and when he spoke she didn't even turn her head.

'I shouted at you because I wasn't expecting to see you there, and you were climbing through the window to the old library, which we had just discovered had a cracked beam. The slightest movement was going to bring it down. The whole place was unsafe. Whoever converted it had ignored every basic rule of building safety.'

If Ellie remembered correctly, the subject of the conversion of Delcourt into the much-disputed flatlets had also given rise to an angry exchange between Aunt Belle and her father. She had only been a child but she still remembered Aunt Belle's immoveable belief that her father had a bunch of cowboys in the house. It didn't seem a good idea to repeat this, so she merely showed what she hoped was a surprised expression, tinged with disbelief for good measure.

'You could have said so then,' she reminded him.

'I might have done, if you hadn't been so determined to tell me what you thought of me. Proper little spitfire. Eleanor, listen to me ... No, please just listen. What happened here tonight was indefensible. Debra's remarks were out of order, I think she just misunderstood – after all you didn't keep it quiet that you were gathering quotes from people who know me.

'To be honest I thought you had given up because everything went so quiet. And then you went back to writing for *Focus* and it seemed to coincide with the meeting that was held in the village this morning.'

Ellie hadn't a clue what he was talking about and said so.

'Any information I may or may not have gathered was done months ago. Why would I need any more? Frankly I've been too busy trying to get a job ... I mean getting between here and London,' she hastily corrected herself, 'to give you much thought.'

'Do I take it you've dropped the idea of – how shall I put it? – a personal view of me?'

Difficult ground had never bothered her in the past. Now she felt a moment's panic. The truth was that she had never, not even in the midst of her depression and the long, dreary days when her mind was concentrated on just surviving, considered dropping the idea. The opportunity had simply been removed. Now she had it back. The one thing she had learned about this man was never to underestimate him.

''Fraid not.' She shook her head. 'I don't know why you think I would drop the idea, it seems a perfectly reasonable one to me, particularly after tonight.'

His eyes closed. Exasperation was written all over him.

Good, thought Ellie, that will show you I'm not a push-over. She sat surveying him calmly.

'Charming room,' she said eventually, chattily. 'Do you bring everyone in here to browbeat them? Or just the ones that are more difficult to bring to heel?'

'Don't be ridiculous,' he snapped. 'You're quite deliber-ately whipping up this ludicrous image you have of me, and you know it.'

Ellie yawned and gazed round.

'Why do you do it?' he asked bluntly.

A Stubbs original over the fireplace seemed to be hold-ing her attention.

'Oh, sorry,' she said, looking innocently at him. 'Did you say something?'

He regarded her gravely.

'You know, Eleanor, I don't wish to get personal.'

Ellie could barely suppress her glee. She'd rattled him.

'Oh, be as personal as you like,' she invited. 'I have – metaphorically speaking – a very broad back.'

He looked relieved.

'Oh well, in which case you won't mind me mentioning that you have what appears to be soot all over your face. These damn chimneys.' Theo shook his head sadly as Ellie shot one hand to her cheek.

'No, no, you'll only make it worse,' he said helpfully.

Ellie scrambled in her bag for her compact, blushing furiously. Oh God, how humiliating, she thought, snap-ping open the gold case and hurriedly searching her face.

It was flawless. Nothing. 'But where . . . ?'

She stopped. Her hand holding the compact frozen in front of her. Slowly, deliberately, she closed the case and as steadily as a deep desire to hurl it hard at his grinning face would allow, returned it to her bag.

'You do seem to have a remarkably inventive mind,' she said coldly. 'First still convinced I'm making enquiries about you and then a schoolboy's trick to gain points. However,' she continued, rising and smoothing her skirt, 'I am now bored with this conversation and with you. You haven't said one single thing that has interested me so far and I think I'd like to go.'

'Oh, shut up,' Theo said bluntly. 'And sit down again. Why do you have to keep making all these dramatic gestures? I only want to talk to you. Okay, okay, okay. Sorry.' He threw his hands up in defeat. 'Truly, completely, even humbly if it helps, sorry.'

It seemed absurd to remain standing, so she sat down on a long couch and looked pointedly at her watch.

Theo got up and came and crouched down in front of her. When he took her hand she made no attempt to pull it away.

'I'll take back that I thought you were making enquiries. I can see perfectly well that you were not and my friends weren't told to charm you. Eleanor, I don't give a damn about good or bad publicity or what you write. But what I do care about is what you think.'

'Excuse me, but what exactly is the difference?' Ellie shot at him.

'The difference is that you believe you have good reason to write adverse things about me. But I don't believe that's what you want to do. What I mean is, I don't want you to judge me without getting to know me on your . . . our . . . own terms.'

Ellie winced. Pointless to pretend her feelings for him were clear cut. She let him go on and simply slid over to make space for him when he moved to sit alongside her. It seemed the most natural thing in the world. She couldn't understand why when he was close to her she

334

couldn't think straight, she couldn't make any sense.

'I want you and I to start again,' Theo was saying. 'Pretend the past hasn't happened, forget the future. Let's just meet in the present, two people who should have the chance to decide for themselves the rights and wrongs about each other. Will you do that, Eleanor?'

He hadn't attempted to do more than lightly hold her hand, just sat and waited for her answer.

Ellie heard Jill's warning voice. This time she heeded it.

'I'm not sure that it's possible,' she told him. 'Really . . . just listen to me for a moment,' and she resisted the urge to reach out and stroke his face as he grinned at her, acknowledging her gentle sarcasm.

'Supposing we decide that we have misjudged each other – and I'm not saying we will – what then? Do you mean you'll back off buying the land next to Oliver, that you'll tell me why your family nearly ruined mine?'

His answer was to put his hand very gently against her mouth. 'It won't work if there is a deal. You and I have got to be honest with each other, not get to know each other against a background of what we're going to get out of it. Let's come to that when we've given it a chance.'

'I'd like to think it over,' she told him, knowing it was ridiculous to pretend she found his request unreasonable. Instead she said:

'I mean, how do we go about it?'

'Well, we could start in the nicest way possible, but I think you might suspect my motives,' Theo laughed, seeing the flash of apprehension in her eyes. 'So we could either rejoin the others and watch the rest of the movie – or I could take you home and have you to myself for a while.'

Ellie blushed, she actually blushed and felt suddenly very shy.

'I think I'd like to go home. I'm not sure I could cope

with Deb . . . any more fun this evening,' she corrected herself. 'But won't Debra mind if you leave with me? She might not understand.'

'That's my problem,' he said easily. 'And it really isn't up to Debra who I drive home.'

'But I thought you . . . I thought she and you . . .'

'What did you think?' he asked as he pulled her to her feet.

'That you and she are, well . . . together.'

Theo was still holding her hands and keeping them firmly clasped he held them to his chest. Looking down into her eyes, he asked:

'Did I tell you that?'

She was conscious of a very strong desire to just slide her arms under his jacket and hold him close but instead she simply shook her head.

'Then let's get one thing straight, only believe what I tell you.'

Ellie had the oddest feeling that believing him was the one thing she wanted more than anything else at that moment. Then very gently Theo bent his head and kissed her, and for someone she had vowed to hate, she didn't mind at all.

Softly, slowly, even tenderly, his mouth moved towards her ear.

Ellie could feel her head swimming, her stomach had relocated itself, she would not have relied on her legs to take her anywhere. She felt his body, needed its strength. She moved her hands but only to wind her arms around his neck. He pulled her to him, she heard him roughly mutter her name and then there was nothing gentle about the rest of the kiss.

This time she didn't try to resist or move away when he raised his head. All the laughter had gone from his face. Ellie wasn't laughing either.

'Don't move,' he ordered and reached behind her to

press a switch on the phone, pulling the receiver to his ear. 'Joseph. I don't want to be disturbed. Tell Lady Montrose I've driven Miss Carter home.'

Ellie should have left then, but as he swiftly kissed her, moving towards the door, she found this impossible to do.

'What are you doing?' she whispered as he turned the key in the lock and rejoined her, pulling her back into his arms.

'I've made sure we're not disturbed.'

There comes a point in everyone's life when they have a split second to make a decision that they might live to regret.

Theo saw the hesitation and handed her the key. 'Take it. You can leave any time you like. But I hope you won't.'

'But Debra's film . . .' she said, knowing that it was the weakest and most unconvincing reason she could proffer and the decision was made. Had been made an hour before when she should have gone home and instead had agreed to all of this.

'I've seen it,' he said, pushing her gently back on to the cushions, slipping the straps of her dress down and running his mouth across her shoulders.

'Oh well, in which case . . .' she said and after that there wasn't much time for talking, except when he suggested they get their clothes out of the way. Then they were lying together, the light from the fire flickering across the curves of her body and she couldn't stop touching him or wanting him and when she heard him groan softly, whispering her name over and over, and he lifted his head to gaze down at her, his face suffused with longing and need, she didn't quite understand but she felt her eyes fill with tears and as he entered her she wept with the knowledge that she had found something she thought would be denied her for ever.

*

Ellie heard a clock chime in the distance. The glow from the fire was warming the glass in her hand. Theo appeared in the doorway, beckoning silently to her.

'Come on.' His voice was unsteady. 'The film's over, I'll drive you home before they come looking for us.'

With that, entwining his fingers in hers, he led from the room a very shaken Ellie who had still to come to terms with the fact that she had no resolutions left to defend. That Theo still hadn't answered any of her questions had somehow completely slipped her mind.

Chapter Twenty-six

The call from Debra Carlysle came at midday on Tuesday. She thought it would be 'useful' for both of them if they met.

Ellie wasn't at all sure she wanted to meet her after Saturday night, but then she wasn't sure about anything any more. Except that she had fallen in love with Theo Stirling.

She had gone through Sunday in a daze. Vaguely aware that Oliver and Jill were exchanging worried glances, it had taken the twins bodily hurling themselves on her to get Ellie's attention.

If asked what she had said to Joe McPhee when they met for a pre-lunch drink, she would have looked blank. But she had retained just enough common sense to take herself off for a long, solitary walk on Sunday afternoon to sort out her own feelings before she confided in anyone or indeed risked anyone suspecting and asking her for explanations she was incapable of giving.

There had been a phone call earlier from Clive, guessing who had been trying to ring him, and for the first time, Ellie had to confront reality. Surely that's what last night had been? An escape from reality, a stupid dream, an impetuous, thoughtless action.

Rubbish. That's what had happened with Clive, high on excitement and relief and the pleasure of getting out of that awful black hole which had threatened to suck her in and take her away altogether.

That isn't what happened with Theo. And, dear God, what was she thinking of? She had once criticized Judith for sleeping with every man who took her fancy, and here she was casting inhibition to the wind, and consigning caution to the bottom of the sea for exactly those reasons. It was little consolation that in the last few months, if the occasion demanded, lying and hypocrisy had come breathtakingly easily to her.

If she had been drunk the night before she couldn't have had a worse hangover.

The overcast, leaden sky, the stiff wind, threatening to become a gale later, the sheer effort of walking in such difficult conditions hadn't helped for one second to clear her head.

If this was love, it was a bloody painful business, she muttered, drawing a curious look from an elderly couple straining against the wind walking their dogs. It wasn't hard to understand the physical attraction she felt for Theo, but it was everything else about him that she knew made him so right for her. His sense of humour, his wit, the way he could read her expression, and a stability that was largely absent with Clive and had never even existed with Paul.

When she looked back on it, she had done very little to discourage him from thinking she was fair game and would not spurn anyone's advances if it helped her career, but she knew instinctively he respected women, liked them, liked her.

But how much did he like her? Impossible to think he wasn't attracted to her. At least she knew that. But was he in love with her?

He said they should get to know each other slowly. Ellie, sitting on her favourite rock idly throwing stones at the grey, swollen sea, sighed and knew he was right. Being in love is like being a little bit mad. And she knew she must be mad.

But there was now nothing she could do. She didn't want to think about Clive, away in Dublin, unsuspecting, so beautiful and kind and clever, who had pulled her up by the roots and made her believe in herself again, to be herself again.

Even less did she want to think about Oliver and Jill. They had been so excited at breakfast about their success the previous evening. The MP Gregory Merton, along with Charles Peterhouse, the historian, had both pledged their support to Oliver's campaign.

In return Ellie had lied and told them that the evening with Theo was entertaining but uneventful and had spared them the details of her private meeting with him later. They wouldn't understand, not yet.

She wasn't sure that she did herself.

Gregory, they laughed, had even asked quite kindly after her and was clearly anxious to improve his image. Charles was genuinely concerned. Both, of course, were influential locally. While neither of them personally knew Conrad Linton, they knew his interest in Willetts Green was now nil since he had discovered the delights of Australia, and warned Oliver that he would simply sell to the highest bidder.

'The only thing we can do,' Oliver continued, seemingly unaware that Ellie's breakfast remained untouched and that the second cup of coffee Jill had poured for her had, like the first, simply gone cold, 'is to save the land from redevelopment whoever owns it. We must just make sure that if Theo Stirling gets it – and he's bound to – that we prevent him doing anything dreadful with it. Or even better, anything at all. At least that way we might be able to hang on to the hotel. What do you think, Ellie? Ellie, are you listening?'

'Hmm? Yes, marvellous,' she said automatically and didn't see Jill raise a significant eyebrow at Oliver.

After that Ellie went for a walk because she could not find the words to tell them that the man they were trying to outwit was not like that.

Why is that, Ellie?

Because he isn't, that's all.

That doesn't make sense, Ellie.

To me it does.

This man wrecked Pa, and threatened you, and is about to damage Oliver.

I know.

You know? And you say he isn't like that?

I'm in love with him and I don't see how I can work against him.

You are *what*?

Ellie looked out over the rocks to the curve in the bay and beyond that to the house where Theo was probably, right now, departing for London.

No, she couldn't tell them. Not yet.

She had half expected to hear from Theo when she reached her flat on Sunday night, although he had said it would be Monday afternoon before he called her.

But the machine simply spilled out messages from Jed – off to New York on flying visit, see her Friday. Amanda, just for a gossip. Roger Nelson. A number where he could be reached. God, Lucy couldn't have been discreet at all. Oh well, couldn't be helped. Two from Paul. Where are you? Will call later.

Extraordinary how Paul didn't even cross her mind any more when once he had dominated her days and she had imagined herself in love with him.

Now she knew that this heady, all-consuming, all-powerful feeling for Theo was something she had never experienced before, not with Clive and certainly not with Paul, and at that moment she believed she would never experience again.

Jerome had to speak to her twice the next morning when they met for their weekly conference before she responded. If she had been more locked on to their meeting she might have noticed the undisguised annoyance that flicked across his face and the slightly clenched teeth as he waited for her to comment on his suggestions for interviews.

No good being sarcastic, he quietly seethed, not wanting to repeat the scene with Ian Willoughby when the boss had politely informed Jerome he wanted Ellie back. You just couldn't tell with her now what she might do.

She was a very different woman to the courteous, sophisticated one who had walked out of his office with such contempt a few months before. Not that she was any less courteous, just not prepared to allow the conversation to wander away from the point, no gossipy foreplay before the meeting, no quiet wit putting a high profile name in perspective.

Lucy eventually stopped putting calls through to her office and Rosie, popping her head round the door at ten thirty to see if Ellie was free for lunch, found her leaning against the window just staring out.

By the time Theo called on Monday afternoon and asked her to dinner, it was doubtful if Ellie would have noticed the building falling down around her.

He picked her up from her flat at seven thirty and took her to what Ellie was vaguely aware was an exclusive and expensive restaurant. She wouldn't have cared if they'd had fish and chips on the Embankment.

They talked about their friends. She told him about Paul. How she was relieved he was no longer part of her life. About Jed, and how she had rushed Gemma to hospital, about feeling restless with journalism.

He told her that he never thought about travelling, it was just something he did, that he rarely read press cuttings, just the business section. And of course Jed's column to see what she was up to.

He told her about Harvard, and how it was so much easier to work in New York because in that city that is what everyone did. You didn't really 'live' there.

She told him about Aunt Belle's visits and how much she liked Alison. She noticed he didn't make any comment. He said both his sisters were now married, one in LA and the other in New York. His mother longed to be a grandmother.

Over coffee he linked his hand in hers and asked her about Clive.

She shook her head quickly. No, not yet, Clive was special, still a no-go area for discussion.

For a minute Theo looked intently at her and then shrugged and changed the subject. She didn't ask him about his brief marriage to Serena and certainly not his relationship with Debra. And he didn't volunteer any information about either.

So instead Ellie switched topics and told him she had almost given up journalism because it had been sort of difficult when she left *Focus*. She gave him a side-splitting account of Jonquil, mimicked Taylor and shyly told him that his flowers had arrived just after she'd met Gemma, and now she thought it was almost unbelievable that all the people who had once filled her life had gone and all these new, nicer, braver, brighter people were in it.

He said he hoped he was one of them.

When the phone call came for him and he told her there was a problem in New York that had to be sorted out that night, she had to insist his driver was sufficient escort to get her home.

'I'm business too,' Ellie had teased him and thought she would expire with happiness when Theo laughed into her eyes and said he was going to enjoy all the overtime.

'Tomorrow, I'll cancel everything,' he said, briefly kissing her as he closed the door of the car and his driver swept her back to her flat.

It was, curiously enough, Debra's call that snapped Ellie out of her trance-like state.

'My dear,' came the drawling voice. 'I find I am not required for any fittings today, I wonder if you would care for lunch? Or if you already have arrangements, a drink before lunch? Please say yes, I have been *so* upset thinking I may have put my foot in it on Saturday.'

Debra refused to be put off. Eventually Ellie simply shrugged and gave Debra the benefit of the doubt – after all, she did sound genuinely concerned – and agreed to a drink before lunch.

Letty had phoned early in the morning to say the response from women to Ellie's frank admission that she had been a victim of redundancy had been so strong, they wanted her to do a live studio discussion with a group of women who had been plunged into the same dilemma but who with varying degrees of success had got themselves out of it.

'We're going to emphasize how to stay positive. One of the women we've got coming in actually ended up buying her old company. They're terrific women.'

Ellie thought it was a brilliant idea and calculated that if she got the seven o'clock train down first thing Wednesday she could spend as long as possible with Theo. Funny how in the space of a few short days, she was planning her schedule around him. It gave her such a warm glow to think of it, she almost didn't need her coat.

Now that she wasn't pinned down to the office, she was able to take off mid morning to collect some cosmetics Amanda had asked her to pick up that she couldn't get in Wiltshire, and to buy presents for Amy before Gemma and Bill left for Scotland to spend the holiday season with their families.

Ellie enjoyed shopping for Amy, packing a huge red stocking full of soft toys, outrageously coloured ribbons for her hair, and a Baby-gro with 'Are You Ready For Me Scotland' embroidered on it. London only days before Christmas was packed with shoppers. Christmas trees hung from the parapets of stores and filled out shop windows. Fairy lights and tinsel trailed the length of Oxford Street and the queue of small children waiting to see Father Christmas at Selfridges stretched for yards.

Miles and Chloe would love it, she thought, pushing her way out of the store into the biting wind of Oxford Street and wondered if there was time to get them up here before Christmas at Delcourt started in earnest.

As she turned round the corner at Marble Arch and started to walk down Park Lane a very pleasing image flashed into her mind of Theo and herself taking two small children to see Santa in his grotto, smiling and laughing at their excited faces. For some reason the two children in question weren't her small nephew and niece. A sheepish grin spread across her face. And to think she once teased Amanda for doing much the same thing.

The block where Debra retained her London apartment was no more than a stroll from Theo's address and Ellie arrived, her cheeks rosy from the wind, laden down with Christmas shopping and ready to be civil to Debra.

The door was opened by a young, painfully thin, raven-haired girl, who might have been described as pretty if it were not for the dark circles under her eyes. Ellie assumed she must be some kind of maid or secretary but she seemed vaguely familiar when she asked Ellie to wait.

The room Ellie was ushered into was long, wide, high, completely decorated and furnished in white, with only vivid splashes of pink and green in the cushions and curtains to relieve the unrelenting starkness. She blinked at the sheer opulence of what was clearly an extensive apartment, dominated by a vast mirror at one end and some aggressively modern paintings on the other walls.

It was not a feminine room, but it had obviously been created by someone with a great deal of money, who had bought art through an adviser, not through personal taste, and had allowed a fashionable interior designer to let his imagination run riot with the decor.

Ellie had seen too many apartments like it, too many homes of newly made wealth or fame not to recognize the lack of the owner's personality. She had also seen enough of Debra to know she was more interested in image than taste.

The actress herself chose that moment to come in, not quite such a dramatic entrance as on the previous occasion they had met but effective enough.

Ellie was wearing a dark blue three-quarter tunic dress over a short matching skirt, her favourite black pumps and black tights. The weather as they approached Christmas was cold, and the day had started with a fine frost, so she had chosen her navy single-breasted coat and pale grey cashmere scarf, which now lay on the sofa beside her.

By comparison to Debra, Ellie was dressed for a summer's day. The furs alone would have had the animal rights lobby screaming for vengeance. White chinchilla and something definitely in mink were draped and strewn about Debra's statuesque figure.

'So sorry,' she gushed. 'I had to rush off to do a little shopping. Let me just get rid of these.'

With that she flung off the top layer to reveal the most figure-hugging all-in-one jump suit that Ellie had ever seen, in the palest blue angora. Debra's long slender legs were tucked into matching suede calf-length boots that even at twenty paces Ellie could see must have cost nearly as much as the suit.

Ellie wondered if she had enough self control to keep a straight face. If Debra was out to let Ellie know that in every way she could never fail to stun, she was wasting her time. Ellie thought her vulgar. Even more puzzling was what Theo saw in her?

She knew that Rosie, with her fastidious eye for style,

would have had a fit. She also knew that Maggie, Jack Ferguson's likeable wife, would have been in hysterics.

As Debra sank into one of the white leather sofas, she reached out a perfectly manicured hand and pressed a bell. The raven-haired girl appeared. 'Suki, my sweet, can you find that idiot Pedro and arrange some drinks?'

Her next remark made the social smile on Ellie's face fade.

'And let me know when Mr Stirling calls. I wasn't awake when he left this morning. He'll be so cross with me – you know what he's like first thing.'

'Of course,' smiled the Suki person. 'Don't I know it, I kept out of his way until he'd gone,' and she departed.

Ellie felt as though someone had hit her in the stomach. She wanted to scream, it's not true. But Debra would never have said it in front of that girl unless it was. And anyway Suki had clearly seen him often enough first thing in the morning to assess his moods.

This couldn't be happening.

'Have I told you that?' is what he had said when she had assumed his involvement with Debra was more than tenuous. No, of course he hadn't told her, but that didn't mean it wasn't true. She had just wanted so much for it not to be true she had believed him.

Now she knew now why he hadn't called on Sunday night. Because he was asleep with Debra. Why he had to leave early last night. Because he was on his way to Debra's bed.

She realized that the actress had spoken to her twice and turned a stricken face to her.

'Is something the matter?' asked Debra. 'You look rather cold. Let me get the heat turned up. Pedro!'

Ellie swallowed hard as Debra summoned her houseman to adjust the heating. The flat was already sweltering.

Concentrate, she told herself fiercely. Just concentrate

on getting out of here. Then you can think. If it killed her she would not let this woman know what a fool she had been. Never would Debra be able to relay to Theo what a dreadful sense of humiliation had swept over Ellie at that moment.

Ellie heard herself speaking in a voice that was normal, if a little curt.

'I'm fine, just a rather hectic morning.'

Keep going, she told herself. Lie, keep lying. It's your only salvation.

'I'm so pleased,' smiled the other woman. 'And delighted you've come over for a drink. I have been feeling rather awful since Saturday. You know Theo is a wonderful man, but so naughty – like most men.' She gave a light laugh.

'I'm afraid you have the advantage over me,' Ellie replied crisply. 'I'm afraid I hardly know him and I hope you won't think me rude, but I'm not sure that I want to either.'

And that at least wasn't a lie, she consoled herself.

'My dear,' said Debra, leaning forward in a confiding way. 'I can't tell you how relieved I am to hear you say that. You see, Theo and I are a good match. I understand him perfectly – and I am delighted to say he understands me. But he was quite wrong to have discussed your work with me. No, no. I'm not going to defend him, I won't insult your intelligence by pretending he hadn't expressed his concern to me over this feature you're writing.

'But,' she shrugged her shoulders in an expressive, help-less gesture, 'I am constantly telling him it is quite wicked to use his charm to get his own way all the time. Of course it doesn't happen with me, I mean if you're going to mar . . . well, that doesn't matter.' She hesitated but the slip wasn't lost on Ellie.

Suki reappeared with the hapless Pedro who was carry-ing glasses and chilled white wine.

'Anything else, Debra?' asked Suki. 'If not, I'll pop out and do those errands.'

What was it about her that Ellie recognized?

Debra followed her curious gaze and dismissed the girl from their conversation.

'Oh, you may have seen her in walk-on parts on television. She is desperate to be an actress and hopes that just being around me she will pick up some tips,' she said carelessly as the door closed behind Suki.

I bet, thought Ellie bitterly. Just like Theo, using people. The girl didn't have a chance in hell of becoming an actress with Debra around. She wondered if Debra knew the girl was clearly on drugs.

'As I was saying,' said Debra, curling up with her drink. 'I was concerned that you might have got the wrong impression about the way Theo operates. That he had invited you on Saturday just so that you wouldn't write anything unpleasant about him. Oh, c'mon.' She smiled coaxingly, seeing Ellie's wooden expression. 'You can't blame me for trying to defend him, I'm stuck with him after all.'

'Don't give it another thought,' Ellie said carefully. 'I'm so used to people thinking they can manipulate me, it rolls off my back.'

'How very sensible of you to realize it,' Debra said, sipping her drink. 'I just thought that with Theo anxious to be in that sweet little village for a while and all these plans that he's got going down there . . .'

'Has he got plans?' asked Ellie politely, though her knuckles were white clutching her glass of untouched wine.

'Oh yes, there are some over there,' replied Debra, waving an airy hand at what appeared to be drawings on a nearby table, casually unrolled and clearly visible to Ellie.

Ellie could hardly breathe. 'How fascinating,' she managed. 'Plans for what?'

'Well, apart from building a new house – that dreadful mausoleum he's got at the moment is hopeless – I believe he mentioned something or other about doing something for the area.'

The actress yawned, clearly bored with the conversation. Ellie had had enough. The plans were in front of her. He was sleeping with Debra. He was a liar and a seducer and she had – like the hapless Caroline, the beautiful Gisella and countless more – fallen for it.

Getting out of Debra's flat was now a matter of such urgency, Ellie didn't care about being rude. She told her Rosie would be waiting for her, grabbed her coat and rapidly began to gather up her shopping and started to leave.

Just as she reached the door, she stopped and turned to Debra, looking curiously at her.

'Just as a matter of interest, what is it that you see in him?'

The question she longed to ask but which would have revealed her for the unquestioningly naive journalist she was, was quite different. What do you see in a man who makes loves to one of his guests, while his soon-to-be wife watched television in another room?

Debra laughed softly.

'Oh my dear, I'm sure you didn't mean that as an insult, but it has rather more to do with what he sees in me. You see, I don't need his money. I'm very rich. And money is the only thing Theo understands. He knows I want nothing from him. And that's very attractive to a man like Theo.'

Ellie walked slowly through Hyde Park, needing time to think. I'll walk up to the Marble Arch entrance. By the time I get there I will know what to do.

It was a game she had played as a child. A way to make a decision. Since there was no logic to what had happened, then why not pick an illogical way to decide? As though the gate at Marble Arch would make any difference.

But then what would?

Leafless trees with branches like grey sinewy fingers clawed bleakly into a leaden sky, a defiant gesture against the chill wind that whipped and flailed angrily at the last remnants of autumn.

A cold, chill December morning unlikely to encourage any but the most stouthearted to linger for more than a moment or two, was no time to be strolling out of doors, but it was important that she was alone and somewhere where she had to keep a grip on her emotions.

The haven of her flat, the safety of her closed office door were designed to sap rather than fuel her resolve.

The first message she got from Lucy when she finally made it back to the office was that Theo had called, and then his secretary, asking if eight o'clock was convenient for dinner.

'No. Phone his secretary, Lucy, tell her, not dinner but a drink at six would be convenient,' Ellie told her.

Hearing that Paul was in the building having a meeting with the advertisers about travel for the January issues, she sent Lucy speeding off to locate him.

Since Ellie had not spoken to him for weeks, except to decline all his pleas for dinner, it was not unexpected that he looked suspicious when he arrived in her office to hear that she thought a drink would be nice, for old times' sake, and arranged to meet him at the same hotel but at six thirty.

Lucy began to look nervous. She didn't like the look on Ellie's face and the way she was drumming her fingers purposefully on her desk as she punched out Oliver's number.

She told him that she had discovered that not only was Theo about to marry the ghastly Debra, but he was planning a house on the site and something noble for the area. The words came out in a cold fury.

Oliver whistled softly. 'So that's why you were so pre-occupied on Sunday. Jill thought you had got yourself too heavily involved with Stirling. She says most women do fall for him. I knew it was nonsense.'

Ellie thought she would scream.

Like a Sergeant Major going into battle she rapped out instructions to him to step up the campaign and promised that every available moment she had she would help him.

Her next stop was in Jed's office where she ordered a startled secretary to get him on the phone instantly.

'Tell him that he can run the story on Debra Carlysle and Theo Stirling. Carlysle herself has just virtually told me.'

'Wha-a-at?' screamed the secretary. 'You're kidding. Jed will flip. Ellie, you are after his job, admit it!'

After that, Ellie told a saucer-eyed Sonya Harvey-Lloyd that she wanted to see Jerome the minute he returned. Half an hour later she was in his office, telling him she would deliver the most crippling, paralysing, condemnatory profile on Theo Stirling if he promised not to use it until she said so.

Jerome looked startled. Honestly, Ellie was really peculiar these days. Yesterday she made the speaking clock sound animated and now today she was like a firework going off.

He gave her the promise she wanted. Next she went to Rosie and persuaded her to let her borrow the tightest and shortest, most seductive little black dress that normally Ellie in a hundred years would never wear, some dramatically bold and gold tasselled earrings, four-inch high heels that were like a foot fetishist's dream and when Rosie asked sarcastically why she didn't just go the whole hog and wear black fishnet tights, Ellie hesitated, looking wistfully at possibly the most vulgar pair ever made.

'Ellie,' squealed Rosie, whipping them out of her grasp. 'I don't know what all this is about, but there is a line to be drawn and these are it.'

'No matter,' said Ellie, surveying herself critically in the tiny mirror in the fashion room. 'I don't want to overdo it.'

Rosie passed a hand over her eyes.

News travels quickly in a magazine office. Gossip makes a streak of lightning look sluggish. By the time she left at quarter to six, it was generally being said that Ellie had flipped.

The tiny foyer of The Burch House, an elegant, exclusive hotel in Kensington, famed for its English Country House charm, where she was to meet Theo, was crowded.

Declining to leave the fur coat which Rosie had begged her to rethink but in the end, almost tearfully, lent her, Ellie peeped in at the bar. Her nerve almost gave out but she was sustained by the knowledge that in a very few minutes Theo Stirling was going to meet his match.

She saw him before he saw her, sitting at the bar in conversation with a man in a pinstripe suit. She swallowed hard. He was laughing at something the man said. He looked happy. He glanced at his watch and then towards the door and saw her.

Instantly Theo was on his feet, his eyes alight with pleasure, and Ellie thought her heart would break.

'Hi,' he said softly, kissing her swiftly on both cheeks. 'You smell nice.'

Ellie wondered why life was so unfair. 'Have I kept you waiting, I'm so sorry.'

'You're worth waiting for. I'm sorry you can't have dinner. Working?'

'No, I'm having dinner with someone else. I haven't got long, I just thought you should know the decision I've come to.'

She did not miss the expectant look that leapt into his eyes.

'Of course. Let me get you a drink and let me take your coat.'

Then and only then did Theo get the full impact of what Ellie was wearing. He didn't even blink.

'Exactly *who* are you having dinner with?' he said, taking in the long legs, the neckline so low Ellie knew if she even coughed she would be courting disaster.

'A friend,' she said, tossing her hair back and crossing her legs, running her hands along her thighs as she did so. She then ordered a double scotch and asked a passing waiter to bring her some cigarettes.

'I didn't know you smoked,' Theo remarked mildly, thus far remaining outwardly unmoved by this quite different version of Ellie.

Ellie looked at him from under her lashes and leaning across the table, giving him the full benefit of her astonishing cleavage, trailed one long, freshly painted red nail seductively across the low neckline of her dress, and ran the tip of her tongue slowly along her top lip. 'There's a lot about me you don't know.'

'Evidently,' he said drily as her cigarettes and drink arrived.

'Okay, Eleanor, what is all this?' he said impatiently.

'This is to say, I've thought over what you said. Yes,' she said, blowing a cloud of smoke across the table. 'We could get to know each other, we could put the past behind us. You could make an attempt to get me to fall for you – you've already done that – and,' she paused for deliberate effect, 'failed.'

'Do go on,' he said icily. 'This is fascinating.'

'I'm so pleased,' she purred. 'Because the good news is that I'm going to save you the bother of trying to charm me. I'm going to let you know now what a waste of time it would be. And playing good little Ellie really is *so* boring. Let's just say you've made me an offer I find no difficulty whatsoever in refusing.'

'You could have told me this on the phone,' he said calmly, but she noticed his mouth was now set in a hard line and he was looking pale.

Matching his calm tone she told him she thoroughly agreed.

'You're absolutely right. But I wanted to make sure there were no misunderstandings. So let me make myself clear. If you make any attempt to build on the land next to Delcourt, I will ruin you. I will repeat everything Caroline Montgomery has told me and print word for word what Matt Harksey says about your father.'

At those names he jerked his head up and looked at her with an odd and startled expression.

'You spoke to Caroline?'

Ellie, who was near breaking point, managed to nod, taking a sip of the whisky she thought was vile.

'Where? And more interestingly, when?'

'I never reveal my sources,' she retorted, seeing Paul entering the bar, scanning the room for her.

'You'll hurt so many people, why can't you trust me? I thought you were beginning to?'

Her answer was to smirk pityingly at him. She saw the confusion flickering in his eyes. She almost cracked.

'Eleanor, why are you doing this?' Theo leaned across the table, gripping her arm. 'What the hell has happened? I can't believe you mean any of this?'

'Oh, ver-ry good,' she said admiringly. 'Very convincing. Nothing's happened. I've just decided we are both too busy to continue with this charade and I've started being myself again. I recommend you do the same, far less strenuous.

'Darling,' she waved at Paul who came across looking startled at being addressed so affectionately by the girl who had so recently dumped him for cheating on her.

As he reached the table, Theo's face for one brief second looked surprised but then he gazed impassively as Ellie stretched her arms invitingly up and Paul leaned down to kiss her.

'I believe you've met,' she said, knowing she was going to settle another score in one evening when she eventually told Paul what she thought of his deceitful nature.

Theo looked at Paul and then at Ellie, who was making a big fuss about putting her cigarettes into her bag and collecting her quite outrageous fur coat from behind her chair. She knew he was completely stunned. Only last night she had told him her relationship with Paul was over and why.

Quietly he got up and shook Paul's hand. 'You certainly are a devil for punishment,' he said to a bewildered Paul, moving away from the table. 'Have a pleasant evening. Goodbye, Eleanor.' He looked steadily at her. His face was pale, his eyes betrayed nothing.

'Oh, are you going?' she said as though she had only just noticed. 'Bye,' and linking her arm through Paul's she walked out of the restaurant, chatting animatedly.

As they reached the pavement, she saw Theo's driver open the door of the Mercedes and as he paused before sliding into the back, she heard him quite distinctly give the driver Debra's address.

When Paul asked her where she would like to have dinner, Ellie pushed him away.

'Dinner with you? God, I don't even want to be *seen* with you,' and she turned, leaving Paul to gape open-mouthed after her as she balanced on one foot, whipping off one and then the other of her impossibly high-heeled shoes and hailed a taxi.

Leaning back against the leather seat, safe in the gloom of the cab, Ellie didn't think her heart would break. She knew it had.

Chapter Twenty-seven

Just before the New Year, Jerome made three announcements. The first was that Jed was going to be an editor at large, which meant he would divide his time between London and New York; the second that Paul was taking a six-month sabbatical to write a book and would be based at his home in Juan les Pins; and the third that in the late spring Rosie was to do a special fashion spread in Venice, where a glittering charity ball was being held at which every society name in Europe was guaranteed to be present.

Ellie and Jed would be going too, he told the assembled staff at the special advance planning conference after the Christmas break.

Ellie was to interview Prince Stefano Ferrucini, who had just taken over as head of a cosmetics empire and was hosting the ball, from which all proceeds would go to environmental campaigns.

'Jed, you can do the social stuff, make sure you get the names right and his wives in the right order.'

Jerome glanced around the room at their bemused faces.

'Yeah, yeah, yeah, I know. Bentley has had another brilliant idea and we are very fortunate that these are all his friends and we won't have any problem getting co-operation.'

The heavy sarcasm was not lost on them as it all became plain. The idea of sending three journalists on one story was unheard of but not when the proprietor of the magazine had decided it was a good idea.

Ellie knew that Roland would never have been coerced in this way, but right now knowing she had a full diary three months ahead suited her. She was thrilled for Jed. His relationship with Ashley was once again on a roller coaster. Putting the Atlantic between them seemed like a great idea. She was simply relieved about Paul.

Ever since the night Ellie had exacted her revenge for the shallow way he had treated her, he had missed no opportunity to try to undermine her. Occasionally she thought it might resolve the whole childish business if she pretended he had managed to score a point, but it had been too long now, and she was too much in the habit of refusing to be reduced to a mass of insecurity, to allow him even a glimpse of anything other than cool indifference.

Jerome watched her file out behind Rosie and Paul, wondering when she was going to crack. It was now three weeks since she had promised to produce the piece on Theo Stirling and so far he had not seen one word of copy. Every now and then he cautiously asked about its progress and every time she just said stonily that the moment wasn't right.

The relationship between her and Ian was cordial. Almost close. Jealousy and insecurity had always been Jerome's weakness and the continuing warmth between his boss and the girl he felt was a walking reminder of his grossest error of judgement occupied him more than was good for him.

Jerome was waiting for his moment, but as each day passed it seemed to slip even further from his grasp. Always slight, Ellie was now gaunt. The slender face looked strained. Her eyes had lost their laughter. It was all tied up with Stirling, but he couldn't piece it together. He knew for a fact that Stirling was back in New York, and his marriage to Debra Carlysle was on the cards for when she finished this movie that Max Culver was directing.

When they had wanted to interview Max, he had said only if Eleanor Carter did it, and she had sent a note direct to Max – wasn't there *anybody* she didn't know – saying it was just not possible with her present commitments.

The news of Theo's impending marriage had been in Jed's column just before Christmas and the nationals had picked it up the next day, but there was still no sign of it. Ironically there had been a picture of Ellie at a reception with Clive O'Connell Moore in one of the tabloids on the same gossip page as the one that featured Stirling.

Jerome wondered what Stirling would do if he knew Ellie had a profile ready that would cripple his reputation. Murder her, he decided, and the thought made him feel a great deal happier for the rest of the day.

Ellie had never known it was possible to feel so dead inside. Christmas had been a nightmare, trying to be cheerful for her family's sake. She had taken the minimum time off, arriving at Oliver's late in the afternoon on Christmas Eve and leaving early in the evening on Boxing Day.

Clive had disappeared in the direction of Joanne's house, seen off like Father Christmas piled high with presents for the boys and some 'offerings', as he called them, for Joanne. Before he went he gave Ellie a Clarice Cliffe bowl that she had spotted one Sunday as they strolled through Rye. She gave him one of her father's watercolours of the lake at Delcourt, which he had wanted to buy from her the minute he saw it hanging in her flat. They were to meet up to spend New Year together but in the event they didn't.

It had been touch and go whether her father and Alison would manage to join everyone at Delcourt for the holiday, but to their delight at the last minute Alison rang to say they would be there for a rare family Christmas.

But a long walk alone with her father along the beach

on Boxing Day had done nothing to reconcile him to the fact that Oliver stubbornly believed that with public support behind him, he could see off both Basil Oldburn and Theo Stirling and protect his hotel. Raw-nerved and still in shock, Ellie was impatient with him and they returned for the first time either could remember totally fed up with each other.

'He just wants the past to stay buried,' sighed Alison, finding Ellie in her room packing to return to London. 'He doesn't want to discuss it, or mention it any more. He was obviously so hurt by it all.'

'And he's not the only one,' Ellie snapped back. But her stepmother's wounded expression made her regret having ever embarked on the subject, and she couldn't help feeling that everyone was relieved when she finally disappeared down the drive and headed back to Fulham.

Only Jill had remained aloof from it all and very sensibly too, thought Ellie savagely as she joined the motorway. Why didn't I do the same?

Her mood did not improve when she pushed open the door of her flat and hastily flipped through the cards and letters that had arrived in her absence. Since none of them had a New York postmark she lost interest in them and tossed them along with all the others into the Clarice Cliffe fruit bowl, chiding herself for clutching at straws.

The campaign in Willetts Green was now a well known cause. True to their word Gregory Merton and Charles Peterhouse had written marvellous tub-thumping pieces for the *Recorder* which had delighted both Joe and Gregory's constituency manager, who had been concerned for some time at his MP's low popularity rating locally.

Car stickers and posters sprouted throughout the area with a distinctive pink and white entwined motif of larkspurs in the corner, which Josie had designed. Those guests to the hotel who had enquired about its significance had discreetly had the campaign brought to their attention and had willingly pledged their support.

Maurice Middleton was now a firm member of the team. Not only had he become an enthusiastic supporter and helper but his days at Delcourt liaising with Oliver and Joe had made him two more unexpected friends. Chloe and Miles, denied a grandfather figure, had virtually adopted him and he was practically one of the family.

Led by Maurice, a local conservation club had held two meetings which Oliver addressed along with Gregory, who was now on to a Good Thing. Sandy Barlow, asking Ellie to talk on his show about a *Focus* profile on the new woman governor of a top security prison, managed to slip in a couple of questions under the pretext of general environmental issues. It was now simply a matter of keeping interest alive awaiting Conrad Linton's return from Australia at the end of March when the planning committee was due to consider its decision.

New Year saw Ellie at Roland's house where he and Thelma gave a wildly successful, not to say drunken, party for their friends and the staff of *Focus*. Lucy came with her latest boyfriend who, she said, had a record out and was big in Tokyo. Rosie brought Piers Imber, a photographer she had been trying to get her hands on for months. Paul arrived with Kiki Stevens, the beautiful but dim model who had cut her hair off and so enraged Rosie.

Ellie watched without a flicker of emotion as Paul kissed Kiki and told him he was pushing his luck when ten minutes later he tried to persuade Ellie to leave the party early with him.

Whatever had she ever seen in him, she thought, and went in search of Jed who was to drive with her to Gemma and Bill's to have a drink.

'Why not,' he agreed. 'I work so hard, I don't have time to find anyone to love.'

'You're very lucky,' she said with such sadness in her

voice that he slipped an arm around her shoulders as they went to collect their coats.

'Sorry, love,' Jed apologized, seeing the pain in her eyes. 'I had to write it.'

She didn't have to ask what he meant. The latest issue of *Focus* had a picture of Debra with Theo leaving her apartment in New York, with a caption saying friends expected an announcement that they were to be a permanent item any day now.

Ellie hugged his arm. 'It's okay,' she whispered. 'After all I started the ball rolling.'

Jed now knew the truth. The whole truth. Two days after he had returned from his brief trip to New York just before Christmas, he had tried to phone Ellie to find out how she had managed to get such a scoop on Theo Stirling and Debra Carlysle, but he was told by the operator her phone had been left off the hook. Not getting any reply from the flat, he rang Oliver's and then Amanda's. Gemma and Bill he knew had already departed for Scotland. There was no answer from Clive and anyway wasn't he still in Dublin?

Jed never knew quite why he'd felt uneasy, but it was more, he said later, Ellie's recent roller-coaster emotions that had set the alarm bells ringing than any real evidence that something must have happened.

As he pulled up outside her flat he could see immediately that the place was in darkness, but her car was there. So too was the milk, uncollected, frozen solid on the doorstep. Pushing open the gate to the area steps he ran down, not at all confident that his journey had been without cause, and leaned on the buzzer.

Nothing.

Bending down, he knelt in front of the letter box and tried to see through to the darkened hallway, calling her name. The windows were secured and the blinds down. But the back, the back by the patio might not be. The only way in was through the house that backed on to Ellie's.

Leaving his car he ran round the block, counting off the houses until he found the one that he guessed lined up with Ellie's, and banged on the door. The owner, a woman, appeared almost immediately and Jed, who rather admired his own ingenuity, poured out a story about looking after his friend's flat and he had gone out leaving the keys inside. The woman, as well she might, was inclined not to believe him, until Jed, seeing her hesitation, added swiftly that he was sure he'd left the gas on.

Within minutes he was scaling the wall at the back, agreeing that she had better waste no time calling the gas board, and was pounding on Ellie's patio windows.

Then the blind was pulled back and at five o'clock on a Sunday evening, wrapped in one of Oliver's old rugger shirts over black leggings, barefoot and clutching a half-empty wine glass, Ellie appeared.

Jed had never seen her look so haggard – or so drunk.

'Okay, Carter,' he said, pushing past her and switching on a couple of lamps. 'Let's get some coffee going, some heat on and then you might as well get used to the idea that I'm not leaving until I know what's going on.'

A swift look round and he took in the empty wine bottles and a glass that had deposited its contents on to the carpet.

Ellie was telling him she was fine. And what was he doing coming in the back? A headache, that's all.

'No, don't give me that crap about colds and flu and headaches,' Jed went on, collecting up the wine bottles and tipping them into the waste bin.

Ellie didn't even protest when Jed ushered her into her bedroom with orders to wash her face, change her clothes and be out in ten minutes. After fifteen, having discovered there was no food in the fridge, Jed phoned a local take away home delivery service, and having turned the heat on full and brewed up some coffee, he went to find her. She was lying on her bed, her arms wrapped around a pillow, and crying as though her heart would never mend.

Silently he covered her with the quilt which had slid down to the floor and, stroking her head as though she were a small child just as she had once done for him when he thought he couldn't face another day listening to the jokes and jibes about his private life, let her cry.

'Sorry, Jed,' she said after a while, propping herself up on one elbow, blowing her nose and giving him a weak smile. 'I thought I could do this on my own.'

'Not as bright as you look sometimes, my flower,' he said and left her to fetch the freshly brewed coffee. 'Now let's have it. Theo, isn't it?' It was a statement more than a question as he handed her a steaming mug of coffee.

She nodded, knowing Jed would understand, not judge her, stay silent.

'Why don't you start from the beginning. You've known him for longer than you've let on, haven't you?' he asked shrewdly and propping himself up next to her on the bed, settled down to listen.

So there in her cosy, tiny bedroom, sipping black coffee, on a cold December evening, Ellie described to her best friend the events that had changed all their lives all those years before.

'We had lived in that house forever. The Stirlings had a house locally, but they mainly lived in the States. I never really knew Theo because he was older and his sisters are only a year or two younger than him, so they were away at school and went to the States during the holidays. I never saw them.

'Besides, they were amazingly wealthy even then, and Dad never had two pennies to rub together. In fact Aunt Belle said she saw more of the bailiff than she did of Dad.

'You see, Theo's father had inherited the company from

his father, Theo's grandfather, when old man Stirling retired to the Bahamas. Robert Stirling had come back to oversee the transition of Stirling Industries to its new London headquarters, so for about a year he lived in the big house, the one I was at on Saturday.'

For a moment her voice faltered, but she drew a deep breath and went on.

'Robert Stirling had seen some of Dad's work and asked him if he would paint a portrait of Theo's mother. Dad was obviously thrilled. It meant money and because Robert was so established locally, suddenly Dad became flavour of the month and all the local bigwigs who wanted to impress Robert, I suppose, were all having their portraits painted. It had begun to look as though we were out of the woods. Dad was happy because Alison was around, looking after him and apparently wanting to marry him.

'I came home from school for the summer and for once I wasn't immediately handed a list of lights I was to remember to switch off and Dad said at this rate when I got back for the winter, we might even turn the heating on.'

'It sounds ghastly,' said Jed sympathetically.

'Oh, it wasn't,' said Ellie quickly. 'It was a wonderful time. You see, Oliver and I didn't know any different. That house was a stable thing in our lives, because Dad was always running out of money and I never knew from one term to the next what school I would be going to, provided of course Dad could scrape up the money – or usually poor old Aunt Belle, I'm afraid.

'It was that summer she fell out with Dad, over Alison's alterations to the house – and the fact that Dad had bought the Lagonda instead of spending the money on the house – so from then, Oliver and I fended for ourselves when we were home from school and Aunt Belle would just come in the long summer break.'

'So then what happened?'

Ellie told him how suddenly everything changed. How Robert Stirling had arrived at the house one afternoon and she and Oliver had overheard the dreadful accusations, the raised voices, and her father protesting his innocence.

'He was accusing Pa of stealing plans that would have seriously damaged Stirling Industries if Oldburns – that was the other property developer locally – acted on them. Which he said they undoubtedly would. And,' Ellie took a deep breath, 'they did. Stirlings lost a huge contract, it nearly wiped them out over here.'

Jed looked puzzled.

'But why would your father want them? He's not in the property business?'

Ellie took a gulp of coffee, shaking her head.

'No. Just that we were so broke all the time, I suppose Robert Stirling must have thought Dad would have sold them to get some money. They'd gone missing, you see, from Stirling's house and a copy – or part of it – had been delivered back to Robert Stirling by the printers who had copied the original. They were somewhere over in Bournemouth, about fifty miles away.

'The cheque paying for the copies was traced to Dad, who couldn't make them believe it was for artist's materials, you know, cartridge paper, that sort of thing – the coincidence was too great.'

'But what was your father doing there? So far from home?'

Ellie shrugged. 'I never found out and neither did Oliver, but Dad was – is – eccentric. It didn't sound at all odd to us. Just to other people. But the coincidence was enough for Robert Stirling.'

'But why blame him?'

Ellie's face clouded over at the memory of the stormy scene in her father's study.

'Because to them it made sense. You see the really awful part about it was that Robert knew that Dad had been commissioned by Basil Oldburn to paint his daughters, and Dad was the only one who had access to Robert Stirling's office up at the house – when he used to go for sittings with Mrs Stirling. Even worse, clearly he needed the money that selling the plans to Oldburns would have brought.'

Quietly she recounted the next nightmare scenario in her young life – how suddenly everyone began to cancel their commissions. Robert had plenty of influence and no-one wanted to be seen to do anything to offend him.

She told Jed how she and Oliver finally stopped going to the village because the humiliation of being studiously ignored by everyone, too embarrassed to approach them, proved too much. Local people who had once automatically included them in invitations suddenly stopped calling, friends found excuses not to come to the phone. Aunt Belle's rapid departure simply adding fuel to their belief that John Carter was guilty.

Robert Stirling had also offered to act as guarantor for a loan John Carter had taken out at the bank to pay off some of his debts and he naturally withdrew the offer.

'The problem was Dad had borrowed against the promise. Enter Theo.' She covered her face wearily. 'He arrived out of the blue, about four weeks later, to see Dad. Dad emerged from the meeting saying he had no option but to sell the house to Theo Stirling, otherwise we would starve – funny that, we already were.

'Aunt Belle had gone and we were reduced to living off Alison. But she wasn't earning much, certainly not enough to pay the bills, which were colossal, and keep us. The tenants were leaving in droves because the rooms needed repairs and Dad couldn't afford to do them up. It was all such a mess. Jed, I was so frightened. There was no-one to turn to. Dad, lovely though he is, was useless.

'Anyway, he emerged from the meeting with Theo saying that he would sell the house for a rock-bottom price to the Stirlings and that as long as we didn't live in Dorset we could go where we liked. No-one actually said it, but I think it was because the Stirlings didn't want to be seen to be grinding Dad's nose in it, that they wanted us as far away from Willetts Green as possible.

'And that's what we did. At first I thought Oliver and I would have to leave school – again – but Dad scraped the money together to keep us there. Just as well really, I don't suppose Alison wanted two teenage stepchildren foisted on her the minute she got married.

'Alison stood by Dad and after they bought the house in Devon where they now live, they got married. I was hardly there. After A levels I persuaded Dad to let me have the rest of the money put aside for my school fees to go back to work for Joe McPhee in Dorset on the *Recorder*. Oliver was in Switzerland in the middle of his training. So that's what happened. I got a bedsit in the town. Best time I ever had.'

Ellie was by now considerably calmer. The relief of unloading such a burden after years of silence and months of anguish was beyond description.

She smiled at Jed and he squeezed her hand.

'But the bit I don't understand,' he said, taking her mug from her and refilling it, 'is why, with all that evidence, didn't Stirling bring in the police? They couldn't have been that certain, could they?'

It was Ellie's turn to frown. 'Oh, they did bring the police in, Dad was interviewed, but then they dropped the case after Dad agreed to sell the land to them. I've always had this odd feeling that it wouldn't have done Stirling any good to prosecute a man and convict him thereby leaving his children high and dry. They're terribly into reputation you know, the Stirlings.'

'Okay, that I can understand, but why didn't your father fight the accusation? After all, you and Oliver and Alison believed him. The evidence was certainly against him, but a good lawyer might have been able to help.'

'Huh!' Ellie's laugh was mirthless. 'No-one would touch him without money up front. Not against powerful people like the Stirlings. Lawyers are expensive. Besides Dad isn't a fighter, he just wanted to go away.'

Knowing John Carter, that was something Jed could readily believe. He simply walked away from reality. Ellie always explained it as being vague, you know, she would say, like artists are. But Jed more than once had thought John Carter's feelings for his children came a poor second to his own.

Briefly Ellie told him how Oliver, many years later, had rebought the house and the real reason why she so desperately wanted to keep Jed from writing about Theo returning to Dorset.

'It was such a scandal at the time. I didn't want to put Dad through it all again. Or us. It was all so squalid. People avoiding us. Aunt Belle storming off simply confirmed everyone's belief that there must be something in it. And it will ruin Oliver if that land is built on. But Theo doesn't seem to care, he just wants to build Carlysle a new house and some other development. She didn't know what, and honestly, she didn't seem to care much. I bet you after all that she doesn't even live in the bloody place.'

'And that's why he doesn't want you to write about him,' said Jed, who privately thought Ellie could make a fortune if she sold her story to one of the tabloids. 'He'd look like such a shit, everyone would be on your – I mean Oliver's side.'

Jed was staring into his coffee. Turning his head, he looked at Ellie and frowned.

'What doesn't make sense is why Theo wants to return to his roots? I mean, with respect, Willetts Green isn't New York or LA and that's what he's used to.'

Ellie shrugged. 'He also owns land in Ireland, Clive told me, and he has a farmhouse in Wales. So why not?'

'There is that, I suppose. Most people do want to go home eventually, except for myself of course. In fact the very idea makes me feel very nervous.'

Ellie smiled for the first time. There were never any secrets between her and Jed and the relief of just confessing to him was giving her a strength she never thought she would find again.

'I believed Theo when he said he wanted a truce,' she told him, describing the previous weekend's events. 'I thought I had misjudged him. He was so gentle and sweet when he dragged me out of the sea, and made me laugh and I had begun to think, stupidly, that we could reach a compromise. And all the time he was fooling me.'

Jed watched her thoughtfully when she recounted her interview with Debra.

The doorbell rang sharply and Jed went away to take delivery of the pizzas he had ordered. He deposited them in Ellie's kitchen which was now warm and comfortable to sit in.

Returning to the bedroom, he started gathering up cups and piling them on to the tray he'd brought in. Just watching Ellie and listening to her he had arrived at a great many conclusions himself. As she swung her legs over the side of the bed, pushing her hair into some kind of order, she followed him into the kitchen where between mouthfuls of the first food she had eaten in days, she told Jed about her final meeting with Theo and the dreadful outfit she'd worn.

'It offended everything Rosie holds dear, I thought she was going to faint with horror.'

'But that isn't why you were sitting in the dark, half drunk, is it?'

The question caught her by surprise and Jed heard her sharp intake of breath.

'Is it?' he persisted.

'No,' she mumbled and then, her voice breaking in a half sob, she pushed her plate away and turned to gaze bleakly at him. 'I've fallen in love with him, Jed. Isn't that the dumbest thing you ever heard?'

Chapter Twenty-eight

January opened with freezing snow. The staff of *Focus* slipped and sloshed their way into the office. Ellie took Jed down to Delcourt and on her return went down with a heavy cold which in her low spirits felt like flu.

She turned down dinner with Brook Wetherby – who had been aware that the interview that finally appeared was too critical for his liking and wanted to polish his image – and watched Paul go through a series of girl-friends, all of whom he flaunted in front of her.

She thought he was boring.

She also ran into Roger Nelson in a restaurant where she was meeting Amanda – on a flying visit to see her doctor – for lunch. Ellie hesitated, not certain she wanted that part of her life to be resurrected, not knowing what else they would talk about but Theo. But in the event he saw her first and insisted that she join him at the bar for a drink since both their lunch companions had yet to arrive.

'Ann Winterman mentioned that you had asked where I had gone, so I rang you. I don't think you were really that interested, you never returned the call.'

So that was it, not Lucy being indiscreet after all. Ellie gave him a vague reply. 'I just wanted to commiserate, after all you had been helpful to me. Getting the sack isn't easy – or being made redundant.'

'Not sacked – far too crude,' he said with a raised eyebrow. 'Just asked to consider a couple of options that were frankly demotions.'

'But why? I got the impression you were invaluable to him?'

'Oh, my dear,' he drawled mockingly. 'What a wonderfully romantic notion you journalists have about city life.'

Ellie flushed. 'I'm sorry. I didn't mean to pry . . .'

'No, no, I'm sorry. Old story, familiar one. I took a week's leave while he was in New York. I was feeling quite wrecked and needed a break, but some crisis blew up and when I got back I found I had been blown out.'

Ellie was shocked. 'Didn't he know you were away?'

'Doubt it. All he knows is whether something is done or not. He really doesn't give a shit about past or present performance. It's what use you are to him at that moment that counts – which is why I laughed when you used the word "invaluable". Doesn't exist for him.' He looked curiously at her. 'Er . . . the word was that you were going to stitch him up, but you never did. Is that why he saw you that day?'

Ellie felt unreal. Sick. She wished Amanda would hurry up. 'I don't think so,' she said quietly and then seeing him expecting her to go on, she lied. 'As a journalist, I was really just interested in a society story, you know, gossipy stuff, about him and . . . and . . . well, his latest companion I suppose.'

Roger Nelson indicated to the barman to refill his glass. Ellie noticed the puffy lines around his eyes, the tiny red veins on his cheeks.

'Who are you working for now?' she asked, glad to be able to turn the subject.

'Oh, you know, this and that,' he said carelessly. 'Matter of fact I'm meeting someone now who's interested in me joining them.'

'Well, lots of luck,' Ellie said, beginning to slide off the stool, seeing Amanda arriving in a whirlwind of parcels and tousled hair.

'It's funny, you know,' said Roger. 'I thought he was

interested in you, but the delicious Debra seems much more his cup of tea. Wasting her time though. He isn't the marrying kind. I don't care what you put in your papers. His first wife could tell you that, poor cow.'

Ellie didn't want anyone to tell her anything ever again about Theo Stirling. It wasn't easy knowing she had served her purpose. She just thanked God that she had got out before she had made a complete fool of herself and that Clive had never known.

As she hugged Amanda and squealed with delight that Amanda's doctor had confirmed her pregnancy, she wondered why though she had escaped with pride and dignity nearly intact it was no comfort at all.

Half way through the month, after his sons had returned to school, Clive came back from Joanne's subdued and bitterly regretting staying in the country instead of bringing the boys back to London.

'We talk, and we agree, and then she always, well, one of us,' he amended with commendable honesty, 'one of us can't help raking over the ashes and then we're off and of course by that time I've promised the boys any manner of things that we'll be doing together so I can't just up sticks. D'ye see?'

It sounded like hell. Just the way they were when they'd been married, if he had given her a reliable description of the troubled O'Connell Moore union. Ellie smiled at him and ruffled his hair.

'No, I don't see. But then I've never been married. I'm sure it's quite different, isn't it?'

'It's different, all right,' he growled. 'And I doubt I'll be repeating the experience.'

Ellie tried to look and sound shocked.

'Mr O'Connell Moore.' Her voice was severe. 'What are you trying to tell me? Have you been having your wicked way with me and no thought of making an honest woman of me?'

They were in bed at Clive's apartment, the television still on after they had finished watching the late movie. The floor around the bed was cluttered as always with evidence of the tasks Clive had been engaged in immediately before they'd fallen into bed.

Clive didn't move, just turned his head very slowly, apprehensively, as Ellie went on eating chocolate chip ice cream straight from the tub, trying not to laugh.

'Is that what you want?' His voice sounded uneasy. 'Because if you did, I would, but it wouldn't work, and then I'd lose you as well.'

It wasn't quite what Ellie had expected. She had just wanted to tease him. But then quite suddenly she had to know. Had to know for once in her life where she stood. What was all this about?

'It's about,' he said, 'me and you and time standing still. Not fraught with decisions, no past, no future, just the here and now. You with that tub of ice cream. Me with no other thought than how beautiful you are, and not wanting to think about anything else. Does that make sense?'

Ellie looked down at him lying beside her, his arms behind his head, eyes closed, very still. And she knew, just knew, that in his own way he was praying that she would not want to change anything, to leave everything as it was at this moment, but if she had wanted something more he would have moved mountains to meet her needs.

And she knew she would do the same for him.

Very gently she began to stroke his head, and eased herself down in the bed beside him.

'And what if I say, it doesn't make any sense, that I want a future?'

He opened his eyes and sighed and flicked the remote control switch on the television to off.

'I would do my best to make you happy. But I don't think you would be. I've got too much luggage in my life and I don't think you'd put up with me for long.'

'Do you know,' she said, resting her head on his chest, sliding her arms around him, 'I have the strangest feeling that it's you who wouldn't put up with me. And no, I don't want to go forward or back or sideways or any other way. I just want to be here, shut away. Not thinking. Not . . . not anything.'

She felt his hand tilt her chin up so that he could look down into her face. A lock of hair had fallen across her brow and he gently moved it aside and when he spoke her heart lurched.

'For someone who should be looking forward to everything life has to offer, you sound remarkably like someone who's running away. Now I wonder why I think that?'

'You think too much,' she said with a casualness that she hoped would disguise the ache that her eyes, her face could so easily betray. 'And I nearly forgot to tell you, Letty's asked me to do a special when Jonquil comes back at the end of the month.'

'Idiot,' he said affectionately. 'And what else have you forgotten to tell me?'

'Apart from the fact that I promised Gemma we would baby sit for her on Saturday, that's all,' she said as he switched out the light.

It wasn't, of course. She hadn't told him about Theo. Not yet. But then what really was there to tell him about something that had ceased to exist?

At the end of February she read in the morning papers that Theo was due in England for a week en route to Paris. Ellie chose that week to go to Lanzarote with Rosie.

Jonquil had returned to her job a week earlier than expected and while Ellie was sad to leave 'PrimeMovers', Letty was keen for her to sign to do half a dozen hour-long specials, so she wouldn't be saying goodbye to them after all. Her career was looking rosy.

But neither she nor Letty were, of course, prepared for the unedifying sight of Jonquil almost blind with fury storming the MD's office, unable to believe the opportunity hadn't been offered to her.

'But Jonquil, it was you who insisted on signing the contract to keep you on "PrimeMovers" for the next twelve months,' Letty pointed out, and stood hastily aside as the new mother stormed out of the office, seemingly incapable of speech unless it was no more than four letters at a time.

It was only because Jerome persuaded her to that Ellie backed off from trying to get out of going to Venice to interview Prince Stefano Ferrucini.

'I know it's just another charity ball,' the editor explained. 'But Bentley's a friend of his and we've got exclusive coverage. And at this stage it would be difficult to explain why you're not going.'

He had long since abandoned any attempt to order her around and it was partly a recognition of that which made Ellie resist the temptation to dig her heels in. She said nothing but she knew he was being leaned on. A society ball did not require three writers to cover it. Bentley Goodman was clearly into social mobility. Ellie had yet only glimpsed him from a distance. The great man rarely visited his footsoldiers and even more rarely invited them to see him.

Knowing she had a busy spring ahead and might not get away again until the end of the summer, Ellie also squeezed in a visit to her father in Devon and reported back to Oliver that he was ridiculously unreasonable whenever she mentioned the campaign.

'I think he feels guilty that he didn't fight to keep Delcourt more than he did,' said Oliver. 'I don't think it hit him until recently how badly affected you and I were.'

The echo of Jill's belief that their father had cared very little how it would affect them came back to Ellie and she was forced to accept that her sister-in-law might be right.

Except that she found it hard to read a newspaper that mentioned Theo, and couldn't bear not to read about him either, nor could she stand to have white flowers in the house, Ellie was happier with her life than she would have thought possible only a few short months before.

Clive was her constant, if unpredictable, companion and if she had ceased to believe that he no longer felt emotionally tied to his former wife, she had learned to accept that emotional luggage could be stored away with a sign saying not needed on the next voyage. She could not, however, bring herself to say not wanted.

Her days were now divided almost equally between London and Dorset, where her reputation was now established, and she had even been asked to open a local fête. She blushingly declined.

As February drew to a close, Gemma and Bill shrieking with excitement came flying down to her flat and dragged Ellie and Clive upstairs to celebrate Bill's new job.

'Not what I wanted,' he beamed, pouring the inevitable Bollinger that Clive had grabbed from Ellie's fridge as Amy promptly woke up and refused to go back to sleep. 'Hell of a journey each day – over to Blackheath,' he said, looking doubtfully at Clive who was cuddling a now content Amy, sucking avidly on his little finger which he had dipped in champagne. 'But so what? It's a start, isn't it, Gem?'

A start. That's all she had asked for, and all Bill had wanted. They smiled at each other. Ellie understood.

So enveloped now in the life she had created for herself out of the ashes of her former existence, she would sometimes try and recall what it was like having a diary that allowed for only a meticulously planned life, no spontaneity, no impulsive treats. If anything she was more ambitious than ever; she loved being at the centre of things, she knew she always would. But Ellie no longer wanted a life that revolved around politically correct organizations, ducking and diving trying to stay one step ahead of office politics and dining with the right people.

Good grief, she smiled a few days later, looking in at Clive inexpertly trying to whip up omelettes in his kitchen, roaring his refusal to accept her help, and wondered how she could ever have thought, before all of this, that she was having fun.

Inevitably she ran into people she no longer regarded as important in her life, and to her shame, but satisfaction, she notched up each encounter as an old score finally settled.

Liz Smedley was mentally ticked off the list when she ran into Ellie in Sloane Street and suggested lunch.

'Lunch?' said Ellie, leaning her head to one side and considering the idea. 'Mmm. No, I don't think so, Liz, but thanks for asking,' and she waved and walked on.

Later as she flopped down in her seat Liz told a frankly disbelieving Anne Carmichael that Ellie Carter was plain bloody rude.

'Anyone would think she was still ruling the roost instead of bloody lucky to have got back into things again,' Liz said, stabbing butter on to a roll that was taking the full vent of her fury.

They were lunching at a newly opened salad bar that had, for reasons no-one could quite fathom, become the rage overnight. Reservations were hard to get and no-one worth their expenses would be seen dead on the waiting list. Liz had one eye on the menu and one sweeping the room for confirmation that she was lunching in the right place and broke off to hiss at Anne.

'Don't look now, Beth Wickham has just come in with Tony Travers. Is it true they're an item? Anyway, bloody Miss Carter said she was too busy. And to think when she was out of work, she was ringing me non stop to see if I could help. I even offered to take her to lunch. Never again,' she seethed.

'And did you?' asked Anne Carmichael, who felt rather uneasy that Ellie had been left to it when she lost her job. But then, she comforted herself, it was probably what she wanted. So embarrassing.

'Did what?' snapped Liz, tapping her foot angrily against the table.

'Take her to lunch?'

Liz eyed her companion with irritation. 'I can't remember. And anyway I'm glad I didn't. Beth Wickham is right, she is an arrogant bitch and it's no wonder Paul D'Erlanger dumped her.'

Anne looked across the crowded restaurant to where Beth was giving Tony Travers her undivided attention, approximately six inches between their noses.

'Paul dumped Beth too,' she said mildly. 'I hear he's trying to get back with Ellie.'

Polly, on the other hand, was made of sterner stuff. You had to admire her, thought Ellie, colliding with her one afternoon as she strolled to meet Clive at the National Gallery and Polly was distractedly trying to get a cab back to her office.

Polly squealed a greeting, grabbing Ellie by the arms and berated her for hiding herself away.

'We've missed you at WIN, you naughty girl,' she scolded playfully. 'How about lunch?'

The first profile Ellie had written for *Focus* since her return had been published that week. She felt she could afford to be more forthright.

'I don't do lunch very much these days,' she told a startled Polly, who continued to measure success in terms of how long it took to fit someone in for that very activity.

'But I thought you were writing for *Focus* again, I mean I heard about your TV show . . .'

Ellie knew that a nasty suspicion had surfaced in Polly's

mind. She groaned as though comprehension had just dawned.

'Oh sorry, Polly, I thought you *knew*. I meant I don't have *business* lunches any more unless I really have to.'

Polly eyed her in alarm. Her voice faltered.

'You don't? What, never?'

Ellie knew she was going to enjoy this.

'Oh, no. It's just that these days I can afford to choose what I do and having lunch is something I choose not to do.'

There was a persistence about Polly which at one time Ellie had put down to professionalism, something she herself believed in. Now she thought it irritating.

'But you really will kick yourself if you don't hear about who I've just taken on. Wait for it ... Are you ready for this? *Trevor Summers*.'

Ellie laughed and started to move on. Trevor Summers might have once rated an interest in her life. But these days Oscar-winning actors were way down on her list.

'If he's that good, Polly, we don't need to waste each other's time meeting for lunch to discuss it.'

Polly made one last attempt to retrieve her position.

'Fine, great. I'll send you his biog. You'll love him. Fascinating guy. And he was thrilled when I told him I knew you well.'

Ellie paused.

'Now there's a funny thing, Polly. I, on the other hand, have discovered in the last few months that I really didn't know you at all. See you.'

Before Ellie left for Venice the sore subject of Kathryn Renshaw and her libel action against *Focus* had to be addressed. For Ellie it was irritating and time consuming, and she hated being used as a tool for a vain, financially ambitious woman to parade her life across the tabloids. The action for libel was to be heard in the High Court and was expected to last five days.

'After which,' she told Rosie, 'Venice may well be exactly what I need after all.'

The press were out in force on the first day of the hearing when Ellie arrived accompanied by Alistair Bell. Kathryn Renshaw turned up with a posse of minders, several relatives and a fierce expression which set Ellie and Alistair into a fit of laughing.

'You ain't seen nothing, yet,' he breathed as the Renshaw brigade swept past and into the oak-panelled court room, settling themselves firmly into the public benches, in full view of the jury. Throughout the next five days they presented a united and totally unassailable front of moral indignation whilst quietly negotiating with the murkier tabloids to do an exclusive story just in case Mr John Carpenter Renshaw's ex- and very irate wife should lose her case.

As Alistair had predicted, Kathryn Renshaw needed her day in court.

What had clearly outraged her was that Alistair had advised their counsel that they saw no point in calling John Carpenter Renshaw as a witness, since it was Ellie's own comment that Kathryn Renshaw had benefited both financially and socially from her marriage to the Ambassador that had caused all the bother.

Clearly determined to have maximum compensation for the loss of seeing her former husband in court, Kathryn Renshaw, a walking tribute to the safer end of the fashion industry but an experienced litigant, skilfully lobbed gratuitous comments into her evidence which she was aware would make a good headline next day, lost no opportunity to describe *Focus* as no better than the gutter press and when Quentin Brough, the QC acting for *Focus*, boxed her into a corner, she resorted to a copious bout of weeping which left everyone wrung out with the tedium of it all.

Quentin had decided to call Ellie first to give evidence and the ordeal was not so much the time that Kathryn Renshaw's counsel took to cross-examine, but the fact that he was so plodding and unimaginative, it was like dealing with a third-rate member of the debating society at school.

'Still, why should he put himself out?' Alistair yawned as they waited for the jury to come back with their verdict. 'He's home and dry. Our only concern now is that the press box is crammed full and the rest are practically swinging from the rafters, which means that the jury may well feel obliged to say something dramatic. It's happened before,' he pointed out, seeing the look of amazement that crossed Ellie's face.

While they waited she had time to observe Kathryn Renshaw and had never felt sorrier for any woman before. John Renshaw had been her one claim to fame, her ticket to opportunities that were now lost to her, a gilded life with a view from the top – and then she had overplayed her cards.

One holiday too many, a bigger house, a faster car and while she was enjoying the fruits of her most ambitious career move, marriage to the Ambassador, he had been consoling himself for the lack of her presence in his life, with his secretary, about to become the third Mrs Renshaw.

Too late Kathryn had seen the trip wire, and since her looks, her ability and most depressing of all her age, precluded the chance of another brilliant match, she had locked herself into a time when life had been better and now she couldn't – and indeed couldn't afford to – let go.

Ellie shivered. What a waste of a life. To hanker after something that is gone. She would never do that, of that she was sure.

384

And it was in that moment, watching the distorted features of Kathryn Renshaw acting for all she was worth, that the futility of loving someone who was no longer there hit her.

Alistair was not at all surprised that the jury found for Kathryn Renshaw, a sizeable sum which, for the moment, seemed to assuage the Renshaw camp's need for income and revenge.

Ellie was just thankful it was all over. 'I must get some-one to libel me,' she said as they left the court and strolled along the ancient corridors, down the shallow stone steps and out into the forecourt. 'I could do with a new car.'

Glancing back as they headed down Fleet Street, they witnessed the sight of Kathryn Renshaw leaning heavily on her lawyer's arm delivering a well rehearsed set of quotes to the assembled press, jockeying with each other to capture the victor. 'Just want a quiet life. My marriage was a mistake but I am paying for it,' came floating after them.

'Getting well paid for it, more like,' muttered Alistair. 'And call that victory? She's the biggest loser I've ever come across. C'mon, a quick drink and then back to the real world.'

The morning papers featured the case very promi-nently, putting a dramatic Kathryn Renshaw on all the front pages. Ellie wasn't surprised but what did catch her unawares was that quite a few of them had used photographs of Ellie herself leaving court with Alistair.

Mid morning, as she was leaving her flat to drive down to Dorset for a production meeting with Letty, Jed phoned and asked who her press agent was.

'For someone who wants to lead a blameless life,' he teased, 'you don't half attract attention.'

Towards the end of March Jed, Rosie and Ellie with Piers Imber, the photographer Rosie was besotted with, left

London for Venice with a couple of assistants and a make-up artist in tow. Rosie was in festive mood. For once she didn't have to drag hundreds of dresses through customs, sorting out carnets, and face the dreary task of ironing everything on location.

'Easy peasy,' she crowed as they stepped into the motor launch at Marco Polo that was to take them across the canal to their hotel. 'I pointed out to Jerome that since most of the guests at the ball will be wearing couture anyway, what was the point? Tra la. No work for me.'

Ellie had thought the break would do her good, but she had forgotten just how romantic Venice was even on the cloudiest of days. You do not come to Venice when you are recovering from a broken heart, she told herself grimly as the hotel launch swung into the wide basin before heading into the grand canal and the brilliant perfection of the city was spread out before her.

A city that is a celebration of beauty and love was no place to help her forget that the man she was unwise enough to have fallen in love with was virtually living with someone else and at any moment might announce they had married.

Ellie steeled herself for that news, but every day that passed without hearing Theo was married she had come to regard as a bonus. What she found impossible to unravel was why she should still care what happened to a man who had treated her so badly, used her and undoubtedly would have discarded her the minute he achieved his aim.

But she did care. It had been nearly four months since she had acted out that outrageous scene in the hotel. She had wanted to punish Theo, let him see how easily he too could be fooled and most importantly never let him know that she had believed him.

The stupid thing is, she thought, as she unpacked an hour later in her luxurious room at the Europa, she couldn't bring herself to believe that she didn't.

He had made no effort to contact her. No sign that his bid for Linton's Field had been withdrawn. Nothing. It was as though everything that had passed between them had never happened.

It had been many weeks since Ellie spent every waking moment thinking about him. She had, she told herself with relief, learned to live with it. The knowledge made it easier for her to stay with Clive, but while they were still deeply concerned with each other, still made love, they had lost the passion of the first heady moments of their affair, and settled – the thought amused her – into a comfortable relationship, which suited them both. Neither of them was prepared to take it further or even find out why.

The phone by her bed gave a low buzz.

'See who's on the ball committee?' came Jed's cheerful voice. 'Lady Montrose, but of course she would be, it's her rainforests at stake. Anyway, she's having a drinks party this evening and we're invited.'

While Jed was speaking Ellie scrabbled among her pile of envelopes to find the invitation from Sarah Montrose, which announced she would be delighted if they could join her at six thirty at the Gritti Palace.

Ellie wasn't sure that she in turn was that delighted. She liked Sarah Montrose enormously, but she wasn't convinced she could handle being with her, knowing how closely connected she was with Theo, and his name was bound to come up. She said so to Jed.

'Got to do it sometime, my flower,' he said, but he wasn't altogether surprised when at six fifteen Ellie rang to cry off and arrange to meet him, along with Rosie and Piers, for dinner at La Madonna.

At eight she boarded a vaporetto to the Rialto Bridge and slipped through the sliding doors that led to the tiny platform at the back. Pulling her collar around her neck, she watched as the quietly majestic, romantic buildings like a series of Canalettos fell away as the boat glided down the centre of the Grand Canal towards the Rialto Bridge.

She didn't mind being alone. Clive was now immersed in his next book, late of course, and since he hadn't the time to come with her she couldn't think of anyone else she would want to share such a moment with.

Alighting at the bus station Ellie strolled back along the quay to the side street where the entrance to the hugely popular restaurant was located.

It was, as she had thought, packed. Rosie, Piers, along with Trixie the make-up artist and Bob, Piers's young assistant, were in fine form at a table towards the back of the main room. She noticed that Jed was looking anxiously at her and smiled at him to let him know she was okay.

Later as they crossed the Rialto Bridge, having elected to walk back to their hotel, stopping off at Harry's Bar for a nightcap, Jed hung back.

'Ellie, I've got to tell you something.'

The cautious note in his voice surprised her, the uncertain expression on his face even more so.

'It's Theo,' he said abruptly. 'He's here. Did you hear me Ellie?' he asked when she simply stood staring at him. 'He's here, with his parents – and Debra.'

'I see.' Ellie's voice was dull. 'He was at Sarah's drink, I suppose?'

Jed just nodded. He loathed having to tell her but at the same time he knew she had to be warned.

'Yes, I spoke to him for a quite a while. He's staying with the Prince at his Palazzo and flying back to New York immediately after the ball.'

Ellie continued walking, feeling a strange sense of calm. It was knowing he was in the same city, probably less than a mile away, that was doing it, but why? Surely she

should be feeling sick with nerves, panic-stricken, ready
to get the first flight out.

It was what Jed finally asked.

'No, of course not,' she said tightly. 'I have to get on
with my life. It was bound to happen. After all, he doesn't
know how much he affected me. And nor will he.'

Chapter Twenty-nine

Ellie watched as the gondolas and motor launches arrived at the torch-lit jetty that formed an archway into the marble-halled entrance to Prince Stefano's sumptuous home.

The mild spring evening, with only a gentle breeze from the water, lent an air of enchantment to the almost too perfect setting. Each new arrival disgorged a glittering army of names and titles dressed in an array of jewels and designer gowns, the sight of which had Rosie and Piers almost fainting with pleasure.

Ellie left them setting up cameras, as Rosie darted around accosting European princesses and socialites with a confidence that made a refusal simply out of the question and demonstrated to Ellie why *Focus*'s fashion editor was so good at her job.

'Your Highness,' Ellie heard her exclaim, 'You look too dee-vine. Gianni must be thrilled you're wearing one of his gowns,' and she turned away to hide a giggle at Rosie's outrageous implication that her acquaintance with Versace was close and personal, and grinned appreciatively as Rosie notched up another conquest.

Ellie's role at the ball was to get some colour to add to the interview she had completed that morning with the Prince. He was barely an inch taller than she was, but quite extraordinarily good looking. In spite of herself Ellie had liked him and found that beneath the outrageously flirtatious manner and quite stunning conceit, he had a razor-sharp brain and was comfortably able to reel off — and dismiss — every single perfume and cosmetic range in the world that he regarded as a competitor to his own exclusive Stefanissimo brand.

'For you, Eleanora,' he smiled winningly as she rose to leave his suite of rooms at the Palazzo, which Jed had privately estimated must be worth millions, being one of the few private residences left in the city overlooking the Grand Canal. 'You musta weara my perfume for tonight and you must dance with me so that I can make every man present know I am not only gifted but irresistible to the most beautiful woman in the room.'

So saying he pressed into Ellie's protesting hand a white satin-finished box, tied with silver ribbon, which Ellie knew contained his most expensive perfume, one she lusted after but would never have bought since the price ran into three figures.

It was impossible to refuse him, he looked so genuinely hurt when she tried to − and so, knowing that she was unlikely to want to criticize him, she accepted it and his impossible compliments with delight and told him mischievously that she didn't how she would last out until the evening when she would make him keep his promise to dance with her.

'You will write wonderful things about me,' he smiled, clasping her hand. 'My good friend Theo − who most mysteriously has disappeared for the morning − tells me you are the greatest journalist in the world, but I will be having many words with him, because he is very sly and did not say also the most beautiful.'

Ellie had managed a faint smile and was relieved the Prince couldn't hear her heart pounding against her ribs as she took her leave of him.

Of course he knows I'm here, she told herself as she dressed for the ball. My name is on Sarah's invitation list, on the one for the ball and Jed must have mentioned it.

'You can't avoid him forever,' Jed said when they had managed to squeeze in a brief visit to the Accademia and were sitting on the verandah of the Gritti Palace sipping coffee in the warm sunshine, lazily watching the river traffic bustling up and down the Grand Canal.

'You must think I'm stupid to be still feeling like this,' Ellie said in a small voice.

'Not at all.' Jed pushed his sunglasses back into his blonde hair and lifted his face to catch the sun. 'Having talked to him at length at Sarah's I understand how you feel. Ellie, I really liked the guy.'

'So did I,' she answered flatly.

'And I'll tell you something else, Miss,' Jed said, without opening his eyes. 'If things were different, I personally think you two would be terrific together.'

'But things are different,' she sighed. 'The difference is called Debra Carlysle.'

'I thought it was Delcourt.' Jed's amused voice made her give a guilty start.

'Oh, that too,' she told him hastily. 'Of course.'

She was going to miss having Jed constantly around. Amanda was wonderful, but now that she was pregnant she had become even more preoccupied with married life and Ellie couldn't blame her. What she was surprised about was that she felt a pang of envy for her friend.

Ever since the night Clive had revealed his fear of another commitment, the subject had lain dormant between them. When Ellie thought of Clive, she thought only of warmth, fun and a life free of complications and anguish. And she wanted to keep it that way. Not going forward, or back.

Slipping into the delicate white lace teddy – which gave her no pang of anguish at all when she recalled the price – she grinned at herself in the mirror. The weight loss she had sustained over the past four months was easily disguised by the smooth swell of her breasts, which she knew owed more to the expertise of La Perla than nature.

On reflection she was pleased that she had dashed off

at the last minute with Rosie to Lanzarote. It had been hot enough to get a light tan, which now made her skin against the figure-hugging honey-coloured silk and chiffon strapless dress she had brought for the ball gleam with a translucent glow.

That evening Trixie had offered to do Ellie's and Rosie's make-up and hair, and when Ellie gazed back at herself, she knew why Rosie paid over the odds to have Trixie on a fashion shoot. The pale-faced, hollow-eyed young woman who had arrived in Venice had been replaced with an ethereal beauty, her eyes gazing luminously out from faintly blushed cheeks, her hair piled into lustrous waves through which Trixie had threaded slivers of gold ribbon which now shimmered in the pale moonlight of the early spring evening.

As Jed handed her into the gondola – commanding a great deal of attention himself in his white dinner jacket and ruffled blonde hair – that was to take them the few hundred yards down the canal to the Palazzo, he told her jokingly she was likely to end up marrying the Prince.

For someone who prides herself on a deeper understanding of life, Ellie thought guiltily, it only took some make-up and a few compliments to restore a sagging ego. Really, you are so easily seduced, she admonished herself, as she began to explore the beautiful Renaissance building, admiring pictures by Tintoretto and Titian, sculptures by Verrocchio and gazing upwards at the breathtaking painted ceilings and, in spite of herself, enjoying the spectacle of so many exquisitely dressed people.

You're meant to be level-headed, seeing all these people for what they are, realizing this is just another job, she sighed.

After which she promptly abandoned all attempts to keep a grip on her sense of reality and knew as she wandered around the ornate rooms, admired the loggia and coveted the view from one of the turreted windows out over the Grand Canal, that the piece she had come here to write was writing itself.

She told Prince Stefano so when he passionately embraced her as she met him in the grand salon where the reception before the ball was being held.

'It is, of course, my perfume that lends enchantment to everything,' he claimed extravagantly, seizing her wrist and inhaling, with a look of reverence on his face, the subtle blend of oils that was the hallmark of his perfume.

Ellie was laughing as he continued to hug her, to the evident enjoyment of his friends, when she felt herself being watched. Standing silently in the doorway gazing at her, Theo's expression was impossible to read.

The smile faded on her lips.

She heard nothing, saw nothing. The room went into orbit. His gaze held hers for what seemed to be at least ten minutes but it was no more than mere seconds before she saw he was not alone.

Debra – in a dramatic black dress which left nothing to even the dullest imagination (and caused Rosie to mutter bitchily that she was surprised she had bothered with the dress at all) – was clinging limpet-like to his arm.

Behind him she glimpsed Lady Montrose and Sir Findlay, and next to them a tall, slender woman whose dark beauty matched Theo's. Ellie knew at once that she was his mother. Beside her stood a much older man, silver-haired, distinguished and who hadn't changed all that much since Ellie had last seen him accusing her father of theft.

He was holding Ria Stirling's arm while talking animatedly to Max Culver immediately behind him. On Theo's left was Jed and somewhere in the recesses of her spinning brain it occurred to her that Jed seemed awfully friendly with Theo.

But for now this meeting was not how she had imagined it would be. Ellie wanted to be able to smile coolly and pass on with a mere nod. And here she was staring numbly at him, clearly in anguish. She found she couldn't move and oh my God, here he was coming over, bringing Max with him to introduce him to the Prince.

In the confusion of greetings, she found herself being warmly hugged by Lady Montrose, pecked on the cheek by Sir Findlay and gathered in a bearlike embrace by Max. Debra's eyes swept over Ellie and she smiled distantly with a languid 'how are you, so lovely to see you,' and then Theo was turning to her.

She wanted to scream, don't do this, take me away, I can't breathe. But instead she found Jed was firmly and loyally gripping her elbow, refusing to leave her and equally refusing to let her run away.

'How are you, Eleanor?' Theo asked quietly, taking her hand briefly.

Just for a second as Eleanor felt the warm clasp of his hand, she didn't blame Debra for fighting to keep her hold on him. If she had someone – him – she knew she would do the same.

With her nerves beginning to restore themselves to something approximating normality, she managed to return his greeting with a polite smile.

'My mother was anxious to meet you,' he offered when Ellie clearly had nothing to say. 'If you have time . . .'

He got no further. Ellie's control began to dissolve. How dare he try to introduce his family, the family who took away her home, as though they had done nothing to her? Was he completely dead to all sense of human decency?

'I'm afraid I must disappoint your mother,' she said icily and then very deliberately added, 'You must excuse me, I have to join the people I came with – my friends.' And with that she turned on her heel and walked away through the crowd, not caring that they were all exchanging startled looks.

'Darling, whatever did you find interesting in her? She is positively rude.'

Debra's amused voice fell on deaf ears.

'You shouldn't listen to gossip, my dear, especially when they get my views out of context,' Theo remarked.

'But you never give your views,' objected Debra, pouting her lips.

'Nonsense,' he said levelly. 'You just don't listen.'

Debra pursed her lips, opened her mouth, thought better of what she had planned to say and gazed around the room. Eleanor Carter had disappeared and with a courteous smile Theo had moved them towards their table.

Prince Stefano was charming Sarah Montrose, the others had departed for the dance floor and Max Culver was laughing at Sir Findlay's attempts to slide away unnoticed.

Having failed to get Theo to dance, Debra was becoming increasingly irritated with his mood. That damned girl would be here. A few months before she had felt Eleanor Carter was a threat. Weeks, months, without a mention of her name had restored her confidence in keeping Theo's attention; that, and the fact that while he never confirmed the rumours that they would marry, he hadn't denied them either.

It occurred to Debra that she might have played her cards badly. Perhaps it would have been wiser to have turned a blind eye, let him get it out of his system at the time.

No-one knew him better. Challenge him with what he couldn't have and he stalked it till he got it. And then threw it away.

Increasingly she was having to rely on the power of a

sexually fertile imagination to keep him at her side. If only the studio would send the car later. God, how she hated those grey early mornings and that bloody make-up girl's tactful silence when she was doing her eyes.

Theo, amused by her silence, glanced at her and spoke softly.

'On this occasion you are absolutely right. I have never given my view of Eleanor Carter to anyone – except Eleanor Carter.'

Debra stiffened. 'And what was that?' she said lightly.

Theo laughed. 'Nothing that would interest you. Or her,' he added reflectively.

'Why not? Did you try to get her interested in you? Oh, poor darling,' she laughed. 'And there she was desperate about Clive O'Connell Moore. Still is, according to Brook Wetherby.'

'He isn't here though, is he?' observed Theo.

'Not sure, but Brook said, she's now virtually living at Westminster with him. Can't say I blame her. He really is the most exciting man – so talented. I gather she met him when she went to interview him. Marvellous ploy for a girl like that to get to meet influential men.'

Getting no response, Theo still sitting gazing lazily ahead, Debra pressed on.

'You'd think they would have more dignity, wouldn't you? It's so obvious and I can never understand why men fall for it. Even you did for a bit, go on, admit it. You thought she was interested in you.'

Her tone was teasing, but her eyes were watchful.

'Oh, I didn't misunderstand her motives,' said Theo deliberately. 'Eleanor Carter was very interested in me – but not the way you think.'

'And now . . . ?' Debra held her breath, but anyone passing their table would never have known.

'Now? My darling, you said so yourself. Now she is with Clive O'Connell Moore – and I am with you,' with which he smiled and held out his hand to lead her to the dance floor.

Debra, smiling brilliantly up at him as they circled the floor, was quite sure he was lying.

For the entire evening Ellie avoided the Stirlings. She glimpsed Theo dancing with a woman who she knew had to be the much talked about young Baroness, Gisella, once so heavily linked with him. She coldly noted that they seemed to be enjoying each other's company rather too much.

Later while dancing with Prince Stefano who, having satisfied himself that his employees were doing their duty, was wasting no opportunity to flirt with every pretty woman in the room, she came within arm's reach of Theo as he listened attentively to something Debra was whispering in his ear as they circled the crowded floor. Ellie thought Debra pathetic and marvelled that Theo could be so attracted to someone so desperate to get him.

Congratulating herself that the danger of running into him was nearly over, she only just managed to beat a hasty retreat as she rounded a corner, escaping the clutches of an over-amorous French Comte, and nearly collided with Theo, grim-faced and deep in a private talk with his mother who – to Ellie's surprise – was looking agitated.

Finally exhausted with trying to pretend she didn't care who he was with, that she never wanted to lay eyes on him again, she found a temporary refuge in the room that had been set aside for Rosie and Piers to work from. Closing the door behind her, she thankfully closed her eyes and leaned her head against the cool marble wall, trying to ease the ache in her head.

At around midnight, she cautiously opened the door and emerged in time to hear the Prince make a charming and amusing speech. He thanked everyone for coming, assuring them that this evening had saved goodness knows how many trees, but his dear friend Sarah Montrose would undoubtedly have an accurate figure if they wanted one.

Then the orchestra began to play a waltz, 'Memory', the signal that the ball was coming to a close. Ellie — escaping both the Prince, who had had far too good a time, and the renewed attentions of the French Comte, who swore she would have a much better one if they left quietly without any more ado and went back to his apartment — had never felt so miserable or alone.

Sighing, she turned to go in search of Rosie and Jed and was totally unprepared for the shock of walking blindly straight into the arms of Theo, who guided her silently but firmly back to the dance floor.

The impact of finding herself being held by him after four months of silence and longing and wanting only to be where she now was, brought a sob to Ellie's throat.

'Don't, Eleanor, it's all right.' His voice was husky, troubled. 'I understand.'

She leaned her head against his shoulder and felt him pull her close to him, cradling her hand against his chest, his arm holding her tightly around her waist. She no longer cared whether he understood or not. Just for this moment, she yearned for the world to go away.

He didn't try to speak. She was aware that his hand was caressing her back as they danced very slowly. As the music died he gazed down into her face and it took every ounce of her self control not to tell him right there in the middle of the room that she loved him.

'Daa-rling, there you are.' A voice cut across them and instinctively Ellie moved behind Theo as Debra, eyes flashing, pushed her way through the throng of people surrounding them with Jed bringing up the rear.

Jed had time only to give Ellie a very broad wink, before Debra was saying: 'Jed was a very persistent and naughty boy and dragged me off to dance – I told him you would be looking everywhere for me.'

Theo, who still held Ellie's hand behind his back, gave it a gentle squeeze as he released it, saying drily, 'Far be it from me to deprive Jed of your company, Debra – I see you've brought Max and Stefano to find me as well – what a search party.'

He had placed himself between Ellie and the others and the screen provided by his broad shoulders had given her time to take a deep breath and look reasonably self possessed.

'I think Jed and I must find the others,' Ellie interjected, attempting a strained smile, not wanting to say one more word or spend another minute in the company of the woman who had more claim on Theo than she ever would.

Ellie's plans for a quick exit were demolished. The Prince, after a triumphantly successful ball, was in no mood to let festivities end there.

'We will go to Florians,' he announced, sweeping an arm around Ellie and the other round Jed. 'And we will have no – how you say – party poopers.'

Ellie looked helplessly at Jed, who just shrugged.

The ride back on Stefano's launch towards the landing stage at St Mark's Square was a nightmare for Ellie. Debra gave a whole new dimension to the phrase 'glueing oneself to another', and Jed, apparently intent on straightening his cuffs, asked Ellie and a giggling Rosie, if Theo decided to hurl himself into the murky waters of the lagoon, would Debra plunge in regardless of the damage it would do to her hairstyle?

'You know, my flower,' he remarked thoughtfully, 'despite all those press reports and indeed my own more modest conversations with him, I'm not convinced he's that taken with the mega star.'

'You could fool me,' retorted Ellie, taking a swift look across the deck to where Theo was standing close to

Debra, shoulders propped under the edge of the cabin. Hands thrust deep into his pockets, he was smiling indulgently at the outpourings of the Prince, who had decided that Piers had not photographed him at the ball in the way that best captured his personality.

'I thinka we shoulda start again, yes?' He gesticulated wildly. 'I stand 'ere, very proud, yes?' and to the hilarious laughter of his guests he struck a pose that would not have shamed an old-time matinee idol.

Ellie couldn't help laughing and instinctively looked at Theo to see if he was enjoying the joke, to find he was already watching her.

'Oh dear, oh dear,' giggled Jed as he caught the exchange. 'Carlysle will have your guts for earrings.'

The boat pulled smoothly into a space reserved for the Prince. The laughing, noisy crowd disembarked, led by Rosie, Piers and Stefano who set off across the nearly deserted square to the world-famous coffee shop that was, even at this late hour, still full of appreciative customers.

How it happened Ellie wasn't sure, but suddenly she found that Jed had swooped the whole party ahead of her including Max Culver and Debra, pouring outrageous compliments into the actress's baubled ears as they went.

The Prince, having noticed Theo walking thoughtfully alongside Ellie, simply smiled to himself, and turned his attentions to Jed. From the moment he had laid eyes on the columnist at Sarah Montrose's, the Prince had decided he was the face to promote his new range of men's toiletries – which was sufficient excuse to be found monopolizing such an enchanting young man.

'That's right,' said Theo's amused voice as he saw enlightenment dawn on Ellie's face. 'I think you'll find he would much prefer Jed's company to yours.'

'Jed is not promiscuous,' snapped Ellie.

'I never said he was, just that Stefano prefers Jed's company – as I prefer yours.'

Ellie could see the high-spirited group disappearing into Florians as she and Theo in unspoken agreement made their way slowly across the Piazza, past the silent, darkened Doge's Palace, and turned left on to the nearly deserted long promenade that by day is filled with souvenir stalls and pavement cafés, and by night with lovers strolling in the moonlight.

'You have an odd way of showing it,' she replied carefully as they left the square behind and joined the Riva degli Schiavoni walking towards the Danieli.

Across the still water of the Canale di San Marco, the wavering reflection of the monastic church of San Giorgio Maggiore on the tiny island of the same name was eerily visible and Ellie wondered how it was that she was in the most romantic city in the world with a devastatingly handsome man and she was actually bickering with him.

'How's Clive?' he asked abruptly.

'Clive is fine.'

'Not with you though?'

'No. I'm working and so is he. This is not a social occasion. And I don't want to talk about Clive.'

'Neither do I, as it happens.'

As they mounted the shallow steps rising over one of the tiny bridges spanning the narrow waterway, he slipped a hand under her elbow. She moved away as soon as they had reached the other side.

'I'm sorry you didn't want to meet my mother,' he said. He sounded regretful rather than censuring.

Ellie's temper got the better of her nerves and she rounded on him. 'What the hell do you think I was going to say to her? "Oh, how nice to meet you after all these years, yes thank you we all survived in spite of your husband's attempts to destroy us?"'

Theo grimaced ruefully in a way that made Ellie's heart turn over.

'I'm sorry, you're quite right. I just thought – hoped –

'seeing you again, that maybe you had changed . . .'

'Changed?' she gasped. 'Why should I change, and change what? Why don't you do a bit of changing. Now there's a novel idea,' she went on sarcastically. 'How about you doing something for someone else for a change? I suppose you're still holding out for Linton's Field, I assume you're still going ahead with that bloody building or whatever it is you're planning.'

His face had taken on a stony look. They were standing on the bridge just in front of the Danieli but as Ellie finished speaking he wheeled round, gripped her by the shoulders and shook her.

'I have never in my life wanted to shake sense into someone as much as I want to do it to you,' he said through gritted teeth. 'I suppose your campaign to vilify me is as strong as ever . . . ?'

'You bet it is.' Ellie winced as his fingers dug into her flesh.

'And if I buy the land and go ahead with my . . . plans, you intend to run a damaging profile on me?'

'You'd better believe it,' she drawled insolently.

'And you would prefer to do all that rather than put your trust in me and back off?'

Briefly she wondered if he wasn't just a little deranged making such an unreasonable demand but her feelings were too far gone to exercise even the smallest modicum of restraint.

'You can bet I would.' She practically spat the words out. 'I'm not Caroline Montgomery, or Matt Harksey or my father. I don't need you like Roger Nelson, or need to be damaged like Serena. I'm me, Ellie Carter. Independent of and totally unafraid of the Stirling family . . .'

'. . . We will leave Serena out of this, if you please. You don't know what you're saying, you . . .'

'. . . Don't I?' she yelled back. '*She* had a nervous breakdown. What did you do to Roger Nelson . . . ?'

'. . . *Nervous breakdown?* Are you quite mad? Announces she's pregnant and then a week after we're married says she isn't? Who the hell is likely to have the breakdown? And as for Nelson, what the fuck do you suppose I'm running . . . a charity for burnt out cases . . . for Christ's sake . . .'

She wasn't even listening. Her fury, the months of pent-up rage that had engulfed her at the memory of their night in his library, came pouring out.

'. . . And just because there was a momentary lapse of common sense — not that hard when someone is out to deceive you on a grand scale — don't delude yourself that it was anything more than a mistake.'

Her shaking voice seemed to calm him. He released his grip on her shoulders, ran a distracted hand through his hair and said harshly, 'Well, I'm glad of that at least. Eleanor, I'm sorry. I didn't mean to hurt you . . . not now or at any time.'

'You haven't,' she flashed back at him. 'You've hurt my family, not me personally. Look, I don't want to do what I'm doing. It's something you couldn't possibly understand, you're so wealthy. But I can't see Oliver hurt — or my father. Not again.'

'Oliver would be just as hurt if Oldburns bought that land,' came Theo's sharp reply. 'But you're not writing a profile on him, or pinpointing him so sharply in your campaign.'

'Possibly,' she conceded. 'But Oldburns' bid is lower than yours and with a bit of luck, Oliver might be able to scrape enough together to match it.'

'I doubt it,' he said. 'If he can't match it now, he never will. Oldburns want it for low-level starter homes and they have enough assets to sell off to raise the capital to underwrite any initial losses they might make on a housing development. What else has Oliver got besides Delcourt?'

Ellie turned away, biting her lip. She knew he had a point, but at least with Oldburns they had a chance of preventing a redevelopment scheme. Local opinion was running quite high and as Joe McPhee had shrewdly pointed out, Basil Oldburn, who was now nearing retiring age and with an eye to living a more relaxed life at his luxury home on the edge of Willetts Green, would be easier to see off.

He would not want his retirement disturbed by local resentment, especially at the golf, Rotary and yachting clubs of which he was a prominent member.

Ellie did not, however, see why she should tell Theo that or that Joe had warned them that Theo's personal celebrity was so high he was extremely likely to gain support for any plans he might have – and he had the finances to make sure he did.

She remembered Joe telling them at the start of the campaign that there were enough go-ahead young people who would willingly swap sides if Theo offered employment locally as an inducement to halting their opposition to his plans.

Ellie tried one last time to appeal to him, impulsively putting her hand on his arm.

'Theo, just listen to me. Oliver and I have always had to work for what we wanted. No bottomless well of money such as you have ever existed for us. We lost our home and we had to fight life with the only weapons we had. Ourselves. Delcourt is all Oliver has, all I've ever wanted for him. Oh, for God's sake, Theo, for the last time, will you just back off?'

She heard him swear softly under his breath and before she knew what was happening, he had pulled her into his arms, his mouth came crushing down on hers. For a brief second she was too stunned to move – and to be truthful she didn't want to.

'Why did you do that?' she said, breathless and visibly

shaken as he released her, wondering for one ecstatic second if he was going to agree. But his next words turned her to stone.

'I kissed you, Eleanor,' he said, 'because after what I'm going to tell you, I think I can predict the end of any relationship we might have had. Oliver will know today that I signed the papers two days ago. I own Linton's Field.'

She stepped back. The sound of laughing voices floated across the silent night air. She could hear Jed, Debra, Prince Stefano coming to find them. She felt the colour drain from her face.

She gazed at Theo, who looked shattered.

'You know, I've felt a lot of things about you over the past few months,' she said in a surprisingly steady voice. 'I never thought I would ever, *ever* have to add hate, but it's just gone right to the top of my list – just above "contempt".'

Turning, she walked away, head held high, back along the quayside, oblivious to the furious gaze of Debra, the puzzled expression on Max's face. She didn't notice the rapid exchange between the Prince and Jed, she just kept on walking and when she heard Jed's footsteps running after her and felt his hand on her arm, she just shook it off.

'Not now, leave me. Just leave me,' she whispered. And disappeared into the darkness of the side street to the safety and sanctuary of her hotel.

Chapter Thirty

The proofs of the profile on Theo stared back at Ellie from Jerome's desk. Alistair Bell was distinctly nervous.

So too was Jerome, trying not to show it, as he dragged on the third cigarette he had lit since the meeting began. The second was lying in the ashtray, a curl of smoke soaring upwards.

'Ellie,' said Alistair earnestly as Jerome glanced anxiously from one to the other, and hastily extinguished the cigarette he had just noticed in his ashtray. 'There is enough in this piece for it to be seen as libellous, and even if we could make the case stand up it is really very dodgy. He could certainly make a case for it to be hugely damaging and he has the funds to go into court. Even if the jury were convinced by what you said, it sounds just about as prejudiced as you can get. And a jury would probably find for him.'

Ellie looked impatiently at him. 'He knows my sources, he hasn't denied them. He can't. He knows I'll run this piece. He hasn't even tried an injunction because he knows it's pointless.'

Alistair tried another tack. The article must have been painful for her to write, it implicated her father and by association her brother and herself. Ellie was white and as immoveable as a mountain.

At Jerome's insistence she had agreed to have 'a personal account' as a strapline, but Alistair was aware that did not exonerate the magazine from any action Theo Stirling might take.

'Ellie, we've had one waltz around the law courts this

year. If he sues he will win. There's no doubt about that at all. Or at the very least we will have to offer him a fortune to stay out of court. I must, as your lawyer and,' he paused and glanced at Jerome who was as frightened by it all as he was fascinated, 'and as your very good friend, recommend that you think very carefully about what this will do to you.'

Ellie looked up at him and her eyes were dead.

'It won't do anything to me. Anything that he could do to me happened a long time ago.'

The two men exchanged startled glances. Alistair was even more nervous.

'Ellie, if this is a personal thing, I beg you, think. Do you want to end up looking like a vengeful woman? Remember how you loathed Kathryn Renshaw.'

Theo's voice came back to her. 'A lot of people will suffer if you do it.'

Too right, she thought bitterly. And all because of him.

'That's different,' she said quietly. 'Kathryn Renshaw was getting back at her husband. Believe me, Alistair, I am prepared to take anything he can sling at me. But after this article is published, unlike Kathryn Renshaw, I can get on with my life. He is meaningless to me.'

The atmosphere was still tense. Ellie noticed that Jerome had made no decisions at all, but had left it all to her. Of course he had. Where Roland would have argued fiercely for a brilliant exposé to be published without further ado, totally backing his writer, Jerome was keeping his head below the parapet and his options wide open.

The silence was broken as Alistair with one brisk movement gathered up the proofs and started to shuffle them together.

'Will this guy Harksey back you?'

'Yes.'

'Any of the others?'

'No. I don't know their names,' she confessed.

Alistair rolled his eyes to heaven.

'What about ... what about your father?'

Ellie smiled wearily. 'No, absolutely not. But that won't be necessary. My brother is prepared to back me to the hilt.'

Resigned to an afternoon of scrutinizing every word and even possibly seeking counsel's advice, Alistair rose to leave. Ellie went with him to the door. As he disappeared into Sonya's office, he put an arm around her shoulders.

'I think you might find life a little difficult getting interviews for a while, once this appears. He's respected in the City and they're a fairly clannish bunch. Anyway,' he said, squeezing her arm. 'Don't forget we're lunching later, if, of course, I have any appetite left.'

That afternoon Alistair and then Jerome okayed the final proofs, Ellie checked the copy once more and resolutely scribbled her initials on the pages so that the subs would know she had seen and approved the text and the captions to the pictures before despatching it on its first stage via the colour repro house to the printers. The courier was already waiting in Angus's office.

Angus had been fully expecting to run Ellie's interview with the Prince, but at the last minute Jerome had ordered him to pull it and replace it with this astonishing profile on Theo Stirling.

The printers were waiting for it; everything else for that issue had been sent down the day before. They were used to Ellie cutting it fine getting the final copy to them, but by anyone's standards this was pushing it.

Since the night in the Europa a week before, when she had sat on her tiny balcony nearly all night, too shocked and distressed to sleep, Ellie had been working on automatic. She had lost. Oliver had lost. She had phoned him the next morning, to discover he had been trying to contact her. Theo and Conrad Linton had done a deal. Planning permission had been granted.

'It took us all by surprise,' Oliver admitted. 'All we can do now is keep opposing anything he tries to do, but as far as we can judge, it's a delaying tactic rather than a solution. Are you there, Ellie?'

She was sitting on the edge of her bed, the white voile curtains of her room billowing in the breeze from the open windows leading to the balcony, where a breakfast tray lay untouched on the table.

'Yes,' she said dully. 'I'm here. What are you going to do?'

She heard Oliver take a deep breath.

'I'm not sure. See the solicitors, check if there is anything we can do. I'm not sure I've got the stomach to go on fighting, have you?'

'No,' she said. 'No, I haven't,' and when she put down the phone she wandered out on to the tiny terrace, leaned her hands on the railing and gazed unseeingly out across the canal and whispered to herself, 'Or the heart.'

Oliver didn't need to remind her that she had assured them that she would never run that feature. He knew that now she had to.

His livelihood was now severely threatened. It was a last desperate bid to stop Theo violating the idyllic setting with unsightly buildings.

Ellie arrived back in England on the next available flight, leaving Jed and Rosie to come back a day later, Rosie because she wanted to take advantage of a Sunday in Venice with Piers and Jed because . . . because, he said, not quite looking Ellie in the eye, Stefano could turn out to be a good contact.

Ellie's responses were automatic.

'Of course,' she said and left. It was only when she was on the plane that she wondered briefly if Ashley was going to find out about the Prince.

Clive was trickier.

After several attempts at getting her attention as they ate dinner in his apartment later that evening, he finally removed her plate, took her hand and led her to the sofa where he waited silently for her to speak.

'I think,' he said carefully, 'I think this has gone on long enough. Don't you? Do you think you could just tell me . . . Ellie, my dear girl, what *is* it?'

Tears were rolling down her cheeks. He gathered her into his arms, rocking her as though she were a child, and waited for the sobs to subside.

'Now,' he said, handing her a fistful of tissues, 'let's have a talk that I think we have both been trying to avoid, is that not so, my precious?'

Switching off the telephone, he moved away from her to the far end of the cluttered sofa, where he failed to see one of Sean's spiked running shoes.

'Jesus,' he howled, leaping up. Ellie started to laugh and thought how endearing and normal and sweet he was. And she just hoped she wouldn't lose him forever, because she knew now it was hopeless to pretend the weight she had been carrying around for months would not make a difference to them.

Taking a deep breath, she began and Clive never took his eyes from her face. It was only when she had finished that he realized he was sitting with an empty glass so he leaned over to reach for the Bollinger, making a big fuss about getting another glass, so that she wouldn't see his eyes had filled with tears.

Chapter Thirty-one

For the first time ever she had fallen out with Jed, who had urged her to reconsider, convinced that Theo was straight in spite of what he had done.

'Let me talk to him?' he urged. 'Let me try and sort all this out. Honestly, Ellie, I'm sure there must be a way out of this.'

Ellie was too angry, in too much pain to listen to him.

'Why should he listen to you?' she demanded. 'He doesn't listen to anyone. He wouldn't listen to me. I think you've done what everyone else has done, fallen for the charm. Probably fallen for him. I wouldn't put anything past him.'

Jed had just swung on his heel and slammed his office door.

Paul, on the other hand, had been delighted she was doing it, which only served to depress her further.

Now Ellie glanced rapidly through the final proofs of the feature, and then ran with the damaging spread down the corridor as though a moment's delay might weaken her resolve and handed them to Angus, the chief sub, who had a motorcycle messenger standing by to rush it to the printers.

'We'll just do it,' he told her, smiling without pausing as he swiftly marked the corrections on to the copy on his screen. 'Haven't lost an issue yet.'

As he spoke he pushed the finalized disk into a folder, sealed it and gave it to the courier saying cheerfully that if the traffic was reasonable he should get it to the colour house and the printers in Milton Keynes would have a set of film before eight o'clock. The presses were due to roll at three the next morning for the issue which would appear on the bookstands ten days later.

Ellie watched transfixed as the final nail in her relationship with Theo Stirling went in, and with a heavy heart went back to her own office, collected her bag and jacket and treated herself to a taxi home to Fulham. Oliver had been in London consulting his solicitors, and was due to meet her there.

A long weekend at Delcourt supporting each other's spirits was what she sorely needed. A heavy dose of Miles and Chloe to take her mind off the fact that she had never before felt that her life was so pointless or aimless.

One swift look at her face was all it took for Jerome to agree that he would only contact her if it was really urgent, and for the first time that she could recall he wished her luck with the filming of her specials with Letty.

On the way home Ellie thought again about ringing Clive. She wanted to talk to him so much, she missed him desperately. But she also knew she had to be fair to him. If only he had been angry, shouted at her, just called her a few names, she would have felt better. But he had said nothing, merely asked her to let him think for a while. Then she had quietly let herself out of the flat, leaving him standing by the window still holding Sean's shoe, absently turning it over and over in his strong, gentle hands.

Oliver had arrived in Fulham shortly before her, letting himself in with the key Ellie had given him, and didn't look exactly ecstatic as he handed her a drink.

'Mark says there is very little we can do. Theo has every right to do what he likes with the land. Local pressure and your feature is all we have left.'

'Then I think,' Ellie said, draining her glass, 'that you and I should get going and maximize what we can.

C'mon, Oliver, we've been in worse spots than this,' she comforted him.

'You're right. Grab your bag and . . . oh hell, you've got a visitor,' he finished as the doorbell pealed.

Frowning, Ellie opened the door, half hoping but half knowing it wouldn't be Clive.

The elegant figure of Ria Stirling standing on her doorstep at six o'clock in the evening was not what Ellie had expected at all.

'May I come in, Eleanor?' she asked.

Ellie, who was too startled to speak, just nodded and stepped back for the older woman to enter.

'Oliver,' Ellie stammered to her brother who had come forward to meet his sister's visitor, 'this is Ria Stirling, Theo's mother.'

The look of amazement that crossed his face was rapidly replaced by one of cold courtesy.

'I don't blame you,' said Mrs Stirling, who had not missed the outraged look that passed between brother and sister. 'In your place, I'm sure I would do the same. May I sit down? I won't keep you long, but I think this meeting . . . discussion, whatever you want to call it, is overdue.'

Slowly beginning to emerge from the shock of their unexpected visitor, Oliver offered her a seat and a drink while Ellie took her coat.

'This is charming, Eleanor,' she said, glancing round. 'And that I do recognize. It's one of your father's, isn't it?' She indicated the watercolour of the garden at Delcourt as it had once been, hanging above the fireplace.

Ellie nodded. 'Mrs Stirling, you must forgive me, I don't wish to sound rude, but will you tell me why you're here? Surely you cannot believe that any intervention from you will stop Oliver and I from fighting your son's plans to redevelop the land next to Delcourt? You, I mean *you*, of all people.'

Ria looked so gravely back at her that Ellie almost laughed and said 'You look just like Theo,' but restrained herself as Oliver handed their visitor a large gin and tonic.

'No, I wouldn't do that. I wanted to see you both. Your wife, Jill, isn't it?' she said to Oliver, accepting the drink, 'told me I would find you here, which is a relief. It will save me the pain of having to repeat all of this.'

'Repeat what, Mrs Stirling?' asked Oliver, as bewildered as his sister.

'Do you think you could call me Ria, you see I feel I know you both so well.'

She didn't wait for a reply and simply continued: 'Theo has for far too long taken the blame — and indeed the pain — for events that were not of his making. I saw you in Venice, Eleanor, and for the first time I realized that it was wickedly unfair to allow the next generation to carry the burdens of their parents' mistakes.'

Ellie and Oliver looked at each other, already bristling at what seemed to be the prelude to another round of accusations against their father.

'No, please, it isn't what you think. I'm going to tell you the whole story — and I have your father's permission. Reluctant permission.' She smiled faintly, reading their disbelieving expressions very accurately.

'John has always shied away from confrontation — I think you know that,' she continued. 'But then so did I. Until this week. Such a mistake to make,' and she smiled so sadly, Ellie found she wasn't regarding her with such hostility, just curiosity.

'Mrs Stirling . . . Ria . . . just tell me what it is you want us to know?'

'I want you to know what you've always known. Your father stole some plans that could have ruined Robert . . .'

It was as far as she got. Brother and sister were on their feet, greeting this news with total, incredulous silence.

Finally in a strangled voice, Oliver said, 'Mrs Stirling, I think you should leave. This is just disgusting . . . to come here . . . to accuse him . . . I just can't believe it.'

Ria's distress was evident. She looked at them and in a voice that was barely audible said: 'You must believe me, because there is so much more to it . . . to understand why he did it.'

They waited in silence as Ria, struggling to find the words, continued. Ellie glanced nervously at Oliver. He was looking at Ria with an odd expression.

'I think we should listen to Ria, Ellie,' he said, motioning his sister to sit down. 'We're listening, Ria, go on.'

She gave him a grateful look and told them the whole story.

'When I came to live in Willetts Green all those years ago, I was there under protest. I hardly saw my husband, he was such a workaholic, and when he wasn't working it seemed to me he spent more time helping out other people who were down on their luck than keeping me company. No, not your father,' she said quickly. 'Robert was attracted to John's talent and had asked him to paint my portrait long before he knew how desperate his financial situation was.

'It was only later that he suggested he re-financed him so that with some of his money worries off his shoulders he would be able to concentrate on what he does best – paint. I was livid. It seemed to me that having my portrait painted was to keep me amused and entertained while my husband worked longer and longer hours. But I liked John – you couldn't help it. He's charming, such good company. We used to talk a lot during the sittings. He told me that Alison wouldn't marry him because financially he was in such a mess . . .'

'But that isn't true,' Ellie protested. 'Dad can't have believed that. It's a family joke he was waiting for Alison to propose . . . he'd never have got round to it himself.'

'I know,' Ria replied. 'But I didn't know it then. Well, and this is the hard part . . .'

She twisted her glass in her hands and looked from one to the other with a look that was hard to interpret. Almost pleading for understanding, thought Ellie.

'What's so hard about it?' asked Oliver gently.

'Well, the hard part is this. Your father and I had a brief, thoughtless, affair.'

Ellie thought a gun had gone off behind her head. Ria Stirling and her father. Impossible. But even as her brain reeled she knew Ria was telling the truth. Her hand flew to her mouth. Oliver, for some reason, didn't look all that surprised.

'Affair?' Ellie finally croaked. 'What do you mean, affair?'

'What it usually means,' said Ria, almost sheepishly. 'It was stupid. Born out of loneliness, a great deal of self pity on both sides and the very selfish actions of two people who didn't know when they were well off.'

'Were you . . . in . . . love?' Ellie could hardly get the words out. Her father, and Theo's mother. The world was falling apart. She wasn't shocked at the morality of it, just the fact that it had never occurred to her as even a remote possibility.

As if reading her mind Ria said, 'You know under any other circumstances, your father and I would have been mildly attracted to each other as some people are, and that would have been it. Far too aware of what we had to lose to risk a meaningless fling. However, the circumstances were not usual. We both felt no-one appreciated us, we were rather spoilt really. So before we came to our senses we, um, well, we were in the middle of an affair.'

Ellie couldn't take her eyes off her.

Ria was looking anxious.

'Oh, believe me, for a very short while we were – I suppose – in lust. But love? No, it was all make believe. We talked for a while about being together, but it was impossible. John had no money to support me and well, I was used to a degree of comfort. I remember it was all rather desperate stuff. We knew without financial help there was no future.

'I was going back to the States with my daughters who had finished the school year, and I wanted to see Theo, who had finished Harvard and was fighting off my husband trying to drag him into the family business.

'John and I agreed to meet one last time – at a restaurant en route to the airport. Robert had asked me to take the plans with me to deliver them personally to the London office – it's often done when something is that sensitive. But I wanted to see John before I left. I didn't have time for both. I thought it would be a simple matter to get him to deliver them for me. Robert would never have known.'

For a moment she stopped and gazing at their intent faces said:

'I'm not very proud of any of this, or what we did. You must believe that.'

Oliver looked down at the carpet and then straight at her.

'It is immaterial whether we believe that or not. Just at this moment Ellie and I want the truth, that's all. Don't we, El?'

Ellie nodded.

'Well, John and I met, all very melodramatic, but we parted, he to take the train to London, me to take a plane to New York. About two weeks later I got this panic-stricken phone call from John. Oh, first of all he lied, then he blurted out the truth.'

Ellie suddenly couldn't conjure up a picture of her father's face. The smiling, charming, often brattish John

Carter was not recognizable in this portrait being painted by Ria Stirling. Or was he?

It was growing dark; Ellie switched on the lamps and even though it was April it was chilly enough for a fire. Ria watched her as she moved around the room.

'You must believe me, Eleanor, please. You can speak to your father . . .'

'No,' Ellie said sharply. 'No. You tell me what happened.'

'Well, John said he couldn't just let me go, not like that. He saw a way of making money. He thought Robert had so much it wouldn't matter if he lost the odd contract. So he took the plans to London, but before he delivered them, he went to a photocopier's and had them copied. It was quite a big document, so he went off for a walk. He didn't want the guy in the shop to become too familiar with how he looked.

'Then he took the train to London and delivered the original to Stirling House as I had asked and took the copy home. After that he contacted Basil Oldburn, whom he had met when he was painting his daughters, and they had a conversation that left John in no doubt that Oldburn would be prepared to pay a lot for the plans.'

'And Basil Oldburn split on Dad,' interjected Oliver.

Ria gave a flat laugh. 'Not on your life. Basil would have carved Robert up at every opportunity. I think he offered John about twenty-five grand for them. A fortune at that time. The plans were exchanged, but before Basil could deliver the cheque – heavily disguised as a huge fee for a special painting commission – all hell broke loose.'

Oliver refilled Ria's glass, Ellie shook her head in bewilderment.

'But how was Dad linked to any of this? Who gave him away?'

'The photocopier's. They ran off the first few pages and apparently they were damaged – or didn't print very well.

The guy in the shop put them on one side and after John had left, some industrious assistant noticed them and the man who did them couldn't remember whether he had replaced them. So they sent them to Robert, assuming he knew all about the copy, with a covering note explaining. Robert was appalled. Immediately he ordered an enquiry. It was a simple matter then to trace the cheque back to your father.'

For the first time Ellie allowed herself a wry grin. Poor Pa, poor stupid, weak, feckless Pa. Couldn't conduct a bus let alone an affair or a theft.

'So when Robert discovered the source, he naturally confronted John and there was, I gather, a terrible scene.'

Ellie didn't even have to look at Oliver. The raised voices, the murderous rage of Robert Stirling. Dad's ashen face. The dreadful silence after Robert had gone. Aunt Belle rigid with anger. Terrible scene? How inadequate.

Aunt Belle. No wonder. Oh God, Aunt Belle.

'Then John phoned me.' Ellie dragged herself back to the present as Ria began to make sense of the last fifteen years. 'I was traumatized. Everything had got desperately out of control. John insisted he had done it for me, so that we could be together. I was horrified. Two weeks back in New York, I was beginning to see what a mistake the affair had been, how much better off I was with Robert. Believe me, please believe me, I never thought John would do such a thing.'

'Neither did we,' said Oliver drily. 'What happened then?'

Ria reeled off a list of events that even Ellie and Oliver realized must have seemed insurmountable at the time: Oldburns whipping a lucrative deal from under Robert's nose with the kind of muscle that could only have come from inside information; Oldburns backing out of the picture; John helpless to make Oldburns honour their agreement without admitting his role in their company coup; Ria begging John not to implicate her, desperate to save her marriage; John facing a future without Alison, who would leave him.

Something, someone had to call a halt to it all. Ria was only too aware that while her reputation remained intact, John Carter's flaky character could not be relied on. So they struck a bargain. In return for his silence, Ria would make sure that Robert dropped all charges against him.

But how to do it was harder to organize. Enter Theo.

Ellie looked quickly at Oliver, who was clearly having his own problem coming to terms with this almost fantastic story.

'So what did Theo do?' asked Ellie.

'He got the first plane over to England, found Robert intent on having John put behind bars and set about convincing him that the scandal would be very damaging to the firm and the family. Oldburns would make sure a theft looked like company incompetence.

'Remember, John was just as much to blame as me. And he was very anxious that Alison should never find out. So Theo took what he considered to be the safest course of action. Your father couldn't sell Delcourt because it was in such a dreadful state of repair – Theo says, he wouldn't have slammed a door in case the lot crashed around his ears – so Theo said he would buy it from him. That way John at·least had a chance of buying a smaller, more manageable property outright, using the rest of the money to pay off his debts and start again somewhere else.

'John jumped at the chance. He had never really liked the house. It had, I believe, been your mother's and after she died he tried to sell it, but it was difficult as it needed so much doing to it.'

Aunt Belle's accusation that the house had been invaded by cowboys came back. Ellie felt as though her teenage years and all that followed were floating into place like missing pieces of a jigsaw puzzle lost after all that time. What puzzled her was how Theo had explained such a generous act to his father, Robert.

'Oh, he didn't,' said Ria. 'It has always been mine and Theo's secret – oh, and John's of course. Theo has always said it was his oddest investment. Robert has always thought John Carter left town under his own steam. And he did, but he drove a hard bargain. Er . . . by this time, I think you've both realized your father and I were united only in wishing we had never laid eyes on each other. He agreed to sell Delcourt provided he could have a cash settlement as well.'

Ellie thought she would faint with embarrassment.

'A cash settlement? What the hell was that?'

Ria eyed her with cynical amusement. 'You've been dealing with Theo and still haven't worked out where he excels? Money, my dear, or at least the investing of it.'

Ellie had no problem believing her.

'Theo refused. But I made him go back and do a deal. In the end Theo agreed to John's demands but only if Alison were the caretaker of the money and the bank. John told Alison that it was from the sale of the house and for tax reasons it should be in her name and remain so. Whether she believed him or not I don't know, but that's what happened. The cash was a lump sum investment for you two. Alison chose to have it invested in the rest of your education. The sale of the house went towards paying off John's debts.

'It was Alison who insisted that she used her own money to buy the house in Devon and take you all there. Oh, don't look so amazed, frankly at the time Theo was glad to see the back of you – and me for a while.'

For the first time Ria's voice broke. She had always known that Theo had loved her but his willingness to help sprang solely from a desire to protect his father.

'Don't forget as a result of Oldburns getting those

plans, Robert – or rather Theo – had practically to rebuild the company from scratch.'

It was Oliver's turn to look horrified. He shook his head, trying to absorb that the man he was campaigning against had been the very man to give him the opportunity in life his own father would have denied him.

'I had half guessed there was something more to the business of stealing plans,' he said in disbelief. 'I was older than Ellie, I could put two and two together. But I could never have guessed what you have just told me.'

Well, that's it, thought Ellie, the final humiliation. She was in a job because Theo Stirling had made sure she had had a decent education and living in a flat that because of him she was able to afford.

And Alison. Thanks to Alison, John Carter had not been able to fritter the money away, as Theo, as anyone who knew him, knew he would.

If there was a dark hole, in a country so remote that it wasn't even on the map, it was unlikely that at that moment, it would have been deep enough or secret enough for her to hide away in. Mortified, she could hardly bring herself to look at Ria, who was addressing an equally stricken Oliver.

'Theo and I were so relieved, you see, that the problem appeared to be solved,' she was saying. 'It never occurred to either of us until he met Eleanor recently just how deeply affected you had both been. John always gave me the impression that you were so gypsy-like you could live anywhere.'

Ellie, who had been sitting staring silently at Ria with the memory of her defiant assertion to Theo that she was independent ricocheting around her head, asked in a quiet voice: 'Why didn't he just tell me all of this? Why bid for the land next to Oliver's?'

Ria sighed. 'That son of mine has an overdeveloped sense of loyalty. I told you. He couldn't break his word to me, he didn't want to betray your father. He couldn't ... never expected ... I mean,' she sounded confused, looking appealingly at Ellie and finished lamely, 'He never expected to meet with such opposition once you inadvertently found out. That was my fault as well.

'What worried me was that I could see history repeating itself. I found out about the piece of land from a chance conversation with Sally. You know, Sally Montrose, his godmother? A dear woman, but really, there are moments when I think it might have been better if I had never discovered anything at all about Linton's Field. Sally knew about it from someone on the planning committee. You know what these environmentalists are. Ears everywhere.

'I was very concerned that once again you might have to sell Delcourt so I told Theo. To be honest, he thought I was overreacting and was inclined to let things shape themselves, but I couldn't let the matter rest. Okay, conscience if you like. So Theo suggested putting a private bid in for the land; that way we could make sure nothing was ever built on it – eventually planning to offer it to Oliver for sale when your resources had improved. And it must be said, the idea of scoring points over Basil Oldburn appealed to him.'

'But why not just say so?' Ellie was fighting off a feeling that, like Alice, she had been dragged into a wonderland where the rules of normal living had been abandoned and the new ones made no sense at all.

'Because after all that had happened, you might with good reason have wondered why the Stirling family cared what happened to you. It wouldn't have made sense. And undoubtedly you might have asked questions. At least this way, the immediate danger would have been removed and Theo would have just registered the land in a company name. You would never have found out.

'But once you did and you wouldn't back off, he didn't

know what to do. He will now. When the time comes you must buy the land from him. But I guarantee there are no plans other than to safeguard your home. Er . . . you may have noticed, he's used to getting his own way. This time he didn't and it threw him a bit. So in the end he said nothing at all.'

And that, Ellie thought with horror, was perfectly true. She had just assumed, just believed. But when had he ever answered any of her questions? Never.

Oliver had his head in his hands. Ellie thought dying was too much to ask for. They looked at each other and read each other's thoughts. Dad. Charming, entertaining, charismatic and utterly, utterly contemptible.

No wonder he had been horrified about the campaign. No surprise he didn't want the past dragged up. How typical of him to hide behind women. Barbara, their mother, then Aunt Belle, then Ria and finally Alison.

Hating him was easy. Knowing she did was hard to bear.

Jill had been so right. No man who loved his children could have left them with an appalling legacy such as the one John Carter had now unleashed on his. Thinking only of his own life being disrupted, uncaring about the quality of theirs, he could not conceive that his children might have inherited a more thoughtful, more caring nature from their mother.

'Theo tried so hard to make you accept him, Eleanor.' Ria smiled sadly. 'And I don't think he blames you for one moment, reacting as you did. I just couldn't bear to see him as unhappy as he was in Venice. I've never seen him so distraught. When you refused to meet me, I knew it was time for the older generation to become account- able for their past.'

Oliver was recovering more quickly than Ellie and in a very subdued voice he asked Ria what would happen now.

'Your father has already told Alison but she had always – like you, Oliver – thought there was more to it. She knew the house couldn't have realized that sort of cash, but she didn't want to lose the chance to solve all the problems going on. Remember she hadn't agreed to marry your father – sorry, asked him to marry her – at that time. She loves John, he's very lucky indeed.'

On the small table next to her, there was a photograph of Ellie as a child standing behind her father in the garden at Delcourt, her arms clasped round his neck, Oliver sitting wedged between his knees. Ria picked it up and gazed at it for a long while.

'Very lucky,' she repeated. 'He clearly was devoted to you both.'

Ellie and Oliver glanced at each other. The photograph had been taken by Aunt Belle. They had searched the house for their father and after much protesting he had been dragged into the garden for the snapshot.

Devoted to them? No, Ellie thought and her childhood ran through her mind. Days of playing alone with Oliver, or being carted off by Aunt Belle so that they wouldn't disturb Daddy painting.

At eight she went away to boarding school and recalled days telling her friends that her father was on an important assignment, which was why he so often missed founder's day or sports day. And even the day Ellie won the literature prize and took home a silver cup, carefully packed in her luggage to proudly show her father, she had consoled herself that he was just busy when he said vaguely, 'Lovely, darling. Tell me all about it at tea.'

Even now she was convinced it wasn't indifference to them. John Carter didn't know his children, because he had never really stopped being a child himself. Looking at Ria, so anxious now to put right what she and her father had set in motion all those years ago, Ellie felt a grudging tug of respect for her, but she wasn't ready to forgive.

'That's the wrong word, Ria,' she said, since honesty seemed to be on the agenda. 'I think he was devoted to an image. The reality was too much trouble. I don't know about Oliver, but I'm not ready yet to decide what I think about all that you've told us.

'You see, for years we lived under this shadow. No child should have to do that. No, I'm not saying it was all your fault. Dad is dreadfully at fault too. But Theo and his sisters didn't have to make sacrifices, they didn't have to leave a home they were secure in. They didn't have to live with the knowledge that the world thought – oh God, *knew* – their father was a crook.'

Ria flinched. There was nothing she could say to contradict Ellie. She looked at the angry young woman and turned pleadingly to Oliver.

'Don't think I don't realize it now. But do you think if we had known any of this, that I would have allowed it to go on? Of course not. But we didn't know. John had told the solicitors that everything had worked out for the best. Remember, unlike you, he loathed Delcourt. Going to Devon and starting the gallery was his idea of bliss. Tell me, if your own father thinks you're happy, how on earth is anyone else to know that you're not?'

The extent of their father's obsession with his own self interest was the hardest part to bear. Both Ellie and Oliver knew that their greatest enemy in life had not after all been Theo Stirling but their own father.

It was, as Ellie much later told Jill, a moment when she had to accept that much of her life had been based on a falsehood. She felt broken, used, that her life had been pure invention, not real at all.

Oliver went over to where she was sitting with her head in her hands and knelt down. Fleetingly she looked at him, gave a little shake of her head and slowly raised her eyes to his.

'I can't do it, Oliver,' she whispered. 'Don't ask me. He's hurt me . . . you . . . all of us . . . so much.'

Oliver leaned forward and placed his hand over hers. 'C'mon, El, give it a chance,' he urged. 'We've been through so much together. I want to try but I can't do it without you. Please, El.'

He waited, watching her, willing her to find the forgiveness that he knew was tangled up in the confusion, the shock, the disbelief that comes in the wake of knowing you have been lied to. It was too soon. Ellie thought of Clive having to come to terms with losing her, thought of Aunt Belle who had loyally remained quiet out of love and respect for her dead sister's children, of Jill who had known John Carter was weak and feckless and loved Oliver too much to hurt him by telling him. And Theo? Theo indeed.

It was too much to ask. Not yet. Ellie looked at Oliver's anxious face and gave him a lopsided smile. 'Give me time, Oliver, let me try and make sense of it all. Just time.'

Silently Oliver watched her. She leaned forward and pressed her cheek against his. And then she addressed herself to Ria.

'Worked out for the best for Dad,' she said bluntly. 'For you, for Theo. But not for me and Oliver. However, I can see that it took great courage to come and tell us all this.'

Oliver nodded agreement. 'But what about you, Ria?' he asked gently. 'What about Robert, does he know? Will you tell him?'

The apprehension on Ria Stirling's face and in her voice told them all they needed to know.

She said simply, 'No, he doesn't know. But I will tell him.'

'What do you think he'll say?'

Ria shrugged. 'I don't know. I know I love him very much and I hope he loves me enough to understand. Maybe even forgive.'

She started to leave. Having started out regarding her with abject hostility, Ellie now had a grudging respect for her. To risk her marriage so that others wouldn't be destroyed was an awesome step. While she was not entirely certain just how deep Ria's feelings went for her husband as opposed to the lifestyle he represented, Oliver appeared to have no such qualms.

'If Robert's got any sense,' said Oliver gruffly, 'he'll just be grateful he's got a wife who cares enough to try and put things right.'

'And a son,' Ria said, looking directly at Ellie. 'Thank you, Oliver. May I come and see Delcourt sometime? Curiously enough it doesn't hold bad memories for me, not any more. Goodbye, my dears,' and she held out a hand to each of them.

'Don't go just yet,' Ellie said. 'There are some things I need to know. Maybe you know the answers. I mean for example why do Caroline Montgomery and Matt Harksey hate Theo?'

Ria looked puzzled and sat down again.

'I know Matt does, but then I loathe him. But Caroline doesn't. She adores Theo. Why?'

Ellie was beginning to panic. 'Because he threw her out. He was going to marry her, wasn't he?'

'Marry Caroline?' she exclaimed. 'Good heavens, no. Caroline is the daughter of some of our oldest friends, she and Theo practically grew up together. Why?'

Fright made Ellie almost incoherent. 'But why did he throw her out?'

Ria was regarding Ellie in amazement.

'Throw her out? Of course he didn't. He made her go home. That's quite different. You see, in New York, Caroline got in with the wrong crowd, started doing drugs. Her parents threw her out so Theo said she could stay with him, provided she worked as his personal assistant and stayed away from cocaine. And with a great struggle that's what she did. She had treatment, started getting her life together and Theo really thought she was on the mend. It's neither of their faults that the press linked their names; after all she was living there.

'Matt Harksey, who was in charge of the US operation, is a different story. You see, while Robert was in England, Harksey became heavily involved in a drug racket – of course we didn't know – all Robert knew was that suddenly under Matt the company was doubling its figures. It was of course drugs – or rather the profit from them – in return for contracts. But when the police began to monitor Matt's activities, they told Robert and he was so shocked, he kind of went to pieces.

'Theo came back from England, fired Harksey and the guys on the board who were turning a blind eye to it all, and said if any of them ever tried to challenge their dismissal he would have them put away for twenty years. It was a pretty awful time. But I suppose they had to tell their families something about why they were fired, so they blamed Theo. Once the drug money went, the figures plummeted. But through sheer hard work and bloody-minded obstinacy, he turned it around.

'As an act of revenge, Harksey got hold of Caroline. She was still vulnerable. Theo arrived back one night and found Harksey and some other drop-outs in his flat and clearly supplying Caroline with drugs. Of course he threw them out. But he didn't throw Caroline out. He just told her she had to go into rehab – and surprisingly she did. After that she went back home to live with her parents in Ireland where she now helps young drug addicts. She's a dear girl at heart, we're all terribly fond of her.'

Ellie sat almost paralysed with fright. Then if it wasn't

Caroline on the phone, who was it? Someone pretending to be her. She stopped dead.

Pretending.

Acting.

It couldn't have been. Dear God, surely not?

Ellie, frantically trying to pull her disordered mind into shape, cut right across Ria telling Oliver about Caroline's new life.

'Ria ... did ... does Debra Carlysle know about Caroline?'

'Debra? Yes, of course. She met Theo through Max Culver at about the time Theo had persuaded Caroline to go back to Ireland. It was common knowledge.'

Ellie barely heard the rest of the discussion. It had to be Carlysle. But what about 'Jessica'?

Jessica! Not Jessica, but Suki. It was the voice, not the face, that was familiar. That whiny, dull, flat voice. But why?

'He's going to marry Debra Carlysle, isn't he?' Oliver was saying as Ellie dived to the phone.

Ria gave him a worried frown. 'I know he wants to build a house in Willetts Green. Our house is lovely but he once said he wouldn't want to take his wife — when he marries — to live there. Besides, Robert hankers after the old place from time to time, and my daughters want to hang on to their English roots. And there's too much of his father there, I suppose,' she laughed.

'But I know,' she said, looking at Ellie frantically punching out a number on the phone, 'that he would like roots somewhere in the area.'

'Jed? It's me.' Ellie was shouting into the phone. 'Have you got a key to the office? Who has? What? What did I say this afternoon? Oh lord, yes, all right, all right, I'm sorry, I shouldn't have said that. Jed, I am prostrate with grief for even suggesting such a thing ... will that do? Good. But the keys, Jed, someone must have a set. Jed, I don't care how you do it, but find someone, *anyone* who's got a set. I may need to get in. I've got to stop that feature. Yes, that one. I'll meet you at the office, but first I've to pay someone a visit.'

Chapter Thirty-two

The cab dropped her outside Debra's apartment. Furiously Ellie pressed the buzzer and kept her finger on it, until a scared-looking Suki opened the door a fraction. Seeing Ellie she immediately tried to slam the door. But she wasn't quick enough.

Ellie pushed past her. 'Where's Debra?' she demanded. 'C'mon, tell me, right now, or believe me I'll make life very painful for you.'

Suki looked terrified. Her eyes were like saucers. 'She's gone . . . gone to the States with Mr Stirling.'

'If you're lying, it will be the worse for you.' Ellie had never felt so violent. And that was just for hearing Debra had gone with Theo to the States.

'Look, you get out of here,' bleated Suki.

Ellie slammed the door shut and pushed Suki ahead of her into the vast white drawing room where Debra Carlysle had gone to such pains to throw her out of Theo's life.

'I will,' she said grimly, 'when you tell me why you allowed yourself to be talked into impersonating someone else. Don't you realize the damage you've done?'

'Damage? What damage?' Suki's face was grey. Ellie thought she looked really ill, but in her anger and panic was too far gone to care.

Suki's voice was a whimper as Ellie backed her against the wall.

'Debra just said she needed to know I could be convincing before she introduced me to her agent. She said I just had to fool you into thinking I was someone called Jessica who had once lived in New York with Caroline Montgomery.'

'Why?' shouted Ellie. But she didn't have to be told. She'd walked right into it. Once she had written a pack of damaging lies about Theo, Debra knew he would never speak to Ellie again. Clearly the woman was prepared to go to any lengths to hang on to him.

'Who pretended to be Caroline?' Ellie asked the frightened girl.

'I don't know. I don't even know who she is!' and quite obviously she wasn't lying. Her face had terror written all over it. 'She said she would tell you. She must have told you? Oh shit, don't tell me you didn't know?'

Ellie didn't even bother to answer. 'Is Debra coming back?'

Suki shook her head and there was a desperation about her that Ellie thought was pitiful.

'I've got to be out of here tonight. I thought she would let me stay, but she's given up the lease of the flat.'

Ellie didn't know who was the most damaged, Suki or Debra. For the first time she looked properly at the pathetic creature in front of her, with her lank hair, dry, cracked skin and who had a greater need in life than to be an actress.

'How much did she pay you?' Ellie asked in a kinder voice.

'Enough,' muttered the girl wearily. 'She helped . . . with some problems.'

Ellie knew it was pointless trying to tell her to get real help. Debra had clearly never troubled herself with anything so positive as getting drug counselling for this pitifully skinny girl, with circles so black around her eyes she looked bruised. Debra had simply used someone prepared to do anything to get the money to fuel a far more dreadful addiction than fame to get her what she wanted.

Ellie and Suki had been the victims of a terrible hoax.

And Theo was going to be the loser. She couldn't think about that now. She had to move fast.

'Look,' she said, rapidly opening her bag and thrusting some money into Suki's hand. 'I expect you'll spend it in the wrong way, but do yourself a favour. Get on a train, go home to your parents.'

Suki just stared at the money and at Ellie's receding back as she sprinted out of the flat and raced down three flights of stairs to the street. Silently cursing how easily she had been duped by Debra, she ran as though her life depended on it along Park Lane, trying to flag down a cab.

Jerome. Oh shit, I've forgotten him. I have to tell him.

A phone. Where? Running like a lunatic she hurled herself into the nearest phone booth. What the hell is his number, she thought feverishly. C'mon, c'mon, she willed him to answer when she finally got directory enquiries to locate it.

'Mr Strachan is at the theatre,' came the irritated voice of what appeared to be a live-in girlfriend who was in no mood to linger. Somewhere it registered that this wasn't Sonya – another time Ellie would have laughed. Roland with Judith, Jerome and Sonya. Some things obviously went with the job.

'Which theatre?' persisted Ellie.

'How should I know?' said the bored voice. 'He didn't say. Just said he'd be back much later.'

Ellie found it difficult to believe. 'Are you telling me he's gone out with no number where he can be located? What if his office needed him?'

The indifference in the girl's voice enraged Ellie. Slamming down the receiver she started to run towards Piccadilly. Typical of Strachan. No editor on press night. Just wanders off into the blue.

Oh grief. She screeched to a halt. The printers. They've got to be stopped.

Racing back to the phone kiosk, she unceremoniously yanked a giggling teenage couple from the box, announcing she was an undercover agent for the drugs squad about to do a bust, and as they scuttled off, she spent a tortuous ten minutes getting the number from directory enquiries and waiting to get through.

They worked through the night. *Focus* was due to start printing at three. It was now nearly ten. The film would have to be redone to take the damaging feature out and insert in its place the totally inoffensive description of Stefano's glittering Venetian society ball.

Ellie ignored the voice in her head telling her it was impossible. New technology may well have speeded up production, but it had made what she wanted to do a dauntingly difficult task. It would also be wildly expensive. The only justification she could think of to satisfy Jerome was that the cost in libel damages and damage to *Focus*'s reputation, if it were published, would be that much again.

When she had assured Alistair that the facts were correct, she had meant it. Now they were not correct. Not ever. Not then. Not now. Oh God.

As she waited for the phone at the printers to be picked up, she swiftly ran through the itinerary ahead of her. If the original film containing the feature on Stefano's reception had been delivered to the printers before they had decided to pull it in favour of the revelations on Theo Stirling, then there was an excellent chance that it would be simply a question of switching them back.

Fred Sommers, production manager at the printers, was an obliging man who wouldn't balk at a last-minute hiccup. Ellie tried to persuade herself it would be okay, but it sounded ludicrous. To hell with it. She couldn't stop now.

She told herself that it was also possible that when the art director had phoned the colour repro house to organize the changes that afternoon the disk was still there and hadn't even gone to the printers. That meant she would have to go via the repro house. That was okay; it was only over in Russell Square. She would pick up the new set of film and take it herself to Milton Keynes. So, add on, say, another hour; that meant she would be at the printers at, with a bit of luck, around one in the morning.

But if it was still in the office . . . hadn't even been sent to the colour house for repro? She didn't want to think any further. If that disk was still in the art director's files at *Focus* – and she had a sinking premonition that it was – the process to get it ready to be printed was brilliantly easy during a normal working day, but at midnight with the rest of the film gone and the colour house totally unprepared for such a bombshell, it became horrendously complicated.

'Fred? Yes, it's Ellie Carter. Fred, I'm sorry . . .'

A bemused Fred Sommers, whose conversations with Ellie were few and far between, was inclined to want to catch up on all the gossip.

'Fred, listen, this is urgent,' she interrupted him. 'Yes, Rosie's really fine, yes, and Jed. Fred . . . Fred, take it from me, the entire office are in terrific shape, just listen, please. The feature on Theo Stirling has got to be stopped. Have you got the original article it was swapped with, the one on the ball in Venice, Stefano Ferrucini's bash?'

Fred Sommers, who had no idea there had even been a switch, spent an agonizing two minutes trying to recall what feature she was talking about. Clearly it wasn't at the printers.

'Fred, if I get another set of film to you, can you make the swap? It's urgent, Fred, we'll be sued out of our brains if that goes ahead, and you'll go down as well for printing it.'

The word 'sued' brought Fred's torrent of social niceties to an abrupt end.

'Does Jerome know about this?' he asked suspiciously.

'Yes,' lied Ellie firmly. 'He's at the theatre, he told me to go ahead. He's even . . .' Ellie paused for just a fraction. Not enough to make Fred notice, not nearly enough to make her lose her nerve. 'He's even talked to Angus, and they both said whatever I could arrange. I expect Angus will ring you.'

Only the knowledge that Angus was a party to this prevented any further opposition from Fred. After all, if Angus had been given the go-ahead by Jerome, then they must know the kind of money it was going to cost them to replace something at such a critical moment. Why should he argue? More money for the printers.

'Okay, Ellie, but it's ten now. By the time you get here, it's got to be worked on . . . you'll never do it before the print run starts.'

'I will, I'll do it,' she said, knowing that Bentley Goodman himself would be harder to placate than Jerome when they discovered what she had single-handedly masterminded.

Directory enquiries were more helpful finding the number of the colour reproduction house. Fingers crossed, Ellie waited for a tortuous five minutes while Chrissie Hewlett, the production supervisor who by sheer chance was working late when the call came through, checked if the film was with them.

'How long will it take you to make a film if I get a disk and trannies to you?' Ellie asked rapidly when Chrissie finally reported back that they didn't have it, never had. The record of Stefano's merrymaking was still on a floppy disk somewhere in the art department at *Focus*.

'Ellie,' Chrissie protested. 'It's going to cost a packet. We've got to . . .' and she reeled off a dauntingly long list of procedures that the copy and transparencies would have to go through before they were made into film.

'At *least* a couple of hours once you get it here. But I haven't got anyone to handle it. We've got other clients with just as many pressing needs.'

Ellie thought she would scream with rage. The others weren't being sued, they weren't about to make the biggest mess of their lives. Make? She already had. But why make it worse? She swallowed hard and as calmly as she could explained the urgency of it to Chrissie.

'Chrissie, we've got to swap it, we'll be sued so hard we'll have to close, I swear. Can't you pull someone in to help?'

There was a brief silence, then a sigh, and Chrissie's reluctant voice said, 'Maybe. Just get here with it and I'll see what I can do.'

Ellie glanced at her watch. It was nearly ten thirty. Ten minutes to the office. Fifteen to find the wretched disk. Twenty across town to the colour house. A couple of hours there, and then what? Just over an hour to get to Milton Keynes. Be there by, say, two o'clock. Easy. Well . . . quite easy.

Fifteen minutes later, a taxi dropped her outside the office. Jed was sitting on the steps with a set of keys and a police officer. For one awful moment Ellie thought he had been arrested.

'No such thing,' he said indignantly. 'Security turned the keys over but only if a policeman accompanied us, and this officer has kindly agreed to do so. Isn't that right, Sergeant?'

'Constable, sir. Now if you'll just get a move on. I haven't got all night.'

Five minutes later all three arrived in the *Focus* office, Ellie and Jed pulling switches as they raced along the eerily deserted corridors towards the art director's office.

Frantically unlocking the door to the room awash with

proofs, layouts, and a filing system that was beyond the combined capabilities of both Jed and Ellie, they gazed nervously at each other.

'Bloody hell,' said Jed, taking in the silent, vast room dominated by four computer screens. 'Why didn't you ever learn how to find your way around an art department? Thank God you've got me with you . . .'

'Then I suggest you find the file,' snapped Ellie, surveying the blank screens gazing unhelpfully back at her.

'No problem,' said Jed, swinging himself behind the art director's screen. 'What's the name of it?'

Ellie looked blank. 'The name? How the hell do I know? Try the date of the issue.'

Grabbing the mouse that would scroll up the screen, Jed found the entry for that week's issue. Nothing in that file. He tried locating Stefano's name. No good. Ellie's by-line? Hopeless.

'Ring the art director,' he suggested. 'Ask him what he's done with it.'

Snatching the phone, Ellie punched in his home number from a list pinned in front of her. She waited until she heard it ring a dozen times and then disgustedly threw it back into its cradle.

'Keep going,' said Ellie, moving swiftly across the room, reaching out to activate another screen. 'I'll use this one. It's got to be here. I wrote it, I saw the layout. I know the trannies exist. Therefore it's simply a question of calmly finding the bloody thing.'

Frenzied precious minutes went by, each file that flashed on to the screen producing lists of features which had either been printed or were being worked on. Of the article on Stefano there was no sign.

'Any luck?' called Jed over his shoulder, as he swiftly loaded another disk.

'Nothing,' groaned Ellie, as she dragged the mouse along lists of files, none of which displayed the magic title she was looking for. She gritted her teeth. 'It's got to be here. It's got to be . . .'

'Hold it, hold it, here it is,' came Jed's triumphant cry. 'It's here, I've got it, under something called "Washout" . . . Oh glory, just look at that.' His voice finished in a wail.

Ellie's heart stopped. 'What is it?' she shrieked, scrambling across the room, sending a chair spinning in her path to where he was sitting. He was peering with such loathing at the screen Ellie was convinced he had found a major flaw in the feature.

'The picture they've used of me and Stefano and Max,' he said, stabbing a finger at a blurred image. 'I told them not to use it. It's one where you can hardly see me.'

'Oh, for crying out loud,' Ellie shouted furiously at him. 'Just transfer it to a disk, will you?'

She grabbed an empty disk and thrust it at Jed, who was still peering resentfully at the computer image, where only his right shoulder was discernible behind the Italian prince. While he did as he was told, she began the relatively easy task of pulling together the transparencies to accompany the text and layout to the colour house. Snatching the disk from Jed, stuffing the whole package into an envelope, she grabbed his arm and together they fled down the corridor to the waiting policeman.

The keys to the building safely in the possession of the law, they raced to the back of the building where Jed's car had been illegally parked for over half an hour.

'Where is it?' she yelled at him as they raced in a frenzy along the narrow street that ran between the office and the back entrances to the buildings opposite.

To their relief it hadn't been clamped. Jed swung the car in the direction of Russell Square, a journey they achieved in the record if illegal time of twelve minutes. Chrissie was waiting for them to despatch the disk and transparencies in their appropriate directions.

'You're lucky,' she threw back over her shoulder as they threaded their way through banks of screens to the scanner, where the transparencies were taken away and the disk disappeared into a computer to be checked. 'I managed to get someone to come in to deal with this. Go on, vanish, the pair of you. Use my office, but don't interrupt.'

There was nothing for it after that, but to pace up and down nervously, clutching cartons of coffee. Ellie remembered another night when she had paced anxiously along an unfamiliar corridor. It seemed so long ago when Gemma had given birth to Amy. Only then, Ellie's whole life hadn't depended on the outcome. This time she knew it did – her professional life, at least. Well, that was something . . .

The minutes, then an hour, then two, ticked by. Ellie had never felt so tired. She glanced across to where Jed was sound asleep, sprawled in Chrissie's big chair, with his blond hair falling across his eyes, his chin resting on his chest. She envied him.

At twenty past one in the morning, Chrissie appeared, handing into their care the film of Stefano's night of revelries. Was that only a week ago? It didn't seem possible.

Jed, roused from his slumber, was ushered hurriedly out of the building with Ellie shouting her thanks as she pushed him to the car. With a promise from Chrissie to ring the printers to say that they were on their way, and with Jed still complaining bitterly about his photograph that would now appear in the magazine they roared off into the night, heading for Milton Keynes.

On the way she told him the whole story.

'You were right, Jed,' she admitted, shamefaced, when just before two thirty he swung the car into the car park at the printers. 'He is straight. Just a little confused about some things.'

Jed, she noticed, was trying not to look smug.

'And,' she said with dangerous calm, 'you needn't look so smart. After all it was you who wrote in your column that Serena had to see a psychiatrist after she divorced Theo – and that's not true. She said she was pregnant to get him to marry her. It was a lie but he fell for it. A week later she said she wasn't. Really, she sounded so neurotic, I'm not surprised he divorced her.'

Jed gave her a quick look as they hurried across the car park. 'And I assume that's not for my column,' he said regretfully.

Ellie didn't bother to reply. Her judgement must be slipping. Roger Nelson had clearly been a company liability, lucky to have been offered a move sideways considering. Amazing how some people looked good at their job but only because of a strong presence behind them. The wisdom of hindsight, she thought bitterly, was very painful and not at all helpful.

They found Fred almost instantly, who once again got Ellie to assure him that Jerome had sanctioned switching features. After all he was going to be presenting him with a sizeable bill for all this. She unblushingly told him he had.

Fred turned to hand over the new set of film, and Ellie leaned against the nearest wall, about to let out her breath.

'Just a minute.' Fred turned back. 'Where's the proof to match it against?'

Ellie had had enough.

'There isn't one. There wasn't time. Just do it, Fred, okay? I promise you, it's fine.'

Fred shrugged. 'Up to you.' And ambled away.

As the night wore on, Ellie realized she had become an accomplished liar – and all for love of Theo Stirling. This surely wasn't how it was in books? Particularly when the hero of the piece was en route to New York about to marry someone else?

It was past three o'clock when Ellie and Jed finally emerged from the printers, Ellie having given final approval on the feature on Prince Stefano and the magical night in Venice, removed the dangerous profile on Theo and heaved a fervent sigh of relief as Fred assured them all was now well. Together they walked across the forecourt and, too tired even to think straight, headed for Jed's car.

'I still think the picture was lousy,' he muttered. 'Stefano looked okay though.'

Ellie gave him a sidelong glance.

'How's that going?'

'Early days, my flower. Early days. Stefano's in London next week and he's offered me his apartment in New York until I can find something for myself.'

'And Ashley?'

Jed thrust his hands in his pockets and kicked a stone into the distance. 'Yes, Ashley. Well, who knows? It won't be the same any more once I'm in New York. Ashley likes having everyone where he can reach them.'

'What about you?' Ellie asked. 'What do you want?'

'At the moment? Weekends in Venice and let the future take care of itself. And I suppose you want me to drive you home now,' he yawned as they reached his car.

'Yes, please,' she said, making for the passenger seat.

'Well, I won't. You can drive me,' he said and before she could protest, he climbed into the back seat, curled up and went to sleep.

Ellie crawled into her bed at four thirty, and when her alarm sounded at seven thirty, she felt so physically disorientated she wasn't sure she would make it through the day. But before she left for the office she made one phone call.

She heard the receiver being picked up and a voice intoned, 'Mr Stirling's residence.'

'Joseph, this is Eleanor Carter. Has Mr Stirling left for New York?'

'He left last night, Miss. I'm not expecting him to be in London for a few weeks. Can I give him a message?'

Suki had been telling the truth, at least about that. Ellie felt exhausted and defeated, but at least now he wouldn't despise her for ever.

Oh, what the hell?

'Joseph, when you next speak to him, will you say Eleanor said, she thought a piece on Stefano would be a better choice so she's dropped the profile on him. I know he'll understand. And Joseph . . . will you also say, I said thank you?'

'Of course, Miss Carter. Would you like me to tell him personally or pass that message on to his personal assistant to tell him?'

'No, you tell him, Joseph,' she said. 'Thank you, good-bye,' and she put the receiver down trying very hard not to break down into tears.

Chapter Thirty-three

Ellie had never seen a more haggard looking face, she decided as she peered into the bathroom mirror and two hours later she had to concede that nor had she ever heard language like it from Jerome or seen him in such a towering rage.

But Jerome had finally recognized his moment. The moment when this girl who had caused him such loss of face with the management, the walking evidence of how far his power really stretched – not nearly as far as he had been led to believe – the moment when he could rid himself of her.

Ian Willoughby would have grave difficulty in defending her. Bentley Goodman would once again revert to his much more sensible opinion that Jerome was a better judge of these people and Miss snooty, bloody unapproachable Carter would be out of his life.

There was another reason for his quite astonishing rage and that had its roots in the knowledge that he should not have been out of touch. His fury was in direct proportion to how much of a defence of his own actions he could make stand up against his all-out onslaught on what Ellie had done.

'I should sack you for this,' he fumed as Jed and Ellie sat silently in front of him. 'I don't give a damn what the reasons are, you have no right to change things at a whim.'

Jerome was conscious of Ellie's white face but her explanation for switching the features just didn't hold water after arguing so vehemently with Alistair earlier in the day to run it. Finally running out of steam, he told them to go, suggesting curtly that they both gave some thought to their futures and he would decide on Monday whether they would be with *Focus* or not.

Ellie looked at him impassively. His wrath had left her unmoved. All she could remember was that she felt very tired, very low and this raging man in front of them had gone off to the theatre on press night leaving no word where he could be found.

Jerome was still standing behind his desk, leaning forward, resting his clenched fists on the top. Suddenly he felt uneasy. This wasn't what he had planned. Ellie was rising to her feet, smoothing down her skirt and glancing at her watch. She didn't even look scratched by such a blistering attack. Her voice was even and unhurried, and for some reason made him feel like an untidy schoolboy.

'If you've finished, Jerome, then with great courtesy and respect I feel I should mention one or two things to you.'

He found it difficult to believe what he was hearing. This woman was something else.

Ellie was not so much something else as someone else.

As Jerome had raged, a voice over and over in her head had been reminding her of a phrase she had come to live by.

'No-one,' she could hear Theo's voice, 'can make you feel inferior without your consent.'

She glanced at Jerome and briefly at Jed's surprised face, where he still sat in the armchair opposite Jerome's desk.

'If you want me to stop working here, you must say so. You had no difficulty doing it once before so I'm sure you will have even less now. If that is not what you want, then you must say that, in terms that I can understand.'

Jerome sat down hard. This was beyond anything he should be asked to tolerate. But for reasons he couldn't later quite recall he listened.

He listened as Ellie let him know that no-one had the right to shout in that uncontrolled manner at anyone who was guilty of nothing more than preventing someone who was very caring and of value from being unnecessarily hurt.

'If anyone had a right to shout as you did, Jerome, it should be him. Fortunately I don't think even he will have to. And frankly knowing him as I do, I don't think he would have lowered himself.'

Jed threw her a startled glance. 'Ellie,' he said warningly. 'Maybe we should . . .'

Ellie ignored him.

'I've learned that the worst that can ever happen to me if I lose this job is that it will be inconvenient, not life-threatening, and it no longer influences the way I live. Redundancy has seen to that. You should try it sometime, Jerome, it concentrates the mind wonderfully on what is and what isn't important. Removing that feature without your permission was wrong of me. But then I couldn't find you to get that permission. That's the worst that's happened here. I haven't killed anyone. The magazine won't fold.'

Jerome felt sick and furious and desperately longed for a freeze-frame button to push on the whole scene while he found the right words to get back on the pitch.

'I've told you, I'll think about it. I haven't said you've lost your job.'

'That's no good, Jerome. If you want me to stay and this is simply an exercise to punish me – and Jed – before you forgive us, then please don't waste my time. I want the decision now.'

'And that goes for me too,' said Jed, rising from his chair and joining Ellie as she walked towards the door.

Ellie tried to prevent him. 'No, Jed . . .' but she was stopped by his lazy grin.

'No good, Jerome, I don't want to work for someone who can't make a decision and more importantly, like Ellie, I will never again hang around while someone else decides on my future.'

Jerome's face was very white.

'Get out, both of you,' he breathed.

Silently they left the room, standing courteously aside as Ian Willoughby came through the outer office en route to Jerome's.

'Blimey,' laughed Ellie. 'Jerome's got them all running around him. Amazing. But Jed, you really shouldn't have done that. It's different for me. I know what it's like to be out of work. I know how to live now without depending on the perks of a job, or not having an expense account. Honestly, ducky dear, with the best will in the world, you don't.'

'Patronizing cow,' he said chummily as they reached his office door. 'Sexist too. I rather enjoyed it and I suspect he won't do too much to me. So, don't give it another thought, my flower,' he yawned. 'I knew what I was doing. You know at this moment I'd kill for a week's sleep.'

The lift down to the foyer was crowded as Ellie left later that day. It was nearly six. It had been a long day. She wanted only to reach her flat and then spend the evening mugging up on the notes for the next day's shoot.

Letty was coming to London with the camera crew and it was going to be another crowded day: filming homeless youngsters on the streets of London, an interview with the Social Services Minister and at least two commentaries to camera.

The lift doors opened and she stepped out, heading for the revolving door.

'Miss Carter, Miss Carter,' called the uniformed hall

porter. 'Phone call for you.' Ellie turned back, trying to think why Lucy could want to stop her.

'Ellie,' came Lucy's frantic voice. 'Boardroom. Bentley himself wants to see you.'

Startled, Ellie headed back for the lift and pressed for the ninth floor to meet for the first time and in uncertain circumstances the man who paid her salary.

Dixie came to meet her. 'So what is it this time,' joked Ellie tiredly. 'My head on a plate, or a public hanging?'

Dixie hurried along beside her but Ellie thought she didn't look too despondent.

'Not sure. But you know he isn't as bad as he's made out to be. Just lacks the human touch. You'll like him. Ian's in there too.'

There was no time for more as Ellie found herself being ushered not into Bentley Goodman's vast office, which had been designed by someone whose enthusiasm for *Citizen Kane* had got out of hand, but across this and into another room where Ian Willoughby was having an early evening drink with his boss.

It was not so much an office as a vast, elegant drawing room. Plump sofas were covered in tea roses, Colefax and Fowler chintz curtains framed three sets of windows looking out over the treetops of a pretty garden square, and in an open fireplace, although the weather was certainly not cold enough, a cheerful fire blazed.

Ellie was taken by surprise. And by Bentley Goodman.

The man himself rose from one of the sofas, doing up the middle button of his double-breasted pin-striped suit.

He was of only average height, with steel-grey hair, but with a light tan, beautifully manicured nails and a tailor who had skilfully combined style with authority, he gave the impression of being much taller.

'Good of you to join us,' he said, coming forward and taking her hand. 'Have you got time for a drink?'

Ellie nodded.

'I'll come straight to the point,' he said bluntly when Ellie, glancing at Ian, took her place in one of the armchairs. 'Jerome is a very talented young man, an editor with a great future.'

Ellie almost choked but, catching Ian's warning look, remained silent.

'You on the other hand have something he doesn't have and that is maturity. Yes, I know what I'm saying. Ian, however, has assured me that you would not misuse such a confidence. Jerome is uncertain with people who know more than he does, he has yet to master the art of listening. I'm not asking you to make allowances for him. I am the one who decides on that. But I am asking you not to allow what's happened to get in the way of what I think could be an exciting working relationship. Think about it overnight and let me have your decision tomorrow, but I think you know what we all hope that will be.'

Ellie put down her untouched drink. It wasn't only Jerome who had to learn the art of listening.

Reading between the lines, Ellie knew this was Bentley's way of saying that Jerome had been well and truly ticked off. He was also asking her to defuse a tricky situation. What had happened to her in the past nine months made scoring points off Jerome Strachan terribly trivial.

She thought of Ria and what it must have taken to confess such a story to her and Oliver. She thought of Clive, so kind and forgiving knowing that she had slept with Theo, and she thought of Theo who had not allowed quite false accusations against him get in the way of doing the right thing. Suddenly everything else seemed very unimportant. Especially Jerome Strachan's wounded feelings.

'Thank you,' she said to Bentley. 'But I don't need to think it over. I'd obviously like my contract to continue. In fact,' she said earning a grateful smile from Ian, 'I think

451

Jerome would too, we've got so many ideas in the pipeline it would be difficult not to.'

Twenty minutes later she strolled through Sonya's outer office and, tapping lightly on the door, went in to find Jerome on the point of leaving for the night.

'I meant to tell you,' she said as though nothing had happened. 'I've got an interview with the leader of the opposition. Would you like to talk about it later in the week?'

Jerome nodded silently. He wasn't going to handle this well, thought Ellie with a groan. Please God, don't let him start trying to apologize or explain.

'That sounds great. Yes, let's talk on Monday.'

Ellie waved a cheery hand at him and started to go.

'Oh, Ellie,' he called after her. 'Maybe over lunch?'

She shook her head with a smile. 'I don't do lunch any more, Jerome, but I would welcome a glass of champagne at the end of the day,' and with that she closed the door.

Jed's car was still parked outside Ellie's flat. Later, after a few hours' sleep, he told her he would come over and collect it.

'I might even give you supper,' she offered, wishing that a few hours' sleep was all that was needed to get rid of the ache she felt at the mess her life was in.

No, that wasn't true. The ache was for the loss of Theo. I'm not going to think about it, she said resolutely and proceeded to do nothing else all the way home.

She let herself into her silent flat, picked up the mail and checked the machine for messages. Once she would have been only too eager to take up any of the invitations from her friends to join them for supper, a drink, the cinema. But tonight she wanted her own thoughts and company. In her bedroom she stripped off her clothes, wrapped herself in a towelling dressing gown and ran a bath, pouring the last of some scented bath oil into the rushing water.

Later, after she had shampooed her hair, she pulled on a white cotton robe and made a very strong pot of coffee. When it was brewed she took it on a tray into the living room, picking up her post and stretched out on the sofa.

Bills, circulars, someone's writing she didn't recognize which turned out to be Josie's commiserating with her and asking her to dinner with her and Joe next time she was down. Her and Joe, eh?

Pouring the coffee with one hand, she flicked through the rest and then her heart stopped. There in sloping letters, black, bold and larger than life, just as he was, was a letter from Clive.

Slowly she replaced the cup and with shaking hands opened the envelope. It had been nearly a week since she had seen him and it felt like an eternity. She missed him so much. Before she had even read it she knew that wouldn't change, but if she could no longer have his friendship, his loving friendship, she needed his forgiveness.

He was writing from the apartment, before going down to Joanne and the boys. He needed his family, he said, and it was then that Ellie knew no matter what they might have been to each other, she would never have replaced that trio of people who represented his security, who drew him back in times of trouble.

She turned the page.

'There is nothing to forgive, and nothing to forget,' he wrote. 'Just a pain that will, in the end, go away. You don't stop loving someone because they cease to fill a need in your life. You love them for having done it. I don't want to pass you in the street without saying hello, or to hear you're in trouble and not offer help. Nor do I care much for the thought of hearing about you second hand.

'If I can't be the love of your life, and you can't be mine, then let me be the friend, the uncritical friend, who will be with you for life. In a while. Not yet.'

Slowly she lowered the page and curled up on to the cushions, Clive's letter clasped in her hand. It was more than she had asked for, but then that's why she had loved him. She still did. Always would.

Intending to close her eyes for just a few minutes, she tried to visualize Clive, dragging her off to an unheard-of exhibition, making her walk for miles until he found a pub he had been told about one day a year ago in Dublin, listening intently as she argued with him and wrapped in his arms as she fell asleep.

The incessant buzzing at the door finally penetrated the mists of sleep. Groggily Ellie rolled off the sofa, trying to focus on her wrist watch. It was eleven o'clock. She had been asleep for two hours. Jed must have been buzzing the door for ages.

'I'm coming,' she called, switching lamps on as she went.

'I just crashed out,' she said, swinging open the door and rubbing her eyes.

'I've just got in,' said the voice she loved best in the world.

Her eyes flew open, one hand flew to her mouth, the other clutching the neck of her gown. She opened and closed her mouth. This must be a dream. Theo was in New York, not Fulham. Jed would be here in a minute and tell her to wake up.

'Do you think I might come in?' Theo asked, and for the first time she saw that even though he was smiling, he was unshaven and his eyes were showing signs of fatigue.

Ellie stepped aside and closed the door after him.

'I'm sorry, I'm just so slow about these things,' she

said, wondering why she suddenly felt terribly shy and Theo was now standing uncertainly in the hallway. 'I thought you were in New York.'

'I was. I came back.'

'Back?' Even to her ears she sounded stupid. 'Why? When?'

'Er . . . why? Well, the view over here is infinitely more attractive,' he said with a wry smile. 'As for when? Well, I've come straight from Heathrow, the plane was late. Otherwise I would have been here earlier. I'm sorry it's so late but I wanted to talk to you.'

He waited for her to say something.

'Joseph gave me your message,' he said helpfully. 'And er . . . I spoke to my mother. And Jed.' He waited.

Ellie had not been able to take her eyes from his face. His expression was watchful, wary. She had seen Theo angry, gentle, amusing and loving. She realized that not until now had she ever seen him uncertain.

'And to deliver something.' He was holding out a solid square box, wrapped in gold paper. Wonderingly she took it from him, glancing from him to the box as she pulled the string. As she removed the lid of the red velvet box that she found inside, she stifled a gasp, and a lump came into her throat.

Carefully, gently she lifted the precious gold horseshoe from its velvet cushion and turned it over in her hand. It was gleaming now; she remembered it had been tarnished. But the inscription was still there. 'Ellie, love always, Mummy.' She noticed something else had been added on the other side. 'Eleanor, forever my love, Theo.' And suddenly tears were streaming down her face.

Brushing them away, she looked at him, exhausted, anxious, not convinced of his welcome.

'Oh, Theo, this is long overdue,' she said huskily and held out her arms to him.

'Oh, my darling girl,' Theo whispered in a voice that

was far from steady and pulled her into his arms, kissing her hair and her face and finally her lips.

And then they just stood clinging to each other, all the pain and misery and confusion of the last six months melting away as they drew strength from each other's bodies.

'I took a chance,' he whispered, smiling down at her and brushing the tears away from her cheeks with his thumb. 'I've had that horseshoe for years. I found it after you ran away that day and just kept it in my safe in New York. I forgot about it until you reminded me that it was there. So I just waited until I could find a way of giving it back to you. I had it engraved, because when you love someone as much as I love you, you just don't give up.'

'There was never, ever a chance I would have let you,' she said, gently gazing up at him, her face drowned in love. 'Not when I plan to love you forever.'

'Miss Carter,' he said in a very unsteady voice. 'I happen to be very much in love with you and it looks as though it's incurable, but I really do think having crossed the Atlantic twice in thirty-six hours, the very least you can do is to waste no more time telling me about it but supply some evidence of how you intend to show me you mean it.'

Suddenly Ellie became very aware of just how little she was wearing, that her hair was still damp and that she had been through a fairly exhausting time herself.

'Just a minute,' she said indignantly. 'I've been suffering as well. And how dare you treat me like a child and not tell me I owe all this to you, and let me go on thinking you loved Debra and what on earth could you possibly see in her and where is she, by the way?'

'New York with Gavin . . . and threatening to expose me for the bastard I am . . .' he said, kissing her. 'And I don't see anything in her . . .'

'And what has Jed to do with this? How come you're so friendly with him?'

'Er . . . I'm not. But Stefano is and the night in Venice when you ran off, they were so bored having to sit with me while I got drunk, they just urged me to find a solution to it all. I wasn't banking on it being my mother. She's very nice, you know,' he said, eyeing her hopefully.

'I'll work on it,' said Ellie carefully. 'But you don't seem to mind in the slightest all the shocks you've dumped on me and letting me believe that you would ruin Oliver. You don't *know* the misery I've been going through and Jed is so fed up with me he made me drive back from the printers and I was so tired, and all you've done is sit in luxury on Concorde flying around the world, and I've got to film all day tomorrow . . .'

'Ellie, Ellie . . .' he laughed, winding his arms round her shoulders and kissing her nose. 'Not the world, just the Atlantic and are you going to talk this much when we're married?'

'Possibly,' she grinned shyly, hugging him to her. 'Unless,' she added mischievously, 'you can find some way of stopping me, which shouldn't be beyond the powers of a resourceful man like you.'

And she was right.

And Then . . .

Ellie walked slowly up from the village to Delcourt. The sun was hot on her back, her bare feet were pushed into plimsolls, a canvas bag was slung casually around her neck, a plain white T-shirt tucked into a long, faded blue cotton skirt carelessly tied at the waist with a narrow silk scarf.

At the top of the hill, the road divided. To the right was the wide gravel drive that led up to Delcourt and beyond that Oliver's house. To the left, the narrow track wound its way to the top of the cliff where rocky steps led down to Willetts Bay Beach.

It was not yet midday. Theo would not be here for hours. For a brief moment she hesitated and then, just as she had when she was a child, the decision rarely delaying her for long, she made her choice. Why not?

Turning left towards the top of the cliff, she climbed down the rocky steps, jumping the last three as she always did, landing with a soft thump in the grainy shingle that further on gave way to moist sand and clusters of rocks. With one hand leaning against the mossy wall of the cliff to steady herself, she bent down and removed her plimsolls so that she could walk barefoot in the soft shingle until she reached her favourite spot.

First she took her bag from around her neck, threw it up and then tucked the hem of her long cotton skirt into her waistband until she had pulled herself up after it, wriggling her bottom into a comfortable position, her back feeling the delicious heat of the sun where it had warmed the rock behind her.

For a while she was content to sit and gaze out over the long stretch of beach, the tide well out, a shimmering haze promising the first hot still afternoon. The beginning of summer. It had been a long week. Three days filming for Letty and a profile for Jerome. Next week was going to be busy too, she knew, but for now . . .

Theo had taken her to dinner with his mother before she left for an extended stay in their summer home at Cape Cod with Robert and this weekend Theo was due at Delcourt. Not to meet Pa. That would have to come later. Later, when some of the hurt and confusion had found their rightful place. As they had with Clive.

As Clive had said, they had a long time ahead to do that.

Gemma and Bill were moving to Blackheath to be nearer Bill's job and to a house with a garden for Amy, and Jed's departure for New York was now only a fortnight away. Everything was changing. But this time the changes were of their own making, not someone else's decision.

Reaching into her bag, she brought out her black diary and began to flick through the pages, her sunglasses pushed on top of her head. Reading back over the last year was like reading about another life. Dinner with Polly, Paul. WIN meetings with Liz or Anne or someone who wanted to get on without giving anything back.

Interviews with the world and his wife, committee meetings. Must go. Don't forget. The terrible dark days of being let go, the painfully blank pages of days she would rather forget, but knew she would always remember as the days when she found the courage to be herself.

It was different now. The diary she used these days stayed with Lucy or on her desk at home. No longer were appointments ringed urgently in black Pentel, no more torrent of commitments that hijacked her time and distorted her thinking. Pages that were filled with reminders about Gemma and Bill, babysitting Amy or dashing down to see Amanda. About Letty, Joe and Josie.

Now it reflected a young woman who had found love, found a career and most of all had found herself.

Slowly, carefully she got up and began to slide down the rock and then she walked, hugging her diary to her chest, right down to the edge of the sea where the waves were lapping gently on to the sand, drawing rhythmically back into the sea, a stiff breeze catching at her T-shirt, flapping it against her sides, tugging at her skirt, the front buttons swinging open to reveal bare, slender legs.

There was a small smile on her face as she shaded her eyes against the brilliant light reflecting off the steady swell of the sea, the water swirling around her feet.

It was time to let go. Ellie opened the pages of her diary.

Very deliberately and methodically she began to rip them out, casting each one as she did so into the wind and watched as the white pages spun and whirled before sinking gently on to the tips of the white foam and began to float out to sea like a flotilla of toy boats, drifting and bobbing away, until finally just the black leather cover was left.

She stayed watching the fast-disappearing pages for some time, until there were just a few white dots and she was satisfied that there was nothing to keep her there any more. Then she turned and made her way back to the rock.

Ten more minutes, she told herself, glancing at her watch, and then you must go and call Letty about next week. With a contented sigh she put the empty cover of her diary down beside her and closed her eyes.

'So this is how you conduct your brilliant career.'

Ellie wheeled round and, shading her eyes upwards, saw Theo standing at the top of the cliff path.

'I don't believe it,' she said delightedly, scrambling to

her feet. 'I wasn't expecting you for hours.'

'Caught an earlier flight.'

'Stay there, I'm coming,' she called and started to slither back down the rock towards the steps, pulling her bag across her shoulders, scooping up her plimsolls, running eagerly to meet him.

'Hey,' he called. 'Not so fast, you've left something behind.'

She paused and looked back to where he was pointing and laughed.

'Don't worry,' she said, glancing to where the black leather diary cover was lying empty and open on the top of the rock. 'It's not important any more, not important at all,' and she began to climb the stone steps to where he was waiting, hand outstretched to pull her up the last three steps into his arms and then to take her home.

Jewels of our Father
Kristy Daniels

Sweeping from the bustling waterfront and gilded mansions
of San Francisco in the 1920s to the intellectual excitement of
de Gaulle's Paris and beyond, *Jewels of Our Father* is a vast
dramatic tale that reveals the sins and secrets, passions and
obsessions of a powerful newspaper dynasty.

Adam Bryant spent a lifetime forging the *San Francisco
Times* into the most powerful newspaper in the country. His
passion for journalism and his love for one woman helped
him build his empire, yet bitterness and despair threatened
to topple it. For on his deathbed, Bryant bequeathed control
of the *Times* to his three estranged children.

And instead of uniting them, as their father had hoped,
the legacy set the stage for a power struggle that would rage
over a decade. Only Bryant's daughter, Kellen, shared
her father's vision and could ride the turbulent wave of a
new generation's passion and betrayal to save his failing
dream . . . and fulfil her own tumultuous destiny.

ISBN 0 00 647167 6

Fontana

Shadows on the Sun
Kathryn Haig

Helen . . .

To Michael, her husband, lonely and reserved, she is both angel and whore . . .

To Adrienne, fleeing the destruction of her homeland by the Kaiser's army, she is an unnatural mother . . .

To Hector, shell-shocked and tormented, she is the woman who has ensnared his brother and brought two families to the brink of tragedy.

After a war that has savaged a generation both physically and spiritually, the affluent classes find themselves cast dangerously adrift from their Edwardian certainties. For Michael and Helen – for all of them – nothing will ever be the same again.

From the last golden summer of a dying era, through the senseless carnage of the Western Front, to the savage gaiety of the jazz age, *Shadows on the Sun* is the story of a terrible obsession.

'An overwhelmingly compelling read. I was captivated.'

Barbara Erskine

ISBN 0 00 647137 4

Fontana

King's Oak
Anne Rivers Siddons

Leaving behind a disastrous marriage, Diana Calhoun and her young daughter Hilary seek refuge in the comforting security of a small Southern town – Pemberton, Georgia, a close-knit, aristocratic community bordered by a primeval forest.

What she discovers, though, is not serenity but Tom Dabney, a magical, passionate man who has renounced his patrician heritage to live close to the land and who worships the wilderness surrounding Pemberton. Despite warnings from friends, Diana abandons herself to a fiery affair that releases within her unforeseen strengths.

She soon comes to realise that Tom will do anything to protect and preserve his world. When an explosive confrontation involving a sinister threat to his cherished wood pits Tom against even his closest friends, Diana must decide if she can follow . . .

'A wickedly good love story, one that soars'
New York Daily News

ISBN 0 00 617922 3

Fontana

Hot Type
Kristy Daniels

When Tory Satterly starts at the second-rate afternoon paper, *The Sun*, she's just a lowly, overweight reporter, relegated to the women's pages and hopelessly in love with Russ Churchill, golden boy of the prestigious rival morning paper, *The Post*. But Tory is tenacious and she soon enters the hard news world of smouldering sex scandals and drug deals. As her career soars, Tory becomes a svelte and sexy woman equally at home at exclusive spas, Swiss resorts, and in the arms of multimillionaire Max Highsmith.

And when *The Post* and *The Sun* are merged, there's room for only one at the top. Russ Churchill becomes Tory's rival . . . as well as her lover. Which of them will get the plum job – the one they have both wanted all their lives?

ISBN 0 00 617811 1

Fontana

Mary Higgins Clark

Mary Higgins Clark's novels have made her – deservedly – one of America's most successful bestselling storytellers. She is superb at conveying the suspense and terror that wait in the wings of ordinary lives of people like us who suddenly find ourselves in mortal danger.

Where Are the Children?
A Stranger is Watching
The Cradle Will Fall
A Cry in the Night
Stillwatch
Weep No More, My Lady

Fontana

The Egyptian Years
Elizabeth Harris

The mysterious disappearance of Genevieve Mountsorrel in the Egyptian desert in 1892 was a longstanding family puzzle. Newly married, the young and vivacious Genevieve had sailed for Egypt, happy at the prospect of a new life. No one could explain the tragic turn of events. Only her parasol had been found, hastily discarded in the hot and dusty sand.

A century later, Willa, a distant relative, discovers Genevieve's diary. Drawn immediately into an astonishing story, she learns of Genevieve's secret life and the child she was forced to abandon, the truth about her sinister husband, Leonard, and the extraordinary drama of what really happened to Genevieve Mountsorrel . . .

Acclaim for *The Herb Gatherers*:

'Enormously enjoyable. Elizabeth Harris writes with sensitivity and skill.'
                                              Barbara Erskine

ISBN 0 00 647191 9

Fontana

Mystical Paths
Susan Howatch

'One of the most original novelists writing today' *Cosmopolitan*

As the Swinging Sixties slide into decadence, young Nicholas Darrow is trying to sort out his private life. How can he marry his girlfriend Rosalind when he is apparently unable to avoid promiscuity? Or face ordination when he finds it impossible to live as a priest should? And how can he break free from Jon, the father whose psychic gifts he shares and upon whom he is so dangerously dependent? At this crucial time Nick beomes involved in the mystery surrounding his friend Christian Aysgarth. Gradually he realizes that, by discovering the truth about this enigmatic and complex man, he will also solve his own baffling problems.

Mystical Paths is a compulsively readable psychological detective story, the gripping tale of a young man's search for spiritual fulfilment and a fascinating examination of the meeting between religion and psychology.

ISBN 0 00 647271 0

Fontana

Magic Hour
Susan Isaacs

Magic Hour – a film-maker's dream – that brief period of enchanted luminescence between light and dark that is perfect for making movies, for making love – for murder.

On the exquisite beaches of Long Island's glamorous Hamptons a blockbuster movie is heading for trouble. One perfect August day, Sy Spencer, the urbane, enigmatic producer, is shot dead beside his swimming pool.

Local detective Steve Brady goes looking for a killer – chief suspect Bonnie Spencer is looking for love. Together they are locked on a collision course of passion, deceit and retribution . . .

'Witty, inventive, elegantly funny and original . . . there really is a sense of mystery here, plenty of edgy suspense and a genuinely satisfying solution'   Anne Tyler, *Vogue*

'Intriguing, humorous, gripping, moving . . . a novel that keeps you guessing, raises your eyebrows, races your motor and makes you laugh out loud, only to bring you close to tears'   *Washington Times*

ISBN 0 00 647093 9

Fontana

Keeping It Up

How to make your love affair last for ever

Cathy Hopkins

Whatever happened to foreplay, flowers and candlelit dinners? If your relationship is more about who puts the rubbish out and who does the ironing than champagne, chocolates and nights of passion, then this book is for you.

Forget the wordy text books and earnest counselling sessions, *Keeping It Up* tells it like it *really* is! From how to compromise and laugh together to how not to kill passion and how to survive infidelity – only Cathy Hopkins, bestselling author of *Girl Chasing* and *Man Hunting* answers all these questions and more.

Hilariously illustrated, compulsively readable, *Keeping It Up* is the essential bedside handbook.

ISBN 0 00 637855 2

Fontana

Fontana Fiction

Fontana is a leading paperback publisher of fiction.
Below are some recent titles.

- [ ] GREEN AND PLEASANT LAND Teresa Crane £4.99
- [ ] KING'S OAK Ann Rivers Siddons £4.99
- [ ] THE EGYPTIAN YEARS Elizabeth Harris £4.50
- [ ] MAGIC HOUR Susan Isaacs £4.99
- [ ] THE RELUCTANT QUEEN Jean Plaidy £3.99
- [ ] TOMORROW'S MEMORIES Connie Monk £3.99
- [ ] WHEN SHE WAS BAD . . . Kate O'Mara £4.99
- [ ] THE CLONING OF JOANNA MAY Fay Weldon £3.99
- [ ] FORBIDDEN GARDEN Diane Guest £3.99
- [ ] KING'S CLOSE Christine Marion Fraser £4.95
- [ ] MEMORY AND DESIRE Lisa Appignanesi £4.99
- [ ] THE ROAD TO ROWANBRAE Doris Davidson £4.50
- [ ] SACRIFICE Harold Carlton £4.99

You can buy Fontana Paperbacks at your local bookshops or
newsagents. Or you can order them from Fontana, Cash Sales
Department, Box 29, Douglas, Isle of Man. Please send a
cheque, postal or money order (not currency) worth the price
plus 24p per book for postage (maximum postage required is
£3.00 for orders within the UK).

NAME (Block letters)_____

ADDRESS_____

_____